NO ESCAPE

Center Point
Large Print

Also by Mary Burton and available from
Center Point Large Print:

Before She Dies
The Seventh Victim

**This Large Print Book carries the
Seal of Approval of N.A.V.H.**

NO ESCAPE

MARY BURTON

CENTER POINT LARGE PRINT
THORNDIKE, MAINE

This Center Point Large Print edition is published
in the year 2013 by arrangement with
Kensington Publishing Corp.

The text of this Large Print edition is unabridged.
In other aspects, this book may vary
from the original edition.
Printed in the United States of America
on permanent paper.
Set in 16-point Times New Roman type.

ISBN: 978-1-61173-909-1

Library of Congress Cataloging-in-Publication Data

Burton, Mary (Mary T.)
No Escape / Mary Burton. — Center Point Large Print edition.
pages cm.
ISBN 978-1-61173-909-1 (Library binding : alk. paper)
1. Serial murderers—Fiction. 2. Women psychologists—Fiction.
  3. Murder—Investigation—Fiction. 4. Large type books. I. Title.
PS3602.U7699N64 2013
813′.6—dc23
                                                              2013032653

NO ESCAPE

Prologue

Central Texas
Ten years ago

Moonlight dripped on the rusted blue '79 Chevy Impala angled at the end of a dirt-packed rural road. Yards ahead a footpath twisted, slithered and vanished into scrawny woodlands. A coyote howled.

Robbie had never been here before but his father, Harvey Lee Smith, had grown up near this property. He'd often talked about it, swearing he could conjure each rock, bump and tree on the field now awash in springtime bluebonnets.

Harvey said the bluebonnets always calmed his racing thoughts and chased away his demons. But imagining the sea of delicate purple flowers did little to ease Robbie's dread.

Setting the brake, Harvey leaned over the steering wheel and stared at the trail that snaked toward the beloved blossoms. "I bet you money that my baby girl would love to see the blossoms. Yes, sir, she would love it."

"She's not a baby, Harvey," Robbie said. "She's twenty-two. A year younger than me."

His smile ebbing, a forlorn shadow darkened the older man's features. "No, I reckon she's not a baby, Robbie. She's graduated. Earned her bachelor's and going to get her PhD. Smart kid. A chip off the old block."

Jealousy stinging, Robbie regarded Harvey. "You should go see her. Tell her you're proud."

Harvey shook his head, staring at his smooth hands gripping the steering wheel. "Thought about it. Thought about it a lot. But like I said before, it's not a good idea."

"She might like to know you're out there thinking of her." Robbie understood he was digging into an old hurt his father carried in his heart. But he didn't care. He was tired of feeling less when compared to the girl Harvey idealized.

Scowling, his father jerked the door handle up and pushed his shoulder into it. The door groaned open. "Come on, boy. The night won't last forever."

Harvey slammed the door hard and moved to the back of the Impala.

Robbie smoothed sweaty palms over his jeans and stared into the rearview mirror, watching Harvey insert a key into the trunk lock.

Robbie's stomach somersaulted and again he hoped his fear didn't upend his stomach. He did not want to be here. Opening his door, he lumbered out of the car and braced against the cool night air. He hovered by the car door.

Key still in hand, Harvey glanced up toward the bright moon as if savoring how the stars popped more in the Hill Country away from the bright lights of Austin. He inhaled, appreciating the cool, soft, spring air. "Lord, but I've missed coming up this way."

Robbie shoved trembling hands into the pockets of his jeans. "Why don't you come back here more often?"

Shaking his head, Harvey twisted the key and the lock released. "Last time I was here, it didn't go well, so I stayed away. I can see now that this trip was a mistake."

"Wasn't this place your family home?"

"Naw. Just a place I liked visiting." The trunk lid rose, cutting off Robbie's view. "Come on, boy. We got work to do." Harvey's voice, darkly polite, had him tensing.

Anxiety rising, Robbie walked toward the back of the car and peered in the trunk. He stifled a wince as he looked at the woman who lay gagged and trussed up like a pig ready for the spit.

She stared up at him with mascara-smudged eyes, bloodshot from crying, her pleas muffled by the gag.

Tucking the keys in his jacket pocket, Harvey delighted in the way she writhed and whimpered. "Picked a fine one this time, didn't I, boy?"

Robbie rattled the change in his pockets. "She's skinny."

"Could stand to gain a pound or two, but she's strong and pretty. Given time, bet she'd grow into a stunning woman." Harvey trailed a hand along her leg and when she jerked away he smiled. "Beauty's skin deep, boy. Remember that. What you want in a woman is spirit. Couldn't coax this one in the car with a fifty-dollar bill like the others. No, sir, this one is leery by nature. Not swayed by pretty words. Careful, cautious. Best kind in my book."

For this one, Harvey had created an intricate backstory, stolen a late-model Volvo wagon with a baby seat in the back and dressed in khakis and a baby blue button-down shirt. "The kind of shirt a safe guy wore," he'd said.

In the end, she'd fallen for Harvey's hoax, wrongly assuming that the outward physical cues reflected the inner man's true intent.

When she'd gotten into his car and realized her mistake, Harvey said she'd fought, landing a hard blow to his face. The pain had snapped his temper, and he'd backhanded her hard across the mouth. Her blood had splattered the windshield. He'd knocked her out cold.

As they'd planned, Harvey drove the Volvo to the empty parking lot where Robbie waited with the Impala. As Harvey tied up the girl and loaded her in the trunk, Robbie had stayed in the car as he'd been told, but it had taken every ounce of control to stay put. He'd wanted to run. Wanted to hide.

Harvey, however, was enjoying himself. He'd

taken care to wake her up. He'd wanted her awake, aware of the danger. She'd jerked and pulled at her bindings, but his knots were sure. Smiling, Harvey had rubbed the tender spot on his jaw before slamming the trunk closed.

For most of the drive up from Austin, Harvey didn't notice her kicks and screams. He talked about the weather, the diner that served the best pancakes, even his upcoming teaching assignment. Just another day for Harvey.

But each thump and shriek had raked across Robbie's nerves, and when he couldn't stand it anymore, he'd turned on the radio, tuning to a country-western station.

Now as Harvey watched her twist against her bindings, he smiled. "Glad to see the ride didn't drain all the fight out of you, girl. Nothing worse than a broken spirit."

Dark eyes narrowed, and he knew this one would go to the grave fighting.

"Robbie," he said, clapping his hands together, "time to get this show on the road."

Harvey grabbed the girl by the midsection, hauled her out of the trunk like a sack of potatoes and hefted her over his shoulder. She smelled of sweat, urine and the faintest hint of department store perfume. She struggled and tried to ram her knees into his belly, but the bindings kept her immobile and easy to handle.

Robbie scanned the darkened road they'd just

traveled. "Harvey, I don't want to do this. I'm not ready. Let me stay in the car."

"Come on, son, we been talking about this for weeks. You're twenty-three. Man enough. We've put this day off long enough."

Fear weighed down Robbie's feet. "I know I said I wanted to do this, but I don't think I can. Not yet."

"Don't be silly, boy. Like riding a bike. Once you get the hang of it, it's as easy as pie."

With the girl on his shoulder Harvey followed the familiar path into the woods. It had been twenty-plus years since he'd been here, but Harvey didn't miss a jutting root, rock or bend on the trail. These were his woods. His home.

Robbie trailed after him. A couple of times he stumbled, muttered under his breath, but he kept moving. Harvey had been his father for eleven years. And Robbie would have matched Harvey against any father. Harvey had taken him away from a crack-addicted mother, seen that he was educated, well fed and clothed. He was a perfect father except for the fact that Harvey liked to kill women. Not all the time, but every so often. Robbie had never questioned or feared his father's obsession, and had assumed he'd one day follow. But now, faced with this second chance to kill, his courage faltered.

When they arrived at the clearing Harvey paused to look at the bluebonnets. "Best time of year to be here," he said more to himself. "Sights like this make a man glad he's alive."

Robbie folded his arms over his chest. His fingertips rubbed his lean biceps, a self-soothing gesture.

"No reason to fret, boy. I know you're nervous, but once we're done tonight, you'll be glad you saw it through." The woman moaned and her stomach contracted against Harvey's shoulder. "Better not barf, girl. It'll come up your throat and the gag will send it right back. You'll be lucky if you don't choke to death."

She tensed as if struggling with her own bile and then relaxed back against him, moaning fear and failure.

Harvey smacked her on the bottom and she jumped. "I think our girl here has finally figured out that there isn't much she can do. We're running the show now, aren't we, Robbie?"

She was gonna die.

No matter what.

"Yeah, I guess."

Carefully, Robbie worked his way through the field of bluebonnets that gently grazed his ankles. At the far edge of the field, he spotted the hole Harvey had dug a couple of days ago and covered with a tarp.

"Boy, go on and pull the tarp off."

Praying he'd not fail his father, he pulled off the tarp and carefully folded it into a neat square.

Setting it aside he peered into the hole. Six feet long, three feet deep and two feet wide. Harvey had said it had taken a few hours to dig, and he'd complained the task had irritated the pinched nerve in his back.

Grabbing the woman's bound hands, Harvey hauled her off his shoulders and dropped her on the ground beside the hole. An unladylike grunt whooshed from her.

The bindings kept her back arched and on her side. She looked up at Robbie, eyes silently pleading.

Harvey pulled a knife from his pocket and flicked it open. Steel glinted in moonlight. She flinched, fear igniting and burning through the pitiful plea dulling her gaze. She tried to wriggle away, but the ropes kept her immobile.

He cut through the bindings that kept her back arched but did not cut the ropes that still held her hands and feet secure. Groaning, she slowly stretched out her body, whimpering as if her muscles and bones protested.

She rolled on her back, her small breasts jutting toward him, and stared up at him with the knowing of a person who called the streets home.

Robbie knelt and removed her gag. Gingerly, he smoothed his hand over her hair. "Scream if you want. No one will hear."

Pent-up fear and rage roared out of her in a loud, piercing howl.

Harvey laughed.

Robbie flinched as he watched her holler until finally she stopped, exhausted.

She moistened dried lips. "Why are you doing this? I don't know you."

"No begging or pleading from this one," Harvey said. "I picked a damn good one for you, boy."

The girl kept her gaze on Robbie, triggering an odd twisting in his gut that wasn't all bad.

"Not too bad, is it, boy?" Harvey stared at him closely.

"Why do you do this, Harvey? It doesn't make sense," Robbie said.

"No, I don't suppose it does. Just an unexplainable need that I stopped questioning a long time ago." He winked and clapped his hands. "Time for the grand finale."

Shadows sharpened the edge of the woman's cheekbones. "You don't have to do this. Let me go. I won't tell a soul."

"You're wasting your breath, girl." Harvey *tsked* as he reached under her armpits and dragged her toward the hole. "I already know you're not going to tell."

Tossing a panicked gaze toward the hole, her body tensed as she tried to dig her heels into the hard dirt. "Please, let me go."

"Robbie, get the shovel. It's lying on the ground over there."

Frowning, Robbie did as he was told and held out the shovel to Harvey.

Harvey shook his head. "We said you'd do it this time. I'm not going to help. Time to make you into the man I know you can be."

Robbie shoved out a breath. The idea of disappointing his father ripped at him. He'd do anything for Harvey. Anything. But this. "Not tonight, Harvey."

Harvey stared at the boy, as if trying to understand his fear. "First time I put a woman in the ground, it scared the daylights out of me. Hell, I almost backed out. I was sure I'd get caught. But I didn't get caught. Neither will you."

Robbie shook his head, slowly opened his fingers and let the shovel drop. "I can't."

Harvey kept his voice calm. "Robbie, no need to test my patience. I gave you a pass last time. Let's get on with this."

"Robbie," the girl said. "You don't have to do this."

"Now, that's enough out of you, girl." Harvey jerked the girl's upper body and settled her entire body in the hole. She lay flat on her back, the moonlight glistening on pale bruised skin.

"Please, let me go!" She sat up.

Harvey pushed her down hard. "Pick up the shovel, boy."

"No."

"You don't have to do this, Robbie." The girl struggled to sit up again.

"Get up again, and I'll hit you with the shovel."

Harvey didn't raise his voice, but his words carried more weight than a madman's rant. He shoved her back with his booted foot.

Gritting her teeth, she ignored him, screamed and again tried to sit up. Without muttering a word, Harvey picked up the shovel and hit her across the side of the head. The blow was enough to send her back, stunned, but not enough to knock her out.

Robbie winced and took a step back.

Harvey dug the shovel's blade into soft dirt. "See what you made me do, boy? If you'd taken care of business then she'd not be half conscious." He shoveled dirt on her midsection. The hard thump sent a lungful of air whooshing from her. He hefted more dirt. "Get over here, boy."

Robbie took another step back. "No."

"Don't disappoint me, boy."

"I'm sorry, Harvey." His hands shook. "I know I said I could, but I can't. Not now."

Harvey cocked his head. "I don't think I'm hearing you correctly."

Tears welled in the boy's eyes. "I can't do this now."

"Time for waiting is over, boy." He held out the shovel. "Now or never. You a man or not?"

Robbie shook his head no.

"You gonna fail me again?"

"I'm sorry."

Harvey was silent for long, tense seconds and

then calmly said, "You don't follow through tonight, then we are done."

Robbie flinched. "Harvey, I can try again."

"If you don't take care of business now, I don't ever want to see you again."

Tears welled in Robbie's eyes as he stepped back. He loved his father. The man who'd saved him from a miserable life. But he couldn't do this now.

Harvey tossed more dirt on the girl. She screamed loud and clear. He tossed dirt on her face. She struggled to clear her eyes, as he ladled more and more dirt on her. She blinked, tried to turn her head, but she was trapped.

Robbie hesitated, stole one more peek at her pale flesh. Lord help him, but he couldn't do it.

Tears spilling, he turned and ran.

Chapter One

Saturday, April 6, 11:00 a.m.
Austin, Texas

If Texas Ranger Brody Winchester had come to see Dr. Jolene Granger on personal business, he'd have come with hat in hand. He'd have been ready to eat a heaping helping of humble pie, or better yet, crow.

But this visit wasn't personal. He'd not come to

apologize or to make amends. He had no intention of digging up the past or rubbing salt in old wounds. This. Was. Business.

He parked the black SUV in the recreation center's parking lot and shoved out a breath. He reached for his white Stetson on the passenger's seat, took a moment to level the silver concho trimming on the hat's base before he stepped out of the vehicle, straightened his shoulders and eyed the large box-shaped building. The sign above the double glass doors read: AUSTIN ROCK CLIMBING GYM.

As he stared up at the sign, hat in hand, he wondered if the boys back at headquarters had sent him to the wrong place and were having a good laugh at the new transfer's expense. The Jo Granger he'd known hated heights and if anyone had bet him she hung out in a place like this, he'd have taken the bet, damn sure he'd win.

'Course, he'd not been face-to-face with Jo in fourteen years. And time changed plenty.

Dr. Jolene Granger was no longer a wide-eyed college student but a psychologist who consulted with the Texas Rangers. In fact, her expertise on violent behavior had landed her several television interviews last year when a reporter had been digging for the motivations driving a serial killer that had hunted along I-35.

He'd seen on television that she'd given up the peasant skirts and flip-flops in favor of dark suits, pencil skirts, a tight bun, and white pearls around her neck. Reminded him of a librarian he'd had in school as a kid. Cool. Controlled. Hot.

Yeah, she'd changed in fourteen years. Maybe heights didn't bother her anymore.

A couple of laughing teens wearing shorts and carrying gym bags raced past him through the front door. He trailed behind them, finding himself in an industrial-style lobby tricked out with a cement floor, solid crate furniture and soda machines. He moved toward a long, narrow reception desk where a young guy was texting. Dark hair swept over a thin, pale face and tattoos covered every bit of skin exposed below his white T-shirt cuff.

If Brody had been in a more charitable mood, he'd let the kid finish his nonsense communication, which likely had to do with gossip or a party. But a foul and dark disposition sapped all patience.

He smacked his hand on the reception desk. "Need to find Dr. Jolene Granger."

The kid jumped, his initial glance aggravated until he took stock of the Stetson, the Texas Ranger's star pinned to Brody's broad chest and his six-foot-four frame. Displeasure gave way to startled deference. "She's in the main gym. Can I tell her you're here?"

"I'll announce myself."

The kid scrambled around the counter and

took a step as if to follow. "Is she in some kind of trouble?"

Brody stopped and eyed the kid. "Why's it your business if she is?"

His Adam's apple bobbed as he swallowed. "I like her. And if she were in trouble—"

Brody's own worries sharpened his tone. "What would you do if she were in trouble?"

Slight shoulders shrugged, but the kid's gaze remained direct. "I don't know."

"That's right. You don't know."

"She's a nice lady."

Jo had always coaxed this kind of loyalty out of folks. Kind, smart as a whip, she drew people. The kid was no different and Brody gave him props for standing up to him.

He softened his scowl. "Dr. Granger isn't in trouble. But my business is official. If you don't mind, I need for you to get back behind that counter and take care of your own business." He took a step toward the kid who hustled back behind the counter.

As Brody turned toward the main gym he imagined the boy on his cell again, texting his friends as fast as his thin fingers could move.

In the main gym, Brody was greeted by the smells of sweat and freshly polyurethane-coated floors. The walls were covered with gray rocklike facings that jutted and curved as a rock ledge might. Dispersed over the wall were colored footholds and handholds, some large and others so small he wondered how his large hands could maintain a grip.

A collection of climbers scaled the walls from the floor to ceiling. Belayers stood at the bottom, feeding climbers their safety ropes. A young, blond girl scaled the wall as if she were part monkey. A couple of guys in their midtwenties moved between the rock ledges with a power and grace he admired. He couldn't imagine that fourteen years had changed Jo so much that she now enjoyed this kind of foolishness.

The shouts and giggles of a group of girls in a side room drew him. The ten girls, who looked to be between fourteen and sixteen, stood at the base of a tall rock wall. Several were pregnant and most had tattoos and piercings. Young, but he imagined they all had a lifetime of experiences already under their belts.

There was no whiff of anger or sorrow radiating off anyone. They were cheering, like kids their age should. His gaze trailed theirs to a woman racing a male climber to the top of the rock wall toward a bell.

Squealing young voices chanted, "Go Jo. Go Jo. Go Jo."

Jo.

Brody stood behind the students, rested his hands on his hips and shifted his gaze from the male climber to the woman. Her chalked fingers clung to slivers of manufactured rock while her feet perched on similar pieces. Tight black pants and a white, fitted spandex top molded a trim athletic body. Long, red hair bound into a ponytail swept across her muscled back as she scrambled haphazardly from rock to rock. Jo? He looked closer.

Damn, if it wasn't her.

When Jo reached the top and rang a bell, the kids cheered. She looked over her shoulder, suspending from a single handhold and foothold and smiled at them. "Now which one of you girls bet that I couldn't win?"

The girls laughed, shaking heads and pointing to each other. None fessed up to having any doubts about her.

Jo surveyed the crowd of girls. "And seeing as I won, ladies, that means you all are going to study real hard for the rest of this semester, correct?"

A rumble of laughter and whispers rolled through the teens. "Yes!" they shouted.

The male climber rang the bell. He regarded Jo, his good-natured appreciation clear as he nodded his concession.

Brody assessed the man, wondering if Jo had really beaten him or if he had held back to win points with Jo. If he had to wager, he'd put his chips on the latter.

"Doug buys ice cream for everyone!" Jo said.

The kids cheered.

Doug grinned. "Rematch!"

Jo's laughter rang clear and bright as she turned her face from the wall and gazed at the girls with tenderness. However, as quickly as she looked down, she looked back up as if the height flustered her. "Gonna have to be a lot of A's and B's to get me up here again."

Brody crossed his arms over his chest, taking inventory of her high cheekbones, pale complexion and full lips. She was more relaxed, and a hell of a lot hotter than the grim woman he'd seen on television last year.

As if she'd read his mind, her gaze shifted from the kids to him. For a moment she stared at him, as if she couldn't believe her eyes. He made a point not to blink or show the faintest sign of curiosity for this new version of Dr. Granger.

Shaking off her surprise, she moved to climb down the wall but missed her handhold and, in a blink, fell. The girls squealed. Brody tensed, moving toward the crowd, ready to shove his way toward the wall's base. But the rope tightened, halted her fall and the belayer held tight.

Jo immediately grabbed for another rock and swung herself back into position on the wall. For an instant, she didn't move.

"You okay, Jo?" Doug asked.

"Fine." She grabbed for a larger rock. Within seconds she'd scrambled to the bottom of the wall. She stared at the kids, and she wiped a bead of sweat off her forehead with the back of her hand. "That's why I harp on preparedness. Never go into any situation without thinking about what could go wrong. You'll live a longer, happier life if you are careful."

The kids chuckled nervously as Doug descended the wall. He moved to Jo, putting his hand on her shoulder. "You're really okay?"

She briefly studied Brody before dropping her gaze. "Yeah, I'm fine. Would you excuse me?"

She moved through the crowd of girls. Several stopped her and asked again if she was okay. She assured them all she was fine. Her back was straight and her gaze direct as she finally cut through the crowd and closed the distance between them.

Wisps of hair framed her face, which had grown more angular over the years. Though she'd always been slim, her body now was trim and nicely muscular. No hint of apology softened green eyes now as sharp as emeralds. The years had been good to her. And he was real glad. The last time he'd seen her she'd been . . . broken.

Jo stopped a few feet shy of him. Her expression was stern, controlled and mildly interested. "I'm guessing you're here on business. A case."

"That's right." He removed his hat as he regarded the kids and Doug who stared at them with raw curiosity. "Mind if we talk somewhere else more private?"

"Sure. Let me grab my bag." She snatched up a gym bag from a wooden bench. "Girls, I'll be right back."

"Are you getting arrested?" one shouted.

Jo glanced up at Brody. "Am I in trouble, Ranger Winchester?"

"No, ma'am." He spoke loud enough for all to hear.

She followed him outside. Sweat glistened from her skin and mingled with a delicate perfume that reminded him of roses. A lot had changed about Jo but not her scent. "What gives?"

"You heard of Harvey Lee Smith?"

"Sure." She yanked out a hoodie jacket from her bag and pulled it on. "Convicted serial killer. I featured him in my dissertation, 'The Mind of a Serial Killer.' You were the original DPS arresting officer, as I remember."

He'd been a Texas Department of Public Safety officer when he'd collared Smith. But the arrest had been the coup that earned him his Ranger's star. The Texas Rangers were an elite group of one hundred and forty-four men and women in the Department of Public Safety.

"That's right. And if you've studied Smith you'd know he was convicted of killing ten women. However, it's believed his murder count is higher than thirteen."

She zipped up her jacket and tucked her hands in the pockets. "When he was interviewed he confessed to killing the women. Ten bodies were found buried in his backyard in Austin. Three victims linked to him were not found. When pressed he wouldn't give details."

"I've interviewed him many times over the last three years. But he kept changing his story and 'forgetting' where the other bodies were buried. It was all a big game to him."

She frowned. "He's dying of cancer, from what I hear. Doesn't have much time to live."

"Docs say the disease spread to his liver. Less than a couple of months."

She was silent for several seconds. "He's going to his grave with his secrets and will deny closure for the victims' families. It's the last bit of control he can exert."

Brody's jaw tightened and released. He'd used every trick in the book to get Smith to open up but endless hours of interviews had been a waste. Smith had taken pleasure in jerking his chain.

"Smith told prison authorities late yesterday that he wanted to talk. He knows time is running out, and he wants to cleanse his soul. He's agreed to tell where the bodies are buried."

Jo shifted her stance. "He's made similar promises before. You said it yourself. It's all a game to him."

"I know. And I'd love to tell him to rot in hell. But this might be my last chance to talk to him and to find those bodies."

She nodded. "And you can't let it pass. I get that."

"That's right."

She met his gaze. "Why me?"

Brody pulled in a deep breath and let it out slowly. "Because Smith requested that you hear his last confession."

She shook her head, her brow rising. "Me specifically? I find that hard to believe."

"He was clear he'd talk to you and no one else."

"I've done some work for the Texas Rangers and I wrote a paper on the guy, but I'm by no stretch the most experienced psychologist. Others have written more about him and have a lot more to offer."

No traces of false modesty in the clear-minded assessment. "Your record has been impressive."

Green eyes narrowed. "I'm building a reputation but again, why me? I shouldn't be on this guy's radar."

He settled his right hand on his belt next to his gun. "The guy's smart as hell. He's had all the time in the world to do what digging he can."

A humorless smile tipped the edge of her mouth. "And he figured out that you and I used to be married."

"That's my best guess. I interviewed him more than anyone and each session he did his best to pull personal information out of me."

"I can't see you discussing personal matters."

He caught the comment's double edge. "No, I did not. But like I said, I'm betting he did some digging."

"And somehow he figured out about me."

"Somehow."

A silence settled for a moment. "Maybe he heard about my dissertation. The university published it online. Maybe this is a quirky coincidence."

Leather creaked on his gun belt as he shifted his stance. "Could be as simple as that. But I've never been a big believer in coincidence. By my way of thinking they are as rare as hen's teeth."

She tightened her hand on her bag. "You've put some thought into this."

"Since the prison called me this morning, overthinking is more like it."

She dropped her gaze to the ground, shaking her head.

"If you don't want to do this, there's no harm, no foul. I'll go talk to Smith again and see if he'll talk to me. He might give in, seeing as death is close."

"And what if he doesn't?"

Brody shrugged. "Then our last shot at finding those three bodies is lost."

She drew in a slow, steady breath and then released it. "I'll do it. I'll go. Least I can do for those families."

Jo might not cross a street to spit on him, but she'd give up her Saturday to talk to a killer to help grieving families. "You sure about that?"

"As I remember, Smith is a control freak who only cooperates if all his demands are met. When does he want to see me?"

"Today."

A brow arched. "Right now?"

"My plane is gassed and ready to go at the airport. I can have you in West Livingston in two hours." West Livingston, Texas, was home to the prison that housed death row for male inmates.

"I didn't bring a change of clothes here. I need to swing by my house."

"I'll follow you."

She fished her keys out of her bag and offered him a less than enthusiastic "Great. Let me tell Doug and the girls I'm leaving."

Without another word she hurried into the gym. She reappeared moments later, crossed the lot and slid into a sleek, black BMW. He wasn't surprised that she was doing well. He'd always known she was meant for a big life. From what he'd heard, and he always made a point to listen when her name came up, her easy style was getting big results.

Brody slid behind the wheel of his Bronco and watched her as she pulled slowly out of her space and through the parking lot. She came to a complete stop at the stop sign, put on her right blinker and turned.

"Still following all the rules," he muttered.

The drive from the gym to her small, earth-toned bungalow in Hyde Park, a central Austin neighborhood, took minutes. Built in the twenties, Hyde Park was now home to mostly university professors, students and professionals.

As she pulled in the driveway he noted her yard had been neatly landscaped at one time, but like everyone else who'd endured the Texas drought for the last few years, she'd had to let her lawn go when the water restrictions had been implemented. Still, even grassless, she managed to keep the place looking tidy.

Because the Rangers had transferred him several times over the last three years, he'd lived a gypsy's life, settling for short-term leases in nondescript apartments. He'd always figured by this age he'd have been in a home with wife and kids. But work, and maybe his own faults, had kept him single.

Out of her car, she grabbed mail from a white mailbox with carefully lined numbers on the side and motioned for him to follow. "Might as well come inside. It's gonna take me about a half hour."

He'd have been fine staying in the car, but now was not the time to put up any kind of fuss. She was doing him a favor when she could have easily told him to fuck off.

"Sure." He shut off the engine and followed her up the sidewalk, cracked in spots by last summer's heat.

He studied the empty window boxes freshly painted turquoise and the front door also newly painted in black. Precise. Orderly. By the front porch a one-hundred-year-old pecan tree had grown so large, its leaves hung over the porch and its roots ate into the porch foundation.

As if reading his thoughts, Jo said, "I'm redoing the porch this summer. Last couple of years I focused on the inside of the house."

"Considering the drought, a good choice."

Jo had always had her shit together. Back in the day, without trying, she had made him feel like a clod. He'd resented her in those days. Maturity had taught him that he, not her, had been the root of his problems.

She opened her storm door and he caught it, holding it open for her as she fumbled with her keys.

"I've three cats," she said. "They won't bother you, but don't be put off when you see them. They're former strays and look a little rough."

"I can handle three cats."

"Great." She opened the door, flipped on the light and set her purse and keys by the front door as she likely did every day she'd lived here. The living room was warm and cozy, an overstuffed chair in front of a fireplace reserved for cold Austin nights. The floors were a yellow pine and the ceiling high and vaulted. A long farmhouse table filled a dining room that led into a kitchen.

"Have a seat on the couch. There are bottled waters in the fridge. Even a soda or two. I'll be as quick as I can."

"I could use a soda," he said. "I came straight from work."

"There's luncheon meat and bread in there if you're hungry. Help yourself." Her smile fell short of warm.

She vanished into the bedroom, and he made his way past several black-and-white photo images hanging on the dining room wall. It didn't take a practiced eye to know they were worth money. The kitchen, glittering stainless steel and granite, looked as if it had just been cleaned. Hell, if a surprise visitor showed up at his apartment . . . well, it sure as hell wouldn't be this nice. He grabbed a cola from the fridge and popped the top. As the cool liquid rolled down his parched throat, he wondered how the hell he'd landed in his ex's house.

Jo turned on the shower, kicked off her shoes and socks, and then leaned on the sink, staring into the fogging mirror. She was grateful her expression looked calm and her cheeks had not flushed with shock. Brody Winchester. She'd heard he'd moved back to town but had hoped Austin was big enough for her to avoid him.

For several seconds she stared until the steam misted over all traces of her.

"Holy shit," she whispered as she turned and pulled off her hoodie, workout top and pants.

She stepped into the shower and ducked her head under the hot spray, barely noticing as it streamed over her body and rinsed the salty sweat from her skin.

Brody *f-ing* Winchester was in her house. Getting a soda out of her fridge. Brody *f-ing* Winchester was sitting on her sofa like it was old home week.

Brody *f-ing* Winchester.

Her ex-husband.

It had been fourteen years since they'd last seen each other. For several years after their divorce she'd dreamed of facing him again and demanding an apology. She'd imagined him seeing the error of his ways and offering sincere regret. The dream had sustained her for a time but after several years, she'd simply grown tired of being angry. And so she'd let Winchester go, truly believing he was out of her system.

And then she'd seen him standing in the gym, staring at her as if she were an odd curiosity. She'd been taken aback, lost her hold, and practiced speeches recited too many times after the divorce were forgotten.

She groaned. She'd invited him into her home. Offered him a soda. And a sandwich. *You were always a pushover around him.*

She willed the water to wash away her thoughts

and disappointments. *Let go. Let go.* The familiar mantra lapped over her, taking with it some of the emotion.

Brody's arrival wasn't personal. It was business. And he was acting like an adult, a professional. He wasn't the newly enlisted twenty-two-year-old Marine who had all the answers, and he wasn't looking at her as if she owed him. Nor was she an awkward eighteen-year-old, grateful for any kind of love and attention. She didn't need him, not as she thought she had all those years ago.

The hot water beaded on her forehead. She was thirty-two. He was thirty-six. If they couldn't act like grown-ups now, when would they ever? The past was the past. Let it go and move on.

This time tomorrow her interview with Harvey Lee Smith would be over and Brody would be out of her life again. Case, hopefully, closed.

She shut off the water, toweled off, dried her hair quickly and dressed in a dark pencil skirt, white blouse and matching jacket. She put on her pearl necklace and earrings and, as she promised, was ready to leave within thirty minutes.

When she emerged from her bedroom, her cats had surrounded Brody. Atticus, a sixteen-pound orange cat, sat at the end of the sofa staring at Brody as if he wanted to attack. Shakespeare, a wiry black cat with a snub nose tail, sat on the floor out of his reach, and Mrs. Ramsey, a small gray tabby, sat in his lap, purring as he rubbed her between the ears.

God, what he must think of her. All these years and she was still not only the nerdy smart girl, but also the single lady with the house full of cats.

She snatched up her purse and snapped it open. "Ready?"

He finished off his soda and gently nudged Mrs. Ramsey back onto the couch. As he rose, his gaze lingered on her a half a beat before he held up the can. "Yep. Where's your recycling?"

Her first instinct was to take the can and throw it out for him. She'd have done it for anyone but him. "Under the sink in the kitchen."

As he disposed of the can, she checked her wallet to make sure she had enough cash as well as her ID. She tucked in a notebook, extra pens as well as a point-and-shoot camera. "I'll follow you to the airport."

He moved toward her, hat balanced in his hand, each step measured.

When had she forgotten he was so tall and broad-shouldered? He'd been like that in college, possessing a room simply by entering. Age had certainly not whittled away his muscle tone. He was broader in the shoulders and his legs and his forearms had grown thicker.

He'd never been classically or pretty-boy handsome. "Very male" had been the best way to describe him. Age had not only wiped away the traces of youth, but had left his face with a raw-boned leanness that bordered on menacing.

"It could be a late night," he said. "Better not to leave an extra car at the airport."

No doubt his frame all but filled the front seat of that Bronco. "I don't mind."

"It'll be easier if I drive."

A rebuttal danced on the tip of her tongue and then she swallowed it. The more she protested, the bigger deal she made out of the whole situation. And this was not a big deal. It was business.

"Fine." Atticus meowed, jumped off the back of a chair. "Let me feed the cats."

He held out his hat, indicating the way to the kitchen. "You've wrangled yourself a real herd here."

"They kinda found me."

"You're a soft touch."

"Maybe." She opened the kitchen pantry, scooped out a mound of dried food and dropped it into three different bowls scattered around the kitchen and den. Atticus took the bowl by the bin. Shakespeare moved to his bowl under the kitchen table and Mrs. Ramsey ate behind the chair.

"That big red one runs the roost," Brody said.

She filled a water bowl and set it beside Atticus. "I've had him a year. But as soon as he arrived he took over."

"Is he growling?"

"He growls when he eats. Defense mechanism,

I suppose. Vet thinks he fended for himself a good while. He was half starved and pretty banged up when he came to me."

"Give the 'ol boy credit for surviving."

"Let me check in with my neighbor and let him know I'll be gone. There's a fifty percent chance of rain this evening, and if we get grounded the cats will need to be fed."

He followed her out the front door. "Still watch the weather every morning?"

Still eat Frosted Flakes in the morning? The unexpected memory had her pulling the front door closed with a too-firm slam. She turned the key in the lock until the dead bolt slid into place. "The first personal reference to our short but brief marriage—the elephant in the room."

He stood at the base of the stairs, one foot on the bottom step. "I never was good at pretending."

"Cutting honesty from what I remember."

He settled his hat on his head. He tightened and released his jaw. "There something between us we need to lance before we get this show on the road?"

"No." Emotions tightened and released. She nodded toward the house to her right. "I'll be right back."

He studied her a moment. "I'll be in the car."

Not sure why she needed to push back over weather and memories of cereal, she hurried, her heels clicking against the sidewalk's cracked cement, toward her neighbor Ted Rucker's front door. A couple of quick knocks and the door opened to a tall, lean man with blond hair and horn-rimmed glasses.

"Rucker," she said. "I'm headed out of town. Could you check in on the cats if you don't hear from me? I should be back tonight, but you never know."

He looked past her to Brody who stood outside his Bronco, arms folded over his chest. "Rangers?"

"Ranger Brody Winchester." She never discussed cases. "I should be back late, but if the weather doesn't hold, we could be delayed."

Rucker grinned. "I'll feed The Three Musketeers. How's that abscess on Atticus's side?"

"The antibiotics you prescribed did the trick. Hopefully he's learned not to tangle with the alley cat down the street."

"We'll see. He has a mind of his own." He frowned. "Safe travels."

"Thanks again."

"Hey, when you get back why don't we get coffee? We've been talking about it often enough and never make the time. We can catch up on neighborhood gossip."

She laughed, already backing away. "Sounds like a plan."

When she reached the car, Brody opened the door for her and she paused. "You've never done that before."

"I have. Just not for you."

No anger. No attitude. Merely facts. Not sure how to gauge his statement, she eased in the car and carefully adjusted her purse as he closed the door. When he slid behind the wheel, the Bronco's large cab did indeed shrink to a far-too-small size. Large wind-chapped hands shoved the key into the ignition. That hand had gripped a baseball bat like it was a lifeline. That hand had once cupped her breast and ignited a need in her that had taken her breath away.

"It helps that you're familiar with Smith," he said as he fired up the engine and pulled onto the street.

Swallowing, she considered the road ahead. "He was one of the four serial killers on which I based my dissertation. I never spoke to him, of course. My sources were based on law enforcement records and some interviews." She'd nearly dropped Smith from the paper altogether when she'd learned Brody had been the arresting officer. Pride wouldn't allow her to seek an interview with Brody and stubbornness had kept Smith in her dissertation. "Is there more I should be aware of?"

"He was a substitute teacher who fancied himself a novelist. The next Poe. He'd sit in his backyard, his burial ground, and for hours work on his short stories and books.

"Born in Texas and graduated from Oklahoma

University summa cum laude. His professors and many of the principals and teachers he worked with respected him. When he had a long-term sub assignment, lots of parents raved about him and requested he be hired permanently. But he refused all offers. He drifted around Oklahoma and Kansas for many years and then returned permanently to Texas twenty years ago."

Brody threaded the car in and out of traffic and soon they were headed east toward the municipal airport. "I asked him why he moved back, but he never answered. My theory is that he wanted more space, more land and better weather, which makes for a longer killing season."

"He was in his late forties when he moved back to Texas."

"That's right."

She stared out the front window, rifling through the facts she had on Smith. "His primary burial ground was his backyard but another is suspected."

"When he was arrested in the suspected disappearance of Tammy Lynn Myers three years ago, we got a subpoena to search his house and grounds. It didn't take much poking around the backyard to see that the land had been disturbed many times. We spent weeks in that backyard excavating ten bodies. However, we never found Tammy Lynn Myers. We also found evidence in his house that suggested there were at least two other victims. They were also never found."

"The medical examiner believed that the victims were buried alive."

"Most of the bodies were so decomposed there was no soft tissue to examine. Then we unearthed a body believed to be his second-to-last victim, a woman he killed weeks before Tammy. The medical examiner found dirt in her lungs and stomach, clearly indicating she'd ingested dirt as she tried to breathe."

A shiver traced her spine, as she thought about those women so desperate to breathe. "He never fought the charges."

"No. In fact, he was helpful at times."

"He was sentenced to death."

"And has used the last two years filing every appeal he can."

"He confesses, then fights," she said. "It's always about control with him."

He clenched his jaw, making a muscle by the joint flex. "Looks like the cancer is the game changer now. It'll kill him before the executioner."

"Karma has its own justice."

Without comment, Brody pulled through the gates of the small municipal airport and followed the winding, flat road past the main building with a control tower and then toward the hangars on the north side of the property. He parked beside a hangar. "I asked them to gas up the plane before I left this morning, so the preflight shouldn't take too long."

"Can I help?"

"Naw, hang tight. I got it." They climbed out of the car, and he unlocked a small door that led into the hangar, closed it and seconds later she heard the gears of the big hangar door grinding as the metal slid up and back. Inside the hangar stood a Cessna 150. The single prop, two-seater was painted white with red and black stripes. Brody took his white hat and jacket and tossed both in the back luggage section of the plane. He attached a hook to the aircraft's front wheel and easily pulled the plane out of the hangar. Within minutes, he'd inspected the plane's exterior as if he had done the preflight check a thousand times before.

He opened the airplane door for her and waited as she climbed the awkward step into the plane. After closing the hangar door, he slid behind the yoke of the plane. His shoulder brushed hers as he leaned over and grabbed another preflight list kept tucked by the seat. The Bronco was spacious compared to the cockpit.

He put on headphones and handed her a set before he primed the engine with the choke and then turned the key. The propeller turned once and stopped, but when he cranked the key a second time it turned and caught, quickly sending the propeller spinning so fast it vanished from sight.

Grateful for the loud hum of the engine that would make any conversation difficult, she settled back in her seat, put on her sunglasses, and for the first time since she'd seen Brody standing at the base of her climbing wall, allowed her mind to still.

As he spoke to the tower, he taxied to the runway and swung the plane around so that it rested on the runway's numbers and faced due east. Without tossing her a quick glance he gunned the engine and the two were hurtling down the runway. Halfway, he pulled the controls back and the front wheels lifted effortlessly off the ground. Her stomach flip-flopped and she was glad now she'd had a small breakfast.

Out the side window, she could see the square, functional buildings of the airport quickly growing smaller and smaller. As they gained altitude, the crystal-blue horizon stood in stark contrast to the brown earth savaged by drought. Glancing at the air speed, it didn't take much calculating to figure they'd be in West Livingston within the hour.

That gave her sixty minutes to prepare herself for seeing one of the most vicious serial killers in Texas history.

Chapter Two

Saturday, April 6, 3:00 p.m.

The gray walls of Livingston State Prison loomed as Jo stared out the backseat window of the Department of Public Safety's trooper car. Brody had called ahead from the plane and arranged for a trooper to meet them. He now sat in the front seat next to the officer and she in the back.

The tall fence topped with curled barbed wire surrounded the prison. Rain droplets now dripped on the window, turning a cool day into a raw one. She'd been in prisons before to interview suspects. She was no novice. Understood the ropes. And still a deep trepidation had wormed its way under her skin and left her edgy and nervous.

Brody caught her gaze in the rearview mirror. He sat tall. Strong. And if he'd been anybody else she might have made a joke to slice the tension. A laugh would've gone a long way right now. But she didn't want to laugh with Brody. She didn't want any kind of connection or link to him. It had been fourteen years since she'd seen him, and until this morning she'd believed all the emotions attached to their relationship were long dead and buried. But like a beast stirring after a long slumber, too many unwanted emotions were awakening.

Damn it.

Worrying over what she felt or didn't feel for Brody Winchester was not how she'd planned to spend her first real day off in two weeks.

"You okay?" Brody said.

"Never better." She tossed him a *whatever* smile that she saw often from the teen girls in her support group. However, she sensed hers didn't mask her worry. She considered a pithy comment, but then rejected it, knowing more often than not her quips sounded more bitchy than witty. "I'm still trying to wrap my brain around why Smith requested me. And I can't believe it's simply my connection to you."

The officer in the front seat, a tall, burly man with a crew cut and a full black mustache, didn't comment but she noted the subtle stiffening in his shoulders when she'd said, "my connection to you." She could only imagine what he'd now speculated.

They passed through the first checkpoint and then a second before she and Brody got out of the car. A breeze blew from the west, cutting through her jacket and chilling her skin.

Brody offered thanks to the officer and then escorted her inside where they passed through another metal detector. A female officer searched her bag while Brody checked his gun with the guards. Fifteen minutes later they found themselves in the warden's office.

As they entered the austere office, a mid-sized barrel-chested man rose. He had a thinning shock of red hair brushed back off a wide, ruddy face. He came around his desk, smoothing his hand over his blue plaid tie, before he extended it to Brody. "Brody. Heard you were coming."

"No rest for the wicked," Brody said.

"That would be you," the warden said, smiling. He shifted his gaze to Jo. "I'm Larry Maddox, warden here at Livingston. Dr. Granger?"

She smiled and accepted his calloused hand. "Pleasure to meet you, Warden. And please call me Jo."

He nodded. "Jo it is. And I'm Larry." He hooked his thumbs in his thick belt. "I hear Mr. Smith wants to have a chat with you?"

She frowned. "He does and I am surprised."

"Not much surprises me anymore." He shook his head. "I hate to see you dragged all the way out here for a wild-goose chase."

"You think this trip is a waste of time?"

"Mr. Smith is one of our wilier inmates. Been known to jerk some chains, as I'm sure Brody has told you. He's likely gonna do that to you."

She'd considered that. "Well, I'm here, so I might as well talk with him. How is his health?"

"Not too good these last couple of weeks. He had a surge in energy yesterday and that's when he called this meeting. Hospital doc says that kind of energy boost often comes before the end." His frown deepened. "A word of advice. Don't let him get in your head. He's good at it, and he will try. The man likely wants to inflict one last bit of pain before he leaves this world."

She arched a brow. "I've interviewed men like him before."

Warden Maddox shook his head. "No doubt you've talked to your share of bad guys, Dr. Granger. But this one is dangerous. A whole new level of evil."

An unexpected chill passed over her body. "I'll be fine."

Larry eyed Brody as if to say, *You've been warned.* "Then let's get this show on the road."

With Brody steps behind her, Jo followed the warden down the long, narrow, gray hallway to the interview room.

The warden stopped at the interview room's entrance. "Smith was clear he only wanted you and Winchester in the room."

"Both of us?" Jo said.

The warden shrugged. "Don't pretend to understand Smith's mind. Likely he wants the arresting officer front and center when he gives his last big speech."

Brody shifted his stance but didn't speak.

Jo flexed her fingers. "The sooner we start, the sooner we'll know."

Brody opened the door and this time walked in ahead of her. His gaze swept the small room, roaming over the glass partition that separated the prisoners from visitors. On this side of the glass, there was a chair in front of a small desk and a phone resting in a wall cradle. His frown darkened. "Have a seat, Dr. Granger."

Dr. Granger. Sounded odd, overly formal, even a bit pretentious when Brody said it. But she realized since they'd met, he'd used her formal title when they'd been in front of others and when they'd been alone, he'd kept his words to a minimum.

She passed by him and took a seat in front of the glass partition. In the glass's reflection, she could see Brody taking his post by the door. He didn't lean against the wall but stood straight, his hands clasped in front. In her home he'd been edgy but now his muscles all but snapped with tension. Brody knew dark facts about Smith, had witnessed events that he'd most likely not share with her because she was technically a civilian. She suspected that knowledge now preyed on his mind.

Jo refocused her gaze into the other room and the door on the opposite side of the glass. For several seconds she stared at the plain door, barely breathing as her heart thumped hard against her chest. The case of unexpected nerves had now grown annoying. Smith couldn't hurt her, and the sooner she stopped giving in to this ridiculous case of anxieties, the better.

The second hand on the wall clock moved in slow motion. Her heartbeat pulsed against her neck and wrists. Finally, the knob that she thought would never turn did and in a blink it rotated, and the door opened. She flinched but settled immediately as wheelchair-bound and shackled Smith was wheeled in by a guard.

In all the pictures she'd seen of Smith, he had been a robust and muscled man with dark, thick hair, penetrating green eyes and a sly smile that suggested he knew many secrets. However, the cancer had left him fragile, a good seventy pounds lighter and his ebony hair had grayed and thinned. His once-attractive face was lean and lined, but the green eyes, though sunken, reflected curiosity. And his trademark smile, hinting of dark secrets, emerged.

Smith's gaze flickered to Brody and back to Jo before he focused on getting settled. The guard waited behind him as he adjusted his shackles and carefully folded his thickly veined hands on the table.

Jo had sat across from her share of hardened criminals, most covered in tattoos, scars and piercings. But Smith's appearance could only be described as mild, gentle. Even if he wasn't sick, she doubted anyone would have crossed the street to avoid him and most women would have joined him in a steel, soundproofed elevator without a second thought. Likely, his victims hadn't sensed their extreme danger until it was far too late.

He picked up the phone on his side of the partition and in a clear, deep Texas drawl, he said, "Thank you for coming, Dr. Granger."

"Mr. Smith." She could have said that his request was a surprise. She could have asked why he'd wanted to see her. She could have asked how he was feeling. But she'd learned to say only what she absolutely had to say when she dealt with prisoners. They had the better part of twenty-four hours in a day to pick apart whatever you said and spin it a thousand different ways. The less said, the better.

He smiled, showing even, white teeth. "You must be wondering why I asked you to visit me here today."

"I was told you had something to tell me."

"That is correct." A slight cock of the head. "Would you mind if I spoke to an old friend? I've not seen Ranger Winchester in some time."

"Please, take as long as you like."

"I do appreciate your patience, Dr. Granger."

Having his gaze off of her gave her a moment to gather her thoughts and to assess him and the situation.

"Ranger, it's been a year at least?" Smith said.

Brody's stance relaxed, and whatever anger

he'd had for Smith vanished like ice under the hot sun. "It's been eleven months, Mr. Smith. Last time I was here was right after your sentencing."

"That's right. Hot spring day from what I remember. Time crawls and then in an instant too much of it has passed."

"That it does, Mr. Smith. That it does."

Jo thought about the fourteen years that had passed since she'd last seen Brody. Those years had indeed passed in a blink.

"They are keeping you busy, Ranger. I've seen you in the news. You are always the man behind the speaker at the podium, but I know your role is never minor."

"I hope they're treating you well here," Brody said.

"They are and thank you for speaking to the warden on my behalf. I do appreciate the opportunity to spend more time in the library. I do love reading books and newspapers."

"Glad I could be of help. I understand your health is not well."

"No, I'm afraid it's not good. Not good at all. The doctors say I have weeks." No hint of self-pity lurked behind the words.

"I assumed your time must be getting mighty short. It's not often you request visitors."

Jo always considered herself an expert at couching her emotions. But as she listened to Brody's relaxed cadence, with no hint of the anger she'd heard in the hallway moments ago, she realized she was in the presence of a master manipulator. If she'd only just met these two, she'd bet they were good friends.

"Well, I am glad you are doing well," Smith said, avoiding the comment. "But if you don't mind, Sergeant Winchester, I'd like a word with Dr. Granger."

"By all means."

Smith shifted his gaze back to Jo. "I've read about you in the newspapers. You were involved in that case last year. What did the paper call that killer?"

She sat silent, knowing he wasn't looking for an answer.

"The Interstate Killer. That's right. Left the bodies along Interstate 35. Interesting fellow."

Jo had no intention of discussing an old case. "Mr. Smith, I understand you summoned me here to discuss the location of three bodies."

He smiled and pulled in a labored breath. "Cut to the chase. Direct. I do like that about you, Dr. Jo Granger."

She resisted the urge to shift in her seat. "I've always found direct works best."

He leaned forward a fraction. "I agree. But as much as I'd like to cut to the chase, I don't want this interview over before it really gets started. I don't get visitors very often."

He flexed the bony fingers of his right hand and

she thought about those same hands holding a shovel and burying his victims alive. She tried to imagine the horror of being dragged away from the world, terrorized and then lying in a shallow grave as this man heaped dirt on your body and finally your face. She tried to imagine fighting for air as every cell in your body screamed for oxygen.

Smith was charming, and he was pure evil. Though she wanted to remind Smith she didn't care a whit for him or this chat, she thought about the three families that had lost loved ones but had never found their bodies. They'd gone for years without closure, and if she could play this game a little longer she might be able to give them some sense of peace.

Taking a cue from Brody's behavior, she leaned into her elbows, the phone pressed to her ear. "What would you like to discuss, Mr. Smith?"

"You."

"Me?" She kept her smile fixed and polite, but tension banded the muscles in her back. "Why would I be of any interest to you?"

His dark gaze sharpened. "My directness has made you uncomfortable."

"No, not at all. However, your interest in me is a surprise."

"On the contrary. You're a bright woman, Dr. Granger. You graduated top of your class from UT a year ahead of schedule and what scholarships didn't pay for, you paid for yourself by working as a beautician."

Discomfort slithered over her skin. "You know a lot about me. Why the interest?"

"I admire your intelligence. I find there is less and less of it in the world, and when I see it I give credit where credit is due."

"Thank you."

"Your parents should be proud."

Discussing her life was one matter, but bringing her parents into the discussion was another. Her father, an electrician, had passed away five years ago. He'd never been thrilled about her choice of psychology as a major, fearing she'd never be able to make a living with such a froufrou degree. Her mother was a beautician and owned her own shop in Austin. Candace Granger had never earned her high school degree, and though she wanted the best for Jo, she didn't understand Jo's interest in school.

"They were always supportive."

Keen eyes narrowed a fraction. "Did you find it tough being the only intellectual in a working-class family?"

Her grip on the phone tightened. "I'm not sure where this is heading, Mr. Smith."

"I see parallels between us. You see, I was the only one in my family to go to college and graduate school. My father was a truck driver, and he did not appreciate a son more interested in books than football. I often had to hide in the fields behind our farm when I wanted to read."

Why had he seen fit to draw a parallel between them? Was it to feed his ego or to unsettle her? "Your academic career was distinguished." The career that followed wasn't exceptional. His itinerant lifestyle had been part of the reason he'd stayed clear of law enforcement's notice for so long.

"Learning came easily and naturally for me, as it did you. I still can spend hours and hours rereading the classics."

She thought about the half-read copy of *Huckleberry Finn* on her nightstand. How many times had she read it? But she wasn't here to vent or to share her true thoughts. She was here to discover the location of the missing bodies.

"What about your writing, Mr. Smith? How has that been going? I understand at one point you wanted to write a novel."

He shrugged. "Without the muses I've not been as productive as I could have been, but I do manage to put pen to paper every day."

"Am I here so you can tell me about the missing muses?"

"In part, yes."

He would draw this out for hours if she allowed it. "I appreciate your need to talk, I do. Time no doubt is dear to you. But it is important that I find out the location of those three women. It's time to offer their families peace."

"Peace for the families?" That amused him. "Those women had no real families or stability in their lives, and they thought I offered it."

He wasn't being entirely truthful. Two of the girls had lived on the streets but Tammy, the last to vanish, had been in a halfway house. She'd had several rough years but was putting her life back on track. "Mr. Smith."

His eyes sparked with keen interest. "You are persistent. I like that. Do you know when you get angry or annoyed your eyes flash a little greener. If you were playing poker right now, I'd have identified that hint of emotion as your Tell. You do know what a Tell is, don't you, Dr. Granger?"

A Tell was a change in behavior that signaled emotion to the opponent. "You don't know me so well."

"I know you, like I know myself." He sighed as he sat back. "But you are right. I summoned you here for a different reason." Without taking his gaze off her, he said to Brody, "Got a pencil and paper, Sergeant?"

"All being recorded," Brody said, his voice smooth and easy.

For a moment Jo had been engrossed with Smith, and she'd forgotten Brody was there. However, her heartbeat steadied at the sound of his voice. All their issues aside, she knew he'd protect her, no matter what.

"When you start talking," Brody said easily, "I promise we won't miss a single detail."

Smith smiled, but before he could speak he began coughing. A minute passed before he caught his breath. "The devil is in the details."

"That is a misquote," Jo said. "The actual quote is, 'God is in the details.' "

Smith laughed. "Quite right, Dr. Granger. Quite right. My only regret is that you and I don't have more time. I'd love to have discussed politics with you or played chess. Are you a good chess player, Dr. Granger?"

"I hold my own."

"You are modest.

"Our games and conversations would have been interesting. I could have given you enough insight to transform your dissertation into a book."

For a moment she imagined wistfulness in his gaze. "The bodies are located off Rural Route Twelve exactly fifteen miles west of Austin. There is an old farm. I've not been there in several years but at the time a large tree marked the right turn off Route Twelve onto a dirt road. Follow the dirt road over three miles and you'll see an old shed or at least what remains. The bodies are buried one hundred and twenty feet due east of the structure. They're lined up in a single row. Find one and you'll find the others."

His casual, easy manner didn't soften the horror

of what he'd said. Three women. Brutalized. Buried alive. And he spoke about them as if they were insignificant.

"Thank you for the detailed information, Mr. Smith," Jo said. She thought about what he'd said about her eyes and hoped they'd not flared and betrayed her anger. "May I ask why you've chosen to reveal the location of the bodies? You've resisted all questions and refused to tell anyone."

"That is a fair question." He traced a deep purple vein running under his paper-thin skin. "I did not come to this decision lightly."

"Why, when you have but weeks to live? Is it that you didn't want this information to go with you to your grave?"

"That is partly true, Dr. Granger. I think as I see my life slipping away, setting the record straight means more."

She studied him closely. "The numbers are that important to you?"

"For the longest time it was enough that I knew what I'd done and where I'd buried the bodies. I was content to take it to my grave. I didn't need the world or the media to know. Most people don't have the brains or the patience to sit still for an entire news broadcast so why do I care what they think of me?"

His soft voice had sharpened with rarely exhibited emotion. Despite his words, he clearly cared about what people thought.

"But you do care now." She leaned closer to the glass, studying his drawn features. For the first time she sensed a crack in his glib armor. "Why now?"

For a long moment he stared at his hands and then slowly he raised his gaze. "Because, Dr. Granger, it is no longer just about me."

"Is this about the victims' families?"

"About them, I could care less."

"Who is this about?"

"Another killer."

"I don't understand."

"There is another killer out there."

Chapter Three

Saturday, April 6, 4:15 p.m.

Jo sat silently for a moment, then lifted her gaze to catch Brody's reflection in the glass. The easy manner gone, a new tension rippled through his body.

She released a breath and focused on Smith. "Another killer? Is he a copycat?"

"No, no." His tone was serious with no hint of manipulation or gamesmanship. But then the best manipulators did it effortlessly.

"He was my apprentice. I took him into my home when he was twelve. I raised him like a son, trained him to be a killer."

Jo's mind ticked through all the background information that had been gathered about Smith. How could they not know about a foster son? "The Rangers never mentioned an apprentice or a child."

"By the time I was arrested he wasn't a child. He was bordering thirty, and we hadn't spoken in years."

A dozen questions crowded to the front of her mind. But as tempted as she was to rattle them off, she steadied herself. She could never be certain when a man like Smith would stop answering questions, so it was important to lead with the most important. "What's his name?"

"Robbie Bradford. Or at least that was the name he used."

"What is his name now?"

A hint of sadness clouded his gaze. "I don't know. I've not seen him in ten years."

Robbie had been nearly thirty when Smith had been arrested. That would put him in his early thirties.

"What does he look like?"

"Medium height. Slender. Light brown hair."

"That's not very specific."

"I trained him not to stand out just like I never stood out. The best hunters blend into the landscape. He was clever at assuming roles."

"How do you know Robbie is killing?"

"He's communicated with me."

She heard Brody shift his stance. "The prison screens your communications."

"He is clever and careful. Like you, Robbie is intelligent, Dr. Granger, which is why I took him on as my apprentice. Fools have their place in the world and they are fun to play with from time to time, but when it comes to serious matters, they are a time waster."

"How did he get messages to you?"

"Newspaper want ads. The guards will tell you I read the paper daily. There are so few of us that actually read the paper these days."

"When was the ad?"

"Last week. Maybe the week before. I'm not as certain of time now. I suppose that's what dying does—makes the memory weak."

"What paper?"

"The *Austin Chronicle*."

"And what did Robbie tell you in this ad?"

"That he had passed the test. Crossed the line. Become a man who was ready to really play the game of life."

"Game? Life is a game?"

Smith smiled. "Of course it is. Some of us are smart enough to realize that and the rest stumble through life lost, confused and joyless."

"Killing women gave you joy?"

"Well, I do understand that what I did does not meet with your approval, Dr. Granger. And I am sorry."

Jo wondered if he'd ever experienced a true emotion.

As if he sensed her anger, he said, "Could we put our differences aside for the sake of this conversation?"

She tempered her fury. "Of course. What did Robbie say in the ad? Did he tell you or hint at who he killed? Where he buried the body?"

He hesitated, as he thought and shook his head. "If I tell you all my secrets, Dr. Granger, what will be left for you to figure out?"

Sick and dying and still he manipulated. It would be easy to get frustrated, but she refused. "I suppose you are right, Mr. Smith. A good puzzle does get the blood stirring."

He nodded. "I knew you'd agree."

Hoping he'd remain open, she shifted tactics. "How do you know Robbie is telling you the truth? He could be toying with you."

A half smile tipped the edge of Smith's mouth. "Well, I must trust his word, shouldn't I?" He rubbed the back of his hands as if they ached. "I've given you quite a bit of information today. But if I may, I'd like to ask you a question."

Jo stiffened. "You can ask, but I can't guarantee that I will answer."

"Well, I do have a few more answers to share, but I want answers from you first."

She walked a dangerous tightrope. One answer always led to another question. Men like Smith liked information because it gave them the power to manipulate. But if she didn't give him something, he'd end this conversation. "Ask your question, Mr. Smith, and I shall decide if I can answer."

He leaned forward in his wheelchair, his tired eyes now sharp with interest. "Have you had a good life?"

She'd expected a more specific question. "I don't understand."

"It's a simple question. And I want you to be honest. Have you had a good life?"

She sat back. "You've asked yourself that question a lot lately, haven't you?"

Her attempt to turn the question around tickled him. "I've put the question to myself, and I know the answer. It's you that I'm curious about."

"Why me?"

His delight at her directness faded to something more menacing. "No, no, no. It's your turn to answer, otherwise I suspect you already know what is next. I end this."

She straightened.

"You don't have to answer his questions," Brody said.

The sound of Brody's baritone voice startled her. Again she'd forgotten he was behind her and that she wasn't alone. Brody was an impossible man to ignore under the best of circumstances, and Smith had made her forget him twice.

Mr. Smith studied Brody. "That's a protective tone, Sergeant Winchester. But given the history you two share, it's understandable."

Smith did know about her marriage to Brody.

Brody folded his arms over his chest. "I think this is another one of your games. That the dump site you gave up so easily is bogus and that there is no Robbie. This is about jerking Dr. Granger's chain because it's your last chance for a dig."

Smith again looked amused, all traces of darkness gone. "You're usually controlled, Sergeant. Interesting that you'd be upset by my simple question to Dr. Granger. Unresolved feelings?"

"You're playing a game with her," Brody said.

Jo sat straighter, sensing a longer delay would drive Smith away. "Yes, I've had a good life, Mr. Smith."

Smith shifted his gaze from Brody back to her, staring at her for a moment. "You would consider yourself happy?"

"I do."

"You are an intellectual, and you grew up in a working-class family."

She stiffened and reminded herself that he was reading what could be found on the Internet. "I had good parents."

"They didn't understand you."

"I didn't understand them, but we all loved and supported each other."

"Hollow support at best, I would guess."

She curled the fingers of her left hand into a fist. "That's getting a little personal."

"We all need family, Dr. Granger. Robbie was my family for many years. In the end I didn't understand his decision, and it didn't go well for us. That's my one regret."

A serial killer pining about a lost son—it was an odd, but not impossible, concept. Though men like Smith had little regard for their victims, they sometimes had special people in their lives. "You loved Robbie."

"He was a good son. Smart. Devoted."

"Was he happy with you?"

"Yes. I saved him from a desperate future."

"What was the falling-out you two had?"

"That's not for me to discuss."

"We could find Robbie. Give him a message."

Smith smiled. "You'd never find him, and he'd never believe you. Actions, not words, matter, Dr. Granger."

"Why tell me about him?"

"It's the only way I can really reach him." He closed his eyes, and for a moment she thought he might have fallen asleep.

"What does that mean?"

Instead of answering her question, he said, "Thank you for coming today, Dr. Granger. But I am tired." Smith lifted his hand as a signal to the guard that he was ready to leave.

Jo gripped the phone, knowing a window was

closing forever. "Tell me more about Robbie."

As if she hadn't spoken, he smiled. "I do appreciate your coming, Dr. Granger. I truly do. But the day grows late and you must understand that I have little energy to draw upon."

She leaned closer to the window, resisting the urge to touch the glass. "There must be more about Robbie."

"I've given you all that I have." Gingerly, he leaned back in his wheelchair, wincing. "It's been nice meeting you, Dr. Granger. And I'm glad you are doing well."

She rose, still gripping the phone. "Why me, Mr. Smith? It makes no sense that you'd single me out for this interview."

He stilled as if he wouldn't answer but then said, "You are a smart woman. If you look deep inside yourself, you'll unravel the puzzle."

"What puzzle?" Frustrated by the subterfuge, her anger sparked. "That doesn't make any sense."

"Once you figure yourself out you'll find Robbie." He hung up his phone.

Jo pressed her phone to her ear as if willing him to return. But without a backward glance he left the interview room.

For several seconds, Jo stood there, not sure what had happened. She hung up the phone and carefully brushed the creases from her skirt, as if somehow the action would also diminish her deep sense of unease.

"He likes rattling people." Brody stepped toward her, stopping behind her. "Don't let him get to you."

She faced him. "I've interviewed my share of bad men. I can handle Smith."

"Really? How many bad guys have asked you to look deep inside yourself for the answers?"

None. Smith's question could have been a cheap manipulative trick, but it still troubled her for reasons she couldn't explain. What did he see? Feigning calm, she said, "You'd be surprised what my interviewees have asked me. I can promise you they can be graphic."

Brody frowned.

"Shouldn't you call someone about the information Smith gave us? Some of it could be genuine."

He opened the door to the interview room and waited until she passed. "Making a phone call is next on my list, Dr. Granger."

She stared down the gray hallway, suddenly anxious to be out of this suffocating place. Smith had tapped into a deep worry she'd harbored for years. "Of course, sure."

His head tilted. "You sure you're okay?"

She offered him a cool, polite smile. "Why wouldn't I be?"

If he'd not been watching her closely, he'd have missed the subtle stiffening of her spine and the flash of green in her eyes that Smith had called her Tell. Smith had gotten inside her head.

Brody was annoyed that she guarded her thoughts as closely with him as she had with Smith. When they'd been together fourteen years ago, she'd been open. She'd liked to talk to him and to joke. During one tutoring session, he'd teased her about talking so much. She'd blushed, tucked a stray curl behind her ear and laughed. He'd liked her openness, and he'd liked listening to her talk.

Now her demeanor was pure ice. Though she had a reputation for professionalism, colleagues in the Rangers had often referenced Jo's kindness and approachability. He supposed she'd never again offer him that openness and candor.

That shouldn't bother him. But it did.

He dialed the Rangers' office in Austin and asked for Sergeant James Beck. Brody had transferred back to Austin three weeks ago. Though he didn't know all the Rangers personally, he knew Rangers had each other's backs and when called upon, help arrived without question.

The phone rang twice. "Sergeant James Beck."

"Jim, this is Brody Winchester."

"Brody. You in West Livingston now?" Brody had briefed Jim as soon as the request from Smith had made it to his desk.

Brody explained the situation to Jim, including

Smith's reference to a new gravesite and Jo's presence. "Jo doing all right?"

"She's fine."

"Can I speak to her?" Jim said.

Brody hesitated, much like an animal who sensed his territory had been invaded. "Sure." He held out his phone to Jo. "Jim Beck wants to talk to you."

She took the phone, careful not to let her fingers touch his. "Jim." For several seconds she didn't speak but listened. Her face softened and this time when she smiled it reached her eyes. "Thanks. Great. No. No. I'm fine. Yes, I'm looking forward to it. See you then."

Brody accepted the phone back, watching as she turned away from him. "What's the weather look like in Austin?"

"Pissing rain," he said. "No one is complaining. God knows we need it. It's supposed to let up in an hour, but the whole region is a muddy mess. There is no way we're going to get a crew out to Smith's site today. It's too rural. Not many paved roads up that way."

Impatience bit. "We've waited this long. Another day won't matter."

"You take the plane to West Livingston?"

"Yeah."

"You should have clear skies our way in an hour."

"By the time we get out of here and back to

the airport it'll be at least that, if not more."

"We'll have a full team ready to hit Smith's site at first light."

"See you then."

Brody rang off and glanced toward Jo who seemed lost in thought. "We need to brief the warden."

"Do you think Smith told the truth? I know he likes games."

"He was a hell of a lot more forthcoming this time. He's revealed more today with you than he has with all our investigators over the years."

"He appeared to like or, at least, respect you," she said.

"I suspect it's because I'm the one who arrested him. I bested him at his game, and for that I get extra points."

"You couch your emotions well around him."

He hooked his thumb in his belt, sensing she was trying to gauge him. "I never forget for a moment I'm dealing with a monster."

She pursed her lips, and he could almost hear the wheels in her brain grinding. "I don't understand his last comment. The answers to finding a killer are in myself? Is he talking about my research? My work with the Rangers?"

Brody motioned to the guard who opened the cell block's heavy door. "I don't know, but remember Smith is an expert at deception."

"If his goal was to knock me off balance, he's done it."

"No one walks away from an interview with him unscathed. Let's get out of here."

He took her by the arm and led her away from the interview room. Minutes later they were in Warden Maddox's office.

Maddox gestured toward the chairs in front of his desk. They all sat. "How did it go?"

"He gave us new information," Brody said. He fully briefed him. "We won't know if it's true until we can follow up."

"No one's obtained a damn bit of information out of him in the time he's been here."

"Has his behavior changed in any way over the last weeks?" she said. "Anything to make you wonder why he chose to talk now?"

Maddox leaned back in his chair. "Since he's been here, he's stuck to a strict routine until lately when his illness became grave. He spends most days in the prison hospital."

"But he still reads the paper," Brody said.

"That's right. Reads it like it were the Bible."

"And he's had no visitors or mail?" Brody said.

"He gets fan letters. We screen them all, of course, before we give them to him, but he's not responded to a one. If he's not getting treatment in the infirmary then he's reading books in his cell. We can search his cell again."

"Wouldn't hurt."

"Let me know what you find."

"Will do."

Brody and Jo's ride back to the airport was strained and tense. Brody made small talk with the officer driving them, but she barely commented, choosing instead to stare out the window.

By the time he'd done a preflight check of the plane and they'd boarded, the rain had passed. The sun now hung low in the horizon, casting a fiery light on the landscape.

"I'd like to go with you tomorrow," she said as he'd closed the hangar door on the plane in Austin just after seven. "I want to know if Smith was telling us the truth or not."

The rain had cleared, but the air was heavy with moisture. Moonlight bounced off puddles. "There's no reason for you to go. It's going to be a long day and could well be a wild-goose chase. No sense wasting your time."

"It's my time to waste. I want to see with my own eyes. I'm happy to drive myself."

Brody shook his head. "Not a good idea."

"You can't keep me from going."

He raised a brow. "I sure as hell can."

Hearing the steel behind the words she retrenched. "The guy summoned me there for a reason. I'm mixed up in this somehow, and I need to figure it out." She tightened her jaw. "Come on, Brody, please."

Please sounded as if it had been torn from her

throat, but it accomplished her goal. "If you go, you won't be driving out there alone. I'll pick you up."

"That is not necessary. I have a sense of the area that he was describing and can find it on my own."

"You won't get inside the perimeter, not tomorrow anyway, without me. Jim Beck is sending in all the troops. You ride with me, or you stay behind."

She frowned and he sensed she wanted to argue. "When should I be ready?"

"Seven."

After Brody dropped Jo off at her house, she called her neighbor, Rucker, to let him know she'd returned and then quickly fed three hungry and vocal cats. In her bedroom she stripped off her suit and uncoiled her hair. She turned on the hot water in the shower and let the steam rise before stepping under the hot spray. Though she'd showered this morning, she was anxious to drown the scents of the prison. She washed her hair twice, scrubbed her skin until it was pink before toweling off and dressing in an oversized T-shirt and a thick, blue robe.

In the kitchen she heated up a can of soup and made herself a cheese sandwich before settling with both on the couch. She clicked on the television and switched to the news.

As she ate, her cats settled around her, waiting and hoping for a pinch of cheese. When Atticus nudged her she smiled. "You've eaten. And I promised the vet I would not feed you too much." She dropped her voice to a whisper. "You are getting fat."

Atticus stared at her as if miffed. He meowed loudly several times. Shaking her head, she gave him and the others small pieces of cheese.

Jo studied a picture on the coffee table taken of herself, her sister and her parents. The picture had been snapped five years ago when she'd graduated from her PhD program. It had been the last picture taken of all the Grangers as a family. Several months later her father had died of a heart attack.

Jo stared at her dad's smiling face. So many times that day he'd said she made him proud. She'd been the first Granger to not only attend college but to earn an advanced degree. Her sister, Ellie, three years younger, had been in her early twenties and had opted to forgo college, attend beauty school and work in their mother's hair salon.

That day she'd been excited for her accomplishment and edgy and nervous for the parents who looked at her as if she were a freak of nature. They simply did not understand why she'd wanted a PhD or why the salon hadn't been good enough. She simply did not fit into her family mold.

Look deep inside yourself.

Smith's words had her shifting her gaze to her mother's face. Tall, blond and stunning, Candace Granger had often questioned Jo's decision to take AP classes in high school. Each time she made the dean's list, Candace had an extra drink at dinner. She was always trying to add highlights to Jo's red hair. And her mother had been really unhappy when Jo was awarded the scholarship to UT.

She loved her mother, but when they tried to talk to each other they never quite connected.

"You need to be more like Ellie," Candace used to say. *"You could win those beauty contests if you'd try a little harder. Your piano playing has got the talent licked, and you are quick on your feet when asked questions."*

"I hate them, Mom. I don't fit."

Jo replaced the picture carefully back on the table. "Why wasn't I good enough, Mom?"

Jo considered calling her friend, Lara Church, but the two had only known each other a year and Lara was in the final days of planning her wedding to Jim Beck. Jo considered calling her sister, Ellie, then rejected the idea. She didn't need the drama.

Finally, she picked up the phone and dialed her mother's number. The phone rang once, twice and by the fourth ring the answering machine picked up. "This is Candace. Can't take your call right now, baby, but leave me your info and I'll get back to you."

Jo closed her eyes and for an instant, wondered what she should say to her mother. *Serial killer said to look deep inside myself. That's right. A serial killer. But the thing is, when I look inside me all I see is your disappointment.*

"Mom, it's Jo. This must be your Bible study night. Thought I'd check in. Call me when you get the chance."

She hung up and padded into the kitchen. She rinsed off her bowl and plate and put both neatly in the dishwasher. The clock on the wall chimed ten times as she eyed her reflection in the polished, stainless-steel refrigerator. Red hair curled around her face and without makeup her freckles peppered her pale complexion.

"How did he know I never feel like I fit? How did he know?"

Brody hung his jacket on the back of his door and tossed his hat in the chair. As he rolled up his sleeves and loosened his tie, he stared at the collection of dusty boxes containing Harvey Lee Smith's case files.

After Smith had been convicted, he'd packed up the files and moved on to the next case. There'd been unanswered questions but there'd been other cases that needed his attention. As much as he'd wanted all the questions answered, he'd had to accept that cases rarely were completely wrapped up.

He chose the box labeled number one. When he'd boxed up the files after Smith's trial, he'd had a gut feeling that one day he'd double back around. There'd been no reason to give him cause, but he'd sensed Smith couldn't go to his grave silently.

And Smith had not disappointed.

Brody set the box on his desk and tossed the top aside. The first file contained every bit of biographical information he'd amassed on Smith.

Smith had been born in Texas to a father who was a long-haul driver and a mother who waitressed part-time. His parents had originally hailed from west Texas but had settled in the Austin area when Smith, their only child, was a baby. By all accounts his childhood had been normal. He'd done well in school. He'd played baseball. His parents held steady jobs and appeared to have a happy marriage.

At fifteen, Smith's father died in an automobile accident. The father's sudden death had left mother and son financially ruined. They'd moved from their country farm to a city apartment. Harvey had been forced to quit school and work, so he drove trucks. The money had been good enough and the two had gotten by. Smith continued to study and earned a GED. He'd also applied to Oklahoma University and been accepted. The boy's mother had died suddenly and he'd been free to study full-time.

The mother's untimely death had been a red flag to Brody, and he'd spent a good bit of time digging into her death. But the coroner's findings had been clear-cut. Mae Smith died of a heart attack.

After graduation, he took a job as a substitute teacher. Several schools had wanted to hire Smith but he'd refused all offers. He'd never married and seemed to be just another normal guy.

Until the recent discovery of Smith's oldest kill. The first known victim had been Sandra Day, a twenty-one-year-old waitress in Houston. According to Smith's statement later, he'd taken Day on a date and instead of returning her at the end of the day had kept her in his house for the next three months before he'd buried her alive. He'd not intended to bury her alive. But she'd fought him hard, landing a hard punch to his nose. He'd hit her back and stunned her enough to get her to the grave. She was about covered with dirt when she'd startled awake and realized what was happening. Excited by her panic, he'd quickly covered her face with dirt.

Brody shifted through the victim profiles and made a list of the children. There'd been nine children between five women. Five boys and four girls. He searched the names of the boys. Two were in prison. One dead. One living in Seattle and working as a cop. And the last . . . unaccounted for. The boy's name had been Nathanial Boykin. Nathanial, not Robbie. He'd been placed in foster care after his mother's death and then there was no more mention of him. He'd be in his early thirties now.

Brody typed up a request for Social Services and sent it out. Maybe he'd get lucky. Maybe Robbie still lurked somewhere in the system.

Chapter Four

Sunday, April 7, 4:00 a.m.

Jo woke up to the pitch black of night. Though she tried to coax herself back to sleep for at least another half hour, she was tossing and turning. Her active brain wouldn't be silenced. Sleep wasn't coming back her way anytime soon.

Out of bed, she dressed in dark jeans, a dark turtleneck and vigorously brushed her hair, hoping to smooth out at least some of the curls and tangles. When her hair refused reason she coiled it back in her customary bun and pinned it in place. Knowing she'd be going to the crime scene, she took time applying her makeup as if it were a business day. Since she'd been a small child her mother had talked about the importance of makeup. "A smart lady looks her best all the time."

Jo had not inherited her mother's sleek, blond locks but thanks to makeup she could look more like a professional woman rather than Pippi Longstocking.

After coffee and a breakfast of eggs and toast, she checked her cell for a text from her mother. No message.

Jo still had an hour before Brody was to arrive, giving her enough time to drive to her mother's salon. For all the differences that divided Jo and her mother, she could honestly say she'd inherited her mother's work ethic. Candace worked seven days a week, often ten or twelve hours a day, and Jo was no different.

She grabbed her purse and a backpack prepped for a day in the field and ran out into the morning chill to drive the three miles to her mother's salon. As expected she saw lights on and Candace inside painting a purple wall blue.

Jo knocked on the door, making Candace jump. When she saw Jo she smiled, climbed off her stepladder and crossed to the front door.

Candace opened the front door with one hand while keeping her blue-tipped paintbrush away from her spotless shirt and ironed pants. Her blond hair was blow-dried straight, and she wore makeup and perfume.

"Hey, baby doll. What are you doing here?"

"I called you last night."

"Saw the message but figured I'd call a little later in the morning. You come here to help your old mamma paint?"

"Sorry, no." Jo kissed her mother on her cheek. "How is it you never drip a speck of paint?"

"Pays to be careful, baby girl." She kissed Jo on the cheek. "I swung by your place yesterday afternoon to tell you about your sister's news."

"News? That man she's dating finally gonna give her a ring?"

"No. In fact they broke up. Ellie ended it."

Ellie had dated a string of losers, but Jo had learned to keep thoughts like that to herself. "I thought he was gonna give her a ring?"

"No. Said he wasn't ready to commit. So she broke it off."

"I'll give Ellie credit. She knows what she wants."

"I'm not torn up about it. The ink on the divorce papers isn't dry, and she was already in love again. Too fast leads to trouble."

Jo and Brody had fallen hard and fast for each other. At the time the attraction they'd shared had made perfect sense. But her mother was right. Fast didn't last.

"As long as she's not knocked up, she'll move on fine."

Jo winced.

Her mother cocked a brow. "You better than anybody should agree."

Jo didn't respond, not wishing to stir up an argument.

"Of you two girls, Ellie was always my open book. Not like you. The girl with the secrets. Sometimes I think gypsies dropped you off on the back stoop."

An edge had crept into her mother's voice. "Where did that come from?"

"I spoke to your neighbor yesterday. Mr. Rucker."

"Why were you talking to my neighbor?"

Candace set her paintbrush carefully in the paint pan. "Because I came by to see you. Mothers do check on their daughters from time to time."

"Since when? Is everything all right with you?"

The lines around her eyes had deepened and her skin had paled. "I'm fine."

"Really? You're not working too hard?"

"Don't deflect the conversation to me. This is about you."

"And my secrets?"

"That's right. Mr. Rucker told me you were spending the afternoon with a guy." The frown lines around her mother's mouth deepened. "Said you were with a tall guy named Winchester." Her mother drew in a breath. "Please tell me it wasn't Brody Winchester."

Jo let a breath hiss slowly from her lips.

Her mother's lips flattened. "It is Brody Winchester."

"It's not like that."

Green eyes narrowed. "What's it like, Jo? Didn't that man do enough damage in your life?"

"As I remember, we accomplished much of the damage together. And we're not dating. Definitely not dating. We're working a case."

"Case? Last time you hung out with Brody Winchester, you said it was about tutoring and homework. All that led to a whole heap of trouble."

"I'm not eighteen, Mom. And I'm not a wide-eyed girl anymore." She stopped herself. "This is not why I came to see you this morning."

Candace picked up a rag and wiped her clean hands. "I don't want to fight, Jo. I don't. But it would make me sick to know you and Brody Winchester were seeing each other again."

"We are not seeing each other. Yesterday was the first time I've spoken to him in fourteen years."

Candace lowered her voice as she did when she was upset. "Fourteen years isn't enough to make me forget, honey."

"I haven't forgotten, Mom. Can we let this go? Please. Brody and I were working a case."

"He's not the reason you came by?"

She'd been unsettled since yesterday and now wondered if those feelings stemmed from Brody or Smith or maybe both. "No, I wanted to see you."

Her mother raised a brow. "It is not like you to stop by and talk, honey. You're self-reliant like me. Ellie is a chatterbox like your daddy. But not you. What is the case you're working on?"

"We went to West Livingston yesterday."

"To the prison."

"That's right. We went to interview Harvey Lee Smith."

Her frown deepened. "Isn't that the killer that's dying?"

"That's right."

Her mother again rubbed her clean hands with the rag. "Why does he have you so turned around?"

"At the end of the interview I asked him why he wanted to make his last confession to me. He said, 'Look deep inside yourself.' It didn't make any sense. Why would he say that?"

She rested her fist on her hip. "Honey, how am I supposed to know why a crazy man says what he says?"

"I don't know, Mom. I thought the statement was odd, and there's no one that knows me as well as you, I guess."

Some of Candace's tension eased. "He's a lunatic, honey. He'll say or do whatever suits him. And my guess is that he wanted to upset your applecart to watch you squirm."

"That's what Brody said in so many words."

Candace glanced at her manicured red nails

and then at Jo. "You don't worry about Smith. From what I read, he's an egghead who doesn't have many more days on the earth."

"Egghead. That's what Dad used to call me."

Her mother's face tensed. "Honey, your dad was a good, hardworking man, but he wasn't a big thinker. He didn't understand why I wanted this shop and why I wanted to work for myself. He'd have been happy to see me doing sets and perms in the garage like I did when you girls were little. You wanted more, like me. Daddy didn't understand."

"Your idea of more for me included winning beauty contests and coming into the business to work."

Candace lifted her chin a notch. "Both are honest pathways to a good life."

"I wanted different than you."

"Jo, what is going on with you?" She shook her head. "That Harvey Lee Smith has gotten under your skin."

Jo sighed. "Maybe you're right. I'm out of sorts."

"Honey, I don't want to fight. If I could help you I would. And I'm sorry for needling you about Brody Winchester. I don't have much use for the guy." She shook her head. "When you were having the miscarriage and he was off with his buddies getting drunk—"

"Please, Mom, he didn't know I was

miscarrying. . . . Look, I don't want to rehash old news."

"As long as it stays old news, baby, then I won't bring it up again."

Jo checked her watch. "Mom, I've got an appointment."

"What kind of appointment would you have on a Sunday morning?"

"It's police stuff."

"Not with Brody."

Jo hugged her mom. "You don't need to worry about Brody. He's history."

Brody was a half block from Jo's house when he saw her driving from the opposite direction and pulling into her driveway. Out and about early on a Sunday morning. And without meaning to, he found himself wondering where and with whom she'd spent the night.

Gut tensing, he parked his Bronco behind her and watched as she scrambled out of her car, grabbed a backpack from the backseat and hurried toward him. She slid into the seat, tucked the pack at her feet and clicked her seat belt.

She straightened her jacket. "Thank you for the ride."

"Sure." He put the gearshift in reverse and backed out of the driveway. "Where'd you come from?"

Jo hesitated. "I went to see my mother."

Unexpected relief softened his mood. An odd reaction, considering the last time he'd seen his ex-mother-in-law she had backed him up against a hospital wall after Jo's miscarriage and threatened to cut his balls off if he ever again looked at Jo. "How was your mother this morning?"

She took extra care to straighten out the folds of her jacket. "She's doing well. Though she did happen to drop by my house yesterday, and she wasn't happy to hear I was out with you."

Brody shook his head. "I can only imagine all the ways she dreamed of gutting me."

"She didn't share specifics, but I get the sense she'll be sharpening her knives this afternoon."

Smiling, Brody kept his gaze ahead. "I'll be sure to keep a lookout for a crazed blonde who favors rhinestones. She is still blond, isn't she?"

"She's still blond but doesn't favor the rhinestones much anymore."

"Good to know." He wove through town and was soon pulling onto I-35 headed south and wondering how he'd managed to start this Sunday morning talking about his ex-mother-in-law.

She pursed her lips. "I mentioned Smith to Mom."

"You discuss your cases with your mother a lot?"

"No, never. But he unsettled me yesterday. I shouldn't be, but I am. I wanted to understand the root of the emotions, and I thought Mom could help."

Brody frowned. "Did she?"

"No."

After a brief silence, he said, "I spent the better part of the night trying to figure out your exchange with Smith."

She twisted in her seat toward him. "It all could have been a game. We don't know if Smith was telling us the truth about the bodies."

He tipped his head. "Care to take a bet on whether Smith was lying or telling the truth?"

She frowned, stared at him a beat and then shifted her gaze back to the road. "No."

"Smart."

They arrived at the crime scene at ten minutes after eight. A dozen DPS marked cars, lights flashing, and several black Ranger Broncos stood parked at the end of a long, winding, dirt road. Last night's rain had cleared but had left the ground soggy and muddy. From her pack, Jo pulled out rubber boots and slipped them on over her flat shoes.

Brody didn't comment but she caught his sideways glance. In school he'd teased her about always being prepared. "You should have been a Boy Scout," he'd said.

Her boots squished into sucking mud and a small, very nasty part of her hoped Brody was now ankle deep in mud. Closing the car door, she hefted her backpack on her shoulder and moved around the side of the car to meet Rangers Jim Beck and Rick Santos.

Jim Beck was tall, muscular, with dark hair. Santos was as tall but his build leaner. Like Brody, both men wore the customary khakis, sport jacket, tie and cowboy boots with their white Stetsons.

Her smile was genuine as she extended her hand to both Jim and Santos. "Not such a great way to start a day."

Jim shrugged and sipped from a black travel mug. "If Smith was telling the truth, it will be worth it."

Santos yawned, covering his mouth with the back of his hand. "More sleep would have been mighty welcome. But I reckon it's not so bad."

Brody stood by Jo, extending his hand to the Rangers. The three had never been assigned to the same office until a couple of weeks ago, but a Ranger's jurisdiction often crossed county lines into another territory. They'd all worked together on several cases, most recently an Austin kidnapping that ended with the suspect's arrest in Houston.

"There is no record of Smith owning this land. However, the registered 'owner' is a corporation, which after some digging offered the name Tate Jones. We drill down a little deeper, I bet we find a link to Smith. But it explains why this property never popped up on our radar during the investigation."

Beck frowned. "I wonder what other corporations he's set up and used as a front to buy property."

Brody stared at the wide-open land around them. "I hate to think." He shifted his attention back to the Rangers. "According to Smith, the bodies would be near what's left of that barn. Are the guys here with the ground-penetrating radar?"

A truck rolled down the long road, kicking up mud. The vehicle parked behind Brody's car and two men in jumpsuits emerged.

"Speak of the devil," Jim said. "Shouldn't be long before they're set up and ready to go."

A wind blew across the flat, scrubby land, and Jo burrowed deeper into her jacket. She'd intended to make a thermos of coffee but had not expected Brody to be in her driveway early.

She rubbed her hands together. "You and Lara ready for the big day? T minus six days and counting."

Jim grinned. "About as ready as you can get. She's been so busy shooting pictures for a new summer exhibit that she's barely taken time for the fitting."

"I've seen the dress, and it fits her perfectly. She'll be stunning."

Pride burned in Jim's gaze. "I've not one bit of

doubt. I hear you're getting together with her and Cassidy tonight."

She'd totally forgotten. Damn. "That's right. Seven. A vegetarian cantina in Austin."

"Try not to get too wild and crazy at this bachelorette party."

"It's not me you have to worry about," Jo said. "It's Cassidy."

"And I'm counting on you to be the levelheaded one that says no. Lara's too nice."

"I promise."

The forensic techs unloaded the ground-penetrating radar, which looked much like a push mower with large wheels and a computer screen mounted on the handle. At first, progress was slowgoing, guiding the device through the muck, but the technicians soon had the machine past the line of police cars and worked their way toward what remained of the barn.

Brody and the Rangers moved closer to the search site. Jo straightened, trying to work the kinks from her back. As much as she wanted peace for the victims' families, a big part of her hoped Smith had been lying. Logic suggested that the summons to West Livingston, the lies about the graves, and all his mind games were intended to stir trouble for trouble's sake.

The slow and meticulous process of pushing the GPR in a gridlike fashion began, and Jo was left with the Rangers to stand and watch the process.

The barn had all but collapsed on itself though stubborn chips of red paint still clung to grayed and weather-ravaged boards that lay in a heap on the ground. Tall weeds peppered the land around the barn's old footprint and had woven their way up through the boards. In five years there'd be no trace of the place.

Across the field Brody stood, his hands on his hips, as he watched the technicians work. Her mother would call her a fool for saying this, but she could see that he'd changed in fourteen years. He wasn't the swaggering baseball player with a quick story or a joke. He was a serious man. Hard to be a Marine and a Ranger, witness what they did, and not grow up.

He'd been the lead for the human trafficking case last year. She'd watched the news, and camera crews caught a glimpse of Brody leading a twelve-year-old girl out of a storage shed. The girl had been crying and filthy, covered in weeks of grime. And she'd been wearing Brody's jacket. He'd had his arm draped protectively around her thin shoulders, as a father would his own child.

She never stopped to ask if he was married now. He wasn't wearing a wedding band but many cops didn't. The less the bad guys knew about you, the better. Picturing him with a wife and children sent a flush of embarrassment racing up her neck and face. He'd been frozen in time for her these last fourteen years. She'd always pictured him surrounded by cheerleaders or, with her studying, trying to find a reason why he should care about Shakespeare. Or children. But because she couldn't picture it didn't mean it wasn't true.

Emotion she'd not expected or wanted rose up in her, tightening her chest. Made sense he'd move on with his life. Most everyone had. Except her.

"I think we found something," the technician called.

She shook off the sting of emotion and watched as Brody, Jim and Santos walked toward the GPR. The technician pointed to the screen and then at the ground, nodding his head sideways as if he were as surprised as everyone else.

The technician placed an orange flag in the ground and continued pushing the GPR over the soggy earth. Ten minutes later he raised his hand, indicating another hit. Another ten minutes and another hit. Three bodies. Just as Smith had said.

A deep sense of unease strengthened and coiled around her insides.

Brody spoke to the technicians and though she could not hear, it was clear from his expression he wasn't satisfied. He wanted the land north of the barn also searched.

A grim frown deepened the lines on the technician's face, but he pushed the machine through the muck.

Brody stood in the center of the first field, three orange flags circling him. He'd been trying to get answers for three families for over three years and now he was close.

However, his grim expression held no hint of satisfaction. He looked sad, and judging by the deep lines at his temples and the dark circles under his eyes, he was exhausted.

"Winchester!" the tech shouted. "I've found another one here."

The hum of conversation silenced and everyone watched as Brody, Jim and Santos moved toward the site.

Four bodies. Not three.

They'd all expected Smith to lie.

And he had.

Robbie stared into the small television, which televised an image from a hunter's camera secured high in the trees above his burial site. His plot of land now swarmed with a sea of cop cars and Texas Rangers. They'd found Smith's bodies. And his.

He sat back, folded his arms over his chest and smiled. The fact that the cops were here meant that Harvey had sent them. No way they'd have found this place without Harvey.

Robbie smiled. Harvey had read his message in the classifieds, and he'd sent the cops. Not to punish him but to say, *I know, boy. I know.*

Pulling in a satisfied breath, he was unable to tear his gaze from the images. For days he'd wondered if Harvey had seen his message. He'd feared his father would go to his grave never knowing that his creation had matured and become the man Harvey had intended.

He watched the cops, shovels in hand, hovering around Smith's graves and his own. He touched the screen, wishing Harvey and he could share this moment together. The old man was sick, dying, and there'd not be many days left.

Robbie tipped back his head and closed his eyes smiling. *Thank you, Harvey.*

Years ago, Smith had tried to make him into a man and he'd failed. After a decade he'd finally proven himself to his father.

Harvey had said there was no sweeter rush than killing. Robbie hadn't experienced a rush; however a deep satisfaction had washed over him when he'd shoveled the last bits of dirt on the grave.

Harvey's days were down to a precious few. He had weeks at most.

If he didn't delay, perhaps he could kill several more times before Harvey died. The old man could read about his exploits in the news and perhaps recapture the thrill that had given him such joy.

For Harvey, he would keep killing.

Chapter Five

"We have three skeletonized remains," Marissa Reardon, the medical examiner's assistant, said.

Brody hitched his muddied boot on the bumper of the medical examiner's van as Marissa cradled a warm cup of coffee in her hands. Petite and in her early thirties, she wore her long, dark hair tied back in a ponytail. She was the only tech he'd met who always wore makeup, perfume and earrings no matter the time of day or weather conditions. Jokes painting her as a debutante made her laugh, but when she was on the job it was all about business.

Brody leaned in. "Just as we expected."

"There will have to be lots of testing at the lab when we get the remains back, but they've been in the ground a long time. You said Smith was arrested three years ago?"

"That's right."

She sipped her coffee. "That would fit the initial findings here."

"Can you identify them?"

"Seeing as you have three victims that were never accounted for, it will be easy enough to match dental records. And if we don't have those records we might be able to pull DNA from teeth or bones."

"One of the victims suffered a fractured femur when she was eight."

Marissa shrugged. "An X-ray can also assist with identification."

A grim sense of satisfaction worked its way through his tense muscles as it did after a grueling workout. "You haven't discussed the fourth victim."

A sigh shuddered through her body as she stared at the grave she'd yet to unearth. "That's why I decided to take a quick break. I'm tired, and I want to be on my game when we excavate the fourth victim."

"What do you mean?"

"GPR suggests those remains aren't old. It indicated the presence of flesh."

"Flesh. That can't be right."

"I excavated part of the skull." Cradling her coffee in both hands, she took a sip. "From what I can tell, the deceased hasn't been in the ground much more than a week."

"What?"

"Your fourth victim couldn't have been killed by Smith. Unless he found a way to sneak in and out of prison without anyone noticing."

Brody's frown deepened. Smith had mentioned an apprentice. Robbie. "When can you excavate that body?"

Marissa stared into her coffee cup, as if willing it to give her strength. "Give me a minute. The men and I will get started again soon."

"Thanks."

In the last seven hours Brody had been so caught up in the crime scene he'd not been able to get back to check on Jo. Now as he moved away from Marissa he caught sight of her pale face, as she stood alone, huddling in her jacket. He now regretted not making the time to check in on her.

"Jo," he said.

She raised her head. Recognition flickered in her gaze but there was no hint of a smile. "How's it going?"

"The forensic team is excavating the first three bodies."

"And the fourth?"

He tightened his jaw. "It's not like the others."

"Meaning?"

"This last victim was killed within the last week."

Her head tipped, as it did when she was a teenager. The slight movement indicated she'd stepped back from emotion, and her brain had turned to computing the issue at hand. "Smith mentioned the apprentice. Robbie."

"I know. I wasn't sure how to take the infor-mation."

"Did you check the paper for the ad?"

"I did. Most look like typical ads, whereas a few appear to be messages. *'In it to win it'* was one. Another was *'Bluebonnets'* and the last, *'Call Rafe.'* Robbie and Harvey aren't the only ones who use the classifieds for messages. We're trying to trace all the purchasers of those ads. But each was paid for with cash."

A furrow creased the delicate skin between her eyes. "I should go back and talk to Smith again. Find out what else he knows about Robbie."

"There's time for that. First, we finish what we have here." He sure as hell wouldn't let her go back to that prison alone. He'd hated the way that monster had stared at her through the glass. Crawled in her head. Whenever he'd dealt with Smith in the past he'd always been able to keep his cool. He could play nice with the animal in the hopes of getting answers. But he'd come close to losing his temper yesterday.

She raised her chin a notch. "This is your investigation, so I'll take my cue from you. But I'm no kid. I know what I'm doing, and I can handle Smith."

"This is no reflection on your professional talent."

He'd never had doubts about her intellect. From the get-go, he'd known she was smarter than most, including himself, and could do or be whatever she wanted. "Trust me on this one."

"Of course."

Stiff, professional, he understood her trust did not extend beyond work.

Marissa, who now worked on the fourth victim, motioned him to come.

"I'll be back as soon as I can," he said.

"Let me have a look. I might see something."

He frowned. "Suit yourself."

When they reached the burial site roped off by yellow crime scene tape, Brody reached for plastic gloves in his coat pocket. He handed a set to Jo and called out to Marissa. "What do you have?"

"I've cleaned off the face and upper body." She rose and stepped aside as a forensic technician snapped digital pictures. "But it's clear she was young. I think her hair was blond. It's so caked with dirt now." She hesitated. "I'm going to let the medical examiner do the cleaning. I don't want to disturb any evidence."

Brody raised the tape for Jo and the two ducked under. Immediately, the heavy scent of death rose foul and putrid from the ground. He'd smelled it enough times and knew he could handle it.

He knelt beside the body and stared at the dirt-caked face of the victim. A woman. No more than thirty. Likely, blond hair. High, sunken cheekbones. The expression frozen on her face telegraphed panic. This close, the odors were thick and heavy.

"Smith buried his victims alive," Brody said. "Was she buried alive?"

Marissa shook her head. "I don't know. There is substantial dirt in her mouth and nose but the medical examiner will have to open her up."

"Dr. Granger," Brody said without glancing back. "Any thoughts?"

Slowly she knelt beside him and cleared her throat. She lifted her hand to her nose. "Can you remove more of the dirt?"

Marissa nodded and with a small brush slowly brushed away the dirt. A half hour later, the victim's clothed torso was exposed.

Jo cleared her throat, raised her hand to her nose. "Smith abused his victims physically and tied the victims' hands at their sides, so they couldn't claw free of the dirt. This victim's bindings are consistent with Smith, but there is no bruising on her face." She swallowed.

Marissa cocked her head. "Dr. Granger, this your first crime scene?"

She moistened her lips. "Seen my share of crime scene pictures, but this is my first active scene."

Jo's face had paled to a pasty white. Her lips were drawn tight. She looked like she wanted to throw up.

Shit. He'd assumed she'd been to crime scenes. "You okay?"

Fire spit from her eyes. "I'm fine."

Marissa cocked a brow, a hint of amusement in her eyes. "The first murder scene is always roughest. I threw up when I saw my first dead body."

Jo moistened her lips again and stood, as if the mention of getting sick unsettled her even more. She backed up, creating distance between her and the body. "I'm fine."

The strong, putrid scent of death rose up as Brody stood and took Jo's elbow in hand. She looked as if she'd topple over. "Let's step back and let Marissa finish her work."

Jo resisted. "I need to observe. There could be valuable observations I'll miss if I'm not here."

"They're taping it all. We can check it out later."

"Seriously, Jo," Marissa said. "Don't get sick on my scene."

Persuaded by the logic, Jo ducked back under the tape and walked stiffly away.

"She's going to be sick," Marissa said.

Brody was already turning to follow Jo. "I know."

Put one foot in front of the other. One. Two. Three. Jo counted the steps, grateful for each new one that put more distance between her, the body, coiling smells and the cops that would never let her forget this day if she threw up in front of them.

She made it beyond the line of cars and behind a bush before she lost control and vomited.

Thankfully, she'd had little to eat today, but humiliation burned as her body took over control, leaving her helpless. When her stomach was empty, she wiped her lips with the back of her hand and straightened.

"Damn it." At least she'd managed this humiliation in private.

She turned to find Brody standing several feet from her, a fresh water bottle in hand. Heat rose over her face. Shit. Shit. Shit. Why couldn't he have left her alone? He knew she was sick. Just like Brody to push.

He held out the bottle to her. "Don't drink it. Rinse your mouth out."

She accepted the bottle. "Thanks."

Carefully, she unscrewed the top and took a small sip. However, the idea of spitting in front of Brody bothered her more than her upset stomach. She swallowed and instantly regretted. She turned and vomited again.

Drawing in an irritated, shaky breath, she straightened. This time she took a sip, but after swishing it in her mouth, spit.

"You always were stubborn," he said.

"Hardheaded was the word you used."

He smiled as if a memory drifted out of the shadows. "You'd been trying to teach me a poem."

"Thematic construction."

A dark brow cocked. "I didn't want to learn,

and you refused to sign the sheet releasing me to play ball until I did."

She moistened her lips, wondering if she could find a ginger ale. "You learned it."

"Forgot it as soon as I took the test."

"But you earned a C minus on the test."

"Enough to play ball. I'm surprised you remember."

"I should be saying that to you. I'm the one with the great memory. Mindful of trivia you once said." They stood poised at memory lane, ready to travel. Mentally, she stepped back as she raised her water bottle, pointing to the scene. "Sorry about that. I thought I could handle it."

"I should have asked you if you'd been to a crime scene before. I assumed you had."

She'd foolishly assumed that the hundreds of gruesome crime scene photos she'd seen were enough prep for real life. "Like I told Marissa, I've seen lots of pictures."

Brody eased his hat back with the edge of his finger. "It's the smell that got me the first time."

"You threw up?"

"Hell, no."

"Oh."

He chuckled. "Don't take it so personally. Not everyone has a cast-iron stomach like me."

"Right." Damn, why couldn't she have kept it together?

"Why don't I take you home?"

Her fingers tensed around the bottle. "Absolutely not. You're working."

He shook his head. "You've been out here for over seven hours."

"As have you and everyone else."

"We're used to it. You're not. Call it a day, Jo."

Brody's kindness flew in the face of angry memories she'd carried of him for too many years. But if she dug deep enough, she remembered that Brody could be nice when it suited. When he'd needed to pass the English exam, he'd called her freckles cute. When he needed his paper edited, he'd called her brilliant. When he'd wanted sex, he'd talked about her hot body.

He was past writing college papers and taking tests now, and considering he'd watched her get sick, she doubted he had sex on his mind. But he wanted insight into this killer. And though she had a weak stomach, she read people especially well.

She scraped her thumbnail against the water bottle's label. "I'm used to working long hours."

Amusement lightened his gaze and eased some of his stiff formality. "Inside. Behind a desk. Different when it's cold and smells like death."

She raised the water bottle to her lips, thought better of another sip and recapped it. "Point taken. Look, I'm fine. You go back to what you were doing. I am not leaving until the scene is processed."

"Stubborn."

"I think we covered that ground."

He looked as if he wanted to speak but thought better of it. "Take it easy."

Her stomach was settling. "I'd also like another look at the body."

Brody raised a brow. "Really think that's a good idea?"

This wasn't about pleasing Brody, as it might have been when she was eighteen. This was about proving something to herself. "I promise not to ruin Marissa's crime scene. Before my stomach got the better of me, a detail caught my eye."

Doubt darkened his gaze. "You're sure?"

"Yes."

He adjusted his hat back over his brow and extended his hand, indicating the path back to the crime scene. "Lead the way."

When they reached the body this time, the medical examiner's attendants were preparing to lift the body from the ground. The face and hair were still badly caked in mud and dirt, rendering them unrecognizable. This time she breathed through her mouth and eliminated the smell.

One of Jo's greatest assets was that she could distance herself from horrific images or a client's wild emotions. She'd come to understand that if she could remain free of emotions, she could really see the facts and sift efficiently through the data. Moments ago, the smell had gotten the better of her stomach, but she was prepared to pull back and really observe.

Holding the water bottle close to her chest, she studied the victim and the crime scene. However, this time Jo convinced herself she was looking at evidence. This time she focused not on the girl's humanity but on the details that needed cataloging.

The victim was dressed. A peasant blouse made of a gauzy, green synthetic, likely from a high-end store. Tattered, stonewashed designer jeans that hugged narrow hips, fashioned to look old but in fact were expensive. Detailed black cowboy boots that cost five hundred plus dollars. Remnants of pink nail polish on long fingernails.

"She came from money," Jo said. "This girl did not live on the streets." She leaned closer, zeroing in on a tattoo on the inside of her left wrist. "Can I get a better look at that tattoo?"

Marissa motioned for an assistant with a video camera. "Shoot this." When the camera was rolling, she slowly cut the bindings enough to release the wrist. Rigor mortis had long come and gone so the arm moved with relative ease. Though the skin had darkened and slipped, it was possible to make out a butterfly tattoo.

Jo's eyes narrowed. At first with the decomposition she wasn't sure but the longer she stared at the image the more certain she became. "I've seen it before."

"Where?" Brody said.

"I volunteered to help find a missing girl."

She studied the girl's pale face, forever frozen in panic and fear. She couldn't imagine what it felt like to have the earth crushing the air from your lungs. "We were looking for a girl named Christa Bogart. Twenty-two years old. Went missing about a month ago. A local business-man started the *Find Christa!* campaign."

Brody frowned. "You're sure?"

"I'm sure Christa had a butterfly tattoo. If you can clean her up, maybe get prints, you might be able to confirm this is Christa."

"We'll get on that ASAP."

She leaned closer. "What's that in her hand?"

Marissa leaned closer. "Looks like a silk flower."

"A Texas bluebonnet," Jo said.

Brody's jaw tensed. "The classified ad read: BLUEBONNETS."

"How did Smith know that she was here?" Marissa said.

Jo took a sip from the water bottle. "I don't think he knew for sure. I think he rightly guessed if his apprentice was indeed killing that he was going to follow in his footsteps and use a burial site they'd visited before. It would have been a place this killer knew, was familiar with and therefore felt safe here."

"But if he'd chosen another site," Marissa

countered, "he might not ever have been caught."

Brody rubbed the back of his neck. "He sent a message to Smith through the paper, and Smith sent one back when he sent us here."

"I suspect Smith knows Robbie as well as Robbie does himself."

"They've not seen each other in a decade," Brody said.

"That will add variables to the equation, but Smith made Robbie. Programmed him. If we want to find Robbie, we need to talk to Smith again."

"I'll see what I can arrange."

When the DPS officer dropped Jo off at her house, it was ten minutes to seven on Sunday evening. Brody had stayed at the crime scene but she'd opted to leave, knowing she'd done all she could for now. She had enough time to shower quickly and hustle into town and make her dinner appointment with Lara and Cassidy.

Hair wet and no makeup except mascara, she made it to the restaurant ten minutes late. A miracle.

"Well, you look like something the cat dragged in," Cassidy said to Jo.

Jo slipped into the booth at the casual, vegetarian Austin eatery, doing her best to look cheery and not fresh from a hurried shower and a crime scene. Sitting across from her was Cassidy Roberts, a tall brunet. Sleek, well-dressed and wearing a turquoise bracelet and earrings, Cassidy looked like a successful art gallery owner. And beside her was Lara Church, a petite blonde, wearing a loose top, jeans and no makeup. She looked like an artist. Several of her photographs hung in Jo's house. The two women were first cousins.

Jo had met Lara and Cassidy last year when she'd been asked to consult on a case. And somehow the three of them, an unlikely trio, had become friends. Tonight they were celebrating Lara's upcoming wedding to Texas Ranger Jim Beck.

Jo accepted a glass of wine from Lara. "Cassidy, be grateful I took the time to shower."

Lara frowned. "Jim told me you were at the crime scene."

Jo took a liberal sip of the wine. "Yes."

Cassidy leaned forward, the colorful turquoise bracelet jangling on her wrist. "You were at a crime scene?"

"I was."

"I can't believe you emerged from behind your desk," Cassidy teased.

"It's been known to happen," Jo said.

"Can I ask for juicy details?" Cassidy asked.

Lara sat back in the booth and sipped her wine. "No, you can't, Cassidy. I'm willing to bet what she saw wasn't nice."

Lara's controlled tone served as a reminder that

she had survived a horrific attack last year. She was far too acquainted with crime scenes.

Cassidy frowned. "Sorry, Lara. Insensitive of me."

Jo smiled. "I'd rather talk about fun things. Like Lara's wedding."

Lara's smile warmed. "Now that is a subject near and dear to my heart."

They chatted about the upcoming event, which was to be casual and held at Lara and Jim's country house. Lara had emphasized from day one that this was to be a stress-free event.

Cassidy sipped her wine. "Jo, have you bought your dress?"

So much for no stress. "Not yet."

"What?" Cassidy asked. "My God, woman, the wedding is six days away."

"That's enough time." Jo tossed a silent appeal to Lara. "Right?"

Lara indicated her own worn jeans and white peasant top. "Don't ask me. Cassidy is our fashionista."

"Mine was ordered and altered weeks ago."

Jo snatched up a handful of nuts from the bowl on the table. Her stomach had settled and she was now hungry. "Don't worry, I'll have something to wear by next Saturday."

Lara cringed. "Jo, don't worry over the dress. I don't want this to be a burden. The wedding is casual. You don't have to drive yourself crazy. I think you'd look amazing in green but, really, wear whatever."

Cassidy sat back, her arms folded over her chest. "And I don't know where you heard that weddings aren't stressful. They were designed to drive people crazy."

"I'm not going there," Lara said. "I am not."

Cassidy pushed long fingers through her dark hair. "Well, Jo will be if she thinks she'll find a dress in less than a week."

"She can wear whatever she wants," Lara said. "Now can we talk about food? I haven't eaten since breakfast, and I am starving."

Jo studied the vegetarian menu. "I'm so hungry I could eat tofu."

The women laughed and Cassidy was able to flag their waitress. The young girl arrived at the table as Jo scanned her menu. She listened to Lara and Cassidy's order before raising her gaze. The instant she saw her waitress she froze. She wore jeans and a green T-shirt that read: *FIND CHRISTA!*

It was after eleven when Jo climbed the steps to her front door, her mind ticking through tomorrow's agenda at the office. She considered tomorrow's unread files, brewing a pot of coffee and squeezing more work out of the day.

As she moved to unlock her front door, her neighbor Ted Rucker called out. "Are you on the seven-day-a-week work schedule again? Thought you were going to cut back."

Managing a smile, she shoved her key in the lock and turned it. "I know it doesn't look like I'm cutting back, but I really am. This weekend was the exception."

He shoved back a lock of thick, blond hair with long fingers and laughed as he walked toward her with a large chocolate Lab. "Isn't that what you said the better part of last year?"

Jo descended the two porch steps and scratched the Lab between the ears. "Hey, Greta. And I meant it. I planned to take this weekend off but work came looking for me."

"You could have said no."

"I could have." It had never occurred to her to say no to Brody. He'd asked, and as if she was a naïve eighteen-year-old she'd come a-running. Not good.

Concern darkened his gaze. "You look beat. Where the heck did you end up?"

The night air here smelled so sweet compared to the crime scene. "I can't get into the details. But it was a crime scene."

"You at a crime scene? I can't picture that."

"Why not?"

"I remember the look on your face last fall when I buried that dead dog. I thought you were going to be sick."

A wry smile twisted her lips. "Safe to say, I

survived, and I've provided my professional opinion to the powers that be." She patted Greta one last time. "By the way, if you see a sparkly little blond hurricane knocking on my door again, pretend you don't know any details of my life."

He grimaced. "I spilled the beans to your mother, didn't I? I should have known. Mention of Winchester's name about sent her into orbit. That's why Greta and I happened by. We came to apologize."

"We?" Jo smiled at Greta as she wagged her tail. "I always took Greta for the silent type."

Rucker shook his head as he scratched the dog between the ears. "She can be a real blabbermouth at times."

Jo chuckled. "Did Greta say anything else to my mom?"

"Only that you looked a little stressed." He grimaced. "She shouldn't have said that either."

"No harm, no foul. You and Greta need not worry. My mom might have blown a gasket, but she's likely forgotten all about it now."

"Why did the mention of Winchester tick her off? Old boyfriend?"

Boyfriend. She and Brody had gone straight from one strong sexual attraction to married. They'd never really dated. And she'd certainly never called him her boyfriend. "Yeah, sorta like that."

He leaned close as if they were coconspirators. "No relationship between you two now?"

"God, no."

"That mean you're gonna finally stop breaking Greta's heart and go on a date with me?"

"Last time we talked it was coffee."

"Greta says I needed to man up and offer dinner. She says there's got to be a night when you're not working or chasing that group of teen girls."

She'd been avoiding Rucker's dates for months, using her busy life as an excuse. But now she wondered why she'd been putting him off. Her mother had attributed her monastic life to Brody. How many times had she heard, "He ruined you for all other men." That was, of course, not true. She had dated other men. But in the last couple of years she'd been so busy, she'd not made time for dating. Brody was a professional colleague, at best.

She studied Rucker's smiling face, noting it was a nice change from Brody's perpetual scowl, which she'd seen a lot of in the last twenty-four hours. "Rucker, I'm slammed this week and I've a wedding to attend on Saturday but I am open weekend after next. We can grab dinner downtown."

He grinned. "It's a date."

Chapter Six

Monday, April 8, 5:00 a.m.

Brody woke early, the clock on the nightstand glaring in red back at him. He shoved a hand through his hair and swung his legs over the side of the bed. Around him he surveyed the unpacked boxes, dirty clothes piled on the floor and collection of pictures that leaned in a neat stack against the wall. He'd made the move to Austin from Houston three weeks ago after an unexpected transfer had landed on his desk. In the last three years, the Rangers had bounced him all the way from El Paso to Brownsville. Most times when he settled in a new place he unpacked immediately. He liked order. But this go-around he'd not found the time to organize his apartment. The chaos grated on his nerves but nonstop action at the office had stolen all his time.

He'd rolled off the mattress, still sitting beside the bed frame he'd not assembled, and grabbed clothes he'd managed to pick up from the dry cleaners Saturday morning. A hot shower went a long way to making him feel human before he dressed. At his dresser he picked up his gun, cell phone and badge before he moved into the kitchen. He didn't have many groceries but had managed to pick up coffee and bagels. He rinsed out the mug he'd used yesterday, snagged a bagel and headed to his car.

The drive into Austin took less than twenty minutes. However, this morning instead of heading to the office, he drove toward the medical examiner's office, grateful to miss morning rush-hour traffic.

Sitting at a stoplight, he shrugged his shoulders, working the kinks from his neck and back. Fixing the damn bed had to be priority number one as soon as he had a spare minute. As a Ranger he'd spent enough time sleeping in bad motel beds, cars and bedrolls in an open field. When he'd been younger his body had been more forgiving. It took the abuse he tossed its way. Not so much anymore. He needed to get his bed together and get his routine back.

His folks lived in Austin and they had offered to put his place together or lend him their spare room, but he'd declined. Lord knows they'd not deny him. Hell, they'd jumped through lots of hoops to get him raised and educated. But going back to that wasn't right.

When he'd been in Jo's house, he'd been struck by the home's comfort. Not fussy, high-priced furniture but comfortable and clean. Her walls had been lined with bookshelves stocked full of well-creased books. Jo had always loved her books, even in college. When he'd first come into the tutoring center she'd been sitting in one chair, feet propped in another, reading. It had been a book on math theories. He'd known instantly he was out of his league.

But that message hadn't reached his dick. From the moment she'd first explained that mumbo-jumbo English literature, his Johnson had pulsed hard. She was pretty but not a stunningly beautiful woman. Not like the cheerleaders and sorority girls who hung around the team. She'd worn no makeup, a gauzy peasant top that silhouetted full breasts while hiding a narrow waist, and god-awful shoes old women favored. And yet his boner made it damn near impossible to think.

He'd figured all the crap that had crowded between them fourteen years ago would have tempered his reaction to her, but when he'd seen her climbing on that damn wall, he'd been right back in the past—dumbfounded and rock hard.

Shit.

Better to let that one go, son. You scorched that bridge a long time ago.

A horn beeped, Brody spotted the green light and punched the gas. Minutes later he reached the medical examiner's office.

Brody pushed through the stainless swinging doors connecting to the autopsy room and found the pathologist, Dr. Hank Watterson, talking to his assistant. Both dressed in scrubs, they stood in front of a gurney holding a sheet-clad body.

Watterson, in his late thirties, had joined the medical examiner's office last year. From Colorado, he'd gone through medical school on an Air Force scholarship.

"Ranger Winchester," Watterson said, glancing up. He wore heavy rimmed glasses, his sandy blond hair brushed back off a narrow face etched with deep laugh lines around his mouth and forehead.

Brody extended his hand. "Dr. Watterson."

Dr. Watterson glanced at the clock. "Beck is sending Santos to work the case with you. And Santos called and said he's running late. Traffic on I-35."

"Always an accident on that stretch of road." He eyed the still, white sheet that draped the body of the fourth victim they'd found yesterday. "A few minutes here or there won't make much difference."

Dr. Watterson reached for a file perched on a stainless-steel table. "I gave Beck a preliminary rundown when he called this morning. Want to hear it?"

"Shoot."

"We've not analyzed the skeletonized remains yet. We're waiting on dental records and X-rays. But I hope to get those in a day or two."

"That's fast."

"When Harvey Lee Smith's name is attached to a case it gets bumped to the front of the line."

Watterson moved toward the stainless gurney holding the sheet-clad remains of the most recent body. He reviewed the stats. "She was in her early twenties, stood five foot six and weighed about one-twenty. I've identified three tattoos: the butterfly, which I understand Dr. Granger spotted on her inner left wrist. She also has a tattoo on her back right shoulder blade. It's the initials CTB. Pierced ears and belly. An old scar on her right hand that was stitched. Blond hair, though her natural color is darker. No implants or any visible surgeries."

"Jo thinks we have Christa Bogart."

"I was able to get a partial print from her right thumb and index fingers. I've sent both off for analysis." Brody shifted his stance as the doctor reached for the sheet and pulled it off the victim's face. "Should have an identification in the hour.

"There was a significant amount of dirt in her nostrils and mouth—consistent with being buried alive. Her fingernails were caked with dirt and her skin marked with rope burns as if she struggled and tried to dig at the dirt around her. When I open her up I'll check her lungs and stomach for dirt."

Brody shook his head. "Hell of a way to die."

"She was not sexually assaulted. No vaginal bruising. No semen. No foreign DNA on her body."

"She was missing for several weeks before she died."

"Yes. But whoever had her did not assault her physically."

The doors to the autopsy room opened to a frowning Santos. "Traffic is a bitch this morning."

"That's what you get for living in San Antonio," Brody said.

"I'd be up in Austin but my sister, Maria, is a senior in high school. Don't want to uproot her."

"She lives with you?"

"Has since our folks died five years ago. All my gray hair can be traced right back to raising a teenaged sister."

There'd been times over the years when Brody had tried to imagine Jo's and his kid. Those thoughts always came around the time of her due date in May. If their daughter had lived she'd have been thirteen. "Can't imagine what it's like."

"Some days I swear it's the worst and other days the best."

Brody tried to picture himself as the father of a teenage girl now. He couldn't imagine how different his life would have been. "Sounds like she's lucky to have you."

"Cuts both ways."

The Rangers shifted their attention to the body. Within minutes, Watterson made the Y-incision in the victim's chest. The doctor added more details to the victim's profile. She'd not had children. Organs healthy and normal. Fit Christa's profile.

Santos studied the dead woman's face. "Now that she's cleaned up, even with the decomposition, she looks like she could be Christa."

Brody reached for his cell and dialed Austin police. "Let's see where they stand on the prints." Seconds later he was connected. "Detective Royals, this is Sergeant Winchester with the Texas Rangers. The medical examiner sent over prints and pictures this morning of a Jane Doe in the morgue. Have you had a chance to look at them?"

"Just did. Looks like we have a match. You found Christa Bogart."

Brody nodded. "Thanks, Detective. Once I'm done with the medical examiner I'd like to catch up with you and your files."

"Anytime. I'm sorry she wasn't found alive. The community put out a hell of an effort to find her."

"I'll keep you posted." He closed his phone and relayed the news.

Santos tipped back his head, pressing his fingertips to his forehead. "Christa Bogart vanished without a trace about a month ago."

Brody shifted his gaze to the doctor. "Do you have an approximate time of death?"

"Based on decomposition I'd say about a week ago. But I can't give you an exact time."

"A week ago," Santos said. "What happened to the other three weeks?"

"The killer held her. But according to the doc he didn't sexually abuse her," Brody said.

"Whereas Smith did abuse some of his victims."

"According to his confessions."

"Could we have someone who's a copycat?" Santos asked.

"If not for the way her body was bound, I'd be thinking that too. But we've got knots exactly like Smith's. And that was never released to the media."

Dr. Watterson bowed his head toward the body. "She showed no signs of malnutrition. No tooth decay. The only signs of restraint are on her wrists."

"He holds her, feeds her, doesn't abuse her but doesn't kill her. Why?"

No one had an answer. Yet.

"And Smith never mentioned this Robbie guy before?" Santos asked.

Brody thought back to the hours of Smith's testimony. The old man had savored the attention after his arrest and had enjoyed sharing what he'd done. "During all the hours of confession, Smith never once mentioned Robbie."

Santos shook his head. "Saying he did get a hold of this kid when he was twelve. Can you imagine how many ways that old bastard could twist a kid's mind?"

"The kid would easily come to believe that this is a sick kind of normal."

Dr. Watterson completed his internal examination and closed up Christa Bogart's body. "I'll run a tox screen and see what comes of it. But it's clear from the dirt in her stomach and lungs. She was buried alive."

Winchester and Santos's first stop after leaving the medical examiner's office was Austin Police. They met with Detective Tom Royals, who'd handled the initial investigation on Christa Bogart. They joined Royals in a small conference room with a round table and metal chairs. Royals, a stocky man with a thick mustache and glasses, set a thick file on the table.

Royals opened the file. "Where'd you find her?" He pushed the file toward Brody.

Brody thumbed through the thick file. "Buried in the ground on a farm about fifteen miles west of Austin." He recapped the details.

Royals sat back, shaking his head. "Shit. And you found three other bodies in the same location?"

"Those murders are much older and we believe Smith killed them. Christa's body caught us by surprise. What can you tell us about her?"

"Worked as a secretary for a financial firm. Engaged to be married. No priors. Lots of friends. Well-liked by coworkers. The night she vanished she'd come home from an office party. Checked in with her roommate, went into her room and vanished. I interviewed her roommate for hours, but she couldn't give us any real leads. We found footprints near Christa's window, but we haven't connected them to anyone yet."

"What about the fiancé?"

"Solid guy. Worked for the same financial management company. That's how they met. Well-liked and respected by peers. We dug into his past. Nothing popped up."

"He have an alibi for the night Christa vanished?"

"He and Christa had been at the same party and when she left he stayed to drink with some of his coworkers. The bartender placed him on site until two in the morning."

After another half hour of discussing the case with Royals, Brody and Santos left, starting their investigation at Christa's apartment where her roommate still lived.

Winchester knocked on the front door. Several seconds passed before the shuffle of feet and the scrape of several locks against the front door. A young, short, stocky woman with blue-black shoulder-length hair greeted them.

Both Rangers showed their badges, and the girl nodded as if she'd done this a thousand times in the last four weeks. "Miss Brittany Long?"

The girl surveyed the two men carefully. "You're the Rangers. The police called and said you'd be coming by to see me. Come on in."

After an introduction, the Rangers walked into a small living room filled with half-packed boxes.

One bedroom door was open but the other was closed and sealed with yellow crime scene tape.

"You moving?" Winchester asked.

"Yes," Brittany said. "I wanted to leave right after Christa vanished, but the landlord wouldn't let me out of the lease. See, I signed for both of us, which meant I was on the hook for the entire rent. I did all I could to get out of here but he said no, and I couldn't afford all this rent and another place. Now my lease is up at the end of the week and I'm leaving. Rented another place across town that I'm sharing with several girls."

"What can you tell us about the night Christa vanished?" Santos asked.

Brittany pushed her hands through her hair. "Didn't the other cops tell you?"

"They did, ma'am. But it wouldn't hurt to hear it one more time."

Brittany shrugged. "I'm so tired of telling this story."

Brody thought about Christa's body lying on the gurney in the medical examiner's office. When he spoke his voice had a sharp edge. "One more time for our sake."

"It was a regular night. She was at a party with Scott, the guy she's going to marry. The party had to do with her job. It was an anniversary party, I think. Ten years in business. Anyway, after it broke up she came home, and her fiancé went out drinking with some of the guys at the firm."

"What time did she get home?" Winchester asked.

"Midnight. And I remember the time because I was up reading. I heard her come into the apartment and looked at the clock. She poked her head inside my room, said good night and went to bed. I shut off my light and fell asleep. That was the last time I saw her."

"Any unusual sounds that night?" Santos asked.

"No. But I must have been extra tired that night because I slept like the dead."

"Mind if we have a look in her room?" Brody's question sounded like an order.

"Sure. The cops have been through it so many times it doesn't resemble the way Christa kept it."

"Her family or friends haven't tried to claim her belongings?" Santos asked.

"No. Her sister, Ester, was clear she didn't want the room touched. She gave me cash for the rent and asked me to leave it be. I took the money and was happy to stay clear of the room."

"I thought you said you couldn't leave because you had both rents to pay," Brody said.

"I kinda spent the cash on new clothes, thinking the landlord would let me out. But he was a hard-ass about it." She shook her head. "I should have given him the money and left. Looking at the tape on her door gives me the creeps."

Brody pulled the tape free and opened the door to a slim, narrow room. The room had a double bed on the far wall by the window, a desk to the right and bookshelves to the left. Christa had lived in a low-rise building in a first-floor unit that faced a back parking lot. Gray gauze curtains that matched a flowered bedspread covered double windows.

He pushed back the curtains and stared out the back window, overlooking a small parking lot rimmed by trees. He studied the lock and flicked it with his thumb, noting it was easily moved.

"Did she sleep with the window open?"

"Not normally," Brittany said from the doorway. "But the heater was on overdrive that night, and we were about to cook. I had my window open and suggested she do the same. It was cold as hell outside, and it didn't occur to either of us that it would be a problem. I mean what kind of nut runs around in subzero weather?" Her full lips compressed with tension as if she would forever replay that last bit of advice to Christa. "She was supposed to be married in two weeks."

Brody checked his notes. "What do you think of the guy she was marrying?"

"I didn't really like him. He was kinda possessive with Christa. But he's been great since all this happened. When a local Realtor organized the *Find Christa!* campaign, he searched right along with Christa's sister. He's called me a few times to see how I'm doing. Not the ass I first thought."

"What specifically didn't you like about him?"

129

Santos said as he studied a bulletin board filled with pictures, ticket stubs and restaurant carryout menus. "You said 'possessive.'"

"He didn't like sharing her. When she first moved in we ran around town together and had a blast. After he came into her life, she wasn't around anymore. But that happens, doesn't it? Girl meets a guy, they're all into him and they fall off the friend radar."

"Anything else bother you about him?"

"He didn't hit her or yell at her, but he let her pick up the tab a lot when they went out. He never had his wallet or enough cash."

"He was a financial planner at the firm?"

"Yeah. Made big bucks. But was forgetful, I guess. She came from a family with money and would have inherited on the day she married."

"And he was involved in the search?" Brody said.

She folded her arms over her chest. "Yeah. He really seemed torn up."

"He dated since Christa vanished?" Santos said.

She shook her head. "No. I mean it's only been a month. But yeah, I guess not all guys wait that long." She frowned. "He's not dating, as far as I know."

"Anybody hanging around this general area that gave you cause to worry?" Brody asked.

"No. And no to anyone stalking Christa. No to any weird notes or phone calls. She never said anything that made me worry about her. One day she's planning her wedding and on top of the world and the next she is gone. Whoever took her came out of nowhere. Neither one of us saw him coming."

Chapter Seven

Monday, April 8, 9:00 a.m.

Normally, Jo arrived at work earlier than seven, but today she'd overslept, which hadn't happened since she was eight weeks pregnant and riddled with morning sickness.

All these years had passed and she could still remember morning sickness. And why they called it morning sickness always puzzled her. She'd had it from the moment she woke up until she went to bed.

The day she and Brody had married, she'd thrown up three times and could only stomach ginger ale. And when he'd dropped her back off at her dorm after the wedding ceremony she'd been relieved to crawl in her bed. He'd offered to stay, but she'd wanted to be alone.

Jo pushed the elevator button for the seventh floor of her office. When the doors opened the receptionist glanced up, relief sparking in her eyes.

"Thank God you're here," Sammy said. Sammy

was in her late thirties, blond, tall and slim. "Dr. Anderson has been asking for you."

Her boss was a renowned expert in forensic psychology and also taught at the university. He'd sat in when she'd presented her dissertation and had been impressed. A week later he'd offered her a job in his office.

Dr. Anderson was a brilliant psychologist, but his lack of administrative skills often created unnecessary drama. Within weeks of joining the firm, Jo had learned to avoid high alert until she assessed the situation. "I have no appointments on my schedule."

"Dr. Anderson had an early morning call from an attorney who wants you to talk to one of his clients."

"What's the issue?" Nothing happened in the office without Sammy knowing it.

"The attorney is an old friend of Dr. Anderson's. He wants to get a psych evaluation on one of his clients. He's worried that taking this guy's case could be explosive."

"Why doesn't he refuse the case?"

Sammy grinned. "A lot of money on the table, from what I understand. And if he defends this guy and gets him acquitted it would win a lot of great PR."

Jo's annoyance simmered. "What if my report is not favorable?"

"I guess he's assuming/hoping it will be."

"The report will be honest."

"Dr. Anderson knows that. And he's warned his friend you can be blunt. I guess he's hoping it will all turn out fine."

"What's the client accused of?"

"His wife went missing, and he's a suspect."

"What's his name?" She dug her phone out of her purse to check e-mail.

"Dr. Aaron Dayton."

The name tweaked memories. "His wife went missing a few months ago."

"He has an alibi for the time she vanished, but the cops still aren't sold."

"Where are they?"

"Conference room."

"Tell them I'll be right there." Jo dropped her briefcase and purse in her office, checked her lipstick and with a notepad and pen in hand went to the conference room. One knock and she heard Dr. Anderson's firm "Enter."

Opening the door, she found two men who immediately stood. Her boss, Dr. Anderson, wore dark pants and a black turtleneck, which made his white hair and beard look all the more dramatic. Across from him sat a tall, slim man in a gray suit. He was pleasant-looking, midfifties and had thinning brown hair.

"Dr. Granger." The familiar Texas drawl belonged to Dr. Anderson. "I'm glad you could join us. I expected you an hour ago."

She directed her gaze toward her boss. "I worked the better part of the weekend. I was running late this morning." She'd tell him later about the crime scene.

He smiled, clearly not surprised. "Dr. Granger is my most dedicated doctor. Dr. Granger, I'd like you to meet attorney Mike Black."

She moved toward Dr. Anderson's side of the table. "How can I be of service?"

"I had Sammy check your schedule and she tells me you have extra time this morning. Mr. Black would like you to speak to his client Aaron Dayton," Dr. Anderson said.

She shifted her gaze to Black. "You want an evaluation. Are you considering an insanity plea?"

"No issue is off the table at this point, Dr. Granger. But I need a full evaluation before I figure out our next move."

"Understood. Where is Dr. Dayton?"

"He's in the other office," Dr. Anderson said. "I'll get him if that works for you."

"Normally, I have more time to prep for evaluations."

"I want your opinion based on what you see here today. I don't want you influenced by police reports or newspaper articles."

"I've seen news reports but haven't followed the case closely. Nor have I formed an opinion."

"I doubt anyone hasn't heard about Sheila

Dayton," Black said. "Your non-opinion is the best I can hope for right now."

"Show him in," Jo said.

Her boss opened another door that connected to a private room, and he invited in a third man. He was younger, early thirties, thick, blond hair, muscular build, and medium height. He wore an expensive dark suit, white shirt and red tie. Gold cuff links winked near his wrists. She recognized Dr. Aaron Dayton from news reports.

"Dr. Dayton, I'd like you to meet one of my best associates, Dr. Granger."

Dayton held out a manicured hand. "Dr. Granger. It's a pleasure."

"Dr. Dayton."

"Dr. Granger," Dayton said, "I'm fighting for my life. My wife is missing, and the cops believe I'm behind it."

From the outset, he put himself before his wife.

"Dr. Anderson and Mr. Black, if you will excuse us. And would you have Sammy send in coffee and bagels? I haven't had a bite since yesterday, and I'm willing to bet Dr. Dayton wouldn't mind a cup of coffee."

Dayton tugged the edges of his crisp cuffs. "That would be nice."

"Great." Dr. Anderson understood Jo wasn't as interested in food as she was in disarming Dayton. "Get right on it, Dr. Granger."

Jo waited until she was alone with Dayton

before she moved around the conference table and pulled out a seat next to his. She didn't want the table standing as a barrier between them. She indicated he could sit as she did. "It's been a rough couple of months for you, hasn't it, Dr. Dayton?"

He relaxed back in his chair and pulled a package of gum from his coat pocket. He held it out to her in offering, but she shook her head no. "You have no idea, Dr. Granger. It's been an ordeal."

She crossed her legs and made no move to reach for her notepad. Note taking often made people so nervous they censored their words. "You must be worried about your wife."

"I wasn't at first. As I told the police, she's taken off before for days at a time. She does that when we've had a fight."

"You two had a fight?"

Carefully, he unwrapped a stick of gum. "We did."

"About?"

"Money. She likes to spend more than we have. I want us to save so we can buy a vacation home."

"And is money the usual root of your arguments?"

"Almost always." He popped the gum in his mouth.

"Almost?"

His gaze bore on her before he sighed. "Last year she had an affair. We fought about that a lot."

"You no longer fight about the affair?"

He folded the yellow gum wrapper in half. "We reached an accord."

"You two are still together?"

"She begged me to forgive her. And I do love her." He creased the wrapper edges with his fingertips.

"When is the last time you saw your wife?"

"You know I've been through this a number of times with the cops."

Impatience snapped behind his words. "I know, and I do appreciate your patience. But go over it again for me."

"I saw her two months ago. I was leaving for work. I'm a dentist. She was dressed for a yoga class. I kissed her goodbye and went to work. When I came home from work there was a note. She said she'd be back in three or four days. Needed to think. I didn't worry."

"When did you start to worry?"

"A week later." He folded the wrapper a second and third time.

A long time to wait before sounding the alarm bell. "And you called the police."

"I did."

A knock at the door had her turning. "Enter."

It was Sammy pushing a cart laden with coffee and bagels. Jo thanked Sammy and rose. "Can I offer you a cup?"

"Yes. Black."

She handed him a brimming cup and fixed herself a cup as well. She dropped three sugars in the cup and stirred in extra milk before sitting. She took a sip.

He grinned. "You like your coffee sweet."

She preferred it black. But sweet suggested softness. "I hate the bitterness."

He took a sip. "It's good coffee."

"So I've been told. I'm not a fan, but it gets me going."

"Long weekend?"

"You've no idea."

She set her cup aside, settled back in her chair and pretended to stifle a yawn as if she were off her game. "The police turned up no leads from what I remember from the news."

"Correct."

"Wouldn't she use her credit cards if she were traveling?"

"That's what I said. When they told me there was no activity on the card since the day she vanished, I knew she was in trouble."

She reached for a bagel and a napkin. "Are you hungry?"

He considered the selection. "If you don't mind."

"Of course not. Please help yourself."

He took a napkin, spit the gum into it and chose the largest bagel. Cinnamon raisin. He took time to spread a thick coat of cream cheese and took several bites. She wondered if she could eat, knowing her spouse was missing.

"Your wife is pretty. They showed pictures on the news."

"Sheila always took pride in her appearance."

Took, not takes. "She work out? You mentioned yoga."

"Yoga, Pilates, cardio. She'd put on weight and was trying to get it off. She'd turned into a regular gym rat."

"Do you carry any pictures of her?"

"I do." He reached into his coat pocket and pulled out a sleek wallet. He removed a picture and handed it to her.

She studied the image of the vibrant, blond woman with a wide smile. She wore her makeup heavy and favored lots of gold jewelry that dipped into a full cleavage. "Very attractive."

"She was that."

Was.

"Tell me about her affair last year. That must have been painful for you."

He set down his bagel. "Hurt like hell."

"You felt betrayed?"

"Yeah. It was a knife to the gut."

"Who was the guy?"

"I didn't ask."

"I find that hard to believe."

"That's what the cops said."

"Can you blame them?"

"Yeah, I can. I wouldn't lie when my wife is missing. I keep saying this lover of hers could be behind all this."

"You have no pertinent details about him, including his name. How do you know he's involved in her disappearance?"

"It's the only logical explanation."

Or you killed her. "Why stay with your wife after the affair?"

"I felt sorry for her."

In all Dayton's accounts, he'd been in control. He'd been the one who'd been wronged, had forgiven, had issued forbearance.

She continued to talk to him about his wife. How they met. How long they'd been married. Her spending habits.

Dayton's answers were smooth, relaxed, rehearsed, and nothing riled him. Nothing. His wife was missing, and he was perfectly calm.

"I wish she'd been more like you, Dr. Granger."

"Why's that?"

"You strike me as a woman who's always in control. I like that."

Jo kept her expression neutral, but she didn't like his assessment. "Your wife was out of control."

He shifted in his seat. "Most of the time, yes."

"In what way?"

"The outfits she wore. Her spending. Too loud. Liked to drink."

"And now she is in more trouble than ever." She continued to ask questions. He answered.

"No quiet exit for Sheila." He offered her a wan smile. "No, that would be too easy for her." He checked his watch. "We've covered the same questions at least three times now, Dr. Granger."

She studied him a beat. "You're right. Thank you for your time, Dr. Dayton."

She escorted him to reception where Dr. Anderson and Mr. Black waited. They exchanged pleasantries.

Dayton extended his hand to Jo. She took it and noted the way he squeezed her fingers with a grip, not painful but firm. He held her hand a beat. "It was a pleasure."

She pulled her hand free. "Nice to have met you."

Jo escorted Dayton to the other office, and Jo and Dr. Anderson watched Dayton and Black get on the elevator. When the doors closed Dr. Anderson's smile vanished. "In my office."

She followed him and when he closed the door he said, "What do you think?"

She folded her arms over her chest. "He knows more than he's saying."

"Do you think he killed her?"

"I'd be guessing at this point. A more complete evaluation is warranted."

"I'll take your guess anytime, Jo."

She flexed her fingers. "I think he killed her."

Dr. Anderson shook his head. "Why come here and jump through the hoops?"

She arched a brow. "You know as well as I do. He loves the drama and attention. This is great theater to him, and he is the actor on center stage. He believes he can do no wrong. He is in control."

"Did he give you any information the cops could use?"

"I thought we were working for him."

"We are. But it's good to know."

"He didn't incriminate himself. But if the cops stay close, he will. He's proud of his secret, and it will be hard for him to keep it to himself forever."

"Scott Connors, age thirty-two," Brody read from the file. "By all accounts devastated by his fiancée's disappearance."

Santos parked in front of the old apartment building. "Let's see how he reacts to news of her death."

Out of the car, they strode down a cracked sidewalk to the front door. They located his apartment on the mailboxes and climbed to the third floor.

Brody knocked on the door. Seconds passed with no sound. "According to his boss he called in sick today."

Santos shrugged. "He wouldn't be the first to lie about an illness."

Brody pounded on the door, and this time they

heard the shuffle of feet. The door opened to a tall, lean man wearing jeans and no shirt. His hair stuck up as if he'd rolled out of bed.

"Mr. Scott Connors," Brody said.

"Look, this is a bad time." He moved to close the door.

Brody blocked it with his boot. "We're Texas Rangers, and we came to talk to you about Christa."

Scott sighed. "I've spoken to all the cops I'm going to talk to. Enough. I can't help you anymore. If you have any questions call my attorney."

Brody put his hand on the door and pushed it open several more inches. "For a guy who was desperate to find his girlfriend, I'd think you'd not be all talked out yet."

Dark under-eye circles made his eyes look sunken. "Yet? Are you kidding? It's been four weeks since she vanished."

Brody wanted to annoy, even anger Scott to force a reaction. "Is that the time limit on true love, Scott?"

Scott fisted his fingers. "What the fuck is that supposed to mean?"

"Means if I really loved a woman I'd think it would take me longer than four weeks to give up on her."

"I never gave up on Christa. But damn, I can't stay in limbo forever. Even the cops now are saying she's likely dead."

Brody eyed Santos. "When did forever become four weeks?"

Santos shrugged. "Everyone's in a rush these days."

Scott's lips flattened. "You know the chances of finding her alive get worse and worse the longer it takes. Everyone is saying that."

"Everyone?" Brody heard the shuffle of footteps behind Scott, and immediately his hand slid to his gun. "Someone in the apartment with you, Scott?"

Scott tensed, glanced back over his shoulder. "No one important."

"Who?"

"A friend."

"Scott. Who's at the door, baby?" cooed a woman.

Brody shoved out a breath. "Tell your friend to get dressed and get out. We need to talk."

"What's this about?"

Brody peered past Scott to a brunet wearing a man's white dress shirt. "Ask your friend to leave."

Scott hesitated, turned and said, "Dee, get dressed. The cops are here, and I have to talk to them."

"About Christa? Again?" She sounded irritated. "Yeah."

She pouted. "It's always about Christa."

"Dee. Get dressed." Scott crossed to her,

whispered in her ear and kissed her on the cheek. Pouting, she vanished into the bedroom.

"Her name is Dee?" Brody said.

Scott shoved out a sigh. "Dee. Dee Anders. She works at the financial company with me."

"How long have you two been together?"

Scott shoved long fingers through his hair. "Last night was the first time."

Brody wouldn't bet on that. "I see."

Dee emerged wearing jeans, a *Find Christa!* T-shirt and a leather jacket. She looked at Scott as if she wanted to speak but thought better of it and left.

Brody hooked his thumbs in his belt. "Dee joined the search party?"

"That's right."

"Dee like to wear that T-shirt often?" Santos said.

"No. No, of course not. She put it on yesterday because it was Christa's birthday. A bunch of us gathered together and celebrated. She was trying to cheer me up. Show me that Christa hadn't been forgotten."

Brody let his gaze roam over the apartment. It was neat, organized and smelled of fresh paint. "When was the last time you saw Christa?"

Scott reached for a T-shirt draped over a couch and pulled it on over his head. "That's all in the file."

"Humor me."

Scott's argument melted when his gaze lifted to Brody. "The last time I saw her was the night she vanished. We'd gone to a party for our office. It was kind of a St. Patrick's Day theme plus a corporate celebration. After I walked her to her car about eleven thirty, I returned to the bar to drink with my friends. Ask her roommate if you don't believe me."

"We did ask her."

Scott stabbed long fingers through his blond hair. "Look, if this is about rehashing ground I've already covered . . ."

"We're into new territory now, Scott."

"What do you mean?"

Brody watched Scott's face closely. "We found Christa. She's dead. Murdered."

Scott stared at the Rangers for long, tense seconds. "Where did you find her?"

"We'll get into that later. Where were you about a week ago?"

"Last Monday? At work and home."

"Alone?"

Scott frowned. "Yeah, alone."

"How long have you and the brunet . . . Dee . . . been together?"

"I told you last night was the first time."

Brody grinned. "Really? Somehow I can't see it. You're a good-looking guy. Gals like Dee can see you're hurting, and they want to make you feel better."

"No. I've been faithful to Christa." Tears welled in his eyes. "Are you sure she's dead? Are you sure you didn't make a mistake? It's hard to identify a body after four weeks."

"Christa was killed a week ago."

"What? That doesn't make sense. She's been missing for a month." His face paled as the information sunk in deep. "Where was she all this time?"

Brody dodged the question. "What was she like?"

He swallowed. "She was sweet and nice. Everybody liked her."

"No stalkers or guys hanging around she didn't know?"

"If there was, she never said." He sat on the couch and buried his face in his hands. "Her sister, Ester, is going to be devastated."

"We put a call in to her, but she's out of town."

"She's exhausted and needed a break. She was talking about going to Galveston."

"And Christa and Ester's parents are dead."

"Yeah. They died when Christa was in high school. Car crash. Ester returned to Austin and moved back into the family home. Christa was fifteen when her folks died and Ester kinda finished raising her. They were tight." He slumped back on the couch.

Brody couldn't get a read on Scott. He was

saying all the right words, but there was a missing piece to this puzzle. "Did you organize the search for Christa?"

"No, Tim Neumann did. He heard she was missing and organized the *Find Christa!* search. He was amazing. Marshaled so many people."

"Does he work with you at First Financial?"

"No. He's a Realtor. Has a small office in our building. I'd never met the guy until he stepped forward to help. Shit happens, and you never can tell who will be on your side."

"We can find Tim at the office today?"

"Maybe. He works really hard and is out of the office a lot. But he always carries his cell and will get back to you pretty quick." Scott rattled off the cell number.

Brody pulled a notebook from his pocket and scribbled a note. "Great."

"Why do you want to talk to Tim? He barely knew Christa."

"We're talking to anyone and everyone who can tell us about Christa and the time she vanished."

"You should talk to the local cops. They've been on this case and up my ass for a month."

"We've been in touch. Right now we're trying to get a fresh take on the case."

Scott rose. "You're gonna talk with the people I work with."

"That's right."

"I'd rather you not tell them you found me with

Dee. I've missed so much work the last month. Patience is running thin."

"I'll keep it to myself."

"Thanks."

"Don't thank me yet, pal. If I find out you've been holding out on me, I'll be your worst enemy."

Hookers weren't Robbie's favorite. They'd always been Harvey's favorite in his later years because they were easy. "Two or three twenties and you can lure one into your car," Harvey would say. "Cheap, easy hunts that offered little or no challenge." That's why it had been such a big deal when Harvey had trapped that girl a decade ago. He'd chosen the best for his son.

Knowing that, Robbie had not wanted his first to be a cheap, easy kill. He'd wanted Harvey to know his kill had been a cut above. Worthy.

When he'd first seen Christa he'd been dumbstruck. She looked so much like the girl Harvey had chosen for him a decade ago. She'd been upscale. Smart.

Taking her hadn't been as easy as cruising for a hooker. He'd had to work. To plan. It had taken some doing to toy with her heating unit so that the temperature soared in her apartment, forcing Christa and her roommate to open their windows. He'd sat in the parking lot in his darkened car and watched as the roommate had cracked her window. He could have taken the roommate, but she wasn't his type. So he'd waited, patient and silent, for Christa who had come home just around midnight. It hadn't taken long before she'd opened her window. After she shut off the lights, he waited another fifteen minutes and then made his move. He'd been in her room and on top of her, the needle in her neck, before she knew what had happened. After she'd passed out it had been easy enough to carry her out the one-story window and across the dark parking lot that had no cameras.

Robbie had been proud of his coup. But when the time came to kill her, he'd been as terrified and scared as he had been all those years ago. That's why he'd kept her tucked away in the trailer on the other plot of land for so long.

At first he would toss her food and leave, but after a few days, he'd linger while she ate. A day or two more and he'd asked if she liked her meal. At first she talked only about him letting her go but after a couple more days she answered his questions. He'd been able to tell her about Smith and the loss of his father's love. She'd seemed to understand.

But in the end, he realized if he did not act, he'd run out of time before Smith died. And it broke his heart to know his father would have gone to his grave thinking him a failure.

When he'd told her he was taking her home,

the relief on her face had almost made him back out of the kill. She'd thanked him over and over again as they'd driven down the country road. "I won't tell. I won't tell. I swear."

She didn't deserve to die. But she was the perfect victim. And she had to die, so his father would know he'd finally manned up.

When they'd arrived at the field, she'd looked confused. But she'd not panicked until he'd pulled her out of the cab and bound her hands at her side.

"I won't tell. I won't tell!"

Gently he touched her face. "I know you won't."

He'd dragged her to the hole he'd dug for her and forced her into it. Each time she tried to get up, he tossed more dirt in her face until her entire body was covered.

Robbie had sat at Christa's grave for hours, weeping for her and for his own success.

Shaking off the memory, he tightened his hold on the steering wheel as he drove toward east Austin.

If the cops had not been to Harvey's dump site, now his, he'd have gone for another one like Christa. He liked the nicer girls, the ones that hadn't been used and soiled by so many before him. But he understood Smith needed to send the cops.

As much as he wanted a better girl, for now he'd have to adapt and make do with what he could easily find. Of course, he could wait until the crime cooled or move to another town, but he needed to act again before Smith died. He'd needed to show his father he was a man. The first kill was not a fluke.

Like any city, Austin had its places where the prostitutes hung out. He drove the city side street past Tequila Shots cantina. Three girls stood on the corner. One was older, skinny and dark. The second wore a red wig and had breasts so large, they threatened to spill out of her green skintight dress. But the third one . . . he knew her. Liked her. Young, blond, and thin but not the emaciated kind of thin that came with too much time out here. She wore faded jeans that hugged narrow hips and a black tank top that showed him and the world that it was cold outside. He'd liked the way she absently scanned the streets, as if she knew her way around. She wasn't easily rattled or emotional.

He slowed and rolled down his passenger window. She caught his gaze, glanced from side to side and sauntered toward him.

"Hey." She snapped her gum. "I know you."

"I picked you up a couple of times before." He unlocked the truck door.

"Yes."

"My truck is warm."

She opened the door and slid into the passenger seat. "Turn the heat up. I'm chilly."

He cranked the heat. This one never made small

talk, and he suspected her brain moved at a slower pace. "Better, Bluebonnet?"

"Better." Her smile didn't reach her eyes. "It's a hundred an hour, like before."

He handed her two hundred dollars. She counted the money. "This is more than you're supposed to pay me."

He pulled into traffic and headed west on East Twelfth. "I'd like more of your time, Bluebonnet."

She tucked the money in her shoe. "Okay."

"Thank you, Bluebonnet."

She cocked her head. "Why do you call me Bluebonnet? My name is Hanna."

"Have you ever seen bluebonnets?"

"They're pretty. Purple."

"Pretty like you."

She stared out the window. "Bluebonnet is not my name."

Chapter Eight

Monday, April 8, 3:00 p.m.

Brody and Santos returned to the burial site to walk the land without Sunday's chaos. They got out of the Bronco. Already the heat had evaporated the moisture from Saturday's rain and dried the air. The area remained secure with an officer guarding the site.

A hundred-foot area around the collapsing barn had been roped off. The unearthed graves remained open and raw and several forensic technicians still worked around the graves.

After Brody and Santos spoke to the officers on duty they started to reexamine the site. "No other bodies were found in the immediate area yesterday or this morning," Santos said.

Brody let his gaze trail over the open land of knee-high grass, brushy trees and rolling hills. Nothing caught his attention.

"What if the killer isn't an apprentice? Hell, we only have Smith's word that there is an apprentice," Santos said. "What if he was one of Smith's fans? Maddox said the guy had lots of people writing him. Women wanted to marry him."

"The warden just sent me a list of Smith's fans. There is one in the Austin area that's been very vocal lately."

"This fan decides to take Christa and somehow Smith tips the fan off about this site."

"Not impossible. Smith never mailed correspondence from the prison, but there are other ways to get messages out."

A cool wind blew over the tops of the grass blades, making them bow slightly. "Off the top of your head, do you remember the name of the fan?"

"Ginnie Dupont."

"A woman?"

"She fancied herself in love with him. Said she'd do anything for him."

"She needs a visit."

"Agreed."

They walked toward the cluster of three empty graves. "When are you going back to West Livingston to see Smith?"

"Tomorrow morning. I wanted to go today but Maddox says that Smith is very ill. He's semiconscious at best. A damn miracle that he got out of his sick bed on Saturday."

"The guy's been gaming the system since he entered it. Would stand to reason he'd take his last burst of energy to jerk our chains."

Brody rested his hands on his belt, tapped his right index finger on his gun handle. "What about Neumann?"

"According to his answering service, he's out showing houses until five. He's promised to return all calls when he returns."

"Right."

They walked the land for the better part of an hour, searching for anything that might shed light on two vicious killers. They found nothing.

Back in the car, Brody fired up the engine and cranked the heat.

"You get the invite to Beck's wedding?" Santos said.

Brody stared at the horizon. "He gave it to me this morning."

"Should be fun."

Brody tightened his hand on the steering wheel. "I'm not much for weddings."

"Can't say I am either, but this one is going to be casual. A barbecue. Jo Granger is going."

Brody shifted into gear and drove back toward the main road. "Jo Granger? How do you know her?"

"We became friends last year when she helped my sister, Maria. Maria's been struggling since our mom died and Jo took the time to talk to her."

Brody stopped at a light. "Might as well hear this from me."

Santos met his gaze. "What, you asked her to go to the wedding? There a snap-crackle-pop between you two?"

Brody shook his head. "No. Our relationship is strictly professional. And I did not ask her to the wedding." He hated poking around in the past. "But Jo and I do have a past. We were married in college."

Santos blinked. "Wait. You the baseball jock and Dr. Jolene Granger, the smartest woman in Texas, were married?"

Brody glowered. "You make me sound as dumb as a box of rocks."

"My friend, most college boys are."

Brody shrugged. "Well, I won't pretend that I was a genius. I was failing English literature and needed to get my grades up to stay on the roster.

Jo was my tutor. We hit it off and one thing led to another. We married."

Santos's gaze narrowed. "I could see you being impulsive, but not Jo. She thinks three steps ahead."

Except for that first night they slept together. But he refused to tell Santos about that, the unwanted pregnancy or the miscarriage. That information was too personal. If Jo wanted to share with Santos, so be it, but he wouldn't. "Lots of kids do foolish things in college."

Santos shook his head. "Shit. I didn't expect that. She's never mentioned an ex-husband, but she's a pretty private gal. And I don't know her all that well . . . yet."

A knot twisted in Brody's gut. He had no claim on Jo. And Lord knows that woman deserved happiness. So why did he want to punch Santos in the face? Damn.

"No lingering feelings between you two?" Santos said. "Cards on the table now. If I'm poaching I'll stay clear."

Yeah, back the fuck off. "No. The last couple of days have been business. I tracked her for Smith."

A curious smile curled the edges of Santos's lips. "Last chance, hombre. I warn you now, I like that lady a lot."

"She's all yours."

"No take-backs."

Fuck.

• • •

It was past four when Jo dashed downstairs to the coffee shop, grabbed a sandwich and returned to her office. Maybe if she hustled, she could make up the lost time and put a dent in the paperwork.

She studied the pink message slips piled high on her chair and groaned. She'd be here until tomorrow at the rate this day was going.

Snatching up the slips, she sat in her chair, placed her purse on the credenza behind her and opened her sandwich.

"I talked to Dayton's attorney."

Her mouthful of turkey and rye, she met Dr. Anderson's gaze, chewed and swallowed. "I assume he's not happy."

"He was hoping for a thumbs up from us. He didn't like your assessment: 'cold-blooded sociopath.' "

She wiped her hands with a paper napkin. "I read up on him after the interview, and I am more convinced of his guilt."

He chuckled. "I pay you for your honest opinion. It's what I admire about you."

"I'll keep that in mind the next time I'm being frank."

"I didn't get a chance to ask but what were you doing this weekend? I heard the Rangers corralled you."

She set her sandwich in the center of her napkin.

Dr. Anderson had contacts in all the local and state police agencies, and she always assumed now he knew more about what was going on than she. "I'm surprised you don't know all the details."

He grinned. "I know the high points, like you identifying the victim."

"I made a guess. Are you telling me I was right?"

"You were exactly right. And now there is talk of the Rangers returning to West Livingston to talk to Smith tomorrow."

She scrolled quickly through her cell in-box for a message from Brody. There was none. "And when are they going?"

"Depends on Smith and how he's doing. He's in bad shape."

Frustration rose up in her. Brody should have called her and clued her in on what was happening. He wouldn't have a crime scene if not for her. "I want to go with the Rangers back to West Livingston."

He shrugged. "You can push off the appointments you have tomorrow, but Wednesday you have court."

"I can be up and back to West Livingston in a day. Even if I have to drive. But when they go I want in."

"Brody Winchester runs a tight ship, Jo. If he'd have wanted you on this outing he'd have called."

"It's not about what he wants. Smith was willing to talk to me on Saturday. He won't talk to Winchester."

"Those two have a long history. Smith had said more than once he respects Winchester."

"Respect doesn't mean much if he refuses to talk."

She reached for the phone on her desk. "Winchester is not shutting me out."

Dr. Anderson pulled off his glasses and cleaned the lenses with the edge of his sweater. "Why did Smith want to see you?"

"I can only assume it's my dissertation I wrote on him a couple of years ago or the subsequent presentations I gave. And there is an added element." She explained her past connection to Brody.

He raised a brow, but made no comment on the marriage. "I remember in your presentation that you said he wouldn't consent to be interviewed."

She'd written him several letters, but she'd received no responses. "That's right."

"And now he wants to talk."

"He did the other day at least. Now, let's hope he will keep talking." She cradled the phone under her ear as she looked up Brody's number in her cell phone. "He's running out of time."

Dr. Anderson shook his head. "I'm not so sure it's about time. Smith always had a second and sometimes third motive."

• • •

Three messages from Jo blinked on Brody's phone by five thirty. He'd listened to the first message seconds after it hit his phone, but he'd chosen not to respond. Jo wanted to see Smith again. She'd received updates on the case and hoped another conversation with Smith would reveal more. She wanted in on his next trip to West Livingston.

Jo was smart, likely smarter than anyone he'd ever met, but he would not expose her to Smith again. The old man had stared at her with a lean, hungry look that had tested Brody's patience. His smile had remained intact but instinct demanded he pummel Smith unconscious.

Smith gave no information away for free and whatever price he expected for his assistance, he'd exact it from Jo.

Brody understood too well how this psychopath could get into a mind. When Brody had been tracking Smith, he'd crawled inside the killer's mind, hoping to anticipate his next kill. He'd done what he'd set out to do and trapped the animal but the cost had been high. He'd lost sleep. Cut off friends and family. His girlfriend had ended their relationship.

Brody didn't want Smith's kind of ruin to burn its way into Jo's life. She might resent him protecting her now when he hadn't all those years ago. But she'd have to get over it. This time he would protect her. Whether she liked it or not.

Brody closed his phone and got out of his car. He studied the mobile home surrounded by a chicken-wire fence adorned with Christmas lights. The dirt front yard was decorated with a collection of pinwheels, and aluminum foil covered the windows of the trailer.

A car door slammed shut, signaling Santos's arrival. Dirt kicked up around his boots as he moved toward Brody. "The home of Ginnie Dupont."

Brody caught a whiff of the garbage pile in the backyard. "That's right."

"Can't wait to meet her."

Hands on guns, they approached the trailer. Brody pounded on it with his fist and both men stood to the side while they waited. Footsteps sounded inside the trailer, the aluminum foil on the window closest to the door raised and the door opened.

The woman standing there was in her mid-fifties. Thin, with wrinkled skin, her hair was as white as snow. She wore jeans, a flannel shirt and flip-flops. "Ranger," she said.

Brody touched the brim of his hat. "Ms. Ginnie Dupont?"

Gray eyes narrowed. "That's right. You come to talk to me about those letters again?"

"We have."

She smiled and moved outside. "I was working

on a new one. Been two days since I've written, and I didn't want Mr. Smith to think I'd forgotten him."

"No, ma'am," Santos said.

"When's the last time you heard from Smith?" Brody knew Smith had no outgoing communication, but sometimes asking a direct question awarded him an unexpected answer.

"I heard from him last night."

Brody remembered the profile the warden had relayed on Dupont on the phone. "Is that direct communication or in your dreams like before?"

"In my dream, of course."

"And what did he say, ma'am?" Santos said.

She twisted a braided bracelet that wrapped around her thin wrist. "That he loves me, of course. And that one day he's gonna come for me."

"And bury you like the others?"

She smiled. "That's right."

Robbie stared at Bluebonnet as she lay on her side, curled in a ball on the bed in his trailer. When he'd refused her sexual advances, she'd lain down on the bed, thinking he'd change his mind. He hadn't and she'd slept while he'd gathered his resolve.

He touched her on the shoulder. "It's time to go."

She rolled on her back and stretched. "I need to get back. Daddy is going to be mad."

"Daddy?"

"My pimp."

"Ah. Well, we wouldn't want to upset Daddy, now would we, Bluebonnet?"

"My name is Hanna." She rose and slipped back on her jeans, top and boots.

"Maybe, but to me you will always be Bluebonnet." He pulled a silk bluebonnet from his pocket. For several seconds he twirled it between his fingers before he gently tucked it in her hair.

She removed the flower and stared at it. "Pretty."

"Like you."

Outside, the sun blazed on the horizon, lighting up the land. Silent, both got back into his truck. He started the engine and headed down the dirt road and turned left onto the main road. Soon they were sailing. However, instead of taking the exit to the interstate, he kept on heading toward open land.

"Where are we going?" Bluebonnet said.

"A quick side trip."

"Daddy said one hundred dollars an hour."

He smiled. "We won't be but a minute."

Pale blue eyes flickered with curiosity. Her emotions were flat, which he'd first thought was drug-related. Now he'd come to see that it was a quirk of her personality.

"You'll take me back?"

"I'll take you."

She faced him, the evening light across her face. "When?"

"Soon."

"Daddy will want more money."

"I understand."

Satisfied, she settled in her seat.

His spirits light, he wasn't so anxious or nervous as he had been with Christa, and he saw the change as progress. They reached the main road and drove for another fifteen minutes before he turned into a development so new, no home had been built yet. There were a handful of foundations in place.

Bluebonnet shook her head. "This isn't a shortcut."

"Yes, it is."

She fisted her hands and frowned. "Keri says johns are tricky. I think you're tricky." She grabbed a hold of the door as if she wanted to jump out.

He pushed on the gas. "You jump out now and you'll break a leg. Don't be such a worrywart."

She clung to the door as if it offered some kind of pathetic moral support. The truck rocked and bumped as he drove deeper into the development.

"It rained the other day. Makes for softer soil. Tough on driving but rain is good. This drought has been rough on Texas."

At the back of the development he parked at the end of a cul-de-sac. He turned off the truck and set the brake.

She jerked on the door latch, but the door didn't open. "The door doesn't work."

"That door doesn't open from the inside. Heck of an inconvenience. I'll come around and let you out."

"Out? Why would I want to get out here?"

He slammed his door and came around to her side. When he opened it she was clinging to the seat. "I am not getting out."

"Yes, you are."

She screamed as if someone, maybe Keri, had told her to do it.

He winced and a second later he had handcuffs out of his pocket and on her wrists. Then he shoved a rag in her mouth. He pulled tape from his pocket and flattened it over the gag. She moaned and struggled. "Now, now, Bluebonnet. Stop your worrying. This isn't going to hurt a bit."

When he'd killed Christa, he'd been awkward and afraid. Now fear didn't overwhelm him. In fact, he felt energized and excited. Harvey would be pleased.

He hoisted Bluebonnet up on his shoulder and walked toward the foundation frame of a house and into the center of the dirt square. He dropped her to the ground and before she could scramble to her feet, he tied her ankles together. "Be right back, darlin'. Need to get my shovel."

He hustled back to his truck, grabbed his shovel from under a tarp in the bed and hurried back to find Bluebonnet had rolled several feet away. He jammed the shovel in the soft earth before dragging her back by her ankles. The tape and gag muffled her screams.

"Where you going, girl? Party is about to start."

It took him a half hour to dig a sizable hole. He'd have finished faster but a couple of times he had to stop and drag her back.

A fine sheen of sweat covered his forehead when he finished his digging and he grabbed Bluebonnet under the arms and hauled her toward the hole. He pulled her upper body in first followed by her legs. Moonlight reflected off a gold charm around her neck and, unable to resist the trophy, he snatched it free and shoved it in his pocket.

Thrashing against her restraints, desperation oozed from her. He grabbed his shovel and covered her in dirt. Harvey had taught him to cover the face last. The panic in the eyes was to be savored.

That is the best part.

He continued shoveling until all that remained uncovered was Bluebonnet's nose and eyes. He stared into those eyes for long seconds before dumping dirt on her face. Within a minute she was completely covered.

The earth cracked the tiniest fraction, and he heard her gagged moans.

He smiled.

The day had gone well and Harvey would have been so proud. "I promise, Harvey, there will be many more."

Hanna held her breath as the dirt plastered against her face, filling her nose. Heart pounding hard in her chest, she moved her head from side to side trying to knock the dirt from her face. But the weight grew heavier and heavier as her heart slammed her ribs and her lungs screamed for air.

Keri had never told her about this. She'd said johns could be tricky. They could hit. Steal. Leave you to walk back to your corner. But Keri had never told her about this.

Thump, thump, thump. Her heart thundered, ready to burst out of her chest.

Unable to hold her breath any longer she snorted a breath but when she inhaled she pulled in dirt, which clogged her nose.

Thump, thump, thump.

Her heart labored now and her head spun. She wanted to scream but couldn't.

Keri, you never told me about this.

"I love you, Bluebonnet." His muffled voice reached below the earth.

Keri!

Her heart pounded.

Her head swam.

And then her mind went blank.

Chapter Nine

Monday, April 8, 7:30 p.m.

The support group Jo ran for the at-risk teen girls was held in the basement of the Catholic church, located in east Austin. As Jo headed into the church's fellowship hall, she checked her messages, expecting to see a note from Brody. Brody had done a fine job of ignoring Jo's phone messages today. After she'd left the first, she'd assumed it would be a matter of time before he called her back. But when she checked the clock hours later and realized he'd not called, she'd made calls to a friend in the Rangers' office and gotten his home address. She'd track him down after this meeting.

Avoidance was his specialty when he didn't want to talk. She understood that. But this was about the case. Not them. And she wanted to interview Smith one more time. So she and Brody were going to talk tonight.

Jo shrugged off her coat and put down her bag of groceries. She had about twenty minutes to set up before the girls arrived.

As she pulled sugar cookies from the bag and plated them, the back door opened to a petite blonde with scraggly hair and eye shadow so thick, it made her look as if she'd been bruised.

Jo had seen her once or twice before in the last six months. She wore leather pants, red high-top tennis shoes, a tank top and a white, furry, bolero jacket that made her thin frame look fragile.

"Sadie," Jo said.

A half smile tweaked the girl's thin lips. "You have a good memory, Doc."

Jo searched her mind for details about the girl. Said she was seventeen but Jo would have guessed younger, closer to fifteen. She'd been on the streets about a year. She didn't prostitute but made deliveries for the drug dealers and pimps. So far, Sadie had stayed away from using drugs but the streets chewed up young girls like her. The descent into drugs was often a matter of time.

"I've brought cookies but haven't had the chance to put the coffee on yet, Sadie."

The girl smiled. "I can do that."

Jo didn't hide her surprise. "You can work one of those big coffeemakers?"

"I wish I had a dollar for all the pots of coffee I made when I was a kid." She shrugged off her jacket and laid it on a chair before vanishing into the kitchen and reappearing with the big steel coffeepot.

Sadie had been cautious about opening up. In fact, this detail about her making coffee was the first Jo really had on the girl. As tempted as Jo was to probe the girl's past, she didn't. She'd made it a rule not to pry but to let the girls open up when they were ready. This was a safe place for the girls where she listened and answered questions without offering unsolicited opinions.

As Jo arranged the chairs in a circle, Sadie made quick work of the coffeepot, filling the cylinder with water, setting the basket of grounds inside and flipping the switch. Within seconds it gurgled and popped.

"Haven't seen you in a while," Jo said.

Sadie picked up a cookie and nibbled on it. "Been working."

It broke Jo's heart to think about the "work" the kid did. "I know it's hard to get away."

"Lots of deliveries to make normally but tonight turned out to be slow."

"I'm glad you could make it. Have a seat. You've got to be tired."

Sadie shrugged and sat. "I'm okay."

"I love tennis shoes but my mother loves high heels. So does my sister. But I'm not so good in them. I've my favorite pumps, but I'm not sure on my feet in any other heel."

"Your mom wears heels?"

Jo arched a brow. "Yeah. Mom's always put a lot of care into her appearance."

The kid cocked her head as she studied Jo. "I'd think you'd have the practical sort of mom. You know, one that bakes cookies and shit."

Jo laughed. "Mom dusts off her stove every few

months and knows the number of a dozen take-out places by heart. She hasn't cooked in years."

"What does she do?"

"Works in a beauty salon. She's one of the best colorists in the state from what I hear."

Sadie stared at her, interest popping from her gaze. "She color your hair?"

Jo sat in a seat across from Sadie and crossed her legs. "No. Mom wanted to color it more times than I can count, but I never let her. In the beauty department, I'm a big disappointment to her."

Sadie shrugged. "You're cute enough. I know a dude named Daddy who could find you clients."

Jo laughed. "Thanks, I think."

"Your bones and cheeks are pretty. Just need to glam it up a bit."

"I'll keep that in mind." Jo watched the girl nibble the cookie and decided to break one of her rules. "Where did you learn to make coffee?"

For a moment Sadie hesitated before saying, "At my dad's church. He was a preacher, and Mama and I were always setting up for some social."

She'd mentioned her father at the last meeting. They'd had a terrible fight, which was why she'd left home. "Have you talked to your dad lately?"

"Not since Mom died. It got hard to live around him."

"How long's it been since he's seen you?"

"A year."

"Think he's worried?" She didn't assume her father missed her. A lot of the girls that came in here had families who'd tossed them aside like yesterday's garbage.

"I don't know." Sadie shifted, as if uncomfortable. "You close to your dad?"

"My dad? My dad died five years ago. But when he was alive, we didn't have a lot in common."

Sadie's eyes widened. "Why?"

"I liked my books. He was a man who didn't care to read. He was an electrician and made his living with his hands."

Sadie studied her, her gaze keen. "Yeah, but he loved you, right?"

Jo remembered a time when her dad had taken her to a bookstore and told her she could spend twenty dollars. He'd waited outside, uncomfort-able in his muddy boots, as she'd run inside. "Yeah, in his way he did. He didn't understand."

"I hear you."

The recreation room door opened and two gals dressed much like Sadie sauntered into the room. "Hey, Doc," one of the girls shouted. "What's shaking?"

"Not much, Deidra. How about you?"

Deidra was five months pregnant and had been ready to drop out of school when her school counselor had referred her to Jo's group. She wasn't making A's but Jo was grateful at this point for the C minuses. "Can't complain. No, scratch that," she said. "Complaining is the reason I come here."

Immediately, Sadie stiffened and the easy openness in her gaze vanished. She rose and put on her coat. "Doc, I better get going. I've been here longer than I should. Folks is gonna be looking for me."

Jo rose, smoothing her hands over her slim skirt. "Sadie, you can stay."

"Naw." She scooped up two cookies and dropped them in the pocket of her jacket. "Thanks, Doc."

"Sadie, please stay."

The girl looked tempted but shook her head. "Not tonight. Next time."

"Come back anytime. You can always find me through the church."

Sadie tucked her hair behind her ear and Jo spotted a bruise on the side of her neck. "I know. See ya."

Jo wanted so much to pull the girl back and demand that she remain. She wished like hell she could do more.

By the time the meeting with the girls ended, it was past nine. Once Jo had done a final check of the room and locked the door, she hurried to her car. She fired up the engine and checked her phone, which had been on silent during the meeting.

No call from Brody.

He'd likely figured that she'd give up and let him have his way. That she'd simply absorb her anger, fear and disappointment and pretend all was fine.

She'd long ago stopped being the girl "that went along." She'd changed. Learned to take control. And now was no different. Brody would not ignore her this time.

Determined, she found Brody's complex with her GPS and headed out. The complex was easy enough to find but at the entrance, there were rows and rows of mailboxes. She spent ten minutes searching for the name Winchester.

As she stood there a young girl came up, key in hand, and opened her mailbox. The girl, dressed in jeans and a heavy dark sweater, shrugged. "What's the name? Maybe I can help you find him."

"Winchester. Brody."

"Don't know the name."

"He moved in a couple of weeks ago. Wears a cowboy hat."

"A couple of weeks." She paused to think. "There is the tall dude in building six. Not cute. Wears a cowboy hat."

"That's him."

The girl nodded. "Building six is that way."

Jo found the tension knotting in her stomach annoying. "Thanks."

The girl cocked her head as she shuffled through her mail. "None of my business, but what did he do to piss you off?"

"I'm not mad."

The girl arched a brow.

Jo swallowed a rebuttal. "He didn't return my calls."

"That would do it. Good luck."

"Thanks."

Her sensible heels clicked as she hurried back to her car and slid behind the wheel. Less than a minute later she was parked in front of building six.

She shut off the car, half wishing she'd stuck to phone messages. A glance in the rearview mirror revealed a harried reflection. Her makeup had worn thin, leaving the spray of freckles over her nose exposed. Her lipstick had worn away as had her blush. "Good going, Jo. Toss in a couple of braids, and you are Pippi Longstocking."

The temptation to fuss and preen nudged her fingers to the lipstick in her purse as a car parked beside her. She released the lipstick and let it fall back in her purse. Just her luck, she'd be applying makeup and Brody would knock on her window. Better to be bedraggled than to be caught fussing.

She trailed the guy who'd gotten out of his car

to the building entrance. He swiped his card and she followed him inside, trying to look as if she belonged here. The man vanished into a first-floor apartment as Jo pretended to climb the stairs. When he was inside she did a quick scan of the doors. None bore the Winchester name, so she climbed to the next floor. Another glance and no Brody. But on the third floor three of the four doors had names while the last did not. It made sense he'd not advertise his name.

Taking a chance, she knocked on the door. For a moment she didn't hear any sound or signs of life and thought the girl by the mailbox had given her an incorrect lead. She raised her fist to knock again when she heard steady steps making their way to the door seconds before it snapped open to Brody.

He wore a University of Texas T-shirt and faded jeans. Dark stubble covered his chin and fatigue had left his eyes bloodshot. He looked as if he'd just woken up.

"God, did I wake you?" Not two seconds into this conversation and an apology underscored her tone.

"I was reading files." He stared at her, knowing damn well why she was here.

"I know you're going to West Livingston tomorrow."

"That's right."

"I want to go."

"No."

The conviction behind the word took her aback. "What do you mean 'no'? If you're going to see Smith, I should be there."

"No."

Heat stoked her temper. "I certainly do not need your permission."

"You do need my permission. I've told the warden I'm coming and because I'm now handling an active investigation, I don't want anybody interviewing my witness without me being present."

Her fingers tightened around the shoulder strap of her purse. "Smith told me more in ten minutes than he told you in three years."

He leaned on the doorjamb and slid his hands in his pockets. "What's your point?"

"My point?" Damn him. A resident came out of his apartment, tossed an amused look at the two and then hurried down the stairs. Lowering her voice, she added, "I can help."

"Maybe. Maybe you're giving Smith one more chance to screw with you."

"I'm fine."

"Those dark circles under your eyes tell me you've not slept real well the last two nights."

"I'm a bad sleeper."

"That's not how I remember it."

Unwanted color rose in her cheeks. "I've changed."

"Yeah, I know. You've grown up. We both have. But that doesn't change the fact that Smith can get in your head and fuck you up. He said the answer is in you, and you haven't let it go."

"That's not true."

He leaned toward her. "It is. That's what Smith does. He plants land mines in your brain, and it's damn near impossible to let it go."

"How did he screw with you?"

He studied her a beat as if he'd answer, but he shook his head. "No thanks, Doc. I don't need a shrink."

"I wasn't—"

"Of course, you were. I've not met a shrink that can resist getting into someone's head." He took a step back and put his hand on the door. "You're not going to see Smith again, Jo. End of story."

She opened her mouth to argue as his door shut hard in her face.

Blinking, she stood there for a moment, staring at the cheap door knocker glaring back at her. Tempted as she was to pound on the door and demand to be heard, she refused to lower herself. Brody Winchester might not want her to see Smith again, but he wasn't the end-all, be-all. There was more than one way to skin a cat.

The digital clock read 11:59 p.m. when Jo slid into her bed and lay back on her pillow. She reached for the light and shut it off.

Light from the full moon shone in through plantation shutters, slashing patterns across her bedroom wall.

As much as her body craved a full night's sleep, her mind buzzed with a fuzzy energy. Too tired to work and too awake to sleep.

Look deep inside yourself.

Smith's words rattled in her head, stoking an unease in her that had her rising and swinging her legs over the side of the bed. She buried her face in her hands and took several deep breaths.

He'll get in your head. Brody's words rattled like a jailer's chain.

"He's not in my head. You are in my head." Groaning, she padded to the kitchen, where she filled a glass with water. She took a sip, peered in the glass, and then poured it out. From the refrigerator, she grabbed a half-full bottle of chardonnay and refilled the glass.

The wine tasted bitter. She'd cracked the bottle six months ago for Thanksgiving at her mom's. The only wine drinker in the family, she'd been left after the festivities with a near-full bottle that she'd shoved to the back of her refrigerator, sure she'd have more occasions to enjoy it. But the holiday season, marketed as a glittering happy time, had a way of escalating sadness into suicide attempts. She'd worked nonstop in late December and early January.

So here she sat, alone, with a half-full glass of stale wine, trying to chase away worries that would not leave.

Tapping her finger on the side of the glass, she moved to the hallway closet, opened it and stared at the top shelf, crammed full of boxes. Setting her glass down, she hauled a chair from the kitchen set and climbed up on it. The first couple of boxes were extra climbing ropes and hooks; however it was the last box she was after. The one shoved deep in the back.

Standing on tiptoes, her fingers barely skimmed the corner of the box and she nudged it forward far enough so that she could grab ahold.

Jo carried the box to the couch and sat cross-legged, the box resting beside her. All her other memories had been carefully cataloged in scrapbooks, but these memories didn't warrant that kind of attention. She should have thrown them out years ago, but for some reason she'd schlepped the box from apartment to apartment until two years ago it had found itself in the back of this closet where it had remained untouched.

She reached in and pulled out a name badge that read: JOLENE S. GRANGER, FRESHMAN, PSYCHOLOGY. Those first weeks at UT had been overwhelming and exciting. She was the first and only in her family to go to college. For the first time in her life she'd been in her element.

Two of her three cats jumped up on the couch

and nestled beside her. The third, she knew, still slept on the bed.

Setting the badge aside, she dug deeper, skimming over pamphlets and dorm assignments and first semester schedules. Finally, she reached her time card from the tutoring center. Not many freshmen were hired at the center and she'd been pleased when they accepted her application.

She thumbed through her logbook and found Brody's signature. Bold. And the ridges dug into the paper with the ballpoint pen remained crisp.

God, but he'd been a force of nature. Larger than life. The most interesting guy she'd ever met.

Jo closed her eyes. She'd not been thinking long-term when they'd slipped back to his room and he'd undressed her. She'd been thinking adventure. Excitement. Feeling so alive it hurt.

The sex had been, well . . . okay. He'd not done a great job of tempering his desire, and she'd been an awkward virgin who'd wished for worldliness. But she'd be a liar if she said she'd not enjoyed the sex. They'd met again and again and for a brief time she'd had the world by the tail.

And then one night after they'd made love, he'd realized the condom had broken. His relaxed muscles had tensed and satiation had turned to horror and disgust. She'd been rattled but had assumed it would be fine. Bad stuff had never happened to her.

Jo shook off the image of Brody's worried

expression. She dug deeper into the box and found the group picture taken of the psychology department. She'd been on the third row, five spots in. Not smiling. Pale. Pregnant.

Stuck to the back of that picture was their marriage license. Her signature had been weak and his not so bold, or deeply grooved.

Tears pooled in her eyes, and because she was alone and knew no one would ever know, she let them spill down her cheeks.

If Smith had meant to topple her life out of balance, he had done it.

Chapter Ten

Tuesday, April 9, 9:00 a.m.

Brody spent the morning on the phone trading calls with the warden, trying to confirm his meeting with Smith, who remained in critical, unresponsive condition in the prison infirmary. He was heavily sedated and wouldn't awaken until later in the day. Brody's visit would have to wait. He sent a text to Jo advising her of the situation.

Brody refocused on Christa and called Tim Neumann's service and arranged for a morning appointment. His hope was that Neumann, the organizer of the *Find Christa!* campaign, would have insight into Scott or anyone else that might have wanted to harm Christa.

He arrived at the nondescript office building that housed Neumann's administrative offices as well as the offices of First Financial, Christa and Scott's employer. As the service had instructed, Brody found a seat in the building's café.

Brody ordered a coffee and took a seat in one of the corner booths. As he sipped black coffee, he stared at gray walls decorated with stunning black-and-white photographs.

In all his life, he never imagined himself working in an office building like this. In college he'd known he'd never make it to the top of baseball, but he'd clung to the sport because it had been exciting. When Jo had gotten pregnant and they'd married, he'd realized baseball wasn't going to cut it. And so he'd joined the Marines without discussing it with her. Days later, Jo had lost the baby and their marriage had crumbled. He'd kept his commitment to the Marines and shipped out to basic before the divorce was final. When he'd returned to Austin four years later, he had joined the Department of Public Safety as a patrol officer, which suited his craving for excitement and a curiosity that focused on real-life issues versus the academic ones of college.

The café door opened, revealing a midsized, olive-skinned man with thick, black hair. He had a fit body and when he spotted Brody he reached out to shake Brody's hand. His grip was firm and his gaze direct. "Sergeant Winchester?"

"Mr. Neumann. Thanks for taking the time. Did I pull you off a job?"

"Managed to squeeze you in between house showings. No worries." Neumann frowned. "I was darn sorry to hear the news about Christa. Scott was devastated when she vanished but for so many days we all thought that we'd find her." He nodded toward the counter. "Let me grab a sandwich and soda."

"Sure."

When he returned he had a large soda, sandwich and a bag of chips. "Don't mind if I eat?"

"Not at all."

"Thanks."

Brody waited for Neumann to sit before saying, "How did you get involved in finding Christa?"

"There are lots of small companies in our building and you kind of get to know each other. I saw Christa in here a lot. News of her disappearance traveled fast in the building. We all felt so helpless. Then I thought that I'm good with people and I can organize. I made up flyers announcing an organizational meeting. Within two days of her vanishing, we had a solid team of volunteers ready to search."

"I understand you started your search in the woods near her apartment."

"That's right. When we didn't find her, we fanned out into the neighborhoods."

"You never came up with any leads."

Folding his arms, he shook his head. "Not a one. And now we all hear that she was alive all this time, and we could have found her. Everyone here is really down today."

"Was there anyone in the search party that caught your attention?"

"We had people from all walks of life. Most were everyday folks. A few were the overeager types."

"How so?"

"Just really determined to find her, as if they wanted to be the one the press interviewed when she was found. But that was just a handful, and we had over one hundred volunteers."

"Any stick out in your mind?"

"There was a dude named Rory who was really into the search. He was a volunteer firefighter from the San Marcos area. There was a lady from San Antonio. Long hair, wore loose-fitting clothes. I don't remember her name."

"Who came up with the T-shirts?"

"A local T-shirt shop that does work for my business donated them. Visibility is the name of the game, so I said yes to the donation."

"How was Scott during your search efforts?"

Neumann hesitated. "Scott was fine. He was too personally involved to be much help to the search group. Don't get me wrong. He wanted to help, but he was upset."

"I ran into a gal named Dee yesterday with a *Find Christa!* T-shirt. You know her?"

"Sure. Dee Anders. She works in legal at Scott's firm. She was one of our most dedicated searchers."

"She and Scott work together a lot?"

Neumann hesitated. "You've heard the rumors?"

"Rumors?"

"Dee has a crush on Scott. From what I understand she liked him long before Christa went missing. Anyway, he was totally cool and kept his distance. He was dedicated to Christa."

"They were getting married in a couple of weeks."

"That's right. Several folks suggested he cancel the reception hall and the caterer, but he refused. Said when Christa came back, she'd want to get married right away."

"You ever see Christa and Scott fight? Did she ever appear upset?"

Neumann's gaze hardened. "I know what you're getting at, but you're wrong. Scott would not hurt Christa. He wouldn't."

Brody wasn't so sure. "He invests money."

"From what I hear."

"I know you two work in the same building, but sometimes gossip gets around. Any word on Scott's work?"

Tim hesitated. "There was an issue about six months ago. Scott lost a lot of money in a bad trade. Several clients threatened to sue. The firm settled."

"How'd you hear this?"

"This café. Be surprised what people talk about in here. They chat in these booths as if they are soundproof."

"What about Scott's family?"

"I hear he's from Oklahoma, but that's all I know. We really don't know each other that well outside of the search." Neumann cocked his head. "Is Scott still a suspect? The local cops really went over his life with a fine-tooth comb."

Brody grinned, not willing to tip his hat to anyone. "Doing my due diligence, Mr. Neumann. I'm reexamining all the angles on the case." He handed him a card. "Call me if you think of new information."

"Sure." Neumann picked up his half-eaten sandwich. "And you know where to find me."

I don't want the wedding to be formal. Wear what you want.

Lara's words, delivered to Jo with such kindness, now haunted her as she made her way during her lunch hour through the mall, searching for a "greenish" bridesmaid dress—her only mandate. As wedding tasks went, this was one of the simplest, and yet as her fingers skimmed the fabric of another unwanted dress she wondered if she'd ever find what she needed.

She had no practice with fashion and weddings, and she wanted to get it right. But worries over making a mistake had kept her from buying any dress. She'd fallen into the perfection trap.

A sleek saleslady had tried to help Jo initially but Jo's indecision had sent her back behind her counter to wait.

"Dr. Granger, what a pleasant surprise. Shopping for a special occasion?"

Dayton's smooth voice had her turning, the watered silk still clutched between her fingertips. An answer to his question could create the threads of a bond she did not want. "This is unexpected."

He looked delighted. "It is odd that we would run into each other here."

He wore a hand-tailored blue blazer, crisp white shirt that set off his tanned skin and black trousers. All spoke to his need to project affluence.

His cool, calm smile shouldn't have set off any alarm bells. By all appearances this was a chance meeting. In fact, many ladies would have sought out or welcomed his attention. Not Jo. Her senses peaked at full alert. "What are you doing here?"

He regarded the boutique, his gaze not reflecting real interest as he pulled a pack of yellow gum from his pocket. "I was happening by and saw you. I thought it would be appropriate to say hello."

Though she'd interviewed countless sociopaths and liars it never failed to surprise her how they could be so utterly charming. "It's not appropriate, Dr. Dayton, considering our recent conversation."

A smile tweaked the edges of his lips. "It was an interview, not an interrogation, Dr. Granger. There's no reason for us to be unfriendly to each other."

She released the dress sleeve and faced him directly. "We have nothing to say to each other."

His smile held, though it took on a chill. Carefully, he unwrapped a piece of gum. "I'm trying to be neighborly."

"No, Dr. Dayton, you are trying to manipulate and to control."

He laughed. "You have a flair for the dramatic, don't you, Dr. Granger? You've dealt with so many criminals that you see them everywhere."

"Not everywhere." But she did here. "Now, if you will excuse me."

"By the way, that shade of green is not your color, Dr. Granger. You'd do better to stay with earth tones—olives, browns. They'll set off your red hair nicely."

The saleslady approached, her smile wide and warm, as her gaze bounced between Dr. Dayton and Jo. "Any luck, hon?"

"I think the olive silk is the way to go," Dr. Dayton said to the clerk. He popped the stick of gum in his mouth and folded the wrapper in half.

The saleslady's gaze brightened. "With her porcelain skin and red hair it would be perfect."

Jo straightened, irritated that Dayton had insinuated himself into her life. "I must go."

"You really should try on the dress, Dr. Granger," he said.

Instead of answering, she turned and left, the saleslady's comment about rude behavior trailing after her.

Bob Killian's construction crews had been working on the new housing development west of Austin for several months. Most days they were on-site and working by seven, but today there'd been all kinds of delays and no work. To top it off, the cement truck had broken down and been delayed.

Finally, by three o'clock the truck had arrived at the site. There was only enough time to dump a truckload of cement, which amounted to one foundation. But one foundation was better than none.

"We're burning daylight," Killian yelled to the Mexican day workers. "Get inside the foundation and be ready to spread mud."

As the Mexican foreman translated Killian's words, the workers grabbed their shovels as the cement truck backed into place. The *ding, ding, ding* of the vehicle's backup alarm was punctuated by the laughter of the men who'd been sitting the better part of the day waiting for the truck.

Killian calculated all the money lost today as he reached for an antacid in his coat pocket. The housing market was getting murdered, and if he didn't hustle and get these houses built he stood to lose a fortune.

The driver leaned out the back of the driver's side window and shouted in Spanish for a couple of the men to step back as he lowered the chute.

One of the workers, a young man with a short, stocky build, stepped back and stumbled. His arms waved wildly as he tried to catch himself but he lost his footing in the soft soil and fell right on his ass. His coworkers laughed and pointed as the young guy struggled to stand in the soft earth.

Killian popped another antacid. "Get moving!"

The worker had righted himself when one of the other men stared at the ground where he'd fallen. Seconds later he pointed and screamed in Spanish, "*La mano*! *La mano*!"

Killian moved toward the men, his patience wearing paper-thin. What the hell were they talking about now? *La mano*. Hand. Had the son of a bitch hurt his hand? He swiped his own hand across his neck, a signal for the cement truck driver to halt while he investigated. "If you are fucking around, I am going to have your ass."

He stepped over the foundation's wooden form into what would one day be the crawl space of a two-story house. As the distraught crewman scrambled to get away, Killian spotted what he had been shouting about. Sticking up from the wet earth were three pale fingers.

Killian motioned for the men to step back before squatting by the object. The fingers were curled in a claw-like manner. Stunned curiosity pulled him closer. The hand's small nails were painted with purple polish that was chipped. Three tarnished silver bracelets dangled from the wrist.

He brushed away the dirt to find the arm of a young woman. His stomach tumbled and he rose slowly, doing his best to remain calm when all he wanted to do was run.

Chapter Eleven

Tuesday, April 9, 6:00 p.m.

When Brody and Santos arrived at the construction site, the uniformed officers had already roped off the crime scene. The lights from several Austin PD and DPS marked cars flashed. Forensics had arrived and the technician was shooting pictures of the scene.

Brody pulled rubber gloves from his coat pocket. He and Santos stopped and greeted several officers. One officer, Sergeant Gary Danner, had been stationed in El Paso about the same time as Brody.

Gary stuck his hand out to Brody. "I heard you'd dragged your sorry ass back to Austin."

Brody grinned. When they'd been in their

twenties the two had torn it up more than once in El Paso, closing a couple of cantinas. "That's right. Slunk into town."

Danner cocked a brow. "And you haven't stirred up any trouble?"

He'd worked nonstop since he'd arrived. "Been doing my best, but I'm getting a little too old to live like I used to."

Gary shook his head. "Winchester, the day you're too old will be the day the sun stops rising."

Brody had been a hell-raiser in his twenties and he still liked to have fun. But the days of pounding back too many beers or shots were over. "Heard you got hitched."

"Sure did." Gary grinned. "Second baby is on the way." He lowered his voice a notch. "Marriage is great, but don't tell my wife, Elaine. Don't need her getting a swelled head."

"I'll take it to my grave, partner." The forensic tech's camera flashed in Brody's peripheral vision. "Like you to meet Sergeant Rick Santos. He and I are working this case."

Santos extended his hand. "Danner. I think we've crossed paths before."

"Sure did. That bank robbery in San Antonio last year."

"That's right. Hell of a mess, that one."

"Yes, sir, it was."

Santos nodded toward the crime scene. "You first on the scene, Gary?"

The laughter eased from his eyes. "One of the first."

Brody rested his hands on his hips, glancing toward the opened mound of dirt. "Fill me in."

"The construction crews were preparing to lay the foundation when one of the workers spotted an oddity. The foreman did a little digging and found a hand, which turned out to be attached to a woman's body. She wasn't more than a foot under the ground and by the looks of it hadn't been in the ground too long. The medical examiner's assistant has already had a look at her and thinks she might have died of asphyxiation in the last twenty-four hours. Forensics is doing their job now."

Brody pulled on his gloves. "The boys that found her have more to add about what they saw or heard?"

"No. They were running behind because of mechanical delays and were focused on getting the foundation in the frames. They might remember details when you talk to them. The foreman is out here a good bit, he says. He might have seen someone yesterday or the day before. He's a little shook up."

Brody eyed the slim, grizzled man who leaned against his truck, his arms folded over his chest and his eyes closed. "He looks okay to me."

"Says he needs to do deep breathing exercises."

Brody muttered an oath. "Let me have a look."

He moved over the muddy earth, and when forensics urged him forward, he ducked under the tape and stepped over the foundation frame. He squatted by the body.

The pale hand stuck up from the earth. As he moved closer he could see fingers bent forward as if reaching for a lifeline. Nails were painted with purple polish. The ring and pinky fingers sported silver rings.

The technician came up behind him. "I can clean the face off now if you're ready."

He rose. "Yeah. Let's see who we have here."

As she knelt and slowly moved the dirt from the face, Brody stood with hands on hips. A long time ago, he'd learned to armor himself from the horrors of crime scenes. Over the years in DPS and in the Rangers he'd seen gruesome sights. Most he could handle, but child deaths still penetrated his hard outer shell.

Using a paintbrush, the tech brushed away the last inch of dirt, moving carefully and slowly in deference to evidence that might be on the body. Soon he saw a shock of blond hair with dark roots and a forehead.

She kept brushing, uncovering the eyes and a mouth taped shut with duct tape. The technician brushed more dirt away. Her hands had been handcuffed together. There'd been enough play in the cuffs for her to raise one hand and dig. Just a little. But not enough to save herself.

He studied her face. Pale skin. A sprinkle of freckles across the bridge of her nose. Big hooped earrings.

Just a kid.

Damn. Damn. Damn.

Jo didn't end up buying a dress. After seeing Dayton she'd been angry at his intrusion and frustrated that he'd left her so rattled. She'd driven straight back to her office and soon was swept up in the buzz of evening appointments.

Minutes before eight, when the last patient had left she had time to sit back and really think about Dayton. He'd been all smiles. He'd made no threats or given any hint that he was dangerous.

But that had all been surface. She dug out the file Dr. Anderson had given her on Dayton from her overflowing in-box and scanned it. A brief peek below and she saw all the telltale signs that she might have a problem. Sheila Dayton had vanished. Neighbors had reported seeing Dayton berating his wife. His wife never spoke much when the two were in public. Always tense. Worried. And she had confided in a friend that she thought he was going to kill her.

But there'd been no signs of physical abuse. And no physical evidence linked Dayton to his wife's disappearance. He had a solid alibi for the day she vanished.

And yet there he was at the mall in a shop

that catered to women, only chatting with her.

Jo released the breath she was holding. The guy had set out to fluster her, and he'd done it.

She drummed her fingers on the desk, reminding herself that she'd dealt with men like him before. How many prisoners after an interview had promised to find her when they were released? How many had made lurid suggestions? Trouble was part of this territory. Dayton would not get in her head like Smith.

Despite the late hour and Brody's morning text about Smith's health, she picked up the phone and dialed the West Livingston prison. She asked the switchboard operator for the warden's voicemail. Jo listened to his brief message, identified herself, and reminded him of her visit days earlier. She hung up, not expecting to hear from the warden until morning. When her phone rang minutes later, she was surprised to see the prison number on her caller ID.

"Dr. Granger," the warden said. "What can I do for you?"

It didn't surprise her he worked long hours. There was always some matter to be dealt with in such a big prison. "I was hoping you could give me the status of Mr. Smith. I understand he has been too ill to receive visitors."

"He's resting comfortably right now, Dr. Granger. Had a better day, meaning more restful, according to the staff nurse. But he's very weak."

She deliberated on tomorrow's calendar, wondering how much she could clear so she could get to West Livingston. "Is he conscious?"

"In and out. He was amazingly lucid the day you came. The nurse thinks he reserved all his energy for it."

She traced circles on her blotter with a ball-point pen. "I still don't understand why he showed an interest in me."

The warden hesitated. "We searched every inch of his cell but found nothing. Brody told me that you and he were married. Brody believes Smith is using you to get to him."

The comment caught her by surprise. Their marriage was no secret, but discussing it was awkward. "Logically, that makes sense."

"And searching for logic in an insane mind is a fool's errand."

So true. "If Mr. Smith improves will you call me?"

"Certainly. I had this same conversation with Winchester this morning and last night. He's explained the stakes and the importance of talking to Smith again."

A last-minute thought occurred to her. "Could Smith be faking? I remember during his trial he faked a heart attack."

"Six months ago I might have said yes, but not now. The disease has progressed too far. It's a matter of days, maybe weeks for him."

"Okay. Thanks." She hung up the phone. The clock on the wall read seven fifty-eight. Her mother was taking her last salon appointment of the day, which meant Jo could swing by. With a day or two under their belts her mother might be more open to conversation.

The drive took less than a half hour in evening traffic. When she parked in front of the salon, the lights in the shop were on, but the CLOSED sign dangled from the door. Arlene, one of the salon's stylists, was finishing up a late-appointment client, but Jo knew her mother well enough to know that she was still on the property. Her mother was always the last to leave and lock up the doors.

Jo knocked on the front door and the stylist, Arlene, glanced up and smiled when she recognized her. She crossed to the door, her wedge heels clunking as her black smock billowed around her jeans and Texas rhinestone T-shirt. Arlene had worked for her mother since Jo was in grade school.

Arlene flipped the dead bolt. "Well, little Miss Jolene. What brings you our way?"

Jo smiled. "Came to see Momma." The women hugged. "How you doing?"

"Can't complain," she said, grinning. "Need to rinse out this last perm before my man and I go dancing tonight."

"Sounds fun."

"You should come out with us sometime. There are lots of good-looking men who'd love to take you for a spin on the dance floor."

Jo grimaced. "My sister inherited the dancing gene. I've two left feet."

Arlene winked. "Baby doll, with that figure of yours and that red hair, it don't matter if you can keep time or not. There's gonna be some fella that wants to take you for a spin."

Jo laughed. "I can't remember the last time a man took me for a spin."

Arlene waggled her brows. "Well, all the more reason to come with us sometime. We'll be going out again on Friday night."

"I have a rehearsal dinner this Friday," she said. "But I might take you up on that offer." She'd not been good at having fun, a trait she'd been trying to change.

"Good girl. Now go and check in with your momma. She's in her office doing the receipts."

Jo found her mother sitting at the small, neat desk in the back of the shop. In front of her was a pile of cash, another with checks and the third with credit card receipts. A lit cigarette sat in a crystal ashtray, its smoke trailing toward a popcorn ceiling.

"Momma," Jo said.

Her mother turned in her swivel chair and smiled. "You visit twice in a week. The dear Lord can take me now."

Jo kissed her mother on the cheek. "I thought you quit smoking."

"I did," she said, her tone sincere. "It's just the one a day now."

"That's not exactly quitting." Her Texas twang always deepened when she spoke to her mother.

"About as close as I'll get, baby doll. What are you doing here in the middle of the week?" She turned back to her stacks, took another drag on her cigarette and pulled out a deposit slip.

Jo sat on a box of beauty supplies sitting by the desk. "I called West Livingston prison today and tried to arrange another meeting with Mr. Smith."

Candace's fingers stilled for an instant while she counted the cash but she didn't raise her gaze. "Why'd you do that, Jo?"

"What he said is bothering me, Mom. *Look deep inside yourself.* It keeps rattling in my brain."

Candace reached for her cigarette, flicked the ash from the tip and inhaled deeply. She released the smoke from her lungs slowly. "He's a crazy man, Jo, who likes to stir up trouble."

Jo drummed her fingers on her thigh. "I know that. And still I can't let it go."

Candace's laugh was brittle, strained. "You always did chew on problems when you were a kid. Don't twist yourself up in knots by thinking too hard, Jo."

She didn't know what prompted her next question. "Did you ever know Harvey Lee Smith? I mean before he was arrested?"

Smoke wafted past a narrowing gaze. "How would I ever get to know a crazy man like that?"

Jo was an expert interviewer. She understood people and could find her way around any roadblock they put up. "I don't know. I'm asking. He's about fifteen years older than you, and he's lived in the area for over thirty years, same as you."

"Lots of people fit that description, Jolene. That don't mean I know them." Her mother shook her head. "You were always asking the oddest questions when you were a kid. Never satisfied. Always curious. Ellie took what I said at face value but not you."

Her mom had a talent for pushing Jo's buttons. She knew her better than anyone, which meant she knew her strengths and weaknesses. One of her weaknesses was any comparison to Ellie, her parents' favored child.

Tension coiled in Jo's gut as she struggled to voice fears she'd long held. "I'm not like Ellie at all. She's a perfect blend of you and Daddy. But not me. I'm the oddball."

Candace pursed her lips and chose to take another drag on her cigarette before grinding the stub into the ashes.

Jo summoned courage to say what she'd avoided all her life. "Lord knows I loved Daddy, but we didn't have much in common. Sometimes I caught him looking at me as if I was the strangest puzzle he'd ever seen."

"Your daddy was a good man."

"I know that. And I'd never speak ill of him. But Momma, he and I . . . we never felt like . . . blood kin."

Candace's face paled a fraction. "That's a terrible thing to say. Did that Smith man put that idea in your head?"

"It's been there for a long, long time. I was too afraid to voice it. Lately, I've been thinking more and more about the differences between Daddy and me."

"You realize what you are saying about me?"

"Momma, I'm not passing judgment. Lord knows I made my mistakes."

"Brody Winchester."

Jo's ire rose. Her mother had repeated this fact more than a dozen times during the years after her divorce. And as much as her temper begged to be unleashed, she kept her smile fixed. "Mom, was Cody Granger my biological father?"

Candace pursed her lips. "He was your daddy through and through, and don't you ever forget it. Now, if you don't have more to say, I have my receipts to finish. It's been a long day, and I'm tired."

A wall of ice settled between the two, and Jo knew from experience that no matter how much she begged, pleaded or wailed right now, Candace wasn't going to say a word.

Jo rose, kissed her mother on the forehead and left the salon.

It was after midnight when Brody lumbered into his apartment. It had taken hours to properly unearth the girl's body before it could be escorted to the medical examiner's office. Judging by her clothes, she'd worked on the streets, so the chances of a missing persons report or identifying her would be close to nil.

He tossed his keys on the kitchen bar and set his hat beside it. Drawing his gun, he ejected the live round from the chamber, pressed it back in the magazine and slid both into a kitchen drawer. He changed into old gym pants and a threadbare Texas baseball T-shirt.

As he peered in his refrigerator at the six-pack of beer and a half-eaten pizza still in the box, sadness settled in his bones. He grabbed a beer, sat on the couch and flipped on the television to ESPN.

He twisted the top off the bottle and tossed it in a trash can by the end table before taking a long swallow. He tipped his head back against the couch cushion.

This victim, according to the medical examiner's assistant, was fifteen or sixteen.

She'd been a damned kid.

He thought about the baby girl he and Jo had made and lost. Likely, she'd have been tall like her folks but would have had his olive skin and dark hair. He'd always hoped she'd be smart like her mother.

He'd been so pissed when Jo had told him she was pregnant. *There goes my life,* he'd thought.

So wrapped up in himself, he'd not thought about Jo and the impact a pregnancy would have on her life. She'd barely been scraping by when she was in college on scholarship. Her parents helped a little but had made it clear if she wanted college it would have to be on her dime.

He'd never asked her if she was scared or worried. He'd never done much, except marry her in a two minute justice of the peace ceremony. In his twenty-two-year-old mind, he'd been a damned hero because most wouldn't have owned up to a mistake. He had. Now at thirty-six, he realized she'd needed emotional support. She'd needed him to hold her and tell her it would be all right.

Brody pressed the cold beer to his throbbing temple. He'd grown up a hell of a lot and knew for a fact that if faced with the same decision now he'd have handled it much differently. But *what ifs* didn't mean shit and no matter how deep the regrets, he'd not done right by Jo.

Robbie didn't really study Jo's house every day. But he made a point to study the house at least once a week. He knew when water restrictions had forced her to quit watering and her lawn had died. He knew when she'd had the kitchen redone. He'd liked the shingle for the new roof. Often he wondered when she'd get around to cutting the pecan tree, which was eating into the foundation of her porch.

But in the last couple of months he paused to study her place more and more. He'd not been inside the house for a while, knowing too much lurking would catch someone's attention. That was the problem with neighborhoods. Someone was always watching. But so many temptations were building inside of him. And soon he'd not be able to resist a tiny peek.

Chapter Twelve

Wednesday, April 10, 9:00 a.m.

The autopsy of Jane Doe revealed what Brody had suspected. She'd been buried alive like Christa Bogart. Unlike Christa, she'd showed signs of living on the streets, likely working as a prostitute.

All the evidence supported the theory that Smith's apprentice had killed again. Brody had ordered a media blackout on the murder. No one was to talk to the press. No one. The only lines of communication Robbie and Smith had now were through the media, and Brody would be damned if they sent signals to each other.

He'd called Missing Persons as a matter of routine, not expecting to get a hit on this victim. To his surprise a woman named Keri Jones had filed a report on a girl named Hanna Metcalf, age fifteen.

Finding Keri Jones had proven difficult. She'd left no contact address, and the cell number she listed on the report had gone unanswered a couple of times. However, the fourth time he'd called, a gravelly voice said, "I'm listening."

"Keri Jones?"

After a moment's pause the woman said, "Who's asking?"

"Sergeant Brody Winchester of the Texas Rangers. I'm calling about the missing persons report you filed on Hanna Metcalf."

"Did you find her?" In the background he could hear traffic passing by.

"No. But I'm looking. Can we talk?"

"How do I know you're straight up with me?"

"My guess is you used your real name on the police report, and that's why you hesitated when I used it."

"I didn't think the cops would take the report seriously if they knew a hooker named Dusty Stardust had filed it."

Prostitutes went missing often. Some left the area to find more work or warmer climates, some overdosed and others ended up with a bad john that killed them. Missing Persons didn't invest a lot of energy in folks who lived on the street. "Can we meet?"

"I'm working."

"Where?"

"Sixth Street."

"I can be there in fifteen minutes."

She hesitated. "There's a coffee shop. We can meet there. Not good for business to have you around." She gave him the address.

"Sure."

Brody found the coffee shop. Outside stood a tall African American woman wearing a short, snakeskin skirt, a black tube top and a white, furry-cropped jacket. Thigh-high boots and a blond wig completed the look.

She spotted Brody in the telltale Ranger uniform and walked into the coffee shop. She took a table in the back, away from the front entrance. Brody sat opposite her in the booth.

"Appreciate you seeing me." This close, Brody could see the lines in her face and neck. Life on the streets aged a woman like Keri, but he guessed her real age to be midthirties.

She searched the shop for anyone that might be staring. A waitress glanced in their direction but Keri shook her head. "Are you really looking for Hanna?"

He reached inside his coat pocket and pulled

out a Polaroid of the girl in the morgue. "I have a picture I'd like you to look at."

Keri tapped a long fingernail on the tabletop and braced. "Okay."

Carefully, he laid it on the table. Keri dropped her gaze and looked at the girl's facial image taken while she lay on the medical examiner's table. Tense seconds passed as she stared, dry-eyed. Finally, she raised her head and her chin trembled slightly. "That's Hanna."

"You are sure?"

Keri turned it over. "That's her."

With trembling hands, she reached in her purse for a cigarette and lighter. In spite of a smoking ban, she lit the cigarette.

Brody tucked the overturned picture back in his pocket and gave Keri time to process. "Is it that unusual for a working girl to vanish for a couple of days?"

"For most, yes. But not Hanna. She always checked in with me each night. Good kid. I looked out for her."

"What can you tell me about her?"

"She was special. Didn't process like the rest of us. What she did on the streets didn't touch her. A blessing, really."

"How do you mean?"

"Mentally challenged, but also smart. Could remember all kinds of odd facts and figures. Ask her what the weather was like five years ago on any day, and she'd know. She was fifteen."

"Did she use?"

"No. Never touched the stuff. Wouldn't even take a cigarette from me. She wanted to make enough money so she could move out to California." Keri shook her head. "They all want to go to California. They think there's sunshine and glamorous jobs waiting. I tried to tell her that was bull, but she didn't want to hear. Kept saying, 'Keri, you should come with me. We can start over.' "

"When is the last time you saw her?"

"Two days ago. We shared a laugh. Then one of her regulars came up, and she climbed into his truck."

"What did the truck look like?"

"Red. Fairly beat-up."

"License plate?"

Two more puffs on the cigarette. "Didn't think about it. He was a regular."

"Any details you can give me about him?"

"Only what Hanna told me."

"Which was?"

"Clean. Nice as any john can be. Never tried to stiff her out of her pay."

"Any quirks?"

Keri lifted an amused brow. "Baby, all johns have quirks." The laughter in her gaze vanished. "He liked to call her Bluebonnet."

"Bluebonnet?"

"Yeah. It bothered her that he never called her by her name, but I told her as far as quirks went, not to worry."

Bluebonnet. Like the flower found on Christa's body. "Any details about the john?"

She took a drag and slowly exhaled smoke. "No. She never worried about him, so I never did."

"What about her pimp? Would he know about this john?"

She flicked the ashes on the floor and inhaled deeply. "Oh, he don't give a shit as long as Hanna pays him his cut each night."

"Did she tell you anything else about this guy?"

"Honey, why talk about an easy john when there are other ones that scared her?"

"Did she mention an accent, a tattoo, hair color . . . ?"

"Sorry, baby, no." She leaned forward. "You think he's the guy?"

"He's the last john you saw her with?"

"Yeah, but there could have been others. I had a busy afternoon."

"And you're sure he called her Bluebonnet?"

"Yeah. Real sure about that. I can ask around, if you think it would help. See if any of the other girls ran into him."

Brody pulled out a card and handed it to her. "That would be helpful. Anything you can come up with would be great."

212

"Why do you think he called her Bluebonnet? Did he have a thing for flowers?"

"Yeah, he liked flowers."

Her brow knotted. "This guy you're looking for . . . has he killed other women?"

He didn't understand the connection. Yet. "Yeah."

Tears welled in brown eyes. "She was a good kid. She didn't deserve to die." Her hands trembled as she stared at the lit edge of her cigarette. "You're not really here for Hanna. You're here for another case like this." When he didn't answer, a half smile quirked the edges of her mouth. "The Rangers don't usually ride to a hooker's rescue."

"No." Hanna's case wouldn't have earned top billing under normal circumstances. "I want to find Hanna's killer. Bad."

She squared her jaw. "At least you're honest."

"She keep a room around here?"

"She stayed in a motel in east Austin. Rented it by the week."

He recorded the name. "I'll pay the place a visit."

"Better hurry. The rent is due today, and if it isn't paid by six, the landlord will throw all her shit in the Dumpster."

"I'll go right now."

"You have my number. Can you call me when you find this guy? I want to know Hanna had justice."

"Sure."

The drive to Hanna's motel took less than ten minutes, and after showing a wiry, leather-skinned man at the front desk his identification, he found himself standing in Hanna's room.

"The rent's due today." The clerk hovered at the threshold, rattling the key in his hand.

"Don't worry about the rent right now."

"If I don't collect, I'm throwing her crap out."

Brody stepped toward the man, knowing he had seven or eight inches of height on him and sixty pounds. "I'm gonna have to ask you to leave this room be until I say otherwise."

He raised his chin. "If I ain't getting rent, I'm losing money."

The stale air in the hallway smelled of cigarettes and urine. "Do the best you can. I don't want anyone in this room until I give the clear."

"That ain't fair."

"Life isn't fair. Touch this room, and I'll be doing a room-to-room search of all your tenants and will arrest each and every one I can. That won't be doing your bottom line much good, will it?"

The man glared at Brody. "Let me know the second you're done with it."

"Sure."

Brody zeroed his attention on the room that had been Hanna's. A small, neatly made twin bed hugged the right wall. The coverlet was purple and the half-dozen pillows all kinds of pink. A threadbare, brown teddy bear with a torn left ear and missing eye nestled between the pillows. Across from the bed was a desk, which sported a hot plate and a coffee machine. Under it was a small refrigerator stocked with a bottle of water, three sodas, a jar of peanut butter and a half-eaten loaf of bread.

The curtains were tan and stained, likely standard with the room. On the windowsill was a crystal heart, a mug from Disneyland and a glass jar filled with jelly beans.

Brody pulled on rubber gloves and moved to the desk, opening the center drawer. Inside was a collection of teen magazines and a guidebook to Southern California with dozens of dog-eared pages. On the right of the small closet hung a collection of skimpy spandex, glittery and gauzy clothes and on the left hung jeans, T-shirts and a sweatshirt from a Houston high school.

He'd seen this story play out a thousand times. Kids getting sucked into a life like this because no one gave a shit about them. As a matter of habit, he reached under the drawer, and his fingers grazed a small book taped to the underside of the drawer. He jerked hard and removed a small red notebook. The edges were tattered and the pages curled but the handwriting inside was neat but full and childlike. He thumbed slowly through the pages. Hanna had given her johns code names and kept detailed records of her appointments. This book was full. A search of the room didn't uncover another book, but he guessed by the threadbare nature of the first, Hanna had carried the notebook with her when she worked. The current book would be with her now.

The last date entered in the book was a month ago, not so far in the past. There was a chance the john who called her Bluebonnet was in here.

"Who the hell is he, Hanna?"

Jo knocked off work at five. And as she passed the receptionist's desk Sammy raised a brow. "You are leaving at five? Are you sick?"

Jo laughed. "I've left at five before."

Sammy raised a dark brow. "Yeah, that was the day the building lost power and none of us could work because it was one hundred degrees inside." Sammy waggled her brows. "Hot date?"

That prompted a genuine laugh. "I must find a dress for a wedding."

Sammy cocked her head. "The wedding that's in three days?"

"The very one."

"This is cutting it close, even for you."

Jo set her briefcase down. "I didn't think it would be such an ordeal. I thought I'd find something but so far no winners."

"Head downtown to Zoe's on Congress. Her

inventory is really cute. And not so young and hip that it will send you running."

Jo straightened. "I'd hardly call myself old."

"Oh, hey, you are the coolest, Jo. Really. But let's face it, you're not cutting-edge fashion for clothes."

"Professional trumps fashion," Jo countered.

"Oh, the boss and clients love the school-teacher look. Dr. Anderson likes the fact that you're kinda stuffy. Gives you an air of authority. But at the wedding. Not so much. Sex it up a notch, Miss Marple."

Jo considered her white blouse and pencil skirt. "Miss Marple? That's going a bit far."

Sammy's gaze reflected honest enthusiasm. "Jo, kick it up a notch."

Kick it up a notch. She had no idea what that meant. "I'll see what I can do."

"Go to Zoe's. They'll take care of you."

Jo thought about the dress shop yesterday, running into Dayton and before him the tense saleslady. The thought of trying on dresses made the muscles in her back tighten.

In her car, she called Zoe's, discovered they were open until eight and opted to sneak in a quick workout at the gym before she braved the store. She'd not worked out since early Saturday morning, and her muscles were tight.

She clicked on the radio to NPR and remembered Sammy's comment about Miss Marple. She switched stations to the local pop channel, managed two songs before switching back to NPR. Jo doubted she was hip even when she was young.

When she reached the stoplight a pickup came up right behind hers, stopping just short of hitting her bumper. Frowning into the rearview mirror she nudged her car forward. The pickup followed.

"Get off my tail, pal." She glared into the rearview mirror, trying to get a look at the driver but found thick glasses and a hat made it impossible to recognize him.

The plates were Texas, but a splash of mud covered up half the numbers.

When the light turned green she drove toward the gym, knowing it would be packed at this time of day. She'd rounded the corner into the gym lot when her cell phone rang. She jumped, and quickly fished it out of her purse as she made the last turn.

"Hello," she said.

"I'm calling for Louis Williams. This is Mortgage Financial in Houston, and he's applied for a loan. I was hoping to get a reference."

She rolled her eyes, willing a thundering heart to slow. "Wrong number."

"You sure?" The man rattled off the number.

"The number is correct, but the contact is not. I don't know Louis Williams."

A moment's silence followed. "We'll take you off our call list."

"Great." She hung up and luckily found a close parking spot. Another peek in her mirror showed the truck veering off to a side street, the driver staring straight ahead as if he'd never seen her.

A breath shuddered from her lungs. She was being paranoid. A near bumper-tap, a wrong number and chance encounter with Dayton yesterday had rattled her. This wasn't like her. She was rock solid. Practical. So why suddenly was she so unsettled, as if the ground had shifted under her feet?

With Hanna's name in hand, Brody had been able to pull an arrest record and fingerprints. He'd delivered both to the medical examiner who had made a positive identification. Tracking next of kin had taken more time, and it was past eight by the time Brody got Hanna's uncle on the phone. From the uncle, Brody had learned that Hanna had run away six months ago. "Always figured she'd get herself killed sooner or later. She wasn't so smart. Didn't know when she was in over her head."

Brody sat back at his desk and stared at the notebook he'd retrieved from Hanna's apartment. A forensic team had gone over the place, but there'd been no other telling discoveries. The book was his one clue to who might have killed her.

Thumbing through the pages, he studied the detailed lists she'd kept of her johns. Each had a name, though he doubted many were real. She'd listed the date they'd hooked up and the money collected. The small notebook was full of single-spaced entries.

Santos knocked on Brody's office door. "I hear you identified the second victim."

Brody's chair creaked as he leaned back in his chair and gave Santos a rundown. "When I searched her place earlier I found a notebook that the kid kept. She listed her johns but not all the names strike me as real. She gave many nick-names."

"Her pimp would know more about who her customers were," Santos said. "And he shouldn't be too hard to find."

"Shouldn't be. I've got his name."

"Let's pay him a visit."

Finding Hanna's pimp turned out to be easier than expected. Keri had said he hung out at a coffee shop on Sixth Street. During the day he spent his time online pimping out his girls for dates and in the evening he put them on the street.

Daddy, as Keri had called him, sat in the back corner of the coffee shop. He had a large mug to the right of what looked like a brand-new computer. Midsized but muscular, Daddy wasn't more than thirty but his mocha skin was scarred and pitted. As Keri had described, he wore a large, gold cross around his neck and the favored white jumpsuit.

When the Rangers entered the café the conversation stopped and Daddy looked up. He sat straighter in his chair, leaning an arm back against his booth while keeping the other under the table.

Brody's hand slid to his gun as he approached the table. "Do me a big favor and put your other hand on the table."

Daddy grinned and draped his other hand over the back of the booth. "Don't want no trouble with the Rangers."

"What's your real name, Daddy?"

He tipped back his baseball cap. "Juan Johnson. Why the Rangers calling on me? I ain't done nothing wrong."

Johnson had likely broken more laws than Brody could count, but he wasn't after Johnson tonight. "When is the last time you saw Hanna Metcalf?"

Johnson's easy grin hardened. "She's gone AWOL. Ain't seen her in two days. You know where she is?"

"I know where she is."

"Yeah?" Annoyance flashed in his dark eyes. "What's she saying about me?" So Keri hadn't told Daddy about Hanna.

Brody propped his boot on the edge of the

booth and leaned in as Santos stood behind him. "What do you think she's saying about you?"

"The girl ain't right in the head. A little slow and can run her mouth long after no one wants to hear her yammer." He shook his head. "Dusty said the girl was in trouble, but I knew she was lying. Lazy bitch is out there lying low and stirring up trouble for Daddy."

Brody ignored the pimp's tirade. "What does she talk about?"

"You seen her, so you should know."

"I want to hear what you have to say."

"She is always giving me lip and attitude. And Daddy don't appreciate lip."

Brody pulled out the tattered notebook and thumbed through it. "She gave this to me. Says it's a list of her johns."

Daddy's hands dropped to the table on either side of his computer. "What the fuck did you say?"

"She's been keeping a list. Any reason why she'd do that?"

He shrugged, pretending as if he didn't care. "I don't know what makes a crazy bitch do what she does."

"Daddy, I'm not after you right now. I'm after a killer, and I think Hanna might be able to help me."

Daddy didn't hide his shock. "What do you mean 'a killer'? I don't know nothing about a killer."

"Hanna did."

"Did?"

"She's dead."

Daddy sat back, shaking his head. "Shit." He held up a bejeweled index finger. "I don't know nothing."

Brody grinned. "I bet you know the number of breaths that girl took in a day. I bet you know when she sneezed and when she took a leak."

Daddy was silent for a moment. "What do you want from me?"

"Always the dealmaker, Juan. I like that."

"What do you want?"

"I want you to take a look at this book, and I want you to tell me if you recognize any of the names."

"How the hell would I know the names that Hanna kept?"

Brody leaned closer, keeping his voice low and even. "I can shut you down in two seconds, Juan. You won't see daylight for years, and your girls will scatter like honey bees."

Daddy's face paled a fraction. "I don't know you, Ranger."

Brody smiled. "I'm new in town."

"You ain't got nothing on me."

Brody moved so quickly that Daddy didn't have time to react. He grabbed the pimp, jerked him out of the booth and twisted his arm behind his back. Before Daddy could squeal, Brody had clamped cuffs on his slim wrists.

Santos reached for his phone and called Austin police. "They're sending a car for Daddy."

Daddy grimaced and tried to get free but the more he struggled, the harder Brody twisted. "Hey, you don't have to be so rough."

Brody hauled the pimp outside. When Daddy tried to jerk free, Brody shoved him against the café wall, pushing hard enough so the pimp's face scraped the brick exterior. "Try it again, Daddy. Please."

Daddy struggled to lift his raw, scraped face from the brick but Brody held it in place. "I don't want trouble, Ranger."

"That's too bad."

Daddy stilled and shoved out a breath. "Let me have a look at those names. I bet I could help you."

"Not sure if you're worth the trouble anymore. When I round up your girls and tell them you won't be out of jail for years, they'll tell me."

"You can't throw me away in jail. This is America."

Brody laughed.

"Let me look at the names!"

Brody gave him another shove into the bricks before whirling him around as an Austin police cruiser, lights flashing, arrived. "Better talk fast, Daddy."

Daddy looked at the open book that Brody held in front of his face. When Daddy shook his head, Brody turned the page. Again nothing.

The Austin uniforms approached Brody. "Looks like Daddy is causing you some trouble."

"Not as helpful as he could be. Mind doing me a favor and dropping him in a cell? I'll come looking for him sooner or later."

"I said I'd help!" Daddy shouted. "You've only shown me a couple of pages. Shit. Give me a chance."

Brody thought about fifteen-year-old Hanna working the streets for this monster. He wondered how many second chances he'd given her. He flipped another page. "Look real hard, Daddy, because I'm running out of patience."

The pimp scanned the page again. "I know one of the names."

"Which one?"

"Earl. He was a regular."

"How often did he come by?"

"Least once a week. Men like Hanna. Young, curvy. She has a lot of regulars."

Anger roiled in Brody. "I'm looking for a regular."

"I know most of them. I don't need a notebook for that."

"Any ever call her by a nickname?"

"Like what?"

"You tell me."

"Blondie. Alice in Wonderland. One liked her because she reminded him of his granddaughter."

Brody's jaw tightened and he wanted nothing more than to pummel the shit out of this guy. Instead, he said in a calm voice, "Who else?"

"One guy had an interest in flowers."

Brody's racing pulse stilled. "What kind of flowers?"

"Shit, I don't know. Roses are red, violets are blue, motherfucker."

"What did he call Hanna?"

"I don't know."

"What did he look like?"

"Medium-sized. Dark hair. Wore thick glasses. Looked like an accountant."

"Did he have a name?"

"I don't take roll call, motherfucker. He picked her up in a pickup and did his business."

"When was the last time he picked up Hanna?"

"Few days."

"Where did he pick her up?"

"Near her corner. Right outside."

Brody had already sent officers to canvass the shops for security cameras that might have captured Hanna and her last john. He grabbed Daddy by the shoulders and handed him to the Austin cops. "He's all yours."

"What are you doing?" Daddy shouted. "I told you what I know."

"I got a notebook full of Hanna's solicitation appointments. And you just admitted that you recognized the names of two clients you sent her way. Something tells me that's not legal in Texas."

"Bullshit, I did. I was helping you!"

"Like you helped that fifteen-year-old on the streets."

"Hey, man, she came to me. She was hungry and needed to work, and I put her to work. She got paid."

Cents on the dollar, he'd bet. "Take him away."

Daddy dug in his feet and craned his neck toward Brody as the officers led him to the car. "Hey, man, you need me. I can help you find this guy."

"Really, how's that?"

"I can ask around. See if the dude gave other girls flower names."

The pimp was right. The killer could have lined up other girls. And Daddy might be able to figure out who'd vanished and who they were visiting. "Sure. You can help, Daddy." He eyed the officers. "If you don't get information from him in twenty-four hours, he goes to jail." Brody clamped his hand on Daddy's shoulder and squeezed.

Chapter Thirteen

Saturday, April 13, 9:00 a.m.

Brody rubbed his eyes and reached for his coffee cup. One sip of the cold sludge had him muttering an oath as he set the cup aside and leaned back in his chair. He'd been looking for days at surveillance footage of the area where Hanna worked. He'd cross-checked the images with her journal entries, which detailed four hundred entries over the month of March. Four hundred entries. Shit. A fifteen-year-old kid. Daddy remained free, and he'd asked around and discovered that the red pickup had been sighted many times over the last few weeks. But no one had specifics. As Brody stared at Hanna's entries he vowed Daddy would go down soon.

Of Hanna's four hundred entries, a good thirty percent were repeats. Hanna also used first and sometimes last names for each entry and made notes in the margin. *$$. Remind him of granddaughter. Bad breath. Small dick. Hates talking.* And the most important, *Robbie: Calls me Bluebonnet.*

When he saw the name Robbie listed, his adrenaline snapped. Immediately, he keyed in on those entries. Robbie had visited Hanna ten times during the month. Hanna also noted, *Calls me Bluebonnet.*

Taking the surveillance footage from a liquor store located across from Hanna's corner and a paycheck cashier situated on a diagonal to the site, he watched and searched for guys that showed up on the dates Hanna had cited.

Hanna always stood on the same street corner under a light. For the most part, she arrived by five and often didn't leave her corner for the day until five in the morning. On cold nights she'd stand for an hour waiting and calling out to passersby. On milder nights she'd get in and out of a steady stream of cars. The lighting and angle made it hard to see the johns' faces, so he paid closer attention to the vehicles. On the nights Robbie visited Hanna, a red pickup truck cruised slowly by the corner. The paint was faded, the back tail bumper bent and pockets of rust had eaten into the edges of the truck. The front and back plates both splattered with mud were illegible, but he could see a couple of shovels and rope in the pickup's bed.

Each time he pulled up, his face remained turned as if he knew the cameras were rolling. It was a precaution he'd learned from Smith who'd done the same when he'd stalked his victims. Smith hadn't gotten sloppy with surveillance cameras until the end and Brody had been there to nail him.

In the images, Hanna always smiled as she approached Robbie's passenger door and leaned in to speak to him. They'd talk for several seconds before she settled into the front cab. Robbie never returned Hanna to the same corner because she'd reemerge in the camera an hour or so after the initial pickup. Many times Dusty stepped on screen and the two women chatted. Both kept a close eye on Daddy's van always parked across the street. Daddy was keeping an eye on his investments.

In all the times Robbie showed up in the red pickup truck, the plates were muddied and his face turned. But Brody at least had a link to Robbie.

Brody stared at the frozen screen featuring Hanna leaning into Robbie's truck.

"I'm going to catch you, you son of a bitch."

An alarm on his cell phone had him straightening and glancing at the message he'd sent himself before work.

"Wedding," the display read.

Brody shut the alarm off and rose, stretching the kinks from his back and shoulders. He'd learned long ago that if he had to be somewhere and he was on a case, he had to set the alarm on his phone as a reminder. Too many times he'd been working and lost all track of time. He'd missed or been late to too many family gatherings or dates. His last girlfriend had grown fed up with his misses and absences. *"You don't need a girl-friend. Work is all the mistress you'll ever need."*

He'd regretted the breakup, but it had not derailed him from work or the case. But since then he'd made a point to be where he said he should be or at least call if he couldn't.

He rolled down his cuffs and buttoned them before grabbing a red tie he'd brought in this morning. Tying a quick knot, he slid on the blue blazer hanging on the back of his door and reached for his Stetson.

He'd told Jim he'd be at his wedding and he meant it.

The weather outside was sunny and bright, a welcome change from winter's cold temperatures. This was going to be one of those rare perfect days between winter's blistering cold temperatures and summer's scorching heat. He'd once heard that rain was an omen of a happy marriage but he'd never bought into it. It had rained the day he and Jo had married and that union had never stood a chance.

Jo spent far too long on her hair and makeup. She wanted to look good, but no matter how much she combed, curled or twisted her hair, it didn't look right. By the fourth hairstyle she knew her primping had crossed over into obsession. Exasperated, she let her hair fall, the curled edges brushing the shoulders of the watered silk dress she'd found Wednesday at the last-minute, panicked trip to Zoe's.

The shop owner had been expecting her, confessing that Sammy had called and told her to expect a crazed woman in need of a dress. Zoe had been glad to see her and had dismissed Jo's apologies for arriving near closing. An hour later, the patient woman, who'd borne all Jo's indecision and worry with grace, had helped her settle on the green silk. The dress hugged her waist and the hem hit her mid-calf. Feeling at home in the dress and relieved to have found it, she'd barely balked at the five-hundred-dollar price tag.

She blew a stray strand of hair out of her eyes and wondered again if she should let it hang or tuck it back into the chignon. One call and her mother would have come over and made it perfect in seconds. But the visit could also stir the tension still simmering between them, and Jo did not want to taint this day.

Thinking about her mother and their last conversation, Jo stared in the mirror, studying her features. This time she didn't pay attention to her makeup or the sweep of her hair. This time she searched for features that matched Cody Granger's.

Her red hair had been a surprise to all, but her mother had always reminded anyone that commented that Jo's red hair came from a great-grandmother who'd had hair as red as the rising sun. Jo knew little else about this great-grandmother and often wondered if she'd ever existed. Her mother claimed Jo's green eyes and the wide curve of her mouth as her own, but her nose and all her other features were only Jo's. She didn't share one physical trait with Cody Granger.

Sighing, Jo turned from the mirror, leaving her hair loose as she grabbed her purse. Today was not a day to wallow or whine.

The drive on I-35 toward Lara and Jim's house took her thirty minutes. She'd volunteered to arrive at the crack of dawn, but Lara had told her not to worry. "The day is not about stressing," Lara had said. "Arrive with the rest of the guests."

However, as a bridesmaid, unwritten obligations compelled her to arrive early. Jo knew the best-laid plans always could be tripped up by the smallest detail. And when she pulled up the long, dirt driveway that led to Lara's adobe-style home, her worst-case-scenario brain was relieved to see the catering truck had arrived, the white tent, tables and chairs had been set up and the band was tuning up. The place was abuzz with the controlled chaos that came before a wedding. Jim stood next to a large smoker grill where a caterer basted a huge pig. Beside Jim sat Lara's dog, Lincoln, a large wolflike shepherd whom she'd heard was now devoted to Jim.

Jo parked off to the right at the edge of a field and walked into the house where she found Lara standing in the living room, her hair in curlers, dressed in a bathrobe. Around her sat dozens of unopened presents.

"Lara," Jo said.

Lara glanced up from a photo image and smiled at Jo. "Hey, girl. Boy, do you look superfine."

A warm blush rose up Jo's cheeks. "Thanks."

"Looks like you solved the dress dilemma."

"Will it work?" Sudden indecision nipped at her. "I know I should have bought it sooner and shown it to you, but life has been kinda crazy."

An appraising smile warmed Lara's face. "It's perfect. Today everyone wears what works for them."

Jo arched a brow. "Which means Cassidy is wearing black."

Lara laughed. "She has a flare for the dramatic that I do not."

Jo laughed. "Never a dull moment with Cassidy. She's as dramatic as I am understated."

"That's why I love you both so much. Now, come help me decide which picture I should frame and display at the reception."

Jo set her purse aside, shaking her head. "Lara, you're getting married in an hour, and you are framing a picture."

"Jim sent me in here and told me to do something productive. He doesn't like a vegetarian offering her two cents while he does his caveman grilling."

Jo laughed. "I'd think you'd be fussing over your hair or makeup."

"Cassidy will be here soon and she can do that." Lara was an artist who had built a reputation for herself as a wet plate photographer. She created her images using a 150-year-old camera that looked reminiscent of a time long past. Jo owned several of Lara's pieces and displayed them in her home.

Jo looked at the image. It featured Lara and Jim sitting side by side in chairs on the front porch. The black-and-white coupled with the rich grain told Jo she'd used the bellows camera. "Did you take this?"

"I set it all up and asked Cassidy to remove the lens cap and count to thirty before she replaced it. I hopped up and quickly processed the glass plate."

"How many times was Jim willing to sit for his picture?"

She chuckled as she held the print up to the light and studied it. "He told me I had him for three images and he was done. The one I liked best was the second shot."

If Jo had looked at only Jim, she would have sworn the image had been taken a hundred years ago. Like Brody he looked as if he'd been plucked out of the old west wearing his white Stetson, lariat tie, jeans and scuffed boots. Brody and Jim's similar attire coupled with their square jaws and stiff gazes, made both throwbacks.

What anchored this picture in the present was Lara who wore jeans, a white button-down shirt and no shoes. Her long, blond hair highlighted the high slash of her cheekbones and the vivid paleness of her blue eyes.

The look of love in Lara's eyes struck a chord deep in Jo. That kind of passion, which had eluded her so far, was rare indeed. "This is really good, Lara. Really a work of art."

Lara inspected the image. "I know it's not the traditional wedding portrait, but I'm not so traditional. My main worry now is that I should have edged in this corner a little more. Maybe if I slip back into the darkroom."

Jo laughed. "The picture is perfect. Stop second-guessing. By the way, have you looked at a clock lately? You have fifty-nine minutes before the wedding."

Lara frowned as she stared at the photograph's corner. "I can always fuss with it later."

"Why don't you put it in that frame, finish the job and stop worrying?"

Lara took one last look at the portrait and laid it facedown in the glass. "I can get a little crazy when it comes to my pictures."

"Which is what makes you such a successful artist. Don't worry so much today. Enjoy."

Lara laid the mat over the picture. "I think I'm nervous."

"What are you nervous about?"

Lara laughed. "That sounds very shrinklike."

Jo shrugged. "Hazard of the trade." She cleared her throat. "What are you nervous about, Lara?"

Lara chuckled as she clamped down the frame fasteners. "Commitment. I can be a Ranger's lover. But to take one on for life . . ."

"You and Jim have done pretty well."

"Oh yeah, we're great. But I worry that I might not be as cool about the dangers of his work once I hang 'wife' around my neck."

Wife. Some said marriage was just a piece of paper and that it didn't change anything, but it changed everything.

Lara continued. "People say marriage is no big deal but it is to me. My mom married four times and each new husband was worse than the last. I swore I'd never marry but now that I am I want it to last forever."

"Marriage is work."

She frowned. "Yeah, but what exactly does that mean?"

Car doors closing had Jo glancing out the window in time to see Brody get out of his Bronco. He moved with steady, determined strides to Jim and shook his hand. "Sometimes I think it means staying and accepting the other person when all you want to do is run. Giving the storm time to pass, knowing smooth waters are ahead."

"That sounds a little bit like experience talking."

Jo turned from the window and found Lara staring at her. "Not many people know this, but I was married once."

"Really?"

She fiddled with the strand of pearls around her neck. "We shouldn't have ever married. We knew we wouldn't last."

Lara didn't prompt Jo for more information but waited silently.

"I got pregnant when I was eighteen. He married me for the baby's sake. But I lost the baby. And when the baby went away, the reason to stay married went with her."

Lara moved from the picture and took Jo's hands in hers. "I'm sorry for your loss."

Jo swallowed unshed tears. Fourteen years of ignoring the marriage and pregnancy had caught up to her in one crashing thud. "Thanks. And I'm sorry. I didn't mean this to turn into a session about me."

Lara hugged Jo with a warmth that somehow eased the lingering loneliness that had stalked her since she'd woken up this morning. "I think that is the first time you've opened up to me."

Jo had maintained such a tight rein over her emotions since she'd lost the baby that she'd not realized her need for control was so isolating.

She pulled away and smiled. "You need to get ready for the wedding."

Lara touched a curler. "Cassidy said she'd be here any minute."

"I can do your hair. You may not know it from my spartan hairstyles, but I grew up in a beauty salon."

"Did you?"

"I could roll a perm when I was eleven, and Mom had me doing her highlights by the time I was fifteen. I can promise you, brushing out curls is a piece of cake."

Lara grinned. "Have at it, sister."

Jo regarded Lara's jeans. "Are you wearing a white dress for the ceremony?"

"No. No white dresses for me. I'm wearing a sundress. It's a light purple."

Jo raised a brow. "The throwback carnivore marries the artsy vegetarian."

Lara and Jo both were laughing when Cassidy burst through the front door. Her dark hair was swept up on her head, and she wore a black dress with a large silver concho belt and red cowboy boots. "Let's get this party started!"

Lara laughed. "My life is gonna be interesting."

Brody's tie coiled around his neck extra tight as he took his seat on a white folding chair under the large tent. He and two dozen other Rangers and their wives sat behind Jim's mother and grandfather. A bluegrass band played standard tunes as a cool breeze blew over the tall grass and into the tent.

Jim stood at the front with his younger brother at his side. Both wore dark blue suits that highlighted the olive complexion they'd inherited from their mother and the broad shoulders from their grandfather. Lincoln sat peacefully beside Jim, his collar decorated with small, rather unmanly flowers, which Jim had announced were coming off right after the ceremony.

When a set of guitars started to play the wedding march, everyone rose and faced the dirt path that led back toward the house. The first to appear was Jo. When Brody spotted her, unexpected tension tightened his gut. He'd always found her business suits a little erotic but today's sweep of her hair over her pale shoulders and the green halter dress had him hardening like a teenager.

Her gaze fixed on the minister, she grinned broadly, moving down the aisle. As she moved past, she didn't spare a glance at him, but his gaze locked on her. He caught the whiff of a perfume she'd not worn before. Spicy. And sensual.

He straightened his shoulders and clasped his hands in front of him as she passed. He'd never been one for looking back or wishing away what was, but right now he'd have paid dearly for a clean slate with Jo Granger.

Next on deck was the brunet with the red cowboy boots. Cassidy. She was one hell of a looker in her own right. Nothing like Jo. Not his type. But stunning.

And then Lara emerged. She wore a purple peasant-style sundress that brushed the ground and her sandaled feet. Her long hair hung loose around her shoulders and someone had woven small flowers into several strands. Woodstock would have greeted Jim's artist bride with open arms.

Lara's gaze locked on Jim's, and she moved toward him with a pace that purists might consider too fast. She looked eager and ready to jump into this marriage. Jim looked equally as happy, and the first twist of jealousy Brody had had in years snapped. Back in the day, he'd coveted a new bike, a new car, better bats, and the number one pitcher job, but now all that was downright meaningless. What he coveted was what Jim and Lara shared.

The reception was the kind Brody liked: an old-fashioned Texas barbecue. The bride and groom didn't have the overstressed expressions he'd seen at too many weddings, and the guests looked comfortable. The men had taken off their sport jackets, and the women mostly wore sandals, not those punishing high heels that sent them searching for Band-Aids halfway through a party.

Brody stood with several Rangers talking about a recent trip to the shooting range. Scores were compared. Jokes made. Challenges issued. The talk rumbled around him as he scanned the crowd for Jo. He found her by the food table, a soda in her hand as she talked to Santos. When she smiled at him her eyes lit up and her posture was relaxed, not stiff and defensive. Santos leaned forward and said something close to her ear, and she tossed back her head and laughed out loud. It struck him that he'd never heard her laugh. He suspected now that the laughter had always been there, but he'd been too bullheaded and self-pitying to coax it.

He took a long pull on his beer and imagined landing a punch on Santos's grinning jaw as the other Ranger held out his hand to Jo and the two went to the dance floor in front of the bluegrass band.

Santos led Jo through a two-step, which she had no talent for. The more she protested and laughed at her own missteps, the more endearing she became to Santos and him. After one sloppy spin, she lost her footing, only to have Santos steady her and pull her close. Her hand went to his chest as her other gripped his forearm.

Brody finished off his beer.

"You don't look like the happiest padre I've ever seen." Jim, who'd taken off his jacket and loosened his tie, stared squarely at Brody. "Looks like you could gnaw on broken glass."

Brody tore his gaze from Jo and shrugged. "Naw."

Jim looked past Brody to Jo. "I didn't realize you had a hard-on for the good doctor."

His temper rumbled. "I don't have a hard-on for Dr. Granger."

Jim laughed. "I'm trained to spot liars."

Brody, like any good cop, could lie as well as any thief, but his tense posture and biting grip on his beer bottle were giving him away. He opted to change the subject. "Lara looks nice."

Jim's gaze locked on his bride who was snapping pictures of her guests. "She's pretty damn perfect."

"You two lovebirds taking a honeymoon?"

"Not now. She's teaching, and I'm in the middle of a couple of cases. We're taking a road trip to Galveston in about six weeks."

"Should be a good trip."

Jim drew his gaze away from his wife. "Looking forward to it."

He pondered his empty beer and wished for a second. "Hell of a party."

"Fussy is not our style."

"Amen."

The band stopped playing and the couples on the dance floor stopped and clapped. The bandleader announced a fifteen-minute break. Good. No more dancing.

"So you gonna talk to her?" Jim said. "Or are you gonna stand there like a yellow-belly coward?"

Brody met Jim's amused gaze. "Is this middle school, pal?"

Jim held up his hands in mock surrender. "I know when a guy is smitten. And padre, you've been bitten by the bug."

Brody rubbed the back of his neck with his hands. "I'm about the last guy that Jo Granger would date."

"Why's that? She strikes me as the type to stand up to your type."

"And my type is?"

"Let's face it. Like any good cop you can be an ass when pushed. I'll bet you hate hearing no and you think everything should stop when you speak."

Brody didn't deny it. The Jo from college days had been tentative and worried about offending anyone. But somewhere along the way she'd grown up into a sharp gal. "More the type to settle with a doctor or a lawyer."

"I don't think so."

"Why'd you say that?"

"Just guessing."

"You might be right. Lots of Rangers have circled and sniffed around her, but she keeps them all at arm's distance."

Sniffing around. Shit. "Santos looks like he's doing his share of sniffing."

"Ah, I wouldn't worry about that. He's a pal to her."

Brody's laugh was dark and mirthless. "Don't seem too pal-like to me."

"She helped him with his sister, Maria, when their mom died. He's more like a brother to her."

"He isn't having brotherly thoughts."

"He can have all the thoughts he wants. According to what she told Lara she sees him as a friend."

Good.

Shit. He shouldn't care one way or the other.

He didn't have the right to stand here moping and wishing away a relationship that would make her happy. He'd lost all those claims a long time ago.

"What is it between you two?" Jim pushed.

Brody's fingernail dug into the label on his bottle. He considered dodging the question but refused to shy away from the plain facts. "Would you believe Jo and I used to be married?"

Jim stared at him openmouthed.

Brody had never shared that bit of information. Never made sense to talk about his past. But the present and the past were getting tangled up and suddenly it mattered. "Son, you're going to catch a fly with that trap."

Jim shook his head. "I've known Jo for two years. Never a word about a marriage. Not that she'd share much anyway. That's not her style."

"It was in college. She was a freshman and I was a senior. We had a lot of emotion and not much common sense. We met in the fall and were divorced by spring."

"Damn." Jim shook his head. "Just too young, I suppose."

Brody shook his head. "As you said, I can be an ass."

"Young men aren't the brightest."

"I sure was not."

Jim stared at Jo as if seeing her with fresh eyes. "No signs of tension between you two at the crime scene."

"She's a class act. A lady to the end. Not in her to be anything but professional."

"Second chances aren't impossible. You sure look like you wouldn't mind one."

Brody watched Jo move to the buffet table and study the selection of foods as if making a life-altering decision. That was Jo. Methodical. Smart. Careful. "I burned that bridge a long time ago."

"Rebuild it."

Brody muttered an oath and something about needing another beer.

Jo had begged off another dance from Santos, crying hunger and fatigue. She stood with her plate of freshly cut cake, watching Jim and Lara dance. She was glad for them. They'd struggled but had found a way to make it work.

She bit into the cake, marveling at how good it tasted.

"Cake good?" Brody said as he came up beside her.

She presented her best professional smile. "If I had to confess a fault it would be that I love cake."

Brody studied her. "I figured you as the perfect healthy eater. Lean protein, vegetables."

"I am. Unless I'm offered vanilla cake with a vanilla buttercream. And then I am helpless."

"I never knew that about you."

The offhand comment caught her by surprise. "There's a lot we don't know about each other." She took a bite. "I haven't heard anything on the case in the last couple of days. What's going on?"

"I been meaning to get up with you on that but been running full tilt. This might not be the place to get into it."

She dropped her half-eaten cake in a trash barrel. "Now is as good a time as any. I called the prison. Smith is in a coma."

He raised a coffee cup to his lips, halted and lowered his voice. "We had a second victim."

The laughter and the music around her drifted away. "When?"

"Several days ago. Found at a construction site. Handcuffed and buried."

"Who?"

"A prostitute. We think the killer was one of her clients."

"There was no mention in the media."

"We're keeping a tight lid on the story. The

newspaper is how Smith and Robbie communicated the last time."

"Why didn't you tell me?"

Brody's gaze held no hint of apology. "The order was that no one know."

Jo was angry with Brody for not telling her. "I thought I was a part of this investigation."

Brody shook his head. "This is my case, Jo."

As much as she wanted to argue, she thought about the suffering this latest victim must have endured. Any grievance over how Brody handled this case felt trivial in the face of such pain. And still . . .

After a heavy moment of silence, Brody said, "Lara and Jim look happy."

She wouldn't let this tragedy or her wounded ego spoil a rare and wondrous day like today. "Yes."

He cradled the coffee cup in his hand. "A far cry from our wedding day."

She stiffened and glared up at him as if he'd confessed a sin. She wasn't sure if the subject change was meant to distract her from terrible news or stoke her temper.

Brody arched a brow. "You look shocked. Think I forgot that day?"

"No. I didn't think you forgot. But it's ancient history." She grabbed a second piece of cake.

He stared toward Jim and Lara dancing a slow dance. "Not so long ago."

"Fourteen years. A lifetime."

Brody sipped his coffee. "It wasn't the best time for us. For me."

Anger and sadness that had been so neatly tucked away rose up. "No."

He was silent for a moment. "I owe you an apology, Jo. That last time all those years ago . . . I was immature. Out of control."

"You were a dick," she said. Normally she censored her thoughts better, but he'd caught her by surprise.

"That about sums it up. I was a dick. Said things that I never meant."

A sigh shuddered from her. "If you never meant it, why say it?"

"When I got the call you were in the hospital, I'd been out with my teammates drinking. We were celebrating my joining the Marines—my solution to our marriage and baby. When the nurse told me you'd miscarried, I was mad. Sad."

Bitterness pulled at her. "You looked furious from what I remember."

Apologies didn't come easy for him. "I was ashamed. I was a poor excuse for a man."

She faced him, her anger rising. "You accused me of not caring about the baby."

"You were cool and contained, and your mother had just reamed me out in the lobby. I came in swinging. When I saw how pale and fragile you were, I got madder at myself. I dumped that anger on your head."

Jo shook her head.

"I told my old man about what happened, and he threatened to put his foot up my ass."

She'd dreamed about this apology for years, and he'd dropped it right in her lap. Over the years she'd imagined herself delivering the perfect line or having a witty response. She made her living using words, and right now she couldn't find any to string together.

She knew enough about men, Rangers especially, that they were a proud lot. It had cost him to apologize and there had to be something in that. "Okay."

He raised a brow. "That's all?"

"For now, yes."

"Sure you don't want to take a swing? Call me another name?"

"I'll take a rain check, just in case."

The muscle in his jaw tightened and released. "That's fair. Be nice if we could find our way to being friends."

"I don't know."

The sharpness of his gaze mirrored the look he'd had at the crime scene. Laser sharp.

She shook her head. "Don't turn me into one of your puzzles, Brody."

"What do you mean?"

"You are trying to figure me out like you try to figure out a killer when you're at a crime scene. I saw that look the other day."

His expression neutral, he didn't respond.

Suddenly, the words came to her. "You were curious about me when we first met all those years ago because I was different than the average gal hanging around the baseball field house. Now I suspect you are curious how the fourteen years have changed me."

"Nothing wrong with curiosity."

She laughed. "No. It's what makes you a great Ranger."

He cocked his head. "But . . ."

"Once you have your answers you lose interest altogether. You lost interest in me long before I miscarried. And I suspect once you figure me out this go-around, you'll lose interest in our friendship."

His frown deepened. "I'm not the same guy I was in college."

"I can see you've grown up. You're not the boy who craves tons of recognition and false compliments. I do see that. But we are who we are. You solve puzzles. That makes you a great Ranger. But I suspect it makes you a lousy friend/lover/husband." A weak smile tugged at the edges of her lips. "Let's be grateful for the civility we've managed and not worry about developing anything closer."

The penitentiary nurse stared at Smith's ashen face. She'd dealt with prisoners for more than twenty years. For the most part, she could handle herself fine and when she couldn't she called a guard. But Smith was different than the other inmates. He'd been charming. Always complimented her. At first she kept her guard up and her cool reserve in place. But he kept on being nice. And after a time, she found herself looking forward to his visits. She'd been warned about revealing any personal information to prisoners. Knew they could use it against her. And she had been careful around Smith. What she'd never counted on was his keen ability to observe.

When he'd first seen her three years ago, she'd been nine months pregnant with her son. She'd seen him one time before she'd gone on maternity leave. When she'd returned, he'd congratulated her on the birth of her child. She thanked him but had made no other mention. But he'd seen the blue ribbon peeking out from a present she'd unwrapped from a coworker. He'd noticed when she'd stopped wearing her wedding band after her divorce. Noticed that she'd lost weight when she'd reentered the dating world.

He collected all those bits of information and pieced them together until he knew more about her than she'd ever dared imagined.

Last month, when she'd been giving him his injection, he'd told her he needed a favor done. She'd told him she didn't do favors for prisoners. He'd not gotten angry or flustered, but he'd smiled and asked about her son, Ethan. Hearing him speak her boy's name had rattled her.

"I need a favor," he'd said.

"I don't do favors," she'd repeated.

"You do. I saw when you took that bottle of morphine."

"I didn't."

"I saw."

How closely had he been watching her? She'd only taken a few little vials. She needed a little cash to tide her over to payday. "I never did."

"Who do you think the warden will believe? Five prisoners will back me up."

"Leave me alone."

"I know you're strapped for cash. Must be hard raising Ethan alone and his father not paying a dime for child support."

Her frown confirmed his statement.

He smiled and laid his head back against the infirmary cot's pillow. "I see and hear so much. I don't sleep as much as people think these days."

"I won't help you."

"When I ask you will." And then he'd told her what he wanted.

Now, her hands trembled as they did each time she was near him. She prayed daily that the cancer would kill him, but he had a death grip on life.

He sat back in his wheelchair, his eyes closed. "It's time for that favor, Debra."

She shook her head. "I won't help you."

"We've discussed this before. What I'm asking is not that difficult."

"I won't."

"Do this one favor for me, and I will leave you alone, Debra." His pale face looked ghoulish when he opened his eyes and grinned.

She stiffened, terrified that one of the other nurses had heard. But as always he was careful.

"It's a simple request."

"I've already covered for you with the warden —said you were too ill to talk when he asked."

"And I appreciate that. But that's not the favor and you know it."

"I could go to jail if I do this."

"If you don't help, I'll see that you do go to jail. And how will you support Ethan?"

She paled and her hands trembled as she moved toward the medicine cabinet. "Don't mention his name."

"Just a simple favor."

Silence hung between them. A clock on the wall ticked. A nurse came and went in the other ward.

"Yes or no, Debra?"

She swallowed. "Yes."

The large envelope was waiting for Jo when she arrived home before nine o'clock. Balancing leftover cake and her heels in one hand and her purse in the other, she knelt and picked up the package. It had no return address or postmark. Her thoughts went first to her sister. Taxes were due soon and Ellie always had trouble with the math.

Tucking the envelope under her arm, she unlocked her front door and flipped on her lights. As she dumped her keys and purse on the table by the door, her cats sauntered out toward her, rubbing against her legs and meowing their hunger and general irritation that she'd left them for so long.

Setting her package aside, she padded into the kitchen, turning on lights as she went. She filled the cats' food bowls, refilled their water bowls and put the kettle on the burner.

Anxious to be comfortable, she hurried to her bedroom to change into yoga pants and an over-sized T-shirt. Carefully, she hung up the dress. "All that trouble and energy, and I'll likely not wear it again." But she'd been there for Lara, and the dress had served its purpose.

The kettle in the kitchen whistled and she fixed herself a cup of tea before sitting on the couch and setting her package and cup on the side table. Her cats gathered on the couch beside her, Atticus nudging her hand until she scratched him between his ears.

"Needing some attention, old guy?" She smiled.

The cats purred and the day's tension melted from her muscles. She leaned her head back against the couch. Steam rose from the cup. Her muscles ached with fatigue. She didn't want to sift through Ellie's receipts tonight or untangle her latest financial mess. And the tea, well, she'd get to it in a minute. She closed her eyes.

When Jo opened her eyes, she had no idea how long she'd been asleep. Atticus slept on her lap but the other two had abandoned her for their nighttime retreats.

Shoving out a breath, she sat straighter, groaning at the stiffness in her neck. Carefully she settled Atticus beside her and rose, stretching her arms overhead. The clock on the kitchen stove read 4:14 a.m. She'd slept the entire night on the couch.

As the seconds passed she grew more and more alert and quickly realized she'd not be falling back to sleep. She picked up her cup of tea, now cold, and padded into the kitchen. She popped it in the microwave and hit two minutes. When the microwave dinged, she moved back to the couch. A glance to the end table reminded her that Ellie's taxes waited.

As steam from her teacup rose, she removed the tab sealing the back flap and opened the envelope. Inside she found a collection of papers covered in a bold, dark handwriting. Not Ellie's.

Her gaze settled on *"Dear Dr. Granger."*

Quickly she flipped to the last page and saw the bold signature. *"Yours sincerely, Harvey L. Smith."*

Her heart froze, and for a moment she couldn't

breathe. She traced her finger above his signature, not daring to touch it at first.

Smith had written her, solidifying her fears that there was a deeper connection between them.

Dear Dr. Granger,

You are an intelligent woman with a keen mind. Like me, you understand the nuances of so much in life. Having now read your dissertation, I realize that you see what the average person is too blind or too undeveloped to see.

For many years I've been keeping a mental journal of my exploits, but it has only been in the last months that I've thought to put pen to paper. The police would find this simple missive interesting, as it will no doubt fill in many pieces of the puzzle for them. But I wanted you, Dr. Granger, to have the first look at my work. I went to a great deal of trouble to make sure the events were as detailed as my memory could recall.

One day I hope to share this missive with you in person. I would like your thoughts when you have read through my work. I can't say for certain when we will meet again but know that you are always in my thoughts.

Yours truly,
Harvey L. Smith

Jo's hands shook as she stared at the letter and handwritten pages behind it. Smith was the master gamester and right now she was his latest victim.

Chapter Fourteen

Sunday, April 14, 8:00 a.m.

When Brody's cell rang he was already at the office and making his second pot of coffee. He'd been here since six to review more videotape of Hanna and the men who bought her time.

Thanks to Hanna he had a lead to Robbie, her suspected killer. Red truck. Texas plates with the letter X and T. The search through the DMV records would take time but at least he was headed in the right direction.

Without taking his gaze from the screen, he picked up his phone without glancing at the number. "Brody Winchester."

"This is Jo Granger."

He sat straighter, leaning back in his chair. "Jo. Is everything all right?"

"I had a package waiting for me when I arrived home last night. I didn't open it until this morning. It was from Harvey Smith."

"Smith." He tightened his grip on the phone. "Nothing should have gone out from that prison from him without Maddox knowing about it."

"Apparently, he has connections that helped him circumvent the system."

"Not for long." Brody would turn that place upside down to find out who was helping Smith.

"The package contained his memoir. This is something you should read."

"I'll come to you."

"That's not necessary. I'm on the road. Are you at your apartment?"

"The office."

"I'll be there in twenty minutes."

To the second, she pulled into the Rangers' parking lot. She parked her car right between the lines and took time to set the emergency brake though the lot was as flat as a pancake. Out of the car she locked the doors, tried the handle to double check before tucking her portfolio under her arm and moving toward him with a steady straight-backed posture. Like in college, she walked as if heading toward her grand purpose. Back in the day, he'd found her purpose-driven ways irritating. Now, he knew she'd been light-years ahead of him.

He opened the front door for her. "Come on up to my office."

"Right."

He followed, admiring the subtle sway of her jean-clad hips. In his office she took a seat and unzipped her portfolio. "Can I offer you coffee?"

"No. Thanks."

He hitched his hip on the side of his desk. "What do you have?"

"A long missive from Smith. As I said on the phone it arrived at my house last night."

"It was there, waiting for you?" He pulled rubber gloves from his pocket and yanked them on before accepting the package. He studied the envelope. It had no address or postmark, but had been at her home. "You're the only one who has handled this since yesterday?"

She frowned. "I didn't think about fingerprints until I opened it, and then I couldn't stop myself from reading it."

"Chances are, whoever smuggled this out for him is in the prison system, and they'd be savvy enough to wipe it clean. But it's worth a shot." He pulled out the papers and instantly recognized Smith's handwriting. "During the investigation three years ago I read through thousands of papers like this one written by Smith."

"When they were released after the trial, I was able to read some of his writing. The older papers could be rambling at times, and I had the sense he was tossing in extra details to manipulate the police, as if he were creating a maze of facts. This letter is specific and detailed. His thought processes are different."

He studied her a beat before dropping his gaze

to the papers. "Can you give me the digest version?"

"It's an accounting of all his victims, why he chose them, how long he held them and where he buried them. There is one woman that never came up in the police investigations. Her name was Delores."

Brody would read each and every word more times than he could count but right now he wanted Jo's take. "Any other impressions?"

"I know prisoners have ways of smuggling goods in and out of prison. But wouldn't someone have noticed him writing these papers?"

"Depends. He might have someone on the inside looking the other way while he wrote. He's also spent lots of time in the infirmary."

She frowned. "I called the prison. Smith is on heavy-duty pain meds. He's comatose."

Brody's lips flattened. "He commented once that he couldn't read as well when he took pain meds. And he's been on the meds steadily for six months."

"And yet he wrote in clear, legible handwriting."

"He wrote these earlier?"

She arched a brow. "I don't think he wrote them at all. Something about them bothered me as I was reading. The handwriting looks so much like his. In fact, there is little variation in the entire missive."

Brody frowned as he stared at the words. "As if someone were working hard to make it look like Smith wrote this."

"Exactly. I don't think Smith wrote this manuscript."

"His apprentice?"

"The student learned all he could from the master, going so far as to mimic his handwriting."

Brody tipped his head back. "How does he know where you live, Jo?"

She frowned as if that notion was finally taking root. "I don't know."

The apprentice or one of Smith's flunkies had stood outside Jo's front door. "You have good locks?"

"The best. And I use them without fail."

"Security system?"

"No."

"Get one."

She considered the order. "I will."

Disliking the worry in her gaze, he struggled to keep his voice steady. "What other impressions do you have from the writing?"

Jo shifted back to the facts, a place he knew gave her comfort. "Smith, or whoever wrote this, mentions Robbie several times. What I can't tell is if Robbie was present at the killings." She leaned forward, her soft perfume floating. "He discusses meeting Robbie, who apparently was twelve when the two met. The boy's mother, according to this, had abandoned the boy. She'd been a prostitute. But there is no telling what is true about the boy and what isn't. He speaks fondly of the boy, as a father would talk about a child. He details examples of the boy's intellect and remarks how quickly he learned."

"Is Robbie writing as he remembered or as he'd like to remember?"

"Assuming Robbie is the author, I would say a bit of both. We all have a way of rewriting history and casting ourselves as the hero/victim."

"Why would Robbie want to confirm all of Smith's kills?"

"Affection for a teacher. A father. He wants us to know exactly what Smith accomplished."

He watched her fold her hands in her lap. A prim and proper move or hiding how fear made her hands tremble? "When we arrested Smith we found nothing that would link him to Robbie. There were no pictures, no letters or e-mails. His mention of an apprentice was the first I ever heard of the guy."

"All the interviews you did and no one mentioned seeing a child or a young man?"

"None. Smith was known for taking out-of-town trips often. He always drove, took plenty of supplies and gassed up in Austin before he left."

"No properties listed under his name?"

"Nothing."

Brody set the letter down. "He was keeping the

kid tucked away somewhere. There's a lot of land in Texas to hide a small house or a trailer."

"I'd like to see Smith again. We are running out of time. If he's as sick as I hear, he's not going to last long. I'm driving up to West Livingston today."

"Unannounced?"

"I was hoping the warden would grant me entrance because we've met. You can't stop me this time."

Brody rose, pulled an evidence bag from his desk drawer and dropped the letters into it. "I'm coming with you."

"That's not necessary."

"I don't like the idea of you on the open road alone knowing Robbie or some other nutcase could be out there."

He grabbed his gun from his desk drawer and slid it into his holster. "I'm assuming you're free for the day."

"I am."

"Then let's go. The weather's good, so we'll fly."

Stick to the plan.

Dr. Dayton had repeated the mantra as he sat in his house alone, his tumbler of Scotch empty. Too early for a proper man to drink, but he'd stopped worrying about proper a long time ago. He refilled his glass and lifted his gaze to the wedding portrait of his wife, Sheila. Taken fifteen years ago, she wore a simple, white silk dress with a scooped neckline and a long lace drape that highlighted her smooth, brown skin, dark brown eyes and ice blond hair. She'd been so stunning when he'd first met her that he'd not been able to speak. He'd followed her around for days on their college campus, standing back and watching her. Finally, he'd gotten the nerve to approach her after a biology class. He could be charming when he wanted to be, and it took little to charm her. They'd become an item immediately, and by their senior year they were engaged.

After graduation he'd convinced her to work while he attended dental school. The plan was that she'd get her graduate degree when he landed his first job. But during that time, the dynamic between them shifted. She lost her zest for fun and became worried about finances. She'd talked of buying a house. Of children. All things he'd not wanted. He didn't want more responsibility than they had, and he resented her constant nagging.

Somewhere along the way she'd transformed from a princess to a hag—the proverbial ball and chain.

And now she was gone.

Stick to the plan.

He'd been telling the police for months that Sheila had run away. She'd been as unhappy with their marriage as he and had met another man.

He tried to convince the cops that she was alive and well and simply hiding out, likely laughing at all the heat he was getting from the cops.

The problem was the cops didn't believe him. They believed that he'd hurt Sheila. Based on bullshit comments from her sister about Sheila's fear of Dayton, the cops had gotten a warrant and searched their house from top to bottom. Shit, they'd swabbed the inside of the drains, searching for blood traces.

But in the end, they'd found nothing.

His dumbass attorney had brought him to Dr. Jo Granger to interview him so that they could use her testimony on his behalf. He'd agreed because he thought he could fool her. Several times, she'd nearly tricked him and made him reveal his secrets, but he'd caught himself. Just barely. But she'd been clever and had somehow peered behind the layers, as if he were made of translucent paper, and seen his true intent.

Dr. Jo Granger. She gave the impression that she was a cold woman. Ice. But she was smart enough to know that any red-blooded male liked a challenge. Liked the idea of melting that ice and seeing how hot she could get.

He'd had his share of fantasies of her since he'd seen her last Tuesday. It hadn't been wise to follow her to the mall, but he'd been unable to resist. The delightful look of shock on her face had fueled his sense of power and desire.

Stick to the plan.

Jo Granger was not part of the plan. She was a diversion he did not need.

And yet, sometimes a man owed himself a treat.

Brody and Jo arrived at the West Livingston prison before noon. He'd offered to take her to lunch, but she'd refused, her stomach too knotted to eat. She'd done her best to keep her emotions tightly wrapped and her thoughts clinical, but she was a little freaked out about the package on her porch.

The more she'd read this morning, the more rattled she'd become. She'd checked all the windows and doors to make sure they were locked, and she'd carried her cell phone everywhere until she'd reached Brody.

Smith, his apprentice or someone else knew where she lived.

Brody secured his gun, and the two were escorted to the warden's office where they were asked to wait.

"This can't be good," Jo said.

"Why do you say that?" Brody stood at the window, his hands clasped behind his back.

"Just a feeling."

He turned and smiled. "I thought you were all about logic and facts."

Her heels clicked crisply against the tiled floor. "Never underestimate the power of intuition."

Seconds later the warden arrived. He shook hands with Brody and nodded to Jo. "I'm sorry you came all this way."

"Why's that?"

"Harvey Smith died two hours ago. Passed away in the infirmary."

Brody's face hardened. "He wasn't expected to die so soon, was he?"

"No. His heart stopped," the warden said, shaking his head. "All the women he killed and the families he ruined, and he not only cheated execution but the cancer."

Brody cursed, shoving his hands in his pockets and rattling the change.

Jo snapped a loose thread on her jacket cuff. "The last link to Robbie. Gone."

Chapter Fifteen

Monday, April 15, 9:00 a.m.

Jo arrived early enough at her mother's salon so that they'd have at least fifteen minutes before her staff arrived for the early morning cuts.

She used her key and let herself inside. "Mom!"

"In the back room, Jo."

Jo found her mom stocking perm and hair dye supplies on the shelf.

Candace's hair was spiked and sprayed in place and her makeup as neat as a mask. "I don't have much time to talk, Jo. Got lots to inventory before the day gets rolling."

"You should turn that over to Ellie."

"I don't mind it."

"You ever considered cutting back on your hours?"

"And what would I do with myself?"

"Have fun. You haven't had fun since Daddy died."

Candace's eyes grew wistful. "Hard to top your daddy, baby. He was one in a million."

Her parents had had a loving marriage. It hadn't been perfect. They'd had their share of fights and tough times, but they'd always stuck together. "I miss Daddy."

"Me too. Every day." Her mother swallowed, as if squashing unwanted emotions. "What's this all about?"

Jo wanted an honest conversation with her mother. No judgments. No finger pointing. "It's not been announced to the media, but Harvey Lee Smith died yesterday in the prison. Doctors think his heart stopped."

Other than a subtle tightening of her jaw, her mother had no reaction. "Why should I care if some crazy man died in prison yesterday?"

The muscles in the back of Jo's neck tightened. "Mom, I don't want to fight. I want to ask you point-blank if Harvey Smith is my biological father."

Candace twisted the silver bracelets on her arm. "That is crazy talk."

"And that isn't an answer. It's classic avoidance."

Candace leveled her gaze on Jo as if she were looking at a misbehaving eight-year-old. "I don't need your doctor talk, young lady. I am your momma."

"I will always love Daddy no matter what, Momma. I want to understand my genetics."

Her eyes widened with anger and a touch of panic. "I don't have to justify myself to you."

"I'm not asking you to." She flexed the fingers of her right hand, wishing they didn't have to have this conversation. "Mom, please, give me a straight answer."

"I don't like your tone."

Jo sighed. She knew her mother well enough to know they'd go round and round like this and they'd get nowhere. "Fine, Momma, fine."

Candace glared at Jo. "And what does that mean?"

"DNA, Mom." Frustration raised the volume of her voice. "That will give me the answers you won't."

The front door of the shop chimed, reminding Jo she'd not locked the front door behind her. Candace's face was strained and angry but she held her tongue, knowing a customer could be in earshot.

"Mom, send whoever it is away so we can finish this."

Candace shook her head. "You know walk-ins are always welcome here. Always."

Jo ground her teeth. "This is bigger than a damn haircut."

"Those damn haircuts put a roof over your head and food in your belly. I've never turned away a customer, and I never will."

Her mother pushed through the curtain into the salon. "Welcome to Candy's Hair Salon."

Jo knew there'd be no more discussion today. Frustrated and more certain than ever her mother was hiding something from her, Jo pushed through the curtain. She expected to toss a passing nod at a customer. What she saw stopped her in her tracks.

Dr. Dayton grinned at her mother. "I was hoping to get a haircut. Sign said walk-ins welcome."

Candace reached for her smock. "Of course."

He looked at Jo, not a hint of apology or surprise in his gaze. "Dr. Granger. Fancy meeting you here."

Jo clenched her fingers around the strap of her purse. "What are you doing here?"

"Getting a haircut," her mother said. All traces of anger in her voice were gone. There was no place for tension or politics in her salon when a client was on the property.

Jo shook her head. "You need to leave, Dr. Dayton."

Dayton looked amused. "Is there a problem?"

Candace stepped forward in front of Jo. "No, there is no problem. My daughter is confused."

Dayton's grin widened. "Daughter. Now, I'd have thought you two were sisters."

Candace beamed.

Jo seethed. He wasn't here for a haircut. He'd been following her again. Had he been outside her house when she'd left this morning? She'd not seen anything suspicious, but stalkers were clever. "If you don't leave, Dr. Dayton, I'm calling the police."

"Jo!" her mother shouted as she moved in front of her. "That is enough out of you, little lady."

Dayton managed to look genuinely confused. "Is there a problem, Dr. Granger?"

"Yes, there is a problem." Jo moved in front of her mother. "Seven days ago I interviewed you about the disappearance of your wife. The next day you show up in a dress shop. And now you are here. What game are you playing, you pathetic jerk?"

"Jo!" her mother warned. "I have never heard you speak with such disrespect." Her patience now threadbare, Jo held up her hand to silence her mother. Intellectually, she could see that she was letting Dayton manipulate her, but her emotions didn't care about reason with such a dangerous threat near her family. "Leave now, Dr. Dayton."

"You're a bit prickly," he said. The laughter had vanished from his gaze.

She clenched her fingers into tight fists. "And you are a stalker. Now leave. Or we let the cops settle it."

Dayton looked beyond Jo to Candace. "Mrs. Ganger, I am sorry, but I won't be able to stay. Perhaps another time."

Candace looked mortified. "Of course."

"No," Jo said. "You show up on this property, and I will call the police."

Dayton snapped up a peppermint from the jar on the receptionist desk and slowly unwrapped it. "You're overreacting, Dr. Granger."

"I don't think so, but if I am, I'll live with it. Now get out."

Gaze narrowing, he slowly placed the candy in his mouth and folded the wrapper in half. "See you soon." He turned, tossed the wrapper in the trash, and left.

Jo shook with anger. She'd written off the mall as coincidence but not this. This place was too far out of his way and too unlike any place he'd frequent.

"Jolene Marie Granger," her mother said, teeth clenched. "If you think you're going to get back at me by insulting my clients, you better think twice."

Jo faced her mother, her fingers still fisted at

her side. "Do you think I'm trying to get back at you?"

"Yes, I do."

Drawing in a deep breath, she silenced the first remark that came to mind and slowly unfurled her fingers. "The man is a person of interest, which really means he's a *suspect,* in the disappearance of his wife. She's been missing for months."

The fire blazing in her mother's gaze didn't cool a degree. "People go missing all the time for all kinds of reasons!"

"Everything I know about body language and interview techniques tells me he knows his wife did not run away. I'd bet my last dollar that he killed her."

She planted hands on her narrow hips. "Innocent until proven guilty, Jo."

Jo tipped her head back, praying for the patience that was her trademark. "Don't let that man in your shop again. He is poison, and he's trying to get to me."

Her mother muttered as she pulled a cigarette and lighter out of her smock pocket. "Why is it always about you?"

Irritation clawed at her gut. "This is not about me. It's about keeping you safe."

Candace shoved the cigarette in her mouth. She flicked the lighter three times before it lit. "You keep telling yourself that."

"That man is dangerous." She spoke slowly, carefully.

"He didn't look dangerous to me, and I can take care of myself."

The front door chimed. Tensing, Jo turned and expected to see Dayton again. It was her sister, Ellie. Ellie was a younger version of their mother. Tall, blond and tanned, she wore her jeans and T-shirt tight. The bemused, happy expression on her face turned to suspicion when her gaze darted between Jo's face and their mother's.

Gold bracelets rattled on her wrist as she tucked her purse in the bottom drawer of her beauty station. "So what did I walk in on?"

"Nothing," Jo and her mother said at the same time.

Ellie shook her head. Gilded hoops peeked out from her blond hair. "That's the first time I've heard you two agree on anything in the last fifteen years. What is up?"

Jo hoped she and her mother could talk, and she could help her see that Dayton was dangerous. But as Jo opened her mouth, her mother turned and stalked toward her station to rearrange her scissors. She'd seen that expression often enough. Candace Granger's arctic blast could cool any sweltering Texas day.

Jo moved past her sister, unwilling to rehash, and reached for the door. "Ask Mom."

Dayton was humming when he started his car. He glanced up at the salon as Jo stood in the center of the store arguing with her mother and another woman who, if he didn't miss his guess, was her sister.

By the looks, Jo was gaining little headway with her kinfolk.

He backed up his car. If Jolene Granger thought she could bully him, she was mistaken. He wasn't going anywhere. In fact, he was just getting started with her.

"Do you want the good news or the bad news?" Dr. Watterson said to Brody.

A headache pounded behind Brody's temples as he stared at the medical examiner's sour expression. They stood in exam room two, the draped remains of Smith's last three victims resting on covered gurneys behind the doctor. "Bad news is dominating the day. Good news first."

Dr. Watterson moved toward the first gurney that held one of the victims' skeletonized remains. He pulled back the sheet to reveal a collection of darkened bones that had been arranged in some semblance of anatomical order. "We weren't able to extract DNA from this victim. She's been in the ground too long."

"How long?"

Dr. Watterson adjusted his glasses. "Thirty or so years."

Shit. "That means she wasn't one of the women on my list to identify."

"The women you were looking for died in the last eight to ten years. She can't be one of them."

The letter that had been delivered to Jo's house had mentioned a Delores. The specifics on her had been sketchy compared to the other victims. He'd turned the letters over to the experts who were now analyzing handwriting, fingerprints and whatever information they could squeeze from the pages. "But you can definitely confirm that the victim was a woman?"

"Yes. Shape of her skull and pelvis confirms gender. I can also tell you that she was Caucasian between the ages of twenty-five and thirty. And I think, judging by the shape of her pelvis, she didn't have children."

Brody studied the brown bones. "But you can't identify her?"

"Not at this time."

Frustration had him clenching and releasing his jaw. "Anything else you can tell me about her?"

The doctor raised his index finger. "As a matter of fact, I can tell you that she suffered an injury to her mouth. Someone knocked out two of her front bottom teeth. For whatever reason she did not seek treatment and an infection set in." He pointed a gloved index finger to her bottom teeth and traced along what would have been the gum line. "She would have been in a great deal of pain. And she would have been sick. That kind of infection will spread with each breath she takes."

"Could the killer have injured her mouth?"

"The injury would have occurred six or so months before her death."

"Anything else?"

"She was a heavy smoker. You can see it on her teeth."

Not a lot to go on, but something. "What about the other two bodies?"

Dr. Watterson carefully covered the first set of bones and moved to the second. "If you look at her right femur you'll see she suffered a bad break early in her life. See the break line and how it mended?" He traced a gloved hand along the visible line in the bone. "Likely the trauma happened when she was a teenager. Tammy Lynn Myers, one of your alleged victims, also suffered the same type of break. And we have dental X-rays for Myers and they do match this victim."

Tammy had been living in a halfway house near one of the schools where Smith had taught. She'd been struggling with substance abuse but had turned a corner. And then she'd vanished without a trace.

The police had assumed she'd overdosed or left

town. It had been Tammy's sister who kept insisting that she had done neither.

Three years ago when Smith had been arrested and his house searched, police had found a locket that had belonged to Tammy.

Immediately, she'd been added to the list of possible victims. But the search team excavating his backyard had never found Tammy's body. Later, Smith had confessed to killing the girl, but he'd never revealed where her body could be found.

Finding her now was another piece of the puzzle and though the news was grim, there was relief knowing she'd been found. "So we have Tammy."

"Yes." Carefully, Watterson pulled the sheet over her body. "You are free to speak to her family."

He sighed, not looking forward to the hard conversation. "Will do. What about cause of death?"

"No way of telling without the soft tissue. But based on the positioning of the hand bones in front of her chest and the presence of rope fibers, she was tied up like Smith's other victims."

She'd been in a shallow grave, bound and immobile. He'd never be able to say with certainty but he knew. She'd suffocated.

One down, one to go. "What about the last one?"

He moved to the next gurney, which held the second set of remains. "The next victim is Brenda Morris."

"She vanished eleven years ago. Prostitute working in downtown Austin. Her ankle bracelet and her driver's license were found in Smith's house. How did you confirm her identity?"

"Brenda had scoliosis." He nodded to the collection of bones. "This person had scoliosis, so given the time frame I'd say this is Brenda. I have a DNA sample from Brenda's son on file and was able to extract some from this victim's back molar. The lab will be able to cross-check."

"We have Tammy and most likely Brenda."

Brody hooked his thumbs on his belt. "But we don't have any remains for Susan Carson."

He covered the remains of the final body. "According to my records, she went missing ten years ago."

"That is correct."

"Carson was petite, standing just over five feet. Judging by the long bones, all three of these victims were over five foot six inches. She's definitely not one of the three."

"Smith gave us two of the three lost victims but not the third." Brody shook his head. "Why am I not surprised he'd hold back?"

"Are you certain Susan was one of his victims?"

"We found her wallet in his house along with a piece of jewelry."

"It's a safe assumption he killed her."

"Yeah." Brody sighed. "Who the hell is the other victim?"

Brody had kept in touch with Tammy's parents and sister because they'd been so involved in the Smith trial. The three had sat stoically in the back of the courtroom every day of his trial. Deeply religious, the family had often been seen praying during the trial, and the only sign of emotion he'd ever witnessed from them had been the day the medical examiner had discussed asphyxiation. Tammy's father and mother had wept as their surviving daughter tried to comfort them.

Now as he pulled up in front of the small adobe-style home, he wasn't sure what to expect when he delivered his grim news. Yes, Tammy had been found but now whatever hope they'd harbored that she might be alive and return home one day would vanish.

He parked and moved up the sidewalk past a couple of tricycles with grim determination. Tammy's parents had both died in the last year, both taken by cancer. That left Tammy's sister, Logan, as the family's sole survivor.

He rang the bell. Inside he heard the rush and clamor of young children followed by a mother's lighthearted warnings. "Scoot or no ice cream."

The door snapped open and the instant Logan Myers's green gaze met Brody's, the laughter died. A red-checked towel in her hands, she quickly finished drying her hands. "It's been awhile."

He touched the brim of his white hat. "Yes, ma'am."

She pushed open the screen door. "I see your name in the paper from time to time. Congratulations on getting that Rangers star. I'm glad you're doing well."

Right now, he didn't feel fine but ham-fisted and lacking. "Thank you."

Logan pushed her hand through disheveled, brown hair. "The place is a mess but come on in and have a seat." The children he'd heard through the door turned out to be two towheaded twin boys who were about five. They halted in their tracks when they saw Brody and stared at him wide-eyed.

"Afternoon, boys."

The boys glanced at their mother and back at Brody.

Logan tucked her towel in her apron pocket. "Travis and Tyler, I'd like you to meet Texas Ranger Brody Winchester."

Travis grinned. "A real Ranger?"

"Yes, sir," Brody said.

Tyler raised his thumb to his mouth before thinking better of it. "Are we in trouble?"

Logan shook her head. "No one's in trouble, boys. The Ranger is here to talk to me about some old business."

"Does he have a gun?" Travis said.

"I do," Brody replied.

"Can I touch it?"

Brody shook his head, smiling. "No, sir. You got to be a might bigger before that can happen."

Travis cocked his head. "I'll be six next month."

Brody considered the new bit of information. "No, I don't believe that will be old enough."

"What about your hat?" Tyler said.

Brody squatted. "I don't see how that could hurt anything. Have a look."

The boys scrambled close, each staring at the hat as if it were solid gold.

"What's that around the band?" Travis said.

"A silver concho. Belonged to a man who was a Ranger for thirty years. He gave it to me."

"You ever shoot a bad guy?"

"Do you have a horse?"

Brody grinned at the rapid-fire questions.

Logan gently touched each boy on the head. "Okay, you two, you've seen enough. Now, I need you to scoot on to your rooms and I'll be in presently."

When the boys didn't budge, Brody raised a brow as he stood to his full six-foot-four frame. "Sounded like an order to me, partners."

The boys' eyes widened and they turned and ran to their rooms.

Logan smiled after them. "I could use you around here more often, especially at bedtime when no one is able to listen to a word I say."

Brody smiled. "Happy to help."

She extended her hand to a well-worn sofa. "Have a seat. Can I get you a cup of coffee or a soda?"

"No, ma'am." He sat, his large frame not quite fitting on the sofa. He waited until she'd taken a seat across from him in a Lay-Z-Boy before easing onto the edge of the couch. "I've come to tell you we found Tammy's body."

She folded her hands in her lap and stared at them for a moment. "I saw on the news last week that they'd found Christa Bogart in a shallow grave and I'd wondered. But every time I hear a story like that I wonder if Tammy's also been found." She raised her gaze to him. "I'm tired of wondering but I can't help myself."

His hat dangled on the edges of his long fingers. "It's natural."

A bitter frown twisted her lips. "Funny you should come here today. I heard on the news that Smith died. Heart attack. Cheated the needle and cancer."

Brody had kept Smith's death under wraps until the midday news. No telling what Robbie would do when he got wind of Smith's death, but Brody hoped it forced a mistake.

"Yes, ma'am."

She met his gaze, all hints of softness gone. "I'm sorry they weren't able to execute him properly. I'd have had a front row seat for that."

He'd seen mixed reactions from those who'd witnessed executions. Some experienced vindication while others remained as hollow as ever. But there was no point in telling her. No one under-stood until they lived it.

"I don't suppose you know how she died."

"No, ma'am. The medical examiner wasn't able to determine cause of death."

"Like the others, most likely."

"Yes, ma'am."

She twisted the folds of her apron in her hands. "Tammy made her share of mistakes, but she was trying to get herself together. I thought she'd made it." She was silent before straightening. "Well, I appreciate you coming to tell me."

Case closed. Killer dead. And still inadequacy gnawed at him because he knew Smith's legacy continued to kill and destroy more families like the Myers family. "I wanted to see it through."

"Thank you."

Smith had skirted justice. But he'd be damned if his apprentice would.

The news of Smith's death didn't reach Robbie until late in the day. He'd been busy all day with work, away from TV and radio. The first time he'd heard the news he'd been driving home.

Stunned and not sure if he'd heard correctly, he'd frantically punched buttons, trying to find another station that was reporting the news. When he couldn't find one he'd rushed home and went straight to his computer. He'd searched Smith's name and immediately the prison's news release popped up.

Convicted Serial Killer Harvey Lee Smith died in West Livingston prison of an apparent heart attack.

Robbie sat back in his chair and stared at the screen. Smith had never had heart trouble. But, of course, since the cancer, maybe he'd weakened.

Blinking back tears, Robbie remembered that Smith didn't approve of emotion. *Keep your feelings hidden, boy, even in private. You never know who is watching.*

Biting the inside of his mouth, he focused on the physical pain. But his emotions wouldn't be corralled and he was left with a burning sense of sadness and loss. Harvey was dead. Harvey was dead.

There'd been a time when he'd thought the indestructible Harvey would live forever.

Harvey had plucked him from a rancid hand-to-mouth existence. He'd given him an education. A purpose.

There was so much he owed Harvey. So much he wanted to give in return. And though he'd killed and shown Harvey he could man up, a deep sense of lacking would not lift from his shoulders.

Robbie tapped the keys of his computer. Harvey had always wanted to connect with that damn kid of his, and as much as Robbie resented the old man's love for that child, he knew Harvey had suffered for not knowing his kid.

He searched her name on the Internet. Dr. Jolene Granger. Images of Jo Granger popped up and he stared at them for a long, long time.

"Sure I'd like to see her," Harvey had once said. "But a scorpion's nature doesn't change. Sooner or later I'd turn on her."

Robbie smiled as he traced her face on the screen. "I can give you this last gift, Harvey. I can see to it that you and your baby girl are together forever."

Chapter Sixteen

Tuesday, April 16, 9:00 a.m.

Jo's support group meeting for the at-risk teen girls had gone well last night. She'd had a good turnout and the girls had been in high spirits. Two of the pregnant girls had talked about making an adoption plan for their babies. Jo had listened and offered to put them in touch with a good social worker if they were serious.

She'd hoped Sadie would show but, not surprisingly, the girl didn't make the meeting. By the time Jo had arrived home, she'd been dead on her feet and still her sleep had been restless.

Yawning, she blinked and refocused on the open case file on her desk. She needed to get her work done so she could slip out in an hour. Today was Christa Bogart's funeral.

When the receptionist buzzed her phone, she was actually glad for the interruption. "Dr. Granger."

"Yes?" She pulled off her reading glasses and pinched the bridge of her nose.

"There is a Ranger Brody Winchester here to see you."

Jo sat straighter. "In the lobby now?"

"Yes. He'd like to see you."

"I'll be right down."

She hung up, rose and tucked her already smooth blouse into her waistband. Moving toward the door, she peered at her reflection in a small mirror. Her gaze looked a little wild. She moistened her lips.

"Good Lord, Jo. What the devil has you riled up? He's here on business, just the way it should be and always will be."

She found Brody standing in the lobby chatting with the receptionist. Sammy, normally jaded and aloof, grinned up at Brody as if she were about to melt. Brody listened as she talked and managed a funny quip or two.

Jo's own excited heart slowed a beat. She'd forgotten that Brody could be a charmer. He'd certainly charmed her in college, and like Sammy, she'd willingly lapped up every honey-coated word. The memory cooled her excitement so much that when she spoke her voice had a chill. "Ranger Winchester."

The easy laughter faded from his gaze. "Dr. Granger."

Aware Sammy watched them closely, she hid all traces of emotion. "What can I do for you?"

"Got an idea I'd like to run past you."

"My office is this way."

"After you, ma'am."

She moved toward the hallway, her shoulders tense and tight as she listened to the steady footfall of his feet. In her office she resisted the urge to move behind her desk, but offered him a seat on the couch as she took the chair beside it.

Instead of sitting right away, he walked around her office and studied the diplomas on the wall. "I always knew you were smart, Jo. But to see it up here in black-and-white, well, I see that I underestimated you. Summa cum laude. That is something. Brain cell for brain cell, I always knew you outgunned me."

"I've read some of your interviews with suspects. You've gotten confessions when no one else could."

He grinned. "You've been keeping up with me, Jo?"

She sat back in her seat, aware that body language telegraphed more than words. And she wanted to tell Brody that he did not get to her. "Sure. I've read lots of reports written by the Rangers."

He faced her, his white hat dangling from his fingers. "Which of my cases did you read?"

Too many of them. "Did you come here to talk about the past?"

He grinned. "No. But now that I'm here, it's a topic worth exploring."

"I don't think much about the past."

"Not even a little?" His tone teased.

She crossed her legs. "Tell me, what did you come by to talk to me about?"

He took the seat on the couch and tossed his hat to the side. Staking a claim. This close she could smell the hint of the same aftershave he'd worn in college. "Christa Bogart's funeral is this morning."

His statement extinguished that flicker of giddiness in her belly. "I know. I'd planned to go."

"Good. So am I. I want to see who shows up."

With effort, she relaxed deeper into her seat. "You think the killer might attend?"

"It's been known to happen."

"Sounds reasonable."

"I'd like you to come with me."

"I'll be there."

"Better if you are at my side. I can get your feedback as it comes to you."

"You know how to read people. You don't need me."

He shook his head. "You're better with people than I am. I'm good at browbeating and can be tricky when I want to be. But most folks go on guard when they see me coming. Not you, though. You disarm people."

She laughed. "You charmed a smile out of Sammy who hasn't smiled at me in the three years I've worked here. You do fine with people."

He winked. "Well, you got me there. I am good at charming the womenfolk. But a funeral's a different beast altogether. Highly emotional time. A lot of raw emotion. That kind of situation takes a special kind of finesse. The kind you have."

She cocked a brow and, unable to resist, said, "You're good at flirting and fighting, where my specialty is . . ."

A smile teased the edges of his lips. "You're good at seeing details I don't."

"The funeral is not for another hour and the church is close."

"If we leave now we'll get there early and can watch folks as they arrive."

"Leave now?"

She didn't want to go anywhere with him. The less they saw each other, the better. This was not a date. It was work.

His gaze winked with the satisfaction of a fisherman who'd caught a big one. "You'll be back in plenty of time."

"All right. I'll go early." She rose and moved

toward her jacket hanging on the back of the door. "Where do you want to meet at the church?"

Grabbing his hat, he stood. "No sense taking two cars when one will do the trick. Besides, we can talk in the car on the way back about what you saw."

She could argue with his logic and sound petty and small. Instead, she slid on her jacket, fastened the center button and grabbed her purse. "Let's go."

"I knew you'd be a team player, Jo."

"That's me. Team player."

He opened the door for her and waved to Sammy as they waited for the elevator. "I'll have your girl back before you know it, Miss Sammy."

The woman's grin broadened. "See that you do. She's one of our best."

"Can I get that on tape?" Jo said to Sammy.

Sammy laughed. "No way."

The doors dinged, opened and Jo stepped onto the elevator, wondering what alternative reality she'd entered. A week ago if someone had painted this scene she'd have laughed. But there it was: Sammy smiling and Jo stepping out with her ex-husband.

It took less than ten minutes to drive to the church, a simple clapboard, whitewashed building. The sign out front listed Sunday's sermon JESUS WANTS YOU! along with a list of hymns.

As Brody predicted, they arrived early enough to get a seat in the back by the door. Jo settled on a wooden pew and stared at the front of the church, shaped like a cross. It was a good-sized sanctuary, likely able to seat a thousand. Pews filled the right and left wings and all the way back to the double doors, now wide open to allow the arrival of mourners. A large wooden cross dangled over the red-carpeted center stage at the church's front. A grand podium was positioned to the right and beside it a large glamour shot of Christa. There were no flowers in the church, and Jo remembered that Christa's sister had requested that flower monies be donated to the Center for Missing and Exploited Children.

Brody removed his hat and settled beside her so close his shoulder brushed hers. The deliberate move was most likely about economy of space.

She eased back, Brody's shoulder touching hers, and focused on the task. "Do you really believe he will come?"

Brody kept his gaze on incoming mourners. "I do."

"Why?"

A half smile tugged the edge of his lips. "Do you ever accept an answer at face value?"

"I do when it's complete."

He lowered his voice and leaned closer to her, his gaze still trailing everyone who entered. "Because, Dr. Granger, if Robbie is our guy, he's had one hell of a week. Not only did we find his kill, but his mentor died."

"He's feeling a lot of emotions," she added.

"Some good and some not so good. Here he not only sees the power of his actions, but here he also can mourn, not for Christa but Smith."

"Right on the money, Doc. Right on the money."

A group of women entered. Jo remembered them from the search. They'd worked with Christa. Dressed in black, they dabbed handkerchiefs to their red eyes as they searched for a seat. More like them followed until soon people packed the church. Jo and Brody were forced to sit so close her thigh brushed his. She'd forgotten about the raw power leashed in his body. The times they'd made love before she'd gotten pregnant she'd savored that power and the power of feeling safe and protected.

Safe. She'd not been safe. She'd been playing with fire. And been burned. She drew in a breath so deep it caught Brody's attention.

"Everything okay?" he whispered.

"Yes, fine."

His gaze bore on her a beat before he turned back to the crowd. "See that couple?"

Jo followed his line of sight to a young, attractive man wearing a dark suit and the woman leaning heavily on his arm.

"That's Christa's boyfriend, Scott, and her sister, Ester."

The couple all but hung on each other as if they could topple any moment. "They appear devastated."

He studied them closely. "They do, don't they?"

She heard the doubt in his voice as a group of folks arrived wearing the *Find Christa!* T-shirts. "Hundreds of volunteers helped search for her. Including myself."

He cocked his head but his gaze remained on the crowd. "You mentioned that. What pulled you into the search?"

"Tim Neumann, the guy headed this way now, sent out a mass e-mail. He sold me my house a couple of years ago. Apparently, he sent flyers to all his clients. It made sense to help."

"He was also helping Christa and Scott find their first house."

"He's good. High energy. Personable. He had a way of keeping everyone motivated and working when the weather would have made it easy to stop. He's the one that found Atticus last year and talked me into taking the cat."

Tim hugged a young woman with long, brown hair and whispered something in her ear that made her smile as more tears flowed. He spoke to others, all willing to rally around him.

Jo's neighbor, Rucker, entered the back of the church. However, the church was full and he was forced to stand with a group of latecomers in the back.

"That your neighbor?" Brody said.

"Yeah. He was one of the searchers too."

Brody studied the man a beat. An organist began

playing "Amazing Grace" and he shifted his attention to the front of the church. A choir, dressed in white, took center stage as they sang. The congregation rose and sang as the pallbearers entered with a casket draped in red roses.

Jo dug a hymnal out of the seat back in front and opened the book to the song. She held it up for Brody so he could see and he accepted the weight of the book. They sang and watched the crowd.

The pallbearers wheeled the casket to the front of the church as the minister, a tall, lean man with a thick shock of white hair, welcomed everyone with a prayer. The minister invited Scott and Ester up to the front to speak.

Ester's hands shook as she unfolded a piece of paper and cleared her throat. Her lips were drawn and tight, and her voice broke when she read. Several times she stopped to collect herself. Scott wrapped his arm around her shoulder, and she leaned into him before dabbing her eyes and reading her prepared words about her sister. Jo noted Scott's right hand at his side. He rubbed his thumb and index finger together. A self-comforting gesture.

The next hour was a parade of people who all had lovely sentiments to share about the young woman who'd had a generous heart, loved school and had been excited about her wedding, which would have been in this church if she'd not died.

When the service ended, Jo watched pallbearers

carry out the casket as the mourners followed. Most, genuinely upset, kept their gazes toward the casket. There were some, especially among the *Find Christa!* group, driven by the event's drama. That was to be expected. Any funeral or tragic event attracted those who coveted center stage.

Scott, she knew, had been a suspect. She had no reason to doubt that his anguish was real, but she'd also interviewed killers who were truly heartbroken after the explosive, violent moments that led to a loved one's death.

When everyone had left, Brody escorted Jo into the bright sunshine. She removed sunglasses from her purse, and he settled his Stetson on his head. In the church they'd gone all but unnoticed but out here there was no mistaking a Texas Ranger. Several folks boldly stared at them while others whispered and pointed.

Talk around them didn't turn to murder immediately, but as folks lingered and watched the casket being led to the hearse, several peered in their direction.

Scott stopped his march to the limo, whispered something in Ester's ear and made his way through the crowd toward them. Several times he was forced to stop as someone offered him condolences. With each delay his face tightened with tension.

"Ranger Winchester," Scott said, not tossing a slight glance at Jo. "What are you doing here?"

"I'm paying my respects." Brody made no move to introduce her, which gave her the opportunity to remain unnoticed by Scott.

"I can't have you questioning these people here today. They are all devastated by Christa's death, and questions would heap trauma on trauma."

Brody's jaw tightened a fraction. He still didn't like hearing no. "I'm an observer here today."

"What is there to see other than grief and sadness?"

"You never know."

Scott's fists clenched at his sides. "You don't belong here. I want you to leave."

Brody didn't budge. "Can't do that."

Scott's jaw clenched as he fumbled in his pocket for his cell phone. "I'm calling your supervisor."

Brody didn't flinch.

Tim spotted Scott and cut through the crowd toward him. His gaze landed briefly on Brody and Jo and then settled on Scott. "Scott, it's time to go. We've got the graveside ceremony."

"I have a call to make first," Scott said.

Tim wrapped his arm around Scott's shoulders. "It's going to have to wait, pal. We need to go."

Scott's face crumpled with sadness. "This Ranger shouldn't be here."

"He's trying to find Christa's killer," Tim said. "He's doing his job."

"This isn't the place." Scott lowered the phone to his side as if all the will had melted from him.

"It's always the place," Tim said. "Let him do his job, and we can do ours and see Christa laid to rest."

Tears welled in Scott's gaze as his head and shoulders slumped. "I can't do it. I can't watch them lower her into the ground, knowing that freak buried her alive."

Jo studied Scott's grief but didn't allow herself to be pulled into it. He was clearly hurting.

Tim glanced at Jo. "Hey, Jo, good to see you."

"You too, Tim."

"Thanks for trying," Tim said.

Jo nodded. "Of course."

Scott looked ahead to the casket now being loaded into the hearse. "God, they are going to bury her again. That's not right."

Tim patted Scott's shoulder. "She's in a better place, buddy."

Scott buried his face in his hands. "This is messed up."

Tim made apologies to Jo and Brody and led Scott away, helping him into the limo.

"He's worried about her being buried in the ground again," Jo said. "I'm surprised he didn't have her cremated."

"Ester didn't want Christa cremated. She wanted her buried next to their parents in the family plot. Scott protested. There was a big fight. But Scott had no legal leg to stand on."

Jo had noted how Ester had leaned on Scott. "They seem close now."

Brody shrugged. "Grief can mess a person up. Makes them say or act out of character."

Heaviness lingered behind the words. For a moment she thought he might have been talking about himself. "What you're saying is that tomorrow she won't need Scott?"

"Let's say soon her head is going to clear, and she'll see the world differently. She will look back on today and wonder why she said and did half of what she did."

Before she thought, she said, "You talking about her now or yourself?"

Brody met her gaze. "Both."

At the gravesite, Jo stood next to Brody, too aware of the energy that he radiated. Raw. Powerful. Dangerous. She had a strong attraction to him. It would be foolish now to deny it. But this attraction had to be exorcised. She'd flown too close to this flame once before and had been burned.

Focusing her attention on the gathering crowd of mourners, she watched as they took their seats at the gravesite. Christa's sister and boyfriend sat in the front row, each clutching a red rose. Ester's eyes were bloodshot, and she still clung to Scott as if he were a lifeline. The woman might have disliked the man before but right now he was her rock. Brody had been right. Grief changed enemies into friends. Friends into enemies.

Tim caught her gaze and smiled.

"I'll be right back," Jo said.

Without a glance at Brody she maneuvered the cemetery lawn in her heels toward Tim. He smiled warmly at her and pulled her into a hug.

"A lot of the searchers showed up at the church," Tim said. "I thought I saw Rucker before but he was on the other side of the room so we didn't get a chance to speak."

"It was touching to see everyone. We all wanted to find her alive. That connects us to each other and to her."

Tim was a handsome man. Pretty almost, though she doubted he'd have liked the description. "I wish we'd done a better job. We failed her."

"You can't look at it that way. Look how many people you marshaled and brought together to search."

A bitter smile twisted the edges of his lips. "Effort is nice, but it's the results that matter. Yeah, we worked hard but in the end we didn't find her." He shook his head. "And she'd been alive all these weeks."

"Tim. You can't live your life playing the what-if game."

Tension deepened the lines around his eyes. "But I will for a long time. I let her down."

She took his hand in hers. Warm. Rough. "Don't blame yourself."

"There is a group of us gathering tonight. The searchers, as we like to call ourselves. At a bar downtown. You should join us. You worked harder than anybody."

Aware of Brody, she hesitated. A month ago she'd not have second-guessed. "Grief often finds some solace in groups."

"You sound like a psychologist."

She smiled. "No getting away from it."

"So you'll come?"

"Yeah. See you." She squeezed his hand and returned to Brody's side.

He kept his gaze ahead but he was frowning. "I didn't realize you two were friends."

"He's a nice guy."

Brody's gaze shifted toward Tim, much like a rifle sight zeroed in on a target. "He likes you."

"Mutual respect."

"Don't kid yourself."

"None of your business."

"Anyone connected to Christa is my business. I saw you nodding. You accepted an invitation."

His attention to detail on such a simple exchange surprised her. "He and some of the other searchers are gathering for a drink in town tonight. I agreed to go."

"I didn't realize it was such a tight-knit bunch."

"Tim's great at building camaraderie."

The hearse arrived and Scott, Ester and Tim moved to the back of the vehicle and unloaded the walnut casket. Jo didn't know the other three pallbearers. Their gazes fixed and solemn, the six carried Christa's casket to the grave. The crowd went silent for a moment before the faint sounds of weeping rose.

Thick, sudden tension rippled through Brody's body, drawing Jo's gaze to his face. He wasn't staring at the coffin but past it to a woman hovering close to a tree. The woman wore all black, including a black lace veil that covered white hair.

"Who is she?" Jo asked.

"Her name is Ginnie Dupont. She's a big fan of Smith's. She's been writing him letters since his trial. She dreams of being buried alive with him."

A shudder passed through her body. "And she comes to this funeral because Christa was murdered like Smith's victims? She's delusional."

"That's being kind."

Jo watched the woman wring a handkerchief between her hands. "I didn't see her at the church."

"She's not fond of crowds."

"She's not broken any laws by being here?"

His jaw tensed. "Not yet."

When the casket was lowered into the grave each searcher placed a single red rose on it. In minutes red rose petals covered polished walnut.

Jo watched the casket lower into the ground. A shiver raced down her spine. "I never want to be put in the ground."

Brody raised a brow and stared at her. "When you're dead, does it really matter?"

"My colleagues would argue that I'm trying to maintain control over life even after I'm gone. Which I suppose is true."

"But logic doesn't communicate too well with emotion."

"No. And it's an irrational fear . . . being trapped in a small space. But the fear is there, and I don't want to be buried."

"Well, here's hoping you have a long and happy life, and when the end does come years from now, if there's breath in my body, I'll see that you don't end up in the ground."

She arched a brow. "You can't keep a promise like that. Who's to say where you'll be?"

"Doesn't matter. If I'm alive, that promise will be kept."

An odd calmness warmed the chill. She trusted Brody would keep his word. "Only fair I return the favor. Any final requests?"

He looked toward the spot where Ginnie Dupont had stood. She was gone. "Don't care what you do with my carcass when I'm gone. Fact, I don't want any fuss made. If you're still kicking, have a toast in my honor and make a donation to your favorite charity."

"You really don't care."

"Not a damn bit. Let the dead bury the dead."

Jo wasn't watching the streets carefully when Brody pulled away from the gravesite. She'd been preoccupied with dissecting the reactions of the mourners. The sense of loss and grief had been palpable, but as she'd told Brody, no one really knew what drove the visible tears. It could easily be remorse as well as loss.

When he stopped at a street corner and a horn honked she refocused her gaze. She studied the tree-lined neighborhood. "Where are we?"

"I need to make a quick side trip."

She checked her watch and thought about her six o'clock appointment. "Where?"

He kept his gaze ahead, his body relaxed as he made another turn. "My folks' place."

"Your parents' home?"

"That's right."

Unease rolled through her, tightening her muscles. She'd never met Brody's parents and she never wanted to. "Perhaps you should drop me off at my office first. I shouldn't tag along for this."

His gaze searched hers. "Why not?"

"I would rather not."

"Why?" His gaze sharpened.

She shoved out a deep breath. "Brody, when we were married, you kept making excuses why you couldn't introduce me to your parents." She swallowed a lump in her throat that she'd not expected or wanted.

His jaw tightened. "I was an immature prick when we were married."

"What does that have to do with this introduction now?"

He arched a brow, half amused by her directness. "I've been stowing a few boxes at their place that need to be picked up, and it wouldn't hurt for you three to meet."

"Yes, but why?"

He shook his head, his exasperation evident. "Does there have to be a deep psychological need behind my actions?"

She shrugged. "Most of us are driven by something under the surface."

He parked in front of a white one-story with a neat front yard and faced her, his expression hawkish. "What is driving you now? Why are you hesitant to meet my folks?"

Jo stared sightlessly out the windshield. "I carried their grandchild, and you were ashamed." The inside thought came out before she thought to censor. "It took me a long time to get over all the emotions that stemmed from that time. I don't want to go back."

He shut off the engine. "You did nothing wrong. The baby was an accident. I know that now. I'm ashamed of the way I acted during that time. I thought marrying you was enough, but I can see now you deserved better."

She closed her eyes as tears clogged her throat. "Why are we doing this now, Brody? It's been fourteen years. And I really, really don't want to travel down memory lane."

He was silent for a moment. "A debt is a debt, Jo. And I owe you."

Her left hand curled into a fist as she faced him. "You don't owe me anything."

He opened his car door. "Yeah, I do."

A growing sense of panic clawed at her as she imagined meeting Brody's parents. A foolish reaction, her mind pointed out. Fourteen years was a long time ago. The past was dead and buried. And here were emotions pulling at her as if it were yesterday.

Brody opened her car door. "Come on, Jo. I never figured you for a coward."

Her temper rose and she swung her legs out of the car and stood. "It takes a big brass set, Sergeant Winchester, to call me a coward."

He laughed. "That a girl."

"Oh, shut up."

Brody slammed the car door and the two walked side by side to the front door. He rang the bell and seconds later the door snapped open to a tall woman with short, gray hair and Brody's dark eyes.

The woman grinned and pushed open the screen door. "Brody!"

Jo stepped back as Brody hugged his mother. She thought about the dozen other places she'd rather be right now. Even listening to her sister talk about her beauty pageant days was preferable.

"Mom, I'd like you to meet Jo Granger," Brody said. "Jo, this is my mother, Del Winchester."

Jo extended her hand to the trim woman with keen eyes and smiled as if she were interviewing a stranger or testifying in a court of law. Polite, simple, impersonal. "Pleased to meet you."

Mrs. Winchester's brows knotted as she eyed Brody. "Jo Granger. *Your* Jo Granger, Brody?"

Your Jo Granger. Damn. Somewhere along the way he'd told both his parents about them. Great. Just great.

Brody removed his hat. "Yes, ma'am."

Mrs. Winchester's smile was as warm and welcoming as it had been when she'd first looked at her son. "It's nice to finally meet you, Jo."

Jo wasn't sure if she should extend her hand, nod or smile.

Mrs. Winchester settled it when she hugged her. At first, Jo remained stiff and unsure, but to her surprise her tension eased. This was the kind of hug she could have used fourteen years ago when she'd been scared. "It's a pleasure, Mrs. Winchester."

What else could she say?

Mrs. Winchester squeezed her tight before releasing her. "Call me Del. And you two come on inside. I've got some iced tea made. Brody, Jo and I can visit while you and Daddy load your boxes in the car."

As her brain screamed *Run!* Jo walked into the

small, modest home. It was neat and orderly and the walls were covered with pictures of Brody. The images spanned his infancy all the way up to a recent valor awards ceremony.

"Nick!" Del shouted. "Brody's here, and he's brought company."

"Be right there." Nick's voice emanated from somewhere upstairs.

"He's putting shelves in the attic," Del explained. "I've been after him to do it for years. Had not a bit of interest. I might as well have been talking to a tree outside. Of course, Brody calls, Nick starts rummaging for boxes in the attic and decides it's time to get organized." She rolled her eyes. "It's all his idea now."

A loud *thump* sounded from upstairs.

"Maybe I better go check on Dad," Brody said.

Del didn't look worried. "Might not be such a bad idea. All I need is for him to cut off a finger or break a toe."

Brody smiled at Jo. "Be right back."

She stared up at him, doing her best to send evil intentions without giving away her frustration to Del. "Sure."

He winked, amused as if he could read each of her dark thoughts. "Be right back."

He'd barely vanished from the room when Del said, "Come on in the kitchen, Jo, and let's have some tea. I also made cookies this morning when Brody called."

Jo followed Del into the kitchen, willing herself not to glance at the pictures on the wall. "Brody called this morning?"

"Said he'd be close by, and it was time for him to grab his belongings." Del pulled two glasses from the cabinet. "He didn't tell you he was coming, did he?"

"No, ma'am. He did not."

Del chuckled. "My guess is he figured you wouldn't come with him if he did. That boy is a sly one."

Jo accepted the glass. She'd never been good at dancing around difficult subjects in her work and refused to now, even though the stakes were personal. "What has he told you about me?"

Del didn't bat an eye. "I'm thinking all of it, seeing as he did not paint himself in such a good light."

She sipped her tea, savoring the cool liquid on her dry throat. She remained silent, not sure what that meant.

"He told me about the baby that you lost." She shoved out a breath. "He told me you two married, but he wasn't much of a man during that whole time."

Indignation on Brody's behalf reared. "He was twenty-two."

"That's a man's age. His dad and I both told him we were disappointed. I wanted to track you down after the divorce, but he said no."

To know strangers talked about one of the most personal and painful moments of her life unsettled her. "When was this?"

"When he filed for divorce he needed money for the lawyer. He came to us and told us everything. It was right before he went in the service."

She stared into the coppery depths of her drink. "I'd forgotten he'd agreed to cover all legal expenses."

Del snorted. "That was about the least he could do, considering how good and well he mucked things up."

"It was not all Brody's fault, Del." No false modesty here but the truth. "We both should have been more careful."

"Bad things happen to us all. That's par for the course. It's how we handle those bad things that measures our worth." She sipped her tea as if she needed a break from the emotions. "But I will give my Brody credit. He's done his level best to be an upstanding guy."

"I know."

"Polite and polished, you are. But you don't believe those words." Del smiled. "I suppose Brody aims to fix that too."

Before Jo could ask for clarification, Brody and his father returned to the kitchen. Son favored father in height, weight and bearing. Only the elder's gray hair and sun-etched skin set them apart as father and son.

Nick Winchester extended his hand to Jo. "Real glad to meet you, Dr. Granger."

She took his hand. "Jo, please."

Nick cleared his throat. "I hear you two were at the funeral of Christa Bogart."

Jo glanced to Brody.

"Dad used to be military police and did twenty years with Austin police. He follows my cases," Brody said.

Nick accepted tea from Del. "I'd bet my last dollar the killer was there today. Too much fuss and attention made over the poor girl for him to resist."

As Brody accepted tea from his mother, Jo accepted the shift in conversation with gratitude. Work was safe. She could distance herself from the emotions. "I agree. He'd be enjoying tremendous satisfaction knowing he was the cause of it all."

Nick studied her closely. "Any theories on who might have done it?"

Jo shook her head. "I wish I did know. I suspect whoever did this is driven by lots of strong emotions, including a need to win his father's approval and a need to make his own mark in the world beyond his father's identity."

Brody sipped his tea. The easy, relaxed charm had hardened into a hunter's steely determination. "Got folks rooting around in the key players' pasts. If any of these guys were Harvey's protégé, there'd be missing time in his past. Harvey kept the kid hidden for several years and that would have created a hole in his history."

"You think you'll really find this guy?" his mother asked.

"You can bet your life on it."

He'd not meant to hunt today. He'd only cruised the Austin city side streets because he'd been restless, and the four walls of his office were crushing. Even his skin squeezed so tight he couldn't draw in a deep breath.

It was the funeral that had thrown him off. So much sadness and grief.

He lacked remorse for Christa and her idiot fiancé, but the casket had conjured images of Harvey lying in a box. Harvey had never wanted to be buried. He'd wanted to be cremated. His mother had instilled a fear of burial in him. But the news reports had said he was to be buried in the graveyard reserved for the unclaimed bodies of prisoners.

How he'd wanted to travel to the prison and claim Harvey. Wanted to see his ashes strewn on the open land filled with bluebonnets. But to claim Harvey would mean undermining every-thing. And Harvey, for all his faults, did not want his protégé arrested and put in jail.

However, knowing he was doing the right thing and feeling it were two different matters. The logic his brain spouted didn't soothe his heartache.

And so he'd pushed away from the computer, showered and carefully dressed in jeans and a dark hoodie.

When he'd gone into town to see Hanna he'd driven the red truck each time out of habit. Now he saw the folly of the move and knew the red truck could not leave the barn for a long, long time to come. So, he'd chosen a '79 brown Ford four-door. He'd maintained the car well enough so that the engine ran smoothly and quietly, and fired each time he cranked the ignition. Reliable but not conspicuous that people might remember it.

As he drove into town he thought about Jo. He'd have taken her but with that Ranger shadowing her these days, he understood the wisdom of waiting.

No Jo today. But soon.

When he reached the street, he slowed the car's pace and studied the girls on the street. They all dressed like whores. Short skirts. High heels. Makeup so thick it might as well have been a mask.

The girls were getting younger and younger. Some so young, they held little interest for him. Hanna's womanly curves and full figure, for instance, had fooled him. He'd thought she was seventeen or older. It wasn't until later when he'd taken the gold heart charm from around her neck that he'd seen the inscription with her name and birthdate. She'd been fifteen.

As he approached a light he spotted the woman he'd been watching for a couple of months. She wore a tight, short skirt, a halter and thigh-high black boots. She was a blonde, though he suspected the hair was a wig.

Glancing in his rearview mirror for traffic, he pulled to the curb in front of her. The windows in the car weren't electric, so he had to lean over the passenger side and manually open the window.

The woman spotted him immediately but she didn't approach the car. He leaned over and rolled down the passenger window. "Sadie?"

Her head cocked.

He smiled. "Jo Granger sent me."

Wariness gave way to curiosity. "You know Jo?"

"She said you could help me find my sister. She's on the streets for a couple of weeks, and I'm desperate to find her. Jo said you might be able to help."

She pushed off from the wall and moved toward him. She smelled of soap. "What is your sister's name?"

He reached in his coat pocket and pulled out a photo. He'd snapped the picture of one of the girls in Jo's support group. "Her name is Kelly. She's fifteen. And she's pregnant." The false story spun from him as if it were the truth. "My mother is frantic to find her. She's a good kid. Just met a bad guy."

Sadie took the picture.

"I heard about Jo's group and I went," he continued. "She's really great. So calm. Makes me think I'll find Kelly."

"I think I've seen her," Sadie said.

"Really?"

"A few blocks from here."

"Look, I'm from New York. I don't know anything about Austin. Jo said you'd help me."

Her jaw tightened and released as she studied his car and him. Getting into his car went against every bit of her nature. But he could see the mention of Jo's name had touched her.

She opened his car door. "I'll tell you how to get there."

He grinned, his relief real. "That would really be great."

"It should only take us a few minutes."

Or maybe a little longer.

Chapter Seventeen

Tuesday, April 16, 5:00 p.m.

The drive from his parents' house to Jo's office had been quiet, but the underlying tension that had simmered between them for the last week and a half had eased. Small progress, but progress nonetheless.

Brody hung his jacket on the back of his door,

tossed his hat in a chair. As he rolled up his sleeves and loosened his tie, he stared at the victim case files in the center of his desk.

His phone rang. He picked it up. "Winchester."

"This is Elaine Walton from Social Services. You asked me to search records for a Nathanial Boykin."

He sat forward in his chair. "That's right."

"Search was a little tougher than I'd imagined. We had a fire about a decade back. Not so much damage from the flames as the overhead sprinklers. A lot of files were ruined."

"Did you find anything?"

"It's not much. A grainy picture."

"I'll take whatever you have."

"I've sent it over. Should be there shortly."

"Great. Thank you."

He didn't have long to wait. Seconds later a picture addressed to him arrived in his computer in-box. He stared at the grainy face of Nathanial, son of Smith's third victim, Ellen Boykin.

He couldn't make heads or tails from the image. The kid could be anyone now. Picture in hand, Brody walked toward April Summers's office. April had joined the Rangers three months ago as their newest sketch artist. He'd heard good reports. And he was hoping for a little magic now.

He knocked on the door and a petite brunet raised her head from a sketchpad. She wore heavy, rimmed, dark glasses that did not suit her slender face or pale skin. The glasses magnified dark eyes that narrowed with annoyance when he knocked.

"Ms. Summers?"

She pulled off her glasses and shoved aside her annoyance. "Yes."

"Ranger Brody Winchester. Got a question for you."

She tugged at the hem of her blue blouse as she rose. She was short, not more than five feet, but possessed an energy that reminded him of a pit bull. "What do you need?"

"Got a picture of a twelve-year-old boy that was sent to me by Social Services. It was taken about twenty years ago. Mighty grainy."

"And you want to know what he looks like now?"

"Yes, ma'am."

She accepted the photo and studied it. "I have a computer program. I can run his picture through. Do you know anything about him? Habits and lifestyle choices affect how we age."

"All I know is that his mother died when he was twelve. She'd been a drug addict for years, but I don't know if the boy picked up her ways or not. He was in foster care briefly before he vanished."

"Vanished?"

"Case workers believe he ran off looking for his father. He didn't like the family he'd been placed with and talked about finding his birth father. They searched for him a bit, but over time he was forgotten and vanished."

"He could have been living on the streets."

"Could be. Could have had a real hard life. But I'm betting on the fact that he didn't have to scrimp and save but grew up in a decent enough home." Brody explained the boy's possible connection to Smith who had said he'd seen to the boy's welfare and education. "I'd assume he also had an education."

"I'll come up with a few scenarios." She checked the clock. "I've got several in the queue before you, so it might take me a day or two."

"Faster, the better."

As Brody strode back to his office his cell rang. He answered it as he stepped into his office. "Winchester."

"It's Santos. I just received the report on that letter delivered to Jo's house."

"And?"

"She was right. Smith didn't write it. Handwriting analysis said it's one hell of a fake but Smith didn't write it."

Brody stood silent for a moment.

"You still there?"

"Yeah, I'm here. Call DPS for me. I want more patrols through Jo's neighborhood. Smith didn't write the letter but some nut did and he knows where Jo lives."

Jo sat in the chair beside the couch in her office staring at the young girl who sat slumped back, her arms folded across her chest. The girl, fifteen, had dyed her blond hair an ink black, wore smoky eye shadow that matched her dark clothing. This was Jo's second visit with Mindy, and she'd not made any inroads with the troubled teen who'd taken to stealing.

The girl had wrapped herself in layers and layers of makeup and anger, and Jo wondered what horrible secret required so many defenses. "Mindy, I understand that you don't want to be here and that you don't like to talk, but your parents are worried."

Mindy glanced at her chipped red nail polish and said nothing.

Jo set her notebook aside and sat back in her chair. Mindy's parents were affluent, straitlaced and a far cry from the girl sitting here. "I never fit in at my house. I wasn't the Goth kid but the geek kid. My younger sister and mother were the beauty queens, and all I wanted to do was read."

Mindy kept her gaze down.

Jo continued. "When I was a little younger than you I told my parents during dinner that I wanted to major in psychology one day. I'd finished a report on the subject and was fascinated." Jo released a breath. "They both laughed and said there were better ways to make a living."

Mindy looked up, and for a split second, hints of curiosity flickered in her gaze, before she looked back at her folded arms. "My mother wanted more than anything to enter me into a beauty contest. I did not want any part of it, but my mother is a stubborn gal. She finally got me to enter. Want to know how?"

Mindy shrugged a shoulder. Though she said nothing, her gaze remained on Jo.

Jo took that as a yes. "She promised me one hundred dollars. Said she'd drive me to the bookstore and let me spend the whole one hundred dollars on books." The memory coaxed a smile. "I jumped at the chance. And I let her spray my hair until it hardened like a helmet. She painted my eyes and cheeks. To be honest, I thought I looked more like a rodeo clown than a girl. I even managed a baton-twirling act. Though I must say I do throw a real nice baton. Boy, how I could make that baby spiral in the air. And did I say I convinced Mom to let me set the baton ends on fire?"

Mindy shrugged. "So what happened?"

Jo didn't point out that this was the first time the kid had spoken in their sessions. "I gave it my all and I had come in . . . fifth place. Beat out by four perky, petite blondes. But I did win a ribbon for the talent." She smiled. "I received more applause than any of the girls that night when I threw my flaming baton in the air."

"Did you get your books?"

"I did. Took me two hours of wandering in that store because I wanted to choose carefully. And the best news of all was that Momma shifted her pageant dreams to my younger sister. Who, by the way, loved every minute of her pageant days."

Mindy rolled her eyes. "It was smooth sailing for you, and you never looked back."

"No, honey, I made some bad mistakes after that. Mistakes I couldn't blame on anybody but myself."

Mindy's brow knotted. "What kind of mistakes?"

Jo checked her watch and realized they'd gone five minutes over their time. "I'll tell you next week."

"What if I don't come back?"

Jo shrugged as she rose. "I guess you'll never know."

The girl rose, pulling her backpack with her. "These sessions are lame. They aren't helping."

Jo put her hand on the doorknob and paused. "The choice is yours, Mindy. I'm not going to make you come back."

"My parents will."

Jo opened the door. "Well, on the bright side, if you have to come back you'll find out the next chapter in my story."

The girl held her gaze a beat before turning to leave. As Jo followed, her phone buzzed. Ignoring it, she met the girl's parents, offered suggestions and updates before escorting them to the elevator.

Back at her desk, she snapped up the receiver and dialed the receptionist. "I have a call?"

"You have a call on line two. A Mr. Morris Gentry, attorney-at-law. He's called four times today."

She'd testified in court for clients and law enforcement and had dealt with her share of attorneys, but the name Gentry did not ring a bell. "Take a message."

"Sure."

Her phone buzzed again twenty seconds later and she snapped it up, annoyed. "Mr. Gentry said this is in reference to Mr. Smith."

"Mr. Smith?"

"That's all he'd say."

"I'll take the call." She punched line two. "Mr. Gentry, this is Dr. Granger. What can I do for you?"

A man cleared his throat. "I was the attorney for Mr. Harvey Smith. I assume you are acquainted with him."

"I am." She clicked through her memory. "And you defended him at his trial."

"That is correct, Dr. Granger."

She picked up a pen and doodled circles on her blotter. "What can I do for you?"

"Before he was arrested three years ago, he contacted me and gave me a package, which I was to deliver to you at the time of his death."

She held her breath. "What's in the package?"

He hesitated. "I do not know. All I know is that I got his assurance that it contained nothing considered illegal."

What did Mr. Gentry consider illegal? When

she'd read the trial transcripts she'd judged his definition as relaxed. "Can you send it to me?"

"You are to come to my office and sign for it personally."

"I don't have time for that. Would you courier it to me?"

"Mr. Smith was specific that I see you sign for it."

She didn't like having her actions dictated by a dead man. But to ignore the package was to ignore possible evidence that could help with the current murder investigation. "I'll be there in fifteen minutes."

"Good. Very good." He gave her his address.

The drive across town took twenty minutes, and by the time she parked, a half hour had passed. Gentry's office was located in a high-rise with sleek glass windows and a marble foyer. A scan of the directory in the lobby and a punch of the buttons and she arrived at Gentry's tenth-floor office.

The offices were as nice as the entryway, and she could see that Gentry's practice was profitable. He'd garnered a great deal of publicity from the Smith trial and had shown himself to the world to be a quick-minded attorney.

The receptionist was as sleek as the office and the moment she saw Jo she announced her to Gentry. The attorney greeted her within seconds of her arrival.

Gentry was a short man in his midfifties with a thick belly and dark hair that had thinned considerably. But his suit wasn't off the rack as it had been during Smith's trial, but custom. Gold, monogrammed cuff links winked in the light from a large picture window behind his desk.

He extended his hand to her. "Dr. Granger. So glad you could come quickly."

She accepted his hand, noting it was too soft for her liking. "You made it difficult to resist."

"I am following my client's instructions."

"Understood."

He escorted her into his office and to a plush mid-century modern chair by a chrome desk. Behind him, glass windows offered a spectacular view of the river.

"Can I offer you coffee or tea? A soda perhaps?"

"I'm fine. I need to collect what Smith left me and be on my way."

"Yes." He reached behind his desk and lifted a small beaten-up shoe box wrapped in duct tape. The box stood in stark contrast to the office's sleek surroundings. A spider in a lush bowl of cream. A cancer. A reminder that no matter how much money Mr. Gentry had spent on his new life, it had been built on the back of something very ugly.

She accepted the box, noting it wasn't too heavy. God, but she did not want this box. Did not want this morbid connection to a dead man who'd dedicated his life to evil.

"I have a letter opener if you'd like to open it now," he said.

She stared at the secured lid. "Thank you, but I'd rather not open it now."

His face frowned his disappointment. "You aren't going to open it?"

"Not now." As he continued to stare she added, "I was to sign for it but I don't need to open it in your presence."

"No."

"Excellent."

He cleared his throat. "If you do not want the box I can take it for you, examine the contents and destroy it."

She really looked at him for the first time. Keen interest sparked in his gaze. "What was Mr. Smith like when you represented him?"

"Honestly, he was delightful. He was courteous. Kept up with the current events and was always curious about what was going on in the world."

"I would think he'd have worried about his defense."

Gentry adjusted a cuff. "He never had a real interest in his case."

"Odd, considering the consequences he faced."

"Believe me, we had this discussion many times. I wanted him to be engaged and to worry about what could happen. But he didn't care, as if relieved to be behind bars. As long as he could read and write he was happy."

She dropped her gaze to the box and smoothed her hand over it.

He leaned forward. "Do you mind me asking you a question?"

"You may ask."

"Why ask me to hold a box for you? Who are you to him?"

"I don't know."

"Only once did he mention you. He'd been convicted and sentenced to death. I'd come to talk to him about appeals, but he showed more interest in an award you'd earned. It had been written up in the paper."

She smoothed her hand gently over the rough cardboard as if it could bite. Finally she rose. "Thank you."

"You'll let me know what is in the box?"

"Why do you care?"

"The most notorious serial killer in the last fifty years leaves a box in my charge. I'm curious. Curious enough in fact to have it X-rayed soon after he gave it to me."

"X-rayed."

"I wanted to make sure there wasn't anything really unseemly in the box." He dropped his voice a notch. "I've read how killers like him like to keep trophies. Body parts and such."

Somehow she doubted Mr. Smith would have left her anything gruesome. It would have been rude, uncouth.

She signed the receipt stating she'd accepted the box and with it in hand, she left a disappointed Gentry. Outside the building, she inhaled deeply, savoring the warm air, which eased the chill seeping from the box.

She didn't think about where she was going because she knew if she thought too hard about her destination she'd find a way to second-guess herself. Going to Brody was getting to be a habit. A bad habit. And if she had sense, she'd find another way. But right now, she couldn't think of another person to be with when she opened the box.

Fifteen minutes later, Jo walked through the main doors of the Rangers' Austin office and stopped at the reception desk. "Is Ranger Winchester here? Jo Granger to see him."

"Let me check." The officer cast her a skeptical gaze when he announced her on the phone. His eyes widened with a startled surprise. Brody was coming.

Seconds later, Brody emerged from a side door. Jacketless and hatless, he had rolled up his sleeves to reveal tanned, muscled forearms. "Jo, is every-thing all right?"

A week ago he'd called her Dr. Granger. Formality had been a polite barrier between them. Somewhere along the way that fence had dropped and awareness had developed. They'd never be lovers again, but maybe there could be room for friendship. She certainly needed a friend right now.

"Is there somewhere private where we could talk?"

"Up in my office." He pulled the box out of her hands as if he understood she hated touching it.

She flexed her fingers as they made their way to his office and didn't release the breath she was holding until he closed the door behind them.

"Who sent you the box?"

She explained about Gentry and the call.

Brody's jaw tightened, released. "First the visit. Now the box. Smith can't stay out of your life."

"Don't forget the letter."

"Smith didn't write it. It's a great forgery."

She smoothed her hands over her skirt, trying to erase the weight of the box from her hands. "They're taking over my life."

"No, they are not." Brody reached in his pocket and pulled out a pocketknife, flipped it open and pressed it to the old, cracked tape. "I'm going to open this?"

A single nod was all she offered as she folded her arms over her chest and watched.

With a quick, sure stroke he pulled the blade over the tape's crease between the lid and the box and sliced it open. Carefully, he removed the top.

Inside were stacks of letters. He picked up the first and studied the address. "It's addressed to you. Dated twenty years ago. March 24."

She frowned. "My birthday."

Inside was a birthday card featuring a pink bunny and a large number twelve. Smith had written a note, which Brody read. "Jo, wishing you all the best on this important day of your life."

It had been her twelfth birthday and the card included a picture of her at her one beauty contest. Her hands trembled a little when she studied the picture of her hideously teased hair and heavy makeup. She'd been holding the fifth-place trophy. Off to the side her mother grinned and beamed.

She closed her eyes, absorbing the enormity of the moment. "He believed he was my father."

Brody studied the other envelopes. They were all birthday cards, written and dated in sequential order.

Her gaze remained locked on the picture. "He couldn't have been more than twenty feet from me."

"Do you remember anything about that day?"

"Only that I did not want to be there. My head itched from the hairspray, and my dress was so tight I couldn't breathe. Mom was in her glory, and I was miserable."

"Did your mother act strange that day? Did she notice anything?"

"If she did, I never knew. She was all about the pageant that day." She shook her head. "And Smith was right there watching." She closed her eyes. "I've asked Mother directly if he is my father and she becomes offended. Which, of course, is classic avoidance."

"Happens in the best of families."

Her attempted smile fell short. "Brody, could he really be my father? I mean I know I never fit into my family, but lots of kids feel that way. Doesn't mean anything. But now as I look at this, I'm afraid."

"Jo, don't borrow trouble."

She lifted her gaze to find his boring into her. "I didn't go looking for it. It came to me."

Brody was all about action . . . the battle plan. "We'll go to the DNA lab and get you tested right now."

We. A unit.

"I'll get by the lab soon." Days ago, she'd have marked the idea insane. Now she couldn't deny a possible connection.

"Let's go now and take care of business."

Absently, she shook her head. "And what if he is my father?"

His expression was as practical as his tone. "You've got a biological fact you can tuck in your file box and forget."

It was that simple, and it wasn't. "I'd be the daughter of a serial killer."

He shrugged. "I remember how you talked about your dad, your real dad. It was clear he loved you."

"Biology is a powerful predictor."

He arched a brow. "I don't buy it."

She tipped her head back. "This is like a bad dream."

He rose and closed the gap between them, coming short of touching her. "*If* it's true. And *if* it is, remember it is a fact you have no control over. A fact that does not undo who you are."

He was right, of course. A quirk of genetics didn't define her. Why did she feel as if she'd done something wrong?

Jo had left Brody's office and gone directly to the medical lab for the DNA test. Brody had wanted to go with her, been annoyed when she'd said no and only been soothed when she'd promised to share the results as soon as they arrived.

She'd picked up the test kit just before the office closed. She'd swipe her cheek. She would. Just not right this second.

Jo arrived at the Austin bar where the *Find Christa!* group had gathered after seven. The bar was loud, smoky and full of laughter. She wasn't fond of bars. All the revelry, the laughter— neither fit her well. Work, dedication she understood, this culture she did not. As tempted as she was to turn and leave, she didn't, reminding herself she knew these folks. Had spent count- less hours in the cold, searching for Christa. Though they'd all come from different walks of life, they'd shared a bond that merited a drink.

Across the bar in a private room she saw a group of folks and behind them the battered *Find Christa!* banner that had hung on the side of Tim's truck.

Straightening her shoulders, she went to the bar, ordered a white wine and cut through the crowds toward the group. She didn't see Rucker but spotted several faces she recognized.

A redhead with pale skin and aqua glasses approached her. "I'm Casey. I remember you. Jo, right?"

She extended her hand. "I think we were on a couple of the search teams together."

"Cold day from what I remember. Wind kinda cut like a knife that day."

Jo sipped her wine and decided it tasted decent. "Not the best of circumstances." Across the crowd her gaze connected with Tim's. He raised a beer and smiled.

"Tim's got a lot to be proud of," Casey said. "A hero in my book."

She smiled. "He does." She glanced around the room. "I don't see Scott or Ester."

"Tim said they were too torn up to come. I can understand. I'm not sure if I could be here if it were my sister." Casey took a deep sip of her beer. "Were you at the funeral?"

"Yeah."

"Sad. Real sad. You see that Ranger there?"

"I did."

"Badass. I'd hate to have him on my trail."

Jo sipped her wine. "Yeah."

Casey finished her beer. "How did you get recruited into the search? Were you a friend?"

"No. Tim was my Realtor."

"Oh, me too." A short guy with thinning hair pushed through the group up to Jo and Casey. He tossed a halfhearted smile toward Jo before focusing on Casey. "Hey, I was hoping you'd be here."

Casey grinned. "Luke. Great to see you, man. Hey, did you meet Jo?"

He tore his gaze from Casey for a moment. "Jo, nice to meet you."

She smiled, amused by his clear adoration for Casey. "Luke."

"Hey, Jo, do you mind if I steal Casey for a moment? I got something I'd like to show her."

Jo shrugged. "Have fun."

Casey stopped and turned. "Jo, I almost forgot. I have a message from one of your friends."

"Who?"

"Aaron. He was on his way in here tonight but received a last-minute call. He told me to tell you he'd catch up with you soon."

Her smile froze. "Aaron?"

"Yeah."

Aaron Dayton. He was out there. Interfacing with people she knew.

Luke tugged on Casey's hand. "Nice meeting you again."

"Yeah, sure."

"Bye." Casey sounded breathless and excited as Luke took her by the hand and led her away.

Anger and frustration prodded Jo. Dayton was like a spider.

Tim shouldered his way through the crowd toward her. He picked up on her tension immediately. "What's wrong?"

If her anger weren't raw and fresh, she'd have done a better job of hiding it. "There's a man. He's stalking me."

Tim cocked his head. "Who?"

"It doesn't matter."

"It does." His gaze scanned the room. "Is he here?"

"No. He was outside and sent a message through Casey, who has no idea what he's doing."

"Jo, who was it?"

"Aaron Dayton." She sipped her wine and struggled to regain her composure. "Hey, I'm okay. It was likely nothing."

He shook his head. "I don't think so. You look rattled."

"No. I'm fine. Really." Grateful for a familiar face, her smile warmed. "Nice crowd."

He searched the room. "Yeah, good group of people. I'm glad they could all come and support each other."

His aftershave hinted of spice. "Weird seeing a Ranger at the funeral. But good Christa's case is still on their radar."

"It is. She deserves justice."

Tim's expression turned grim. "The day I heard about her death was one of the hardest of my life. I was sure that we'd find her alive."

"You did an amazing job. How many volunteers did you muster?"

"A couple of hundred. I wish we'd found her. Damn."

Casey and Luke called out to Tim. They wanted him to say a few words.

Tim tried to wave them off but finally nodded acceptance. "Sorry, got to go."

"Don't be sorry. You should speak."

She watched him weave through the crowd. Men patted him on the back. Women shook his hand. Jo set her glass down, suddenly a little suffocated by the crowd.

As Tim spoke, she turned and made her way through the bar. Outside, the cool air washed away the stale air and the tightness in her chest. She dug her keys out of her purse and took two steps before she heard a familiar voice.

"You should have had those keys in hand before you came outside." Brody.

Tensing, she turned, grateful it wasn't Dayton. She thought about telling Brody but caught herself. He was a habit she had to break. "Do you always follow Texans around and offer safety tips?"

His hands tucked into the pockets of a heavy, worn, brown jacket, he pushed away from the pub's wall. "Only ones who have their nose stuck in books."

"I wasn't studying. I was socializing." Being close to him steadied her.

"Something I've heard you don't do too often."

She shrugged. "Times change."

Amusement danced in his gaze. "See anyone of interest?"

His height and size tempted her to step back, but she didn't. "Why are you here?"

He leaned a little closer. "Thought you might have picked up something of interest with that group."

"The noble cause that brought them together is quickly vanishing, and they are fast becoming a group of people enjoying a drink and a laugh."

"Nothing that caught your attention?"

As she tucked a stray curl behind her ear, she considered telling him about Dayton but rejected it. She did not need him hovering. "There is a guy inside who looks like he wants to score with a chick named Casey."

He cocked a brow. "Imagine. A man in a bar looking for a woman."

"Tim was giving a nice speech when I left about community spirit and commitment."

"Why didn't you stay for the show?"

"I've heard his speech before. He used it to rally the volunteers before each search. A little bitter now knowing Christa is dead."

"We wouldn't have found her if not for you. Smith only spoke to you."

"He wanted to talk. He knew he was dying, and he didn't want to take his secrets with him."

"Don't bet on it. He'd have taken the secrets to the grave." He hesitated. "Did you go to the lab?"

She moved toward her car. "I did."

"Take the test?"

Astute. "I will in the morning."

He followed, slowing his pace to match hers. "Results take two or three weeks, which gives you an end date."

"If the test is negative. But if it's positive, the trouble's just getting started. My mother will not be happy."

"She'll survive. Better to have the truth."

With a click of a button, she unlocked her car door. "That's what I always tell my patients. But after a lifetime of lying, the truth is scary." She stopped at her car. "This is my stop."

"Always better to know, Jo."

"I'll keep telling myself that."

He opened her door for her. "Be careful, Jo."

"You keep saying that."

"Smith tangled you up in this mess. And he might be dead and gone but his little helper is not."

She slid behind the wheel. "You think his apprentice has a bigger plan?"

"I do." He braced one hand on the door and the other on the roof of the car. "Did you call the security company?"

"In the morning right after the DNA test."

"Don't delay on that, Jo."

"I won't."

He slammed her door closed, and she started up the engine. As she pulled away, she glanced in the rearview mirror. He was staring at her.

Jo's head throbbed when she pulled into her driveway after nine. The day had not only been long but chock-full of so many unwanted emotions.

Her heels clicked on the sidewalk as she sorted through her keys. She found the gold key, and as she pushed it toward the lock, the dog next door barked and howled, startling her. She looked toward Rucker's house. His Lab, Greta, was inside and had heard Jo arrive. As with most nights when Jo arrived home the dog barked.

A smile twitched the edges of her mouth. No matter what happened in the world, pets had a way of keeping anyone grounded. Her cats didn't care about the box or Smith. They cared that she was here, ready to feed them and scratch them between the ears.

It wasn't until her hand was inches from the

door that her smile vanished. The door was closed and locked, but Jo had the strong sense that something was off.

She drew back her hand as if she'd happened upon a rattler ready to strike. She checked the door again. Locked. She thought about Rucker. He had a key as she had a key to his place. Just in case. Her mother had a key. Both had access. Both could have stopped by.

She dug her cell out of her purse and called Rucker. The phone rang three times and went to voicemail. Greta was barking, but he wasn't there. "Rucker, this is Jo. When you get a second, call me. Just double checking. Were you in my house today?"

Instead of sliding the phone back in her purse, she kept it in her left hand as she unlocked and opened the door. There was no reason to call the cops. The door was locked. There were no signs of trouble. She had a feeling. Calling the cops would not only make her appear foolish but would lead to hours of unnecessary waiting and questions.

Atticus meowed loudly from inside the house. He sounded agitated and upset. "Damn it."

Clutching her phone, she entered the house and flipped on the lights. The place looked as she'd left it, not a vase or pillow out of order. And yet the sense that someone had been in her house nagged her. "Atticus. Here, kitty, kitty."

Atticus meowed again and this time she heard scratching from the hallway closet. She moved carefully toward the door. "Atticus."

Meow.

She drew in a breath and yanked open the door, ready to dash back out the front door. Instead of an intruder she found her fat, yellow tabby glaring up at her, clearly beyond annoyed. He sauntered out of the closet, brushed against her legs and meowed his displeasure all the way into the kitchen.

Jo stared at the closet, wondering how the cat had gotten locked inside. "Did Rucker or Mom close the door on you?"

She flipped on all the lights as she made her way into the kitchen, Atticus following. She found her cats sitting by their bowls staring up at her. They weren't meowing and acted as if they'd been fed. But not sure, she doled out food from a bin into their bowls.

As she watched the trio eat, clearly unharmed, she shook her head. "I must be losing my mind."

She dumped her keys and purse on the kitchen table and with cell phone still in hand moved down the hallway, her gaze still sharp for anything out of place. Nothing was out of place. Could she have been so careless this morning when she'd left? She had been rushed. Frazzled. Maybe she had locked Atticus in the closet. She shook her head. No, she always did a head count of the cats. It had to be Rucker. If he'd gotten an emergency call from the vet hospital, he could easily have raced out of here half-cocked.

She crossed the threshold to her room. Her bed was made as crisply as the moment she'd left it this morning. Nothing was out of place.

Chalking this all up to her day, she changed into sweats and a T-shirt. Back in the kitchen, she dug a frozen dinner out of the freezer and tossed it in the microwave for eight minutes. Her stomach grumbled. As she waited for her meal to cook, she opened her laptop. All the questions that Smith carried within him were gone. Robbie. Her paternity. The identity of the unexpected victim.

She thought about her mother. Could there be a connection to Smith? Was she lying?

They'd have met thirty-three years ago. She'd been living in Austin and would have been a junior at Hanson High School. Jo opened the computer file on Smith she'd set up when she'd been doing her dissertation. In the file was a detailed time line of the man's life. She'd done a painstaking search of his life. There'd been some gaps but for the most part she'd re-created most of it.

Thirty-three years ago. Where had he been substituting? She scrolled through the spreadsheet. There was nothing for September, but in early October he'd been hired as a long-term sub at . . . Hanson High School.

Jo felt the air rush from her lungs.

Her mother and Smith had been at Hanson at the same time.

A chill raced down her spine and she stood. She paced the kitchen. Needing fresh air, she crossed to her front door and stepped outside.

Again she thought about the uneasy feeling she'd had when she'd arrived home. She ran her finger over the lock, wondering if there'd be a nick or a glitch indicating that someone had broken into her house. But the wood was as smooth as it had been when she'd had it installed last year.

"Call me back, Rucker. Tell me I'm being paranoid." God, she was losing her mind. Lord knows there was enough to distract and agitate her these days. Cases. Clients. Her mother. Smith. There were a lot of reasons to feel out of sorts. "Let it go, Jo."

As she turned to go back in the house, she dialed her mother's number but stopped when the whisper of a warning brushed her neck. Later, she'd wonder what made her look down. She'd wonder how her gaze so easily found the flutters of folded yellow gum paper in the mulch bed by her front door.

Slowly she knelt, leaned over into the bed and picked up three pieces of paper. They were yellow gum wrappers. Dayton's brand of gum. Neatly folded into squares, as he liked to do. Had he been to her house?

Crushing the paper in her fist, she scanned the interior of her house, too terrified to enter. She dialed 9-1-1.

Chapter Eighteen

Tuesday, April 16, 10:00 p.m.

The officer came out of Jo's house, his face grim. His swagger coupled with a chagrined look stoked her annoyance. Now that her nerves had calmed, the wrappers seemed a paltry reason to panic and call the police. She was annoyed for being a Nervous Nellie, as her grandfather used to say. Irritated that it was late and she'd lost so much time.

The officer stopped and hooked his thumbs in his belt. "Dr. Granger, there is no one in the house. All the windows are locked and all the doors are locked. I checked the closets and the attic crawl space. There is no one, and by the looks, no sign of an intruder."

"But I found the wrappers."

"Gum wrappers. You said it belonged to a man you interviewed. Dr. Dayton."

"That's right. He's a person of interest in his

wife's disappearance and I've seen him around town several times in just the last week."

"Has he threatened you in any way?"

"No. Nothing like that. But the wrappers by the front door . . . I know he was here."

The officer had bagged the wrappers, but had made no promises. "Ma'am, anyone could have dropped those wrappers. A mailman. A deliveryman."

"I had no deliveries. And there were three wrappers, as if someone had been standing here for a time."

He sighed. "Ma'am, I can't find anything in this house or around it to prove there was an intruder."

Several of her neighbors peeked out their windows. "How do you explain the cat locked in the closet?"

He hooked his thumb in his gun belt. "Cats crawl into closets all the time. Easy to be in a rush and close the door on them."

She shook her head, annoyed at his logic.

He sighed. "Ma'am, I didn't find anything in your house other than three annoyed and vocal cats. We've already put extra patrols in the area, but I could step it up more for a day or two."

The officer believed she was being silly. That she was scattered. Emotional.

And if she were to examine the pure facts, she couldn't blame him. She looked a little crazed standing here in her sweats.

She shoved a shaky hand through her hair. "I look like a crazy woman."

Her comment eased some of his tension. "Not crazy. And we're here to take care of trouble."

She looked toward the open door. "I've never been so foolish, but maybe there's a first for everything."

"Like I said, we'll step up patrols in the neighborhood. Try to keep an eye out."

"Thanks." She held out her hand and he accepted it. "I appreciate your help."

He touched the brim of his hat and moved past her toward his car. Her gaze on the open front door, she moved slowly toward her house. Once a place of safety, the space cast a tainted aura.

She went inside her house, closed and locked the door. Atticus came out from under the couch and rubbed against her. He meowed his annoyance as the other two cats scooted out from under the couch. "I don't like having the police in my house any more than you three. Believe me."

Her cell phone buzzed with a new text. She flinched, surprised she still clutched it.

The text was from her sister. Jo glanced at the subject line. *On a date!!* A smile tugged the edges of Jo's lips. Ellie had had a rough go since her divorce.

Another text followed and this one had an image attached. Jo opened the text and saw a picture of her blond, beaming sister sitting next to the man.

She recognized the man instantly. It was Dayton.

"Damn it!" Her hands trembled as she dialed Ellie's number. The phone rang twice before going to voicemail. "You've put the phone on silent. Call me when you get this."

The first meeting with Dayton could have been considered a happenstance. But a second and then a message from Casey at the bar. The wrappers. And now a date with Ellie. It all added up to stalking.

Calling the police again wouldn't be effective. What was she going to say? Her sister was on a date? Who could she call?

She needed a friend.

Someone that believed her.

She dialed Santos's number.

Brody was in his office going through the collection of birthday cards Smith had sent to Jo. He'd bought a card for each of her birthdays starting at age twelve and going all the way up to her thirtieth birthday. In each he'd written a note detailing how proud he was of her accomplishments. Some included pictures of her taken from some distance. One included a picture of a woman Smith claimed was his mother. He'd included the picture in her sweet sixteen card. The black-and-white had been taken forty years ago and scribbled on the back was the name *"Rachel"* and the note, *"You remind me so much of her."*

Brody studied the image, searching for resemblances to Jo. There might have been some likeness but nothing definitive to make him take note. The bottom line was that Smith believed he was Jo's father.

A knock on his door had him looking up to find Santos standing in his doorway, his cell phone in hand and a frown on his face. "Guess who called me?"

Brody tore his gaze from the card. "Not in the mood for games."

Santos moved into his office, not put off by Brody's foul humor. "Dr. Jo Granger called me. She was trying to sound cool and collected, but she's rattled."

Brody's gut tightened as he rose. "Where is she?"

Customary good humor had vanished in the wake of worry. "At home. She thinks she's got a stalker."

"What?"

Santos had the look of a man who itched to take action. "Dayton. Remember him?"

Brody paused. "Sure, he was implicated in his wife's disappearance."

"Jo interviewed him last week. Dayton's defense attorney hired her firm for an analysis of his psychological makeup. Her report wasn't favorable and since their only official meeting he's been showing up." He detailed the sequence of events including the date with Jo's sister.

Brody reached for his gun in his side drawer and holstered it. "And she called you."

Not me. You.

"She called the local PD first who came and did a search of her house. They offered to patrol her neighborhood more."

Brody shook his head. "I'd already ordered more patrols in the neighborhood. Dayton is in his midthirties, right?"

"You're thinking about Smith's apprentice."

"Do we have a profile of Dayton's past?"

"He's a dentist. Went to dental school and undergrad in Texas. He moved to Texas when he was sixteen, from Tulsa."

"Foster care? Gaps in his past?"

"None local police found. No red flags as far as Smith is concerned."

"That doesn't make him any less dangerous." Brody grabbed his jacket from the back of his chair and slid it on. "Why'd you come to me? I can see you want in on this."

A dark smile curved the edges of his lips. "Jo's a great gal, and I'd like nothing better than to track Dayton and school him on some manners. But I don't poach."

Poach. Santos believed Jo belonged with Brody. Brody could deny the claim on Jo. He could insist that the past was the past. That what they had was a mistake. Over.

But he didn't. There might not be much between Brody and Jo now, but that was something he'd planned to fix.

Santos took his silence for indecision. "But if you don't consider it poaching I'll move in on her faster than you can blink."

Brody met his gaze, a half-unfriendly smile lifting the corner of his mouth. "I'd hate to beat you to a pulp."

Santos's gaze sparked with amusement and challenge. "You sure could try."

"I'd whoop your ass."

"Not on your best day." His lips flattened. "If you hurt her, I will beat your ass to a pulp."

"Understood." Brody picked up his hat.

Satisfied for now, Santos said, "I'll ask around about Dayton. See what else I can find out."

"I want to know all there is to know about this son of a bitch."

Brody couldn't drive to Jo's fast enough. The urge to protect her was primal, and he didn't question it.

When he rang her bell, he listened to her hurried footsteps and the scrape of the chain against the door. A moment's hesitation told him she was looking through the peephole. *Good. Be careful.*

Her expression was grim when she opened the door. "Brody, what are you doing here?"

He'd mucked up their chances good between

them back in the day. Going forward he'd do some serious digging to get himself out of the hole he'd dug. "Santos told me you called."

She folded her arms over her chest. "I called him. Not you."

He searched the front porch, looking for signs of an intruder. "He told me you called."

She wore loose-fitting yoga pants, a tank top and no shoes. Her hair hung loose around her shoulders. "Why would he do that?"

He met her worried gaze. "You gonna let me in or not?" No sense getting into the winning her back part. Right now he suspected she'd slam the door in his face if he did. "I want to hear all you have to say about Dayton."

She hesitated and pushed open the screen door. "Thanks for coming."

He removed his hat and stepped into the house, which was as neat as it had been the last time he'd been here. "Where are the Three Musketeers?"

That coaxed a smile. "Scattered in their favorite hiding spots. They are not happy about the upset to their routine."

"Neither are you." Without her heels the top of her head barely reached his shoulders. And without makeup she looked younger and more vulnerable. He could see now that she wore both like coats of armor, and it wasn't lost on him that she'd answered the door without both because she'd expected Santos, not him.

"Can I get you a coffee? I put a pot on, and it should be ready."

"That would be great. Been a long day."

He followed her into the kitchen. She'd already pulled out two mugs. For her and Santos. He didn't dwell on what might be or what had been. He focused on what he had in front of him. And right now he had Jo all to himself.

She poured the coffee and without asking splashed a bit of milk in the cup before handing it to him. "Good and hot."

His gaze lifted from the cup to her. "You remembered."

Frowning, she shrugged. "I didn't even think."

He sipped the coffee. It tasted good.

She held up her cup. "You remember how I take mine?"

He arched a brow. "You're asking if a twenty-two-year-old remembered how you took your coffee?"

She smiled. "A stretch, I know, but I thought I'd ask."

Brody laid his hat on the table. "I never claimed to be the most observant kid unless it had to do with baseball."

She sipped her coffee black, a fact he'd not forget again. "You were always like a laser on the ballfield. I was surprised when you gave it up."

"The Marines made sense. I'd finished up

school. We had a baby on the way, and I could count on a steady paycheck and benefits."

Her gaze dropped to the coffee as she swirled it. "I didn't mean for you to give up baseball."

"I'd expected us to talk about it once you finished exams. But you lost the baby."

"And it all fell apart." A furrow formed between her brows as she absorbed the information. "Then the Marines, DPS and the Rangers."

"That's exactly right." He nodded toward the kitchen table and when they were both seated he said, "Life can throw a curve, but sometimes that's just fine."

"I suppose."

"What did you do after I saw you that last time in the hospital?"

"Mom insisted I move home. I thought about quitting school after. Mom put me to work in the salon. Two weeks in the shop of setting perms and doing comb-outs and I was at college registration."

"Suppose she knew the right motivation to get you back to school."

Jo frowned. "I never thought about it that way. But I think you're right."

Silence hung between them before he said, "Tell me about Dayton."

Jo leaned her elbows into the table, cradling the mug in her hands. She injected no drama and several times admitted she'd thought she was being paranoid, but when she'd seen the picture of her sister on a date with Dayton, she'd called Santos.

Santos.

Not again. Brody was the man she needed to call going forward when trouble rode up. "Santos is digging into Dayton's business right now."

She shook her head. "Dayton is clever. He thinks he's smarter than everyone."

A smile lifted the edges of his lips. "I wish I had a nickel for all the smart guys I've locked up. I'll nail Dayton."

She arched a brow. "You sound pretty sure about that."

"I am."

"You can't say for sure how it will go."

"We might have been married back in the day, but you don't know me well now. You'll learn that when I make a statement I back it up. Don't you worry. Consider Dayton taken care of."

She stared at him a long moment. "I'd like nothing better than not to worry."

Brody had failed Jo once badly. And now he wanted to right that wrong. He wanted to protect her. Touch her. "I will stop Dayton. Trust me."

She lifted her gaze to his, and he saw the doubt. Carefully, she set down her coffee cup. "This isn't such a great idea."

For a moment, he thought she'd peered into his

mind and read his thoughts. "What isn't a great idea?"

She dropped her gaze to her cup as if carefully considering and weighing the words. "I can take care of myself, Brody. I don't need your help."

"I want to help."

She drummed impatient fingers on the table, as if trying to restrain emotions she didn't want released. "I called Santos for a reason. You should have let him come here tonight."

A growl rumbled in his chest as he set his cup next to hers. "Why him?"

"Because he's a friend. Because I trust him."

"You don't trust me?"

Delicate brows rose. "I did once. And"—she attempted a smile—"it didn't go well."

"I fucked up. In my ham-fisted way I tried to fix it. I didn't. Now I want to make it right."

She tilted her head. "Your being here is about paying back some kind of debt to me?"

"Sure. In part. I also care about you, Jo. I don't want to see you hurt."

"Why do you care about me, Brody? We barely know each other."

"We were married."

"Ancient history. You aren't the kid you were, and I'm no longer a pushover."

"You were never a pushover, Jo."

Tears welled in her eyes, but they glistened with anger and frustration, not sadness. "I stood there in that hospital room and listened to your accusations. For weeks and years after that night I replayed it over and over, wishing I'd told you to go to hell." She swiped away an escaped tear. "But I stood there, dazed and quiet like a half-wit."

"You shouldn't have had to fight me. I was out of line. I still cringe when I think back. Christ, you'd suffered a miscarriage, and I took my anger and frustration out on you."

She shook her head, rose from the table and moved to the counter as if needing the space. "I swore I'd never be that helpless again. I swore I would never need or want anyone as much as I needed you in that moment." She tipped her head back but that didn't stem the rush of tears that spilled down her cheeks. "I thought you'd be the one person who might come close to understanding the loss."

Needing to touch her, Brody took her hand in his. She jerked away but he stood and moved behind her, putting both hands on her shoulders. Her soft skin didn't disguise the tension rippling in her muscles. "I am sorry."

Her head downcast now, she was so still he wondered if his words had registered. "I will not need you."

"I'm not asking you to." *Yet.* "I am not asking anything of you. But I am going to take care of Dayton. And Robbie."

Jo turned and glanced up at Brody. Like it or not, she did need him right now. She was smart as a whip but she was too much of a straight shooter to really deal with the likes of Dayton. Whereas he'd take the bastard apart piece by piece, even if it meant using every nasty trick in the book.

As he stared at Jo, he wanted to kiss her. To taste her. Looking at her made him hard. But he'd never make the first move. Not again. Their past dictated his restraint.

She didn't move away either.

She raised her hand to his, the touch feather soft, exploratory. The sadness had vanished from her gaze and something darker burned in the green depths. She caught her lower lip between her teeth and he remembered the subtle gesture —temptation warring with reason.

He could step back and end this. He didn't.

"I never stopped to ask." Her voice sounded throaty, raspy. "Are you single?"

Tension rippled through his body. "Very."

Bitter amusement lit up her gaze. "I wish you weren't."

"Good excuse to end this?" he challenged.

"Common sense is telling me to walk away."

Her scent wafted around him. Silent, he traced circles on her shoulder with his thumb, knowing if she pulled away he'd not follow.

Instead, she rose up on her tiptoes and kissed

him on the lips. The kiss was light, exploring, even as a frown furrowed her brow. She still searched for an excuse to stop.

He wasn't going to give her a reason. If she well and truly wanted him, he wasn't moving a damn inch.

She nibbled her bottom lip and lifted a hand to his face, tracing his jawline with her fingertips. "I can come up with a thousand reasons why this is a bad idea."

He traced her cheek with his knuckle. As a kid he'd thought she was pretty enough but now he realized he'd not really taken a hard look. If he had, he'd have seen she was stunning. "I can't think of one."

"We've traveled this path before." She clung to reason like a drowning man did to a raft.

"Seeing as we aren't the people we were fourteen years ago, it's easy enough to argue that we're on a different trail."

"You're rationalizing."

"As fast as I can."

She kissed him again, this time her touch more insistent. Unable to resist, he leaned into her, coaxing her lips open with his tongue. A soft moan rumbled in her chest as she wrapped her arms around his neck.

His right hand dropped to her shoulder and then down her arm. He savored the way she shivered and the way her breath grew a little ragged. At her wrist her pulse thrummed wildly against his fingertips.

When he'd first touched her all those years ago, she'd shivered. She'd been tantalized and afraid by her reaction to him. He'd been so lost in his own desires that he'd not thought to ask and didn't realize until later that she'd been a virgin. He'd not realized what she'd given him that night. But he did now. No matter how many men she'd had since they'd split, he'd always be her first, and maybe if he were really damn lucky, her last.

He kissed her at the nape of her neck, savoring the rapid race of her pulse. He slid his hand up under her loose shirt and cupped her lace-covered breast. Her nipples hardened.

"God, Brody, you are killing me," she rasped. "I'm going to explode."

He raised his head to search her gaze. "Too fast? You want me to back off?" And God, he would if she asked.

Laughter bubbled in her chest. "Too slow."

A smile hitched the corner of his mouth. "I can fix that right quick. Where's your bedroom?"

"Down the hallway. First door on the left."

He kissed her lips hard before taking her hand and leading her to the bedroom. Details other than the large, neatly made bed escaped him as he backed her toward the mattress, tugging off his jacket as he did and dropping it. She reached for the edges of her top as he unfastened his shirt. Both dropped to the floor in unison, mingling in a puddle on the floor.

He stared at the demure lace bra and the swell of her breasts. "I feel like a buck in heat."

She moistened her lips, her hair a tangled mess framing her face. "You did this to me the last time. Made me lose my mind."

"Darlin', this ain't gonna be nothing like last time. Gonna be a lot better." He unfastened his belt buckle as he kissed her again. His hand traced the column of her spine toward the waistband of her pants. He slid his hand under the rough fabric and cupped her soft bottom. He wanted to savor this moment because he considered this their first time. A new beginning, and he didn't want to screw it up.

"Please tell me you're not going to take your time," she said, breathless.

A cheerless chuckle rumbled in his chest. "I'm doing my best, ma'am. God help me, I am."

She shook her head, trembling fingers reaching for the zipper of his pants. "I'd like you to move a little faster."

As tempted as he was to toss her on the bed and drive into her, he forced himself to stand still as she slid her hands over his flat belly. He hissed in a breath but managed a calm tone. "No, I think we're gonna take our time."

She frowned, but before she could complain,

he kissed her and backed her up to the edge of the bed. His kisses moved from her lips to her throat and to the hard peak of her right breast. He suckled as she moaned and threaded her fingers through his hair. Only after he'd had his fill did he shift his attention to her other breast.

She arched, her pelvis pushing against his. "I swear to God, Brody, I'll go insane if you drag this out."

"I promise it will be a good kind of insane." He slid his hand back under the waistband of her yoga pants and cupped her. She was moist, readily encouraging his male pride. He teased, played and kissed, and when her knees buckled he caught her and chuckled.

He eased her to the mattress. When he stepped back to kick off his boots and undress, he missed the heat of her body. She stared at him, her gaze an odd mix of pleasure and fear. He didn't like the fear and made up his mind to make it disappear. He lay beside her and stroked her flat belly.

His touch made her muscles jump, twitch and finally calm. Soon he had her pants and under-garments off and in the center of the bed. He moved on top of her, his erection hard. It took all his self-control not to enter her. And then he remembered . . . no condoms.

He shoved out a breath and rolled on his back beside her. Mother of God, to be so close and to fall short.

She looked at him with dazed doe eyes. "What's the matter?"

"No condoms." He pinched the bridge of his nose. No sense saying when he'd used the last or taking a chance in a roulette game they'd played and lost before.

A smile played on her lips as she stroked his thigh. "I'm on the pill."

"Really?"

"No accidents this time."

He rolled on his side and laid his hand on her belly. "You're sure?"

Her gaze sharpened. "Very. And I'm . . . discriminate, so no worries about the other stuff."

"Me either."

She hesitated, and he knew she'd reached a moment that required trust.

"I can be an ass, but I am no liar."

That made her laugh. She lay on top of him, and her bare breasts flattened against his chest. His hand instinctively cupped her bottom. "Stop talking."

Brody chuckled and rolled her on her back, covering her body with his. Kissing her, he took his time stroking her body and taking time to know it.

He was trying to take his time, but when she opened her legs for him he needed no more prompting. He settled between her legs and pushed into her. She was so tight. Wet. And he thought he'd come in that instant. But he waited for her to stretch and accommodate him. She'd said she'd been discriminate, and her tight body more than confirmed it. When he knew her better, he might ask, but for now he simply cared about moving inside of her and savoring it all. He wanted this to be perfect for her.

She moaned and smoothed her hands over his back and cupped his buttocks. "Go much slower, and I am going to have a stroke."

He didn't chuckle this time but gave in to his own urgency. His strokes grew faster and faster as a fine sheen of sweat glistened between them. When she moaned his name and her body tensed under him he released the hold on his control and came.

Jo's heart hammered in her chest as Brody lay on top of her, his head tucked in the crook by her neck. His breath was warm and labored. Her body was relaxed and her senses satiated. She didn't dare think too much about what they'd done. She had taken no chances with her heart all because of him. And now here she was taking the biggest chance of all.

She drew circles in the center of his back, wondering if he'd be up for round two soon.

As if reading her thoughts he said, "Lady, I think you damn near killed me." Chuckling he rolled onto his side beside her.

"Nice to know I've got the touch."

He lay on his back and closed his eyes. "Have no doubt. You do."

To tease she said, "You're not so bad yourself."

He opened an eye and looked at her. "Not so bad?"

Color rose in her cheeks. "Okay, very, very good."

He shook his head. "Tough audience."

When overtaken by passion, she'd not been embarrassed or thought too much at all. She simply reacted. But now as the fires cooled, reason took hold of the reins.

When she didn't answer, he stroked his hand over her flat belly, his expression serious. "It was great for you, right?"

When he looked at her with such intensity, she had trouble stringing thoughts together. "Yes."

"Yes, what?" he prompted.

"It was great."

He nodded, satisfied. "That's more like it."

"Don't get too sure of yourself, cowboy!"

He winked. "A wise man knows his talents."

This easy humor warred with old visions that still rose up naturally. Last time she'd cuddled against his side, she'd thought she'd found a missing piece of her soul. This time, she accepted that what passed between them was casual, terrific fun, but casual. And she wasn't going to hitch her heart to him.

She pushed up, aware her hair now covered her breasts. "I'm starving." She wanted to get dressed and do something other than lie next to him naked and vulnerable. "I can make a bowl of pasta. Want a plate?"

As she sat up, he trailed his fingers lazily down her back. "Sounds good."

He took a hold of her hand as she moved to slide away. "Jo, I want you to be careful."

"Little late for that." His calloused fingertips rubbed the underside of her fingers as she tugged them free. The scramble to find her clothes proved a little more awkward. Her shirt was on the floor but her pants were tangled in the coverlet. And her panties . . . who knew where they'd landed. She snagged her pants and rolled off the side of the bed away from Brody. After quickly tugging them on, she moved to the other side of the bed and snatched up her shirt. Not bothering with her bra, she slipped it on.

"I mean in general." His expression had darkened as it did when he was on the job.

"Did you ever identify the second victim?"

"We did."

Frowning, she sat on the edge of the bed. "Why didn't you tell me?"

"I didn't want to scare you." Annoyance flared, and when she moved to stand he took hold of her hand, keeping her close.

She tried to snatch her hand away but his grip

tightened. "I'm not a kid, Brody. I can handle the bad news."

Brody sat up. Light brown hair covered his chest and forearms. A C-shaped scar curved around his right knee and his right bicep sported a Marine tattoo. "It's not about what you can handle."

"What is it about?"

"It's my investigation. I reveal only what I need to." His lips flattened.

She knew he'd not compromise on this. She could make an issue or accept that with Brody the case came first. "Who was it?"

"I told you before. A young prostitute."

"What was her name?"

The question surprised him. And she understood. When most people heard "prostitute" they didn't ask any more questions. But Jo had worked with a lot of these girls.

"Hanna Metcalf."

She cocked her head. "Blond. Slim. Liked purple?"

His gaze sharpened to a knifepoint. "Yeah. How did you know?"

"She sometimes came to a group I run on Monday nights. I'd not seen her in a while but that's not unusual. The girls come and go."

"You knew Hanna and were connected to Christa's search."

"Yes."

He muttered an oath. "I don't like this one damn bit, Jo."

"He's out there circling."

"Yeah."

He rose and dressed. "What can you tell me about Hanna? Her uncle didn't know much."

Jo shook her head as sadness for the lost girl crept through her. "She was a runaway. That uncle you spoke to was the reason. She didn't come regularly, but when she did I noticed she took everything literally. She cataloged facts when she was nervous. I suspect a mild form of Asperger's syndrome."

"Did she ever talk about her clients?"

"None of the girls talked about work at the church. It was their chance to get away from all that. Their chance to be kids."

"Those girls at the gym. Any of them know Hanna?"

"Sure."

"Could I talk to them?"

"We have a meeting next Monday."

"You can't get them before?"

"I can try. But it's like herding cats. The girls come and go for a lot of reasons. But there is a core group that's stuck with me. I can call some of them."

"Okay." His body tensed as if his mind worked in overdrive. "Any way you could go stay with your mother or sister right now?"

"I'm not leaving my house."

"You already suspect Dayton was here."

"I'm calling a security company first thing in the morning. I'm having a security system installed."

"I can pull a few strings and get it done faster."

"Thanks."

"You'd be better off living with someone."

She shook her head. "Not my mother or sister."

"I don't want you here alone."

"I appreciate your help, but you are not the boss of me, Brody."

"Jo." His tone threatened.

"Jo nothing. I've taken care of myself for a long time, and I've managed fine."

"Jo," he said, hesitating. "I care about you."

She shook her head. "Don't do this."

"Do what?"

"Turn what happened into something personal." Maybe it had been for a split second, but the moment had passed.

"Seemed pretty personal to me, Jo." He tucked in his shirt, studying her face as if she were a prime suspect in a murder investigation.

"Let's not kid ourselves, Brody. This isn't forever. This was for today. It was fun. Lord knows it's been a while for me, and I had forgotten how nice it is to touch a man. But we both know what we had the first time wouldn't have lasted if not for the baby. Let's enjoy it for what it was."

A frown creased the lines around his face. "A quick roll in the hay?"

A chill shivered down her back, cooling the last embers of sex. "You make it sound cheap."

"No, you make it sound cheap."

She folded her arms over her chest. "The last time you didn't want forever."

"I'm thirty-six now. Not a twenty-two-year-old twit. I've changed."

"What are you saying?"

"I've wanted you since the instant I saw you on that climbing wall. Been thinking about you more than I should." His jaw tensed and released. "I thought that maybe we could give it a whirl."

"A whirl?"

"No one is promising forever right now. I get that. But I like you. I respect you. Why can't we see where this takes us?"

She shook her head. "Brody, I don't think that is smart thinking."

He moved toward her, clearly using his height to his advantage. "Now I always figured you were smarter than me when it came to book smarts, but I thought when it came to street smarts I had you licked."

"You make me sound like a cloistered nerd."

He grabbed the edge of her shirt and rolled the soft fabric between his index finger and thumb. "I think you've kept your nose in the books too long, and you're a bit gun-shy."

"Gun-shy? Yeah, you are right. I'm gun-shy of you. I'm not gonna lie. Last go-around was too tough for me, Brody. I don't want to hurt like that again."

He tugged her a little closer. "I don't want to hurt you."

"I don't think you did when you were a kid. You were being you. Just like you didn't tell me about Hanna. You put work first. And it's okay if you do."

"You're mixing me up with the twenty-two-year-old."

"That guy wasn't all bad. He married me when another guy might have walked away. He never denied that the baby was his. He joined the Marines so he could take care of that baby. Granted, his delivery could suck but at least he stepped up to bat."

He held up his hands. "Stop it right now."

"Stop what?"

"Stop thinking about the past so much. We've got right now. Not yesterday and not tomorrow, and right now I want to make sure you're safe."

She cocked a brow. "I'm not going to change my mind, Brody."

His grin was sly. "Not asking for anything now other than maybe a meal. I'm hungry. We can commit that far, can't we?"

"Sure." She studied him an extra beat and moved away, wondering if she'd been hoodwinked.

Sadie shook off the haze of drugs that ass had given her. He'd wanted her quiet and compliant, and so he'd forced pills and bourbon down her throat until she'd been too dazed to offer resistance. She'd seen her share of nasty on the streets but feared the worst was to come.

She reached for the chain that kept her leg tethered to a hook bolted in the wooden floor. She tugged hard at the chain but it didn't budge. On the other side of the room, moonlight trickled in through a curtained window. Judging by the clarity of the night sky, they were far from any town.

Outside the room, she heard footsteps. Her heart leapt in her chest as fear bubbled fresh in her blood. She lay back and closed her eyes, doing her best to keep her breathing smooth as if she were sleeping. *Leave me alone. Leave me alone.*

As his steps moved closer to her door, she heard a cell phone ring. His footsteps stopped. He cursed, hesitated, and answered the phone with a pleasant "Hello."

Sadie opened her eyes and saw the shadow of his feet in front of the crack where he stood.

The man outside shifted his stance from side to side, and she listened as he spoke. "I look forward to it. And tomorrow works for you?" Again silence and a friendly "Great. See you then."

His cell phone closed with a snap seconds before the lock on the door twisted open. She pressed her back into the corner, held her breath and kept her body as quiet and steady as she could. Still her thoughts raced and her heart rammed her ribs hard.

His face backlit from the door behind him, she could see dark stubble covered his chin and thick bangs swept over downcast eyes as he reached for the chain around her ankle and unfastened the lock. He slapped a hand on her butt. "Time to wake up, princess. Time to get this show on the road."

She didn't move at first, hoping against hope that he'd leave. But he grabbed her by the arm, crushed her flesh in his calloused fingers and hauled her to her feet. Forced to open her eyes, she stared at him through blurred vision.

He grinned and captured her face in his hands, painfully squeezing her cheeks. "Time to play. Time to play."

"What do you want? Is this about the delivery I made last week for Daddy?"

He chuckled. "No. This has nothing to do with anybody you know."

"Then why?"

"Something I do."

She stared into determined dark eyes. "You asked about Jo."

"Yes."

"How do you know her?"

"She's my sister."

"No way."

"Believe it."

She stared into his dark eyes a long time. "You don't have to do this."

Without answering he lifted her and carried her outside. The sky was clear and the stars bright. She'd been right about being in the middle of nowhere. The drugs made her head spin, and she thought she'd get sick.

"Please put me down."

Silent, he carried her a short distance before lowering her into the car trunk. He smiled at her and then slammed the lid closed, encasing her in darkness.

The trunk had a foul smell and made her gag. The ride in the trunk was a haze. Bumps, the sounds of tires crunching gravel and dirt kicking up. She tried to stay alert, but the drugs grabbed ahold and pulled her under.

When Sadie woke a second time, a weight pressing on her chest made it tough to breathe. She pulled at the restraints that bound her arms against her chest. Raising her head she realized she lay in a grave and he was burying her alive. She screamed, but the night absorbed all the sound. In the distance a coyote howled.

"You don't have to do this! Come on, mister, please! Whatever I did wrong, I can fix it!" The cold, clammy dirt made her skin crawl and she wriggled her shoulders, trying to get the dirt off as if it were a thousand bugs crawling over her skin.

He jammed the shovel blade into an earth mound and loaded it. He turned and slowly dusted her body with the dirt. He wasn't in a rush. He enjoyed this. "You can wiggle all you want, but it won't make a difference. My knots are sure."

He shoveled more dirt on her feet and chest this time; the weight pushed her deeper into the dirt and made breathing hard and her nose was filling.

Sadie rocked her head from side to side. "Mister, you don't have to do this. If I did something wrong, I'll make it right."

He tossed the dirt on her chest and face. Her nose filled with dirt, and she snorted several times to clear her nostrils.

"I wish my father could see me now," he said. "He'd be proud."

She spit out dirt. "He wouldn't like this. He wouldn't."

His smile was tender. "No, he'd be proud."

"Jo would hate this!"

"I know. She wouldn't understand."

A clump of dirt hit her face, landing in her nose and eyes. She tried to shake the dirt from her head but more dirt walloped her face until she could barely breathe.

The drugs didn't stem the panic, which now cut through her like a razor. As more dirt hit her face, her last thought was she was a nobody. There wasn't a cavalry coming. No last-minute rescue. She was lost to the world forever.

Chapter Nineteen

Wednesday, April 17, 11:00 a.m.

Luke and Tommy should have been in school. Today they were supposed to take the midterm in history. But after a long, cold winter, the warm weather had been too tantalizing. Each had been talking about skipping and going fishing at Sweeney Lake, and last night when Luke had heard the weather forecast, he had decided today would be the big day. Today they'd skip. He'd opted not to tell Tommy last night because the kid couldn't keep a secret worth shit. He'd waited until this morning when he knew Tommy was eating his bagel and watching Cartoon Network like he did every day.

It's the day!

Tommy had laughed when he'd seen the text. He'd been scared. He'd worried. He'd almost said no but Luke's next text had arrived. **Pussy?**

Tommy had laughed and known he couldn't back down. They'd talked about this day for months. So he had kissed his mom good-bye, taken his lunch and headed out as if he was taking the bus to school. Luke had picked him up in his older brother's truck at the corner, and they'd headed out of town.

Now as they sat on the dock jutting into the lake, neither one could have designed a more perfect day.

Tommy cast his line into the water. "What do you think those poor slobs are doing in school right now?"

Luke closed his eyes and tipped his head toward the warm sun. He'd wedged his pole between the open slats of the pier. "Staring at the clock and counting the seconds to the lunch bell."

Tommy laughed. "If they could see us now."

Luke's stomach grumbled as he thought about lunch. He'd already eaten the school lunch his mother had made and was ready for more food. "We should go get some burgers."

"God, man, we just got situated. Soon we'll be snagging fish."

Luke sat up and stared over the calm, clear waters of the lake. "We're gonna toss 'em back. Not like we could eat them."

Tommy turned the handle on his reel. "All you think about is food."

Luke shrugged. "And sex with Rene Rogers. God, what I wouldn't give to suck her tits."

Laughing, Tommy dug in his pocket for his can of dip. "I'd definitely pay money to see those tits. You think they're real or is she all padding?"

"My sister says they are real."

"Shit."

"Yeah. I know."

Tommy pulled a wad of tobacco out of the silver can and wedged it in the side of his cheek. He'd offered the can to Luke who did the same.

Minutes passed before Tommy reeled in his line a little more. This time it caught. "Hey, I've got something."

Luke yawned. "Catch the big one and toss it back, then we can go get something real to eat."

Tommy reeled the line in more, noting the heavy tension weighing the line. "Yeah, sure. Get off your ass and help me with this one."

Luke stretched his arms before reaching for the net, ready to scoop up a fish.

The fishing line bent and groaned and a couple of times Tommy had to release tension for fear it would snap. "This one has to be the granddaddy of all fish."

Luke's eyes snapped with more interest. "I heard there are twenty pounders in the lake."

"Cool. If I catch one."

Luke pulled his cell from his back pocket. "I'll take a picture and post it."

"Yeah. And every douche in the county will know we skipped."

"Good point. I'll post it on Saturday."

Tension stretched Tommy's line to snapping. "That's a plan."

Luke leaned over the dock and stared at the

end of Tommy's line, which pulled from the water as if an anchor were tied to it. "God, is that like the creature from the Black Lagoon?"

"Shit. I think you're right."

Luke watched Tommy struggle, and the fishing line growing tighter and tighter. "It can't be a fish."

"Maybe it's an old tire."

Tommy frowned. "I think I see something."

Luke stared at the surface and the black object rising toward it. He lay on the dock, his belly flat, as he reached for the object. His fingers brushed wet canvas. "It's a bag."

Tommy grimaced as he backed up, pulling the bag closer to the dock. "See if you can grab it."

Luke reached out and with long fingers grabbed a fistful of canvas and hauled the waterlogged bag to the dock.

Water gushed as Tommy unfastened his hook from the bag. "What the fuck?"

Luke's heart raced with excitement. "Think it's loaded with money or something?"

"That would be awesome. But it smells like shit."

"Nobody tosses a bag like this in a lake if they aren't trying to hide something."

"Like stolen money." His grin froze. "Or maybe it's a body."

Luke laughed. "Yeah, right. Shit, man, nobody tosses a body in Sweeney Lake. It's like the most suburban lake in the world."

His lips compressed. "Yeah, well who would toss money?"

"I don't know. But it's gonna be one bitching story either way."

Tommy set his rod aside and wiped his hands on his jeans. "Open it, and let's see."

"You open it."

"I caught it."

"I dragged it in."

Tommy shoved out a breath. "You're such a pussy." He knelt and reached for the zipper, only to discover it had been sealed with a plastic holder.

Luke pulled a knife from his back pocket. "Kinda drastic." With a flick of the knife blade he released the bit of plastic and unzipped the zipper.

Tommy peered in the bag for a split second before he recoiled. "Fuck!"

Luke leaned over his shoulder and looked. "Shit!"

Inside the bag was the headless torso of a woman wrapped in plastic. Her arms and legs were gone and her skin was a grayish white texture and she looked more like a prop from a horror film than anything close to human.

Both boys scrambled off the dock, each knocking into the other as they rushed toward dry land.

Tommy was breathing so hard he nearly hyperventilated.

Luke turned to his side and vomited up the lunch he'd just eaten.

Brody arrived at Sweeney Lake after one. Cop cars, lights flashing, crowded the open land around the lake and the dock had been roped off with yellow crime scene tape.

He was annoyed he'd been called away from his desk, where he'd spent the better part of the morning reading up on Dayton and digging into his past. He'd found nothing to link Smith and Dayton. Evidence didn't link the two killers but that didn't mean Dayton wasn't deadly. The Austin cops were certain he'd killed his wife, but just couldn't prove it.

Before he'd left Jo's early this morning, he'd made her promise she'd call if she saw Dayton. He didn't care how benign the circumstances. If she saw him, he wanted a call.

Brody put on his hat and moved across the open land toward Santos. "Why the call?"

Santos squinted as the sun bounced off the lake. "You said you wanted any information I could dig up about Dayton."

Behind Santos, attendants lifted a black body bag onto a stretcher. "You found Sheila Dayton."

A half smile that held no humor twisted the edges of his lips. "Looks like it."

"I heard all that the boys found was a torso."

"With a distinct tattoo on the right shoulder

blade. Twin butterflies and the initials SD."

"Sheila Dayton."

"They'll need to run DNA, but right now it's looking like we found her."

"She's been missing for two months."

"Vanished late February."

"Has anyone told Dayton?"

Santos shook his head. "I asked local PD to hold off making a notification. Thought we might want in on it."

Brody flexed the fingers of his right hand like he used to before a pitch. "I want in on it."

"Thought you might."

Brody drove to Dayton's office with Santos trailing behind in his own SUV. He'd been itching for a confrontation with this guy since last night. And as much as he'd like to take the guy apart, he would keep his cool. He owed it to Jo and Sheila Dayton.

He and Santos got out of their cars and entered the medical building. Dayton's office was on the third floor, and soon they stood in Dayton's office presenting their badges to the receptionist.

Dayton quickly emerged from an exam room. He wore suit pants, a white dress shirt with the sleeves rolled up and a loosened red tie. "Rangers. I can't say I'm glad to see you. Something tells me you don't have good news."

"Why would you say that?"

"Rangers don't make social calls."

"There a private place we could talk?" Brody said.

Dayton's face constricted with worry. "The conference room."

Under the watchful eye of the receptionist, Brody and Santos followed Dayton to a small consultation room. As plush as the rest of the office, it sported a long, mahogany conference table surrounded by a dozen upholstered chairs. A flat-screen television dominated the back wall and the sleek credenza under it displayed a crystal decanter and glasses.

"Let's have a seat," Brody said. He studied Dayton's body language, looking for the most basic signs of deception—a nervous flexing of the fingers, a shifting gaze, sweat, or rapid breathing. He saw none. Dayton was calm and composed.

Dayton's expression turned grim. "I'd rather stand."

If it had been anyone else Brody might have cut him or her some slack. The news he was about to deliver was a punch in the gut. But this son of a bitch had crossed the line when he'd shown a perverse interest in Jo.

Brody shot straight from the hip. "We found a torso today in Sweeney Lake. No head. No arms or legs. But the body sported a butterfly tattoo that was exactly like your wife's."

Dayton blinked before closing his eyes. He

fisted his hands at his sides as if he were trying to hang on to control. He met Brody's gaze. "All you have is a tattoo?"

"The medical examiner is running DNA tests today and we should have a solid answer soon. But the tattoo is distinctive."

Dayton pulled out a chair, sat and buried his hands in his face. "I was sure she'd be found alive. I thought she'd run away as she always did in the past."

Brody had seen lots of tears in his three years as a Ranger and DPS officer. Some had torn at his heart. Others had left him cold. Dayton's tears didn't stir a flicker of emotion. "When was the last time you saw your wife?" Brody asked.

At first Dayton acted as if he didn't hear, but he pulled a handkerchief from his pocket and dried his eyes. "I know you have to ask these questions. You are only trying to help Sheila. But right now I can barely think."

"You're gonna have to push yourself, Dayton."

He stared at Brody with red-rimmed eyes. "How long am I going to have to answer these questions? I've spoken to the police more times than I can count."

"I keep asking questions until the killer is behind bars."

"I told the cops about her mystery lover. He is the man you should be trying to find."

Santos pulled a notebook from his breast

pocket and flipped through notes. "According to you the man was a vagrant. African American. Over six feet. In his late twenties." Santos glanced up from his notes. "Austin PD never found anyone matching that description."

"That doesn't mean he wasn't out there." No hint of frustration or anger tinted the words, as if they'd been spoken and rehearsed too many times.

Brody shook his head, folding his arms over his chest. "Would have been nice to have found him."

"Would have been nice to have found my wife alive," Dayton snapped. "You two have made your death notice or whatever it is you want to call it. But I'm not up for another round of grilling. Not today. Not now. I need to grieve."

Brody clapped his hands. "That was a mighty fine performance, Dr. Dayton. Those actors in Hollywood ain't got nothing on you."

Dayton's eyes narrowed. "I don't like your tone, Ranger Winchester."

"Too bad, because it's gonna get a lot nastier. I'm not giving up the hunt until I prove you killed your wife."

Dayton raised his chin, his eyes narrowing. "I need to call my attorney."

"From what I hear, he didn't take you on. Didn't like the report on you. But there are lots of attorneys out there that aren't as particular about who they represent."

The mention of the *report* triggered a slight widening of Dayton's eyes. "I know how the cops work. You pick a suspect and rush in with blinders."

Brody pressed. "It's a matter of time before I prove your guilt."

Dayton's jaw tightened. "You can't prove what is not true."

"That report on you says you're capable of cold-blooded murder." He hadn't read it, of course. Jo wouldn't breach professional courtesy. But he wanted to push any button that might make Dayton lash out and say the unplanned.

Dayton's jaw tightened and released. "I won't be made a patsy because I'm convenient. Now if you don't mind, you need to leave the building."

Brody smiled. "I spoke to the medical examiner's technician on the scene. She figures whoever cut Sheila's arms and legs off used a hacksaw. The blade couldn't have been so sharp 'cause it tore the hell out of her flesh. The head, she figured, was hacked off with a hatchet." Brody shook his head. "Hell of a mess."

Dayton's face tightened. "Christ, man, don't you have a conscience?"

Brody unfolded his arms and absently slid his hand to his belt loop, inches from his gun. "When it comes to men who hack up women, my soul is blacker than coal."

Dayton's controlled expression slipped for a

moment, revealing raw anger and hatred. "Get out."

Brody smiled. "You haven't seen the last of us."

Santos shoved his notebook back in his pocket, his face a mask of controlled fury. "Don't know about you, Ranger Winchester, but I'm looking forward to catching this killer. This kind of hunt makes me hard."

Brody smiled. "I smell blood."

Dayton straightened. "If you think you are going to intimidate me, think again. I'll be lawyered up in the hour. I'll have you both brought up on conduct charges."

Both Rangers laughed and turned to leave.

Brody stepped back, stopped and retraced his steps back to Dayton. He lowered his voice so that not even Santos could hear. "If I hear that you go near Jo Granger or any of her family again, I'm coming after you."

Dayton's gaze reflected cold steel. "What's that pretty little liar saying about me now?"

Brody's teeth bared in a snarling smile. "I won't warn you twice."

Candace's hand trembled as she raised the cigarette to her mouth. She inhaled deeply, letting the smoke burn through her. She looked at the letter on the kitchen table. The neatly handwritten letter had come yesterday. It was from an attorney, and she'd had to sign for it. Now she regretted ever opening the envelope.

She rose, and from the kitchen cupboard pulled out a bottle of whiskey. She filled a coffee cup to the brim before taking a liberal sip. For over thirty years she'd been running from her past, doing her best to make up for her sins. Most days were filled with so much activity that she fell into bed at night exhausted. And most days she didn't think back.

Now her days of running were over. The past had caught up.

After Brody had left at sunrise, Jo had received a call later that morning from Rucker about the message she'd left on his phone last night. He'd been in surgery when Jo had called and not checked messages until the morning. He'd not been in her house. Was she all right? Did she need anything? She'd told him about Dayton and calling the cops. He'd listened quietly and told her he'd be keeping his phone close for the duration.

The next message on her phone had been from Ellie. She was home, safe and pissed. "Jesus, Jo, the first nice guy I meet in months and you have to ruin it. Shit, stay out of my life, okay?"

Jo stared in her bathroom mirror. She traced the line of her eyebrows, studied her nose in profile and peered into green eyes her mother always credited to her father.

"But which father?" she muttered.

She reached for the plastic DNA container,

pulled out the cotton swab and rubbed it against the inside of her cheek. Satisfied she'd collected enough cheek cells, she replaced the swab in its plastic holder and dropped it into the mailing envelope. One way or another she'd have her answers in a couple of weeks.

She turned from the mirror, dragging the packet with her. Minutes later, she was in her car and driving to the post office where she deposited the sample in the box. She had enough friends in the police department to get her DNA done locally and faster. But she didn't want to face the inevitable questions, and God help her if Smith was her father and the results leaked out.

Instead of heading straight to the office she decided to visit her mother at the salon. They'd been round and round about Smith for over a week, and Jo doubted she'd ever get a straight answer from her mother, who rewrote history at will. Despite that, Jo wanted to tell her mother about her choice to have her DNA tested. Candace would be angry. She'd accuse Jo of disloyalty. But the time for pretending was over.

Jo parked in front of the salon. Out of her car and across the lot she could see that the shop buzzed with chaos. The front lobby had seven or eight women sitting, some standing and all looking impatient.

The one time in her life she remembered the shop being in turmoil had been when the pipes had burst and flooded the place. It had taken two days to clean up the mess, but her mother had maintained a cool head, even setting up a tent in front of the store and cutting hair for her regular clients.

The bells above the door jingled when Jo entered. Her mother's station was vacant. Frowning, Jo made her way to her sister's chair.

Ellie rolled a strand of her client's hair onto a roller before she stepped away and said in a low voice, "And what the hell was that message about last night?"

"That guy you were out with is trouble. Stay away from him."

"I can take care of myself."

"Yeah, yeah. You told me." Impatience nipped at her. "Where's Mom?"

Ellie frowned. "She called in sick this morning. We're on our own all day."

"Sick?" Jo rattled her keys in her hand. "Mom is never sick."

"Hey, I know it better than anyone. We've been scrambling all morning to cancel her appointments and to take the ones we couldn't reach."

Worry tightened Jo's nerves. "Did you talk to her? Did you check to see how she is doing?"

"I took her call this morning. She said she was under the weather. Said she needed a day."

"Did she say specifically what was wrong?"

Ellie rolled her eyes. "I didn't play twenty

questions with her. She's entitled to a day off every twenty years."

Jo was not amused by Ellie's attempt at humor. "I'm going by her place."

Ellie whispered something in her client's ear before nodding for Jo to follow her into the back. When they were alone, Ellie said, "Why don't you butt out? I'm sick of you thinking you have all the answers. Christ, Jo, I can go on a date and Mom can take a day without you sounding a damn alarm bell."

Frustration scraped against Jo's nerves. "Ellie, I don't have time to get into a game of who is right and who is wrong."

As Jo turned to leave, Ellie hurried to block her path. "What's going on with you and Mom?"

"That's between us."

"Not when you upset her so much that she doesn't come into work. Then it's my problem." She dropped her voice a notch. "The truth is she's likely hung over this morning and not sick. I went by last night, and she'd had a few bourbons."

Jo frowned. "I thought her drinking was under control."

"What did you say to upset her?"

"My intent was not to upset her. I had some questions."

Ellie shook her head. "Shit, Jo, you been stirring the pot in this family since as long as I can remember."

"Excuse me?"

"You could never go along. You were always rocking the boat. The pageants weren't good enough for you. High school wasn't enough. Shit, you even messed it up so I couldn't compete in the Miss Texas pageant."

"How did I mess that up?"

"The year you got knocked up and miscarried. Mom and Dad covered your hospital bill. Ever wonder where the money came from?"

She'd been upset and so confused she'd never asked. "No."

"My pageant fund. I missed out that year."

Jo's bitterness rose up, choking off her breath. "Yeah, I screwed up. Big-time. But you make it sound like I went on a shopping spree. My life was in shambles, and I needed help."

Ellie's jaw set. "If you'd had more sense, we'd have all been better off."

Jo held up her hand. "I'm stopping this before we say something that can't be taken back."

Ellie's eyes narrowed. "Why? Maybe it's time you and I have it out."

"Over what?"

Ellie pulled a cigarette from her smock pocket and lit it up. "Over the fact that you've always looked down on this family. We were never good enough for you. Shit, it's like you were never one of us."

A hard lump settled in Jo's throat as unshed

tears burned behind her eyes. For a moment, she stared at her sister, too afraid to speak.

Ellie's gaze widened as if understanding dawned. "Jo. Does this have to do with Dad?"

Before Ellie could voice Jo's worst fears, she turned. "I need to go, Ellie."

Ellie hurried after Jo. "Look, I know I can be a bitch, but what I said. I didn't mean—"

"Of course you meant it. You've been thinking it for years. I have. And I know Dad did."

"Mom has her faults. But she wouldn't lie about that."

"Lie about what? My paternity?"

"Shit. Jo."

"This is between Mom and me."

"Do you really have to open that can of worms? It's not like you are a kid. And Dad is gone. What difference does it make?"

Jo moved toward the shop's back door and let it slam hard behind her as she strode out toward the alleyway and her car. She barely remembered the drive to her mother's house, a one-level rancher. Her parents had bought the place when she was six. When she'd been twelve and her dad had been hurt on the job and forced to take leave without pay, her mother had worked two jobs so they could hold on to the house. She remembered lying in bed at night while her sister slept, listening to her parents talking about their tight budget. Her mother had been a rock and told her dad that they'd find a way "together" just as they always did.

Jo knocked on the front door and when there was no answer, she used her key and let herself inside. "Mom!"

The house was as neat and organized as the salon. The couch was covered in plastic and doilies covered polished tabletops. On the wall were pictures of Jo and Ellie. When Jo had been six and Ellie two her mother had splurged on a professional portrait featuring all four Grangers. She and Ellie had worn matching blue sailor dresses, her mother sported a green dress, and her dad donned a suit he'd borrowed from the neighbor. Ellie sat in their mother's lap and Jo in her father's.

Ellie looked like a true blend of their folks whereas Jo's red hair and pale skin set her apart. She remembered when the picture had been taken. Her sister had loved preening and posing, whereas she could barely sit still. In fact, Jo could see now the way her right black patent leather shoe was angled up as if she were ready to jump out of her seat. Her mother had said many times that right after that picture was taken Jo had gotten up and said she wanted to leave. Only the promise of two extra stories at bedtime had lured her back.

She turned from the picture and headed to her mother's room. She pushed open the bedroom door and found her mother lying in her bed, curled on her side.

Jo moved to the bed and touched her mother's cheek. Cold to the touch. "Mom."

At first her mother didn't open her eyes, but when Jo called out "Mom!" she opened one droopy lid.

"Jo?" She sounded groggy and tired.

"Mom!"

Jo's alarm grew as she knelt by the bed. "Mom, what is wrong with you?"

Her mother looked at her through hazy, dazed eyes. "Jo?"

"Yes, Mom, it's me. What is wrong with you?"

Her mother scrunched up her face. "I'm sorry, honey. I'm sorry."

"What are you sorry for, Mom?"

Her mother's eyes drifted closed. Jo rose and scanned the nightstand and floor for pill and booze bottles. She had dealt with enough suicide attempts to recognize one when she saw it. As she reached for the phone she spotted the white envelope that had fallen between the side table and bed. She picked it up and immediately recognized Smith's handwriting. The letter began, *"Dearest Candy, It won't be long now before all your lies are exposed. May you rot in hell with me." Harvey Smith*

Hands trembling, she looked at the envelope. It had been sent from the attorney's office.

She reached for the phone on the bedside table and picked it up. No dial tone. A quick search and she saw that the line had been pulled from the wall. "Damn it, Mom."

She fished her cell out of her purse and dialed emergency services. As soon as she told the 9-1-1 operator what was happening and gave her mother's address, she hung up, kicked off her high heels and shrugged off her jacket. She tossed off her mother's comforter and pulled her mother's limp body into a sitting position. "Mom, what did you take?" Another visual search around the bedside revealed nothing, but her mother would have been the kind to toss away a bottle before its effects kicked into action. "Mom!"

She hefted her mother up on her feet. She dragged and pulled her toward the bathroom. "Mom, I need for you to wake up!"

Balancing her mother against the vanity, Jo turned on the cold water in the shower. She grabbed her mother by the arms, pulled her into the stall and dunked her head under the frigid water, which soaked Jo's blouse and hair and set her own teeth to chattering. Her mother's head rose, and she moaned her protest as the water drenched her hair and pajamas.

Her mother coughed and sputtered but her eyes did not open. "Come on, Mom, open your eyes. Nothing is so bad that you have to do this."

Her mother's head dropped limply to the side,

and Jo's own panic exploded. God, this could not be happening.

Outside, the distant wail of sirens grew louder and louder. And then she heard a loud knock on the front door. Jo eased her mother to the shower stall floor, shut off the water and ran to the front door and opened it. "My mother is in the bathroom. She's taken an overdose."

A tall, female paramedic with a wide face and dark hair bound in a ponytail glanced at her partner who rushed up to the house with a med kit in hand. "Do you know what she's taken?"

"I don't." She hurried toward the bathroom. "She's been on antidepressants since my dad died a few years ago. But I can't find the bottle."

"And you are her daughter?"

"Yes."

"I need for you to step back and let us work. Okay?"

Spouting facts was all Jo could think to do to help. "She's fifty years old. She has normal blood pressure and she drinks . . . sometimes too much. She does smoke. Works sixty-plus hours a week."

"We got this."

Caught in her own thoughts Jo didn't move as more inane facts sprung to mind. Her mother loved pink. Talked about gaining weight when she ate ice cream. Used to line dance but hadn't since her dad had died.

The paramedic checked her mother's pulse. "Out of the room now, ma'am."

Jo backed out of the room, barely noticing that her shirt and face were drenched from the shower. A cold chill settled in her bones, and her teeth chattered. She pushed the damp strands of hair from her face as she listened to the paramedics work on her mother.

What had Smith known that was so bad that her mother would try something like this? Could his letter and her questions really have pushed her mother to attempt something so drastic?

Her hands trembling, she went to the kitchen and opened the trash can lid. She dug through the rubbish, found an empty fifth of Scotch but didn't see a pill bottle. Frustrated, with nerves frazzled and strung tight, she upended the can, dumped it in the center of the kitchen and dug through the discarded cigarette cartons, yogurt containers and fried chicken scraps. At the bottom she found the bottle of tranquilizers. It was empty, and judging by the very recent date on the bottle, it had been nearly full.

She quickly replaced the trash in the can and washed her hands. As she hurried into the living room with the bottle, the paramedics wheeled her mother out of the bathroom, strapped to a gurney. Her mother's face, mouth and nose covered with an oxygen mask, was as pale as the sheets on the gurney.

Jo hurried to the female paramedic. "I found this in the kitchen."

The woman read the bottle as she pushed it in her coat pocket. "Good. That will help the docs."

"Can I ride with you?"

"No, ma'am. No civilians in the ambulance."

"Then I'm going to follow you."

"Yes, ma'am."

Jo retrieved her purse and phone from her mother's bedside and hurried to her own car.

A police officer was by the waiting fire truck. "Ma'am."

Jo clutched her keys in her fist. "I need to follow the ambulance."

"Can I get your name?"

"Jo Granger." The lights of the ambulance bounced off her windshield. "You can ask all the questions you like at the hospital. But I need to follow."

His gaze roamed over her wet hair and soaked shirt. "Are you fit to drive?"

"Yes. Yes, of course." It wasn't until she was behind the wheel of the car and caught her reflection in the rearview mirror that she understood the concern in the officer's voice. Her hair was plastered against her head and her mascara was running. She looked crazed.

Brody got the call from DPS patrol that Dr. Jo Granger had called in a 9-1-1 for her mother.

After he'd left Jo's house, he'd put the word out that if her name ended up in *any* report, including parking tickets, he wanted to know about it.

It took him less than twenty minutes to reach the hospital, park and push through the emergency room doors. His boots clicked, hard and purposeful, on the tiled hospital entrance floor. He stopped at reception long enough to introduce himself to the duty nurse and find out Mrs. Granger's status. Resting comfortably and her daughters were with her now.

He spotted Jo the instant he rounded the corner of the waiting room closest to Mrs. Granger's room. Jo leaned against a wall, her arms folded over her chest, her head cocked to the side as a tall blonde spoke angrily and waved her arms as she spoke. In contrast Jo was quiet, virtually emotionless, as she stood there and listened. He'd seen that same look on Jo's face before. It had been when she'd told him she was pregnant, and he'd lost his cool. At the time he'd thought she was cold and unfeeling, but now he could see the reaction was purely defensive.

He approached in time to hear the blonde say, "I blame you for this, Jo. If you'd left well enough alone she'd have been fine."

"If I'd left well enough alone, Ellie," Jo said evenly, "she'd be dead."

"Mom wouldn't have done this if you hadn't

pushed." Ellie's face wrinkled with anger. "It's all your fault."

Brody stepped up. "Jo."

At the sound of Brody's voice Jo looked up at him, relief and sadness flickering before she caught herself. "Brody. What are you doing here?"

His gaze was only for Jo. "Word gets around. I came to see how you're doing."

She offered a wan smile. "I'm fine."

"Jo's always fine," Ellie said. "It's our mother that's not fine and in the hospital bed."

Brody shifted his sharp gaze to the blonde. "I don't believe we've met."

Jo straightened. "I'm sorry. This is my sister, Ellie Granger. Ellie, this is Sergeant Brody Winchester with the Texas Rangers."

Ellie folded her arms over her chest. "This is a family matter, Ranger Winchester. I'm not sure why you feel like you need to be here, but I think it's best you leave."

Brody didn't budge. "If you would excuse us, Ms. Granger, I'd like to speak to your sister."

Ellie's gaze narrowed with such contempt that his ire bristled. "She's needed here."

Jo pressed her fingertips to her temple. "Mom is stable, Ellie. I can step away for a moment."

"Yeah, like always. Do what you want."

Jo stiffened and faced her sister. "Be quiet, Ellie. Be quiet and go sit with Mom. I'll be in soon."

When Ellie looked as if she'd protest, Jo's frown deepened. "Go."

After Ellie flounced back into the hospital room, Brody took Jo by the arm and guided her to a small waiting room. "Can I get you coffee or something to eat?"

"No, I'm fine. And I can't be gone from Mom long."

"Won't kill your sister to wait a moment or two. Tell me what happened."

Jo drew in a breath as if she were conjuring strength from thin air. "Mom tried to kill herself."

He'd only met Candace Granger once and that had been in the hospital right after Jo's miscarriage. Tense and emotional hadn't come close to describing their sole meeting. He'd offered to pay the hospital bills, but Candace had told him to get out of her daughter's life. She'd take care of Jo going forward.

"Did she leave a note?"

"No. And I had to dig through the trash to find the pill bottle. This was no idle attempt."

"Is this because of your questions about Smith?"

She fumbled in her purse and pulled out a crumpled letter. "I should have taken better care of this, but in the rush with Mom and the paramedics I didn't think."

The letter trembled in her hand. He took it.

"It's a letter from Smith. He found a way to get a letter to my mother."

He read the letter, his anger growing with each second.

"It makes no sense," Jo said. "Dad has been dead five years, and I wouldn't be the first child that found out her father wasn't her father. It would have been difficult but not life shattering."

Brody chose his words carefully. "There could be more between your mother and Smith."

"I thought about that, but I have no idea. If anything happened between them, she never breathed a word to anyone." She shoved out a breath. "And it takes a lot to rattle Mom. She's as tough as a rock." Her hands shook as she ran her hands over her hair. "What did Smith know?"

Unmindful of the nurses, doctors, their past or moving too fast, Brody pulled Jo into his arms. She didn't resist but relaxed into him, accepting his touch easily. "I'll get to the bottom of this, Jo. We'll figure out why your mother did this."

She sighed. "This isn't your problem, Brody. It's mine, Ellie's and Mom's."

He pulled her back and looked into her eyes. "I want to help, Jo. We're in this together."

Her brows furrowed as she searched his gaze. She didn't want to believe.

"That statement is a long time coming, Jo, but I mean it."

Tears welled in her eyes. She didn't speak but simply relaxed back into his embrace.

He tightened his hold, his mind quickly turning

to the problems circling around Jo. Dayton. Smith's apprentice. And the secret her mother believed unforgivable.

The cops had found Sheila's body.

Dayton dropped his gaze to his manicured fingers as he sat in the hospital coffee shop, his latte untouched. He ducked his head to the side as he saw Ranger Winchester stride out of the elevator toward the hospital's main exit.

Dayton checked his phone and noted the GPS tracker in Jo's car still placed her at the hospital. Good. At least she remained close by.

The cops would be turning the heat up on him soon, and he was a fool to follow Jo. But he couldn't let her go.

All his well-laid plans were unraveling, and he didn't know how to fix them.

Never in a million years had he thought Sheila would be found. He'd been planning her murder for months. He'd purchased supplies with cash in another town and scouted disposal sites. He'd been extra kind to her, especially in public.

And when she'd planned her trip to that expensive resort he knew his opportunity had arrived. On the premise of painting, he'd lined the den with plastic and unloaded cans of beige paint.

Bags packed and loaded, she'd moved to kiss him good-bye when he'd driven a knife into her chest. The look of pure astonishment and fear in her eyes had been thrilling. She'd clawed and kicked but he'd plunged the knife in again and again until her eyes had rolled back in her head and she'd stopped breathing.

He'd taken extra care to cut her body up into small pieces and load her into thick plastic bags, heavily weighted with rocks. He'd waited until midnight to row onto Sweeney Lake and dump the bags, including the canvas one that had held her torso.

Dayton could now see the lake was a bad choice. He should have put her deep in the ground. There'd have been no accidental discoveries if he'd buried her well below the earth's surface. But hubris had guided him to the lake. The lake. It would have been the last place Sheila would have gone because she'd hated the water. Feared it. But the final resting place was so fitting he couldn't resist.

Dayton traced his thumb over the flecked pattern on the café table. The cops had a body, but they didn't have a link between him and the day Sheila had disappeared. They could have all the theories in the world but without proof they didn't have anything.

Yet.

Winchester was smart. Like a dog with a scent he wasn't going to give up easily.

Panic rose in Dayton. He thought about his wife and all the trouble she'd caused him and the trouble she was still causing. So like Sheila not to do what was expected. All she'd had to do was stay at the bottom of that bloody lake.

Bitch deserved all that she got. If she walked in here today, alive and well, he'd kill her again. His fingertips trembled as he thought about squeezing the life from her. He balled his hands into fists and slowed his breathing.

Killing Sheila had been worth it, and if he were careful, he would get away with it all.

For now, he'd stay away from Jo Granger. As much as he wanted to follow her, to watch and to terrorize, he had to pull back. When the current situation cooled, he'd circle back. She was arrogant. Thought she knew all the answers. Like Sheila.

He'd enjoy watching her die.

Scott Connors shifted the gears of his Mercedes, grinding from second to third as he headed toward downtown Austin. Cursing, he shoved the gear into fourth and revved the engine. He was angry, upset and wanted a pound of flesh.

He had creditors up his ass. There was a repo man out there looking to take the Mercedes, and his credit cards were about at their limit. And to add a cherry on top of this pile of crap, his firm had fired him, by text, an hour after he'd left the office today. His boss's message had been terse and abrupt. You have been terminated. I'll deliver your belongings to your house. If you show up again at the office you will be arrested for trespassing.

He'd considered driving straight back to the office and having it out with his boss. The ass had no idea of the pressure he'd been under this last month. No, he'd not done a great job, but shit, he didn't deserve to be tossed aside.

As tempted as he was to go by the office, he kept driving. He didn't need the cops breathing down his neck. Between the local cops and the Rangers, he'd had no peace in weeks, and he knew they weren't finished with him yet.

How had his life gone to shit so fast? Two months ago, he'd been on top of the world. He had it all. And now Christa was gone. The job was gone. Dee still lingered around, but it now made him sick to look at her.

A red light ahead, he slowed and reread the handwritten note. *Police saying Dusty knows who killed Christa. Tall, red hair. Works Sixth and Congress.*

Scott shoved the paper in his pocket and studied the girls working on the street corner. First Hanna. Now Dusty.

A tall African American woman dressed in a leather skirt and halter top walked toward him. "Want to party?"

He couldn't manage a smile. "I heard from a friend Dusty is good."

She grinned as her eyes assessed. "Depends on what you want."

Nerves and anger clawed at his gut. "You Dusty?"

She offered a half smile. "Yeah, baby. I'm Dusty."

Scott pulled three hundred dollars from his coat pocket. "Heard good things about you."

Her grin softened. "Now you're talking."

"Get in."

Chapter Twenty

Thursday, April 18, 5:00 a.m.

Jo had been at her mother's side most of the night while Ellie had sat and finally dozed in the room's corner chair. The sisters had managed to suspend their anger for now. Ellie had gone to get coffee for both of them. But it was only a matter of time before the bell dinged, and they came out of their corners swinging.

Candace opened her eyes and for a moment stared sightlessly at the ceiling.

Jo sat forward in her chair, her gaze zeroing in on her mother. "Mom. Mom, can you hear me?"

Her mother turned toward her. Without makeup and her hair done, Candace looked a decade older. Jo had always figured her mother to be eternally young, but now could see that life's hardships

407

had left their mark. She smoothed her hand over her mother's hair. "Jo?"

"Hey," she said, forcing a smile. "You gave us a scare."

Her mother moistened her lips and closed her eyes. Failed suicide attempts often led to a deepening depression. More attempts. "I'm not supposed to be here."

Jo cupped her mother's hand. "I'm glad you are. I'd hate to lose you."

Candace shook her head. Tears rolled down her cheeks. "You don't know me that well."

Jo wiped the tears away with her fingertips. "Mom, don't worry about anything right now. I want you to get better and stronger so we can talk."

"Does Ellie know?" Her voice sounded hoarse and raw, a side effect of the tube the medical personnel had stuck down her throat to pump out the pills.

"Yes. She went to get coffee, but she'll be right back. She's as worried about you as I am."

Her mother shook her head. "I didn't want you girls to know. I wanted to leave."

Her mother's hand looked pale and fragile against her own. "Why did you want to leave us? What could be that bad?"

Candace swallowed and turned her head away from Jo. "I want to leave."

She straightened the covers over her mom. "I

saw the letter from Smith, Mom. I know he contacted you."

Her mother, her face still turned away, closed her eyes. She didn't speak.

"Mom, he sent me letters, too. They came a few days ago." She squeezed her mother's hands. "If it turns out he's my biological father I can survive that. I know you did what you did to protect me."

"Smith." She spoke the word as if it were a curse. "I regret the day I ever met that man."

Jo sat quietly by her mother's bed, letting the silence prod the story from her.

Candace let the breath trickle from her lips. "I was seventeen when I first met him. He was substituting in my high school. He was my English teacher." A bitter smile tipped the edge of her lips. "I thought he was so handsome. Dashing. And he made all those dry novels sound romantic. I couldn't stop thinking about him. I was dating your daddy at the time but I was taken with Smith."

"Smith would have been in his late thirties."

"That was part of his charm. So much older and knowing. Made the high school boys look foolish." She swallowed. "I made sure that Smith noticed me. I asked lots of questions in class, and I was always offering to help. He liked it when I wanted to help."

"How long did this go on?"

"Months. He substituted at the school from October until April. Your daddy noticed how much I talked about Smith. He was on the football team. Big, hulking boy. Strong as an ox. Not much sense, or so I thought. But he was smarter than I ever realized. When Cody said Smith was trouble, I wouldn't listen to him or my friends. I wanted what I thought was a real grown-up man."

"Smith."

"Yes. I heard Smith talking to another teacher about a party he was having. I asked my parents if I could go. Of course, they said no. I argued. They forbade me. Nothing tastes as sweet as forbidden to a wild teen girl." She moistened her lips as if parched.

Jo turned to the plastic pitcher by the bed and poured water into a matching cup. She put a straw in the cup and held it to her mother's mouth. Candace drank deeply.

When Jo had set the cup aside and leaned back, her mother continued. "I snuck out of my parents' house. I thought I was all grown up at seventeen. Thought I understood the world and how it worked."

Seventeen. A baby.

"When I saw him at the party he saw me immediately. He watched me as I talked to other people . . . men. Even in those days I looked mature for my age. Finally, when he could break away he motioned toward the kitchen. We met there, and he pulled me outside. The night was cold. And he took off his jacket and draped it on my shoulders."

"What happened?"

"He told me I was beautiful, and I fell for it all. I drank up his lies as if I'd been lost in the desert." She closed her eyes, but the tears spilled free. "He took me to his room that night. I was scared. But he kept asking me if I was as grown up as I claimed." Her mother swallowed. "In the morning before he woke up, I left and snuck back in my bedroom window. I never told anybody."

"Smith didn't let it go after the one night."

"No. He kept giving me looks at school. Kept telling me I was pretty when no one was looking. I snuck out with him a few more times." Candace cleared her throat. "I had no shame."

Jo sat silently for a long moment waiting for her mother to finish the story. There was more. There had to be. Finally, as gently as she could, she said, "What happened? How did it finally end between you two?"

She closed her eyes. "I'm tired."

"Mom, please tell me."

Her mother turned her face away from Jo. "Not now. I can't talk now."

The truth was but millimeters from her finger-tips and yet it remained out of her reach. "Was Smith my biological father?"

Her mother's head snapped back. Her gaze

blistered Jo. "Never use the word *father* and Smith in the same sentence. The man was a monster."

"What did he do to you?"

"Be grateful he is dead. Be grateful."

"Mom, you can tell me anything."

"I read all the newspaper stories about him. People tried to figure out why he did what he did. The truth was he didn't need a reason. He craved fear like a drunk craves booze." Her mother squeezed her hand. "I thought if I worked hard enough and was a good enough mother to you and your sister and a wife to your daddy, I could make up for that time. But I've never been able to work hard enough to forget."

Her mother wept, drawing herself up into a tight ball. What had happened? What had Smith done to her mother? As much as Jo wanted to push for answers, she knew they'd not come right here and now. Soon, she told herself. Soon her mother would release her terrible secrets. "It's okay, Mom."

Jo kissed her mother on her head and let her sleep. Out of the room and to the waiting area, she went and sat with her face buried in her hands. Her mother hadn't said the words but she knew. Smith was her father.

A solid night's sleep had calmed Dayton. He'd now realized how news of Sheila's death had left him frazzled. But this morning, he felt like a million bucks. As if he could tackle the world.

Dressed for a run, he cut through the kitchen and into the garage. He took two steps toward his car when he heard footsteps behind him.

He turned as the *pop, pop, pop* of suppressed gunfire ripped into his chest. For a moment, Dayton stared at the man, stunned, as a bloom of blood blossomed, a growing patch on his white shirt.

He stumbled back against his car. "What the hell?"

"I don't appreciate poachers."

Dayton listed sideways and slid down the side of his car. Blood oozed from the holes in his chest and pooled on the floor.

The man glanced at his gun. "I've always liked the .22. It's not expensive, easy to hide and not fancy. But low-caliber bullets can bounce around a man's insides like a Ping-Pong ball, tearing up organs and smashing bone. It's a good caliber."

Air bubbles gurgled from Dayton as he gasped for air. He was drowning in his own blood. Like Sheila.

"It won't take long." The man replaced the gun in his coat pocket. "And you aren't going to kill Jo Granger."

Dayton rolled on his side. He tried to claw his way across the cement garage floor but he couldn't summon the air to move. "Why?"

The man smiled. "You've been watching Jo Granger. And you're smart enough to get around the law. I see the way you look at her. You want to kill her. Like you killed your wife."

Dayton swallowed. "No."

He smiled. "Just us here now, Dayton. No need to lie. You want to kill her. But you're not going to. I am."

Knowing Jo would be at the hospital all night and safe, Brody had spent most of the night watching surveillance footage of Hanna's street corner. He'd caught images of "Robbie" but nothing concrete. He was determined to find the needle in this wretched haystack.

He'd taken a break after dawn to go home, shower and grab a quick bite before heading to the hospital to see Jo. He found her in the waiting room, alone, her eyes closed and her head tipped back against the wall.

"Jo," he said.

She opened her eyes immediately and looked up at him. She stood and he pulled her into his arms. She clung to his shirt.

"How's she doing?"

Jo nestled close to him. "She's going to be okay. Physically."

He stroked her hair, savoring the soft scents. "Did she say why?"

Jo hesitated a moment. "Something happened

between my mother and Smith, but she won't tell me. I asked her again if Smith was my father but she wouldn't answer."

Silence stretched between them. "Biology doesn't change anything, Jo."

She searched his gaze. "It can be a huge predictor."

He stroked the hair off her face. "Jo, you are a good, kind woman. You are not him."

"I know."

"Do you?"

"I know." She sighed. "I just want all the missing pieces to come together. Mom's not telling me everything."

"What could she be holding back?"

"I don't know. But I'm thinking it's pretty awful."

Brody hated leaving Jo at the hospital, but she'd insisted she'd be fine, and she needed to spend more time with her mother.

Now he sat at his desk and pushed yet another surveillance disk CD into his computer. The tapes were taken from the store that overlooked Hanna's street corner.

A dark Mercedes pulled up to her street corner, and she walked over to the window. She was smiling as the driver leaned toward her. And then her smile vanished, and she stepped back from the car door. A male driver got out of the car. He flipped a dark hoodie over his head as he hurried toward Hanna. He pulled money from his pocket and tried to shove it in her hand. For several tense seconds they stood, his arms wrapped around hers. She took the money and got into the car.

He closed her passenger door and hurried to the driver's side.

"Turn around, you son of a bitch." From this camera angle, Brody had never seen the man's face before he drove away with Hanna.

Brody popped the disk out and searched his stack, finding the footage from a camera mounted at a light two blocks away. He loaded the disk, tapping his fingers on the desk as he waited for the image. He fast-forwarded to the moments where the other tape stopped.

The Mercedes stopped at a light. And this time he could see the driver's face. In that instant, the camera caught him in profile.

There was no mistaking the man's identity.

Scott Connors.

Brody and Santos quickly discovered that Connors had been fired yesterday. He'd not only missed huge blocks of time in the last five weeks, but he'd screwed up several key stock trades.

At Connors's apartment, he didn't answer the front door. Brody called the landlord who promised to be right up.

Minutes later, a tall, lean man with a white shock of hair fumbled through a ring of keys as he walked up the steps to Connors's apartment. "Connors owes me a couple of months' rent. He kept saying, 'Once I get married I'll settle my debt.' But then that girl vanished. He kept promising she'd be back. When she turned up dead, he didn't have any more excuses. I served him with eviction papers two days ago."

The landlord opened the door. "Technically the place belongs to me again. So have at it."

"Thank you, sir," Brody said.

"Mr. Connors," Brody shouted. "Texas Rangers. Mr. Connors, are you here?"

No answer.

Santos shook his head. "This is not right."

"No, it is not." Brody walked into the living room.

Pizza boxes and empty Chinese takeout cartons were scattered over the living room coffee table and the floor. A kitchen trash can overflowed with beer cans. The place smelled of stale air and spoiled milk.

Brody flipped on the kitchen light switch. A large, square fluorescent bulb flickered but didn't fully illuminate. "What happened to the furniture?"

"Taken back," the landlord said. "All rentals."

Santos wrinkled his nose. "I don't remember it being so rank last week."

Brody looked back at the landlord. "Thank you, sir. We'll take it from here."

The older man nodded. "Let me know if you need anything."

After Brody closed the door behind the landlord, he looked at Santos. "He's coming apart."

"World's caving in fast."

Brody moved through the living room, now furnished only with an old television and a couple of lawn chairs. The bathroom looked as if it hadn't been cleaned in weeks.

The Rangers moved to the single back bedroom and flipped on the light. A mattress on the floor and a single floor lamp furnished the room.

Brody spotted a pile of papers on the floor by the bed and moved toward them. They were newspaper articles. Brody immediately recognized Christa's smiling face. Above the picture was the headline: MISSING FIFTEEN DAYS.

He pulled rubber gloves from his back pocket. Once gloved, he picked up the top article. The next several pieces concerned Christa. Below Christa's articles were several on Sheila Dayton.

"His fiancé vanishes and he collects articles about another missing woman."

"Did the local PD vet this guy?"

"They did, thoroughly. He has no record. And I know this place has been searched." Brody flipped over the next article and saw the name *Hanna* written in bold ink on an Austin Realty sticky.

"Look at this. Hanna. We never released her name to the media."

Santos studied the room's bare interior. "He was marrying Christa for her money. Why kill her? Her death left him high and dry," Brody said.

"Smith was dying. Robbie was running out of time if he wanted to prove himself to his father. If Connors is Robbie, then he realized he couldn't wait for the wedding."

"He gives up a big payout to please Smith."

Brody flipped through the articles. The last concerned Smith and his death. The article detailed Smith's dark past and his battle with cancer.

"He'd be about the right age for Robbie. Height and build also fit," Santos said.

"How far did local police dig into his past?"

"Fifteen years."

"Maybe not far enough." Something about all this did not feel right. "Smith was smart as hell. Always thought steps ahead of the cops. That's why he was hard to catch. Doesn't make sense that he trains a guy who leaves a stack of incriminating articles behind. Seems he'd have done a better job of coaching his successor."

Brody and Santos found Christa's sister, Ester, at the elementary school where she worked. She taught first grade.

The Rangers stood by their Bronco, waiting for

the kids to file in for morning assembly. Half a dozen young boys walked up to Brody and Santos. The shortest of the group pushed through his friends to face Brody.

The kid glanced back at his friends and then squarely at Brody. "Are you a Ranger?"

Brody touched the tip of his hat. "Yes, sir, I am."

Excited whispers spread through the boys. "Are you here to arrest a bad guy?"

Brody kept his expression stoic. "Not arresting anyone today, pardner. Here to have a look around."

"There's a fifth grader who likes to take my lunch. I don't like him."

Brody didn't dare glance at Santos, fearing he'd smile. He cocked a brow. "That so?"

The boy nodded. "His name is Colin. We figured you were here to arrest him."

"Not here for Colin today but"—he pulled a notebook from his vest pocket—"I'll make a note of it."

"Good. It's Colin Bainbridge. He has red hair and lots of freckles."

"Got it."

The boy smiled. "Thanks."

"If I don't catch up to him," Brody said, his expression stern, "you tell him Ranger Brody Winchester was asking after him." He handed the boy his card. "In case he doesn't believe you."

The boy's eyes narrowed. "Will do."

Brody and Santos found Ester Bogart's room easily. She was writing the morning assignment on the board as the children put their lunches and books in cubbies.

"Ms. Bogart?"

The woman turned, her smile dimming when she realized it was the law. She met them at the doorway and escorted them to a teacher's lounge where they could speak in private. "I'm sorry. I don't have much time. The bell is ringing soon. Did you find Christa's killer?"

"We're working on it, ma'am," Brody said.

She set down her eraser and folded her arms over her chest. "What do you need to know?"

The weariness in her voice testified to the number of times she must have been interviewed about Christa's disappearance and death. "When is the last time you saw Scott Connors?"

Surprise flashed in her gaze. She'd not expected that question. "The day of Christa's funeral."

"You two walked arm and arm out of the church that day."

A crease in her brow deepened. "We had lost the most of anyone in the room. We understood each other."

"I hear you weren't too fond of Scott when Christa dated him."

"I didn't like him. I thought he was after her money. Christa was to have taken control of her trust on her wedding day. It's a substantial sum. I told her to keep that detail to herself, but she wasn't good about that. When she vanished he was devastated. And he and his friends organized the *Find Christa!* campaign. It was clear he was devoted to her. After the funeral all he could talk about was finding her killer. Tim and I tried to talk to him but he wouldn't listen."

"Did he mention he was leaving town?"

"No." Her brow wrinkled. "In fact, he and I were supposed to have dinner tonight."

"That so?"

Color rose in her cheeks. "We're really good friends. We get each other. The loss of Christa, I mean. We're friends."

Santos studied her. "But you'd like it to be more."

Her fingers tightened around her arms. "No! I mean I like him, but I get that he loved my sister."

Santos shifted his stance. "I heard you two fought before the funeral. He wanted her cremated."

She lifted her chin. "I convinced him it was better for Christa if she was at rest with our parents."

"How much money are you worth now that Christa is dead?" Brody said.

"It's not like that." Her words sounded clipped, angry. "I can't believe you are asking me these questions. I loved my sister."

Brody shook his head. "Never said you didn't."

"What is your point?"

"Have you ever been by Scott's apartment?" Brody said.

She frowned. "No."

"We found articles in the back bedroom of the house."

Her hand rose to her slender neck. "What kind of articles?"

"Articles that dealt with Christa's disappearance along with articles on Harvey Smith."

She shook her head, her lips flattening into a frown. "I'm not sure what you are getting at."

"We've not released it to the media, but there was another woman buried like Christa. Surveillance tapes show this last victim getting into his car the day she vanished."

Her face paled. "No."

"Is there anything you're not telling me about Scott?"

"No. I don't think so."

"He ever tell you anything about his past?"

"His mother died when he was young. Christa told me she tried to talk to him about his childhood, but he was always guarded about it. He prided himself on being a self-made man."

Muscles in the back of Brody's neck tightened. "Where is he, Ms. Bogart?"

"I don't know. Like I said, I haven't seen him since the funeral. Have you checked his work?"

"He was fired yesterday. And the GPS on his car and phone aren't working."

Her shoulders slumped, as if the weight of the news was too much for her. "I don't know. I don't know. He always seemed to care about Christa."

Brody pulled his card from his pocket and handed it to her. "You call the instant you talk to him or see him, you hear me?"

She accepted the card, nervously flicking the edges with her fingertip. "Did he kill Christa?"

Brody rested his hands on his hips. "I don't know anything for sure yet, ma'am. But he is number one on my list of people to talk to."

Two years of thinking and planning and the pieces were coming together for Robbie. Smith had taught him how to plan dozens of steps ahead and it was finally paying off.

Chapter Twenty-One

Friday, April 19, 9:00 a.m.

Jo yawned as she leaned over the kitchen counter, her chin resting on her hand as the coffee machine dripped out her third cup of the day. Her head pounded and her eyes were bloodshot. She couldn't put in her contact lenses. She'd been with her mother all night and had hoped to coax out more information. She thought once or twice her mother might talk to her but her sister had returned and her mother shut down completely. Her sister had stayed through the early morning hours until their mother had fallen into a deep sleep. Both sisters, at the urging of the nurses, had left just before dawn.

The coffeepot stopped gurgling, and she poured herself a cup, hoping the caffeine kick would get her through the day. She'd finish her coffee. Shower. There'd be paperwork to do at the office for a couple of hours. Shift appointments. Postpone meetings. By noon or one she could get back to the hospital if she hurried.

Her doorbell rang. Annoyed by the unexpected, she took another gulp of coffee, set the mug down and went to the front door. She peered through the peephole and saw her sister standing on her front porch.

Jo groaned. She needed coffee before getting into round two with her sister. She unlatched the door and opened it. "Is Mom okay?"

"Just called the hospital. She's resting comfortably." Her sister came in as if she owned the place. "I smell coffee."

"Made a fresh pot. Would you like a cup?"

"God, yes. But I can't stay long. I've got to get to the salon and get ready for the day." Ellie followed Jo into the kitchen.

"Can you manage the place by yourself?"

"With my eyes closed. I've been working in the place since I was twelve. I'd go back to the hospital, but I know Mom will rest easier if the shop is taken care of."

Jo poured Ellie a cup of coffee and handed it to her. She dug sugar out of the cabinet and milk out of the refrigerator. Ellie liked her coffee sweet and cut heavily with milk.

While her sister doctored her cup, Jo sipped from her own cup. There'd been a strained truce between Jo and Ellie at the hospital in the early hours but she suspected Ellie was here to finish the argument.

Ellie took a long sip of coffee. "I was a bitch yesterday. I was freaked out about Mom and was still mad about the stuff you'd said about Aaron."

A heavy weariness settled on her shoulders. "My intent was to protect you from him."

Ellie frowned into her cup. "I've called him several times since we talked, but he's not answered. I did a little digging on him. Didn't take much. The story of his wife is everywhere."

"He's not a good man, Ellie."

"I really feel stupid now, Jo. And when I think about our date I realize he was kinda creepy. I brushed it off. Bad habit of mine."

"What did he say?"

"He railed on about his wife, but a lot of guys bitch about their wives." She sipped her coffee. "But then he said he hoped wherever she was that she was happy. Maybe near water because she loved the water."

Jo remembered from Sheila's file that she'd hated the water. She couldn't swim and was terrified. And yet she'd been found in water. "I'm sorry."

Ellie released a sigh as if letting go of a dream. "What's the deal with you and Mom? And please, Jo, don't bullshit me. I know there is something simmering between you two."

"Honestly, Ellie, I don't know what exactly is going on." She thought about Smith's letter and wondered if he'd written it or if Robbie had made another forgery.

"Shit, Jo, I hate being on the outside of this."

"When I know the whole story the three of us will talk."

Ellie set her cup on the counter hard. Coffee splashed on her hands. "Mom tried to kill herself yesterday. Mom, the-rock-of-all-rocks, cracked. You must know what is going on."

"I thought I knew, but I don't have the whole picture."

"If there was a big problem, Mom would tell you. She always talked to you about money matters, Daddy's estate . . . big picture. Our conversations go as deep as perms and hair dyes. But you two. There's always been a kind of respect. You may drive her crazy, but she respects you."

Jo grabbed a paper towel and handed it to Ellie. "You're more like her than you realize. I'm like Dad. I'm easily fooled. Not you or Mom."

Jo sighed. "When Mom opens up . . ."

Ellie shook her head. "You'll keep me out of the loop like always. Big picture Jo. Little picture Ellie. I am not stupid, you know."

"I never said you were."

"Not with words but your actions. I can handle what Mom is going through."

"I don't know what it is exactly."

Colorful bracelets jangled on Ellie's wrist as she threaded her fingers through her hair. "I may not have a huge IQ but I saw things when I was a kid."

Jo remained silent, not sure if she could speak without betraying emotion.

"I know Mom wanted you in pageants and you hated it. I know you'd try to talk to Dad about a book you read or something you learned. He'd listen and be patient. But he never got it. Never got you."

"Mom thought the pageants were my ticket to success. And Dad, he was tired after a long day."

"It was more than that, and you know it. She didn't push the pageants for you because it was a ticket to success. It was like she was trying to mold you, change you from a brain child into a beauty queen." She shook her head. "I'm sorry I said you weren't one of us. You are totally us."

"Thanks."

"I tried to imagine what it would be like for me if both our parents were like you."

"Like me?"

"An egghead." Her brow rose at Jo's frown. "What? It's the truth. You'd rather read a book than get your hair done. God, I can't imagine a life where I was forced to study all the time."

Her sister's backhanded compliment made Jo smile.

"I'm not as smart as you, Jo, but I'm not stupid. I get that you were out of sync with the family." She hesitated. "Is Dad your biological father? Is that what this is all about?"

Jo stilled, fearful the smallest change in her facial expression would reveal her own worries.

Ellie sighed. "It's not the first time I've thought it. Only seven months separate their wedding date and your birthday."

Jo folded her arms over her chest. "We shouldn't have this conversation without Mom."

Ellie planed her hands on her narrow hips. "Can't you take the shrink hat off for a moment and tell me?"

"I can't talk about what I don't know. Mom is holding a secret, but I don't know what it is. I swear to you, I don't know what it is."

The tension in Ellie's body eased. "I can't believe a paternity test would freak her out like this. Even if Dad were alive, she'd have figured a way around it. She could make him believe anything."

"Whatever she's facing now is not easily dismissed."

Ellie nodded. "We can figure this out together. We can double-team Mom."

Jo smiled. "I don't think we should push hard right now. But we need to encourage her to talk."

"Understood." She pointed a manicured finger at Jo. "But don't shut me out, Jo. Let me help you and Mom. Troubles and all, we are all each other has."

"I know. I know. And when Mom is ready to tell us what drove her to this, I'll encourage her to include us both."

"Thanks." Ellie hugged Jo. "I need to head to the salon. I plan to go back to the hospital around noon."

"Me too." Jo squeezed Ellie close.

"See you then?"

"Yes."

"Okay."

Jo walked her sister to the door and hugged her again before she watched Ellie head to her car. She waved good-bye and closed the front door.

She'd returned to the kitchen, finished her coffee and poured what remained of Ellie's coffee down the sink. She'd wiped up the counter when the doorbell rang. *Ellie. What have you forgotten?*

Jo did a quick sweep for Ellie's bejeweled purse, glasses or wallet but she didn't see anything.

Jo hurried to the front door, anxious to deal with Ellie and get into a hot shower. Her muscles ached and her head throbbed. She opened the door.

Immediately a blast of a foul-smelling mist struck her in the face. She squinted her eyes, rubbing them as they burned. She coughed and staggered back as she stared through the blinding haze to the person at the door.

Strong arms gripped her. The front door slammed closed, trapping her inside with her attacker. Jo, blinded by the spray and eyes burning, kicked and blindly lashed out, hoping to do some kind of damage. Once or twice she heard a grunt but her attacker recovered from her assaults.

He hit her hard across the face and she stumbled back against the wall. Blood trickled from a gash on her lip.

He jerked her forward and as she opened her mouth to scream he pressed a cloth soaked with chloroform over her face. She scraped her fingers over his hands. He grunted and responded by pressing the rag tight against her face. The chemical smells burned up her nose and quickly her head swam. Her world went dark.

Brody's phone buzzed, and he picked it up on the second ring. "Winchester."

"Officer Raynor with DPS. I have orders to contact you if Dayton crossed our paths."

Brody checked his wristwatch. One o'clock. "That's right. What has he done?"

"Got himself killed."

Brody stiffened. "Say again."

"Dayton's body was found in his garage. He had three shots to the chest."

This was the last bit of news he'd expected. "When was he found?"

"Three hours ago. The medical examiner's assistant has already cleared the body for transport. It should be in the ME's lab within the hour."

Brody rubbed the back of his neck with his hand, annoyed that it had taken this long for him to be notified.

"Any witnesses?"

"None. A neighbor noticed his garage door was open. He went to investigate and found Dayton dead."

"Thanks." Brody hung up and immediately dialed Santos. He explained what had happened and asked Santos to get a copy of Dayton's phone records.

"Consider it done."

Brody leaned forward in his chair, a theory prowling in the back of his mind. "Be on the lookout for calls to Connors."

"Connors?"

"Dayton was stalking Jo."

"And Smith's apprentice, a.k.a. Connors, didn't like the fact that Dayton was messing with her."

"I think in an odd way Robbie/Connors thinks he's protecting Smith's legacy by protecting Jo."

"Robbie/Connors shoots Dayton."

"Fits." Brody rubbed the back of his neck with his hand. "But don't limit your search to Connors. I want to know of any connection Dayton might have had to any specific person that doesn't make sense."

"I'll get right back to you."

Brody spent the next hour calling contacts, trying to track Connors, but the more calls he made, the more frustrated he became. It was as if Connors had fallen off the face of the earth. He'd not used his cell and his credit cards had showed no activity. An attempt to ping and locate his phone had failed. Connors had switched it off.

After he hung up he dialed Jo's cell. It went straight to voicemail. No doubt she was at the hospital. He thought about driving over there, but decided to give it a few more hours. Seeing him would spike Candace Granger's blood pressure.

April knocked on Brody's door after three. "Your sketch is ready."

He shook his head, annoyed that he'd forgotten about the age progression. He rose from his chair and came around his desk.

April opened a file full of computer printout forms. "I plugged in all kinds of variables. Twenty years can change a person a lot of ways depending on their habits."

"Let's assume he was disciplined and stayed trim and fit. His mentor would have drilled that kind of behavior into him, so it makes sense he'd have held on to the habits."

She shuffled through several pages. "Here is your Robbie, provided he lived a clean life and didn't have any major reconstructive surgeries."

Brody studied the picture. He recognized the guy instantly. "Shit."

Jo's head felt as if it had been stuffed with cotton and her mouth was so dry she thought her tongue had swollen. She drew in a breath and tried to lift her head but found the slightest movements made her head throb.

Groaning, she rolled on her side, aware that she lay on the damp ground. Opening her eyes, her vision filled with the view of freshly tilled soil.

Tilled soil. Her mind jumped to Christa. And Hanna. Buried alive.

Her heart kicking into high gear, she pushed through the pain and forced herself to sit up. The sun burned bright and hot, scorching the barren horizon. The surrounding land was covered in brush and low-lying trees. Crickets sang. A coyote howled. She appeared miles from any permanent structure.

As she shifted, she heard the clink of a chain and felt the pinch of metal against her skin. Wrapped around her ankle was an iron manacle and chain tethered to a tree.

Panic rising, Jo grabbed at the manacle and tried to pry it free from her ankle. It held fast, scraping her fingertips and breaking her nails. She jerked at the chain but it held firm.

"Help!" she screamed over and over, her head splitting with each syllable.

In the distance an owl hooted. But no human responded back to her. She was alone. Chained.

Brody, Santos and a dozen DPS officers converged on the one-story rancher located at the end of the cul-de-sac. Lights flashing, weapons drawn, the Rangers approached the house with the neatly manicured lawn.

Brody knocked on the door, and when there was no answer, he ordered the uniforms with the battering ram to take down the door.

Inside the house, he reached for the light switch but found that it didn't work. He held up his flashlight and searched the living room furnished with a neat modern sofa, a couple of chairs and a television. Curtains covered what looked like a patio door, and the shag carpet looked smooth and even as if it had been vacuumed.

Flashlights and guns drawn, the cops moved into the house, searching every room and closet. Every few seconds someone would yell, "Clear!"

Finally an officer shouted, "Found the electric box." A click of the circuit breaker and the lights in the room snapped on.

Brody stood back and surveyed the room, which was as neat and clean as the lawn. On the mantel above a scrubbed fireplace rested a collection of photos. All were of Robbie and Smith. The photos were organized in chronological order with the last photo snapped about ten years ago, shortly before Robbie's falling-out with Smith.

On the end table was another picture. One glance at it and rage overtook Brody. Jo was in the picture wearing a *Find Christa!* T-shirt and standing next to her was Robbie, a.k.a. Tim Neumann.

Santos came up behind Brody. "What the fuck is he doing with Jo?"

Brody dug his cell from his pocket and dialed dispatch. "Send officers to Jo Granger's house, and if they don't find her there, go to her office or any place she might haunt. No one rests until she is found."

Brody studied the picture more closely. Jo was smiling at the camera whereas Tim was staring at her. The apprentice and the master's daughter. He thought about the forged letters found on Jo's front porch. They'd been dusted for prints but were clean, whereas the box of cards held by the attorney had been covered in Smith's fingerprints. Robbie had gone to a lot of trouble to communicate with Jo.

His stomach curled. "What better way to best the master than to kill the daughter?"

Brody's phone rang. "Sergeant Winchester." As he listened to the voice on the other end of the line his scowl deepened. "What do you mean her door is open? Go door-to-door. Find me any witnesses."

He snapped the phone closed and glared at Santos. "Jo's neighbor found her front door open and her cats wandering around."

Brody moved quickly to his vehicle and slid inside. Gripping the wheel, he fired the engine and shoved his foot into the accelerator. Dirt and gravel kicked up. "She never lets those cats out. She's in trouble." He shook his head. "It's Robbie. Tim. Whatever the hell name he's using. Smith's apprentice had gone after Jo."

Santos swore. "The ultimate prize in his mind?"

"He always wanted Harvey's approval. Maybe he figures he can really win it by reuniting father and daughter." Brody picked up his phone and dialed another number.

"Where the hell did he take her? We ran a property search, and this is the only place that surfaced."

"He's a Realtor and has access to dozens of properties."

"I'm betting this place is special. Where he has a connection to Smith."

Frustration ate at him. They had so many pieces to pull together and so little time. "I don't know. But there might be someone who does."

Chapter Twenty-Two

Friday, April 19, 5:00 p.m.

Brody shoved out a breath as he moved to the nurse's station at the hospital. He'd been calling Jo for the last couple of hours and no answer. So he'd come to the hospital looking for answers. He flashed his badge at the station, got Candy's room number and knocked briefly. When he heard a clear "Come in," he entered to find Ellie sitting at Candy's bedside.

The Candy he remembered had been a formidable woman. She'd been tough as nails and had sworn up and down she'd skin Brody alive if he ever came near Jo again. He'd backed off, expecting that once Jo healed they could talk. Candace had seen to it that they never did.

The woman before him now wasn't the woman who'd faced him down fourteen years ago. Without makeup and with her hair brushed flat against her head, she looked broken and years older.

Pushing aside whatever resentments he had or didn't have for Candy, he pulled off his hat. "Mrs. Granger, I am—"

She sat up a little straighter. "I know who you are. You look exactly the same."

Ellie rose. "You're Brody Winchester. Jo's ex."

"That's right."

"What do you need, Mr. Winchester?" Candace asked.

He kept his gaze on her. "I'm looking for Jo."

"She isn't here. Hasn't been all day. I thought maybe you'd pulled her into another case."

His stomach knotted. "She hasn't been with me, and she's not been at work."

Ellie flexed her fingers at her side. "It's not like Jo to flake. She always calls. Kinda OCD that way. What's going on?"

"That's what I'm trying to figure out." He shifted his gaze back to Candy. "I need to know what you know about Smith."

The older woman lowered her gaze. "I don't know what you are talking about."

Brody cursed, knowing there was no time for gentle coaxing or hand-holding. "Smith had an apprentice. A kid named Robbie who we believe now goes under the name Tim Neumann."

Candace's lips flattened. "I don't know the name."

Brody advanced on the bed, looming over her. "I think Robbie has Jo."

The old woman's eyes widened and filled with tears. "Why would he care about her?"

"Because Smith believed she was his daughter." Ellie laid her hand on her mother's shoulder. "Time to stop hiding, Momma. Tell what you know."

Candace's pained gaze shifted to her daughter. Her fingers held a white-knuckle grip on the sheets. "You will hate me, Ellie."

Ellie sat in the chair by the bed so she could be eye level with her mother. "I won't hate you, Mom. But you must talk. Is it that Smith is Jo's real daddy?"

Candy closed her eyes. "No. It's not that."

"What is it, Momma?"

"When I met Smith I was seventeen. I thought he was the best man in the world. He listened to me. Told me I was beautiful. We started sneaking around."

"You were dating Daddy then?"

"Yes. I thought I loved Cody until I met Smith. Smith made me see your daddy as small town and simple."

Ellie frowned but didn't say anything.

"I got in Smith's truck and thought I was headed to a great adventure." She shook her head. "It wasn't a great adventure but a horror show."

"What happened?" Brody said.

"We drove for a half hour outside of Austin toward the hill country. Lots of twists and turns. He took me to a field of bluebonnets. Smith kept saying how much he loved bluebonnets." Her chin trembled. "But to this day I can see the road signs as clear as day in my head. What he had to show me made me sick."

"What was it?"

"A woman. He'd tied her up and had her lying in a hole in the ground. He told me he had always dreamed of burying a woman alive. He'd wanted to share that dream with me because he loved me." She squeezed her eyes closed, as if trying to block the memory.

"What next?" Brody said.

Ellie squeezed her mother's hand tighter. "Mom, please tell."

"I was upset. I threw up right there. The girl was squirming and trying to scream. There was such terror in her eyes." She shook her head. "Smith just laughed at her and me. He picked up a shovel and tossed dirt on her."

"Did he bury her?" Brody asked.

Candy shook her head. "God help me, I don't know. I ran to the truck and started the engine. I backed out of there. Smith was yelling and chasing after me. I drove as fast as I could. Ditched the car in town and ran to your daddy's house. He could see that I was scared, and he took me in his arms right away. I'd been so hateful to him for weeks but he took me in his arms and told me everything would be all right. I was sorry for all the bad thoughts I'd had for him."

"You married Granger soon after?"

She moistened her dried lips. "Days later."

"You were pregnant with Jo when you married Daddy," Ellie said.

"Yes." Candy looked at Ellie. "I told your daddy the truth about the baby. I never lied to him. But he said he'd marry me anyway. I saw what a good man I had in him. I'd been such a fool. We swore we'd never speak to Jo about her real daddy."

"What about the girl in the grave?" Brody said.

"Cody said we had to go back and see. He gathered some of his buddies from the football team and we all rode out there that night. We found the hole in the ground but no girl. I prayed she got away." She closed her eyes. "I can still see her."

Brody thought about the unidentified woman who'd been found with the others. She'd been buried thirty plus years. "Did you know the name of the woman in the ground?"

"Delores Jones. She lived in town. Worked in a bar."

Delores. Mentioned in the letter. "And Smith?"

"I never saw him again. Until the pageant when Jo was twelve. When I saw him, I just about threw up. I ran from the room but when I came back, he was gone."

"Where was the land Smith took you to all those years ago?"

She gave him the directions, not missing a beat. "I tried to forget where that terrible place was but I couldn't forget."

"Your memory might save Jo."

Jo wasn't sure how long she lay on the dry ground but she guessed it had to be hours. Her skin had grown cold and she'd begun to shiver. She'd tugged so much at her manacle, she'd rubbed the skin around her ankle raw to the point of bleeding.

In the distance she heard the rumble of a truck engine before the glow of headlights appeared. She scrambled to her feet, jerked at the chain, wincing as the metal rubbed the raw skin of her ankle.

The truck ambled down the road as if the driver had all the time in the world. When the vehicle came to a halt in front of her she flinched as her eyes adjusted to the bright lights, which fully lighted up the land around her.

With the engine still running, the driver got out of the truck. She couldn't see his silhouetted face. She shielded her eyes, trying to see past the light.

"Tim?" she said.

He stepped forward into the light. "Hello again, Jo."

She straightened her shoulders, doing her best to look composed. Composed. She was chained to a tree. In the middle of Texas with a madman, and still she clung to control. "Tim, why are you doing this? Help me to understand."

Tim tossed a set of keys at Jo. "Unlock the manacle."

She eyed the keys lying in the dirt inches from her fingertips and then at the grave now lit up by the headlights. Her heart slammed against her ribs. "So you can drag me to the grave? No, Tim, I'm not going to help you."

A half smile tugged at the edges of his mouth as if he were expecting—even welcoming—a fight. "We can do this easy or hard. But either way that manacle is going to be unlocked."

She scooped up the keys from the dirt and hurled them into the dark woods. "Then it's going to be hard. I won't help you."

He closed the gap between them, grabbing her throat with his hand and slamming her body against the hard ground. Air whooshed from her lungs and her head hit against a hard root. He squeezed so hard she could only blink as her hands came up to his fingers and tried to pry them loose. She coughed and sputtered to catch her breath, but could not break his grip.

He squeezed harder, laughing as her eyes bulged. "I used to tell Harvey that he was a fool to love you. I told him I was the best child he could ever have. But that never stopped him from talking all the time about his perfect little girl. Jo earned straight A's. Jo was accepted into college. Jo is earning her master's."

Jo's gaze dimmed and she could feel herself losing consciousness.

"I told him to go see you, but he was afraid. Kept saying he didn't do well with women. Said it was a matter of time before he turned on you. But he wanted more than anything to be with you."

She struggled to breathe.

"Well, now I have a chance to give Harvey what he always wanted. Eternity with his little Jo. And then he'll finally know that I was the best child."

Seconds later she blacked out.

While Santos worked the radio, Brody drove as if the devil bit at his heels. They'd called in every available gun and badge to back them up.

Dirt kicked up around the car as he raced off the highway onto a rural route. Candace's directions had been frighteningly clear.

"You're betting the whole game on one hand," Santos said.

Brody tightened his hands on the wheel. "It's the only hand I've got to play."

"God, I hope you're right."

Santos's phone rang, and he answered it immediately. "Santos." And then after a moment's pause. "Shit. Yeah, I'll tell him."

"What is it?"

"Austin police found Connors. Shot dead in a seedy motel along with a prostitute."

"Damn." Brody couldn't think about the consequences of him being wrong or too late.

When Jo awoke, she sucked in a deep breath. Lying on her back, her throat ached as she searched the darkness for Tim. Instinct had her reaching for the manacle clamped around her leg. But a thick rope bound around her hands and body, making it impossible for her to move her arms. She tried to sit up, digging deep into her core muscles. She'd made it up several inches before Tim pushed her back against the dirt and smiled. "Jo, you don't want to leave yet. We're just getting started."

Bands of panic tightened around her chest as she surveyed her surroundings and realized she was now in the grave. "Tim, don't do this. Please don't do this."

He knelt beside the grave, trickling a handful of dirt onto her belly. She flinched.

"But it's what I've dreamed of doing for a long, long time. Harvey loved you so much but he feared if he reached out to you, you'd reject him. He didn't want his baby girl looking at him as if he were a monster."

"Harvey was my father."

"Yes. He took great pride in your successes."

446

Her thudding heart all but drowned out his words. "And you are his son."

His brow knotted. "Not his real son. Foster son."

"But he loved you."

"Not like he loved you. As hard as I tried or as hard as I worked I'd never had that biological connection you two shared." He scooped up another handful of dirt and scattered it on her body. "Did you know we actually met twenty years ago? Harvey spotted your mother by accident in a drugstore. She was buying hairspray. We followed her into a nearby hotel. He was nervous and angry all at once. I wasn't sure what he'd do, and then he saw you come out on stage, in that blue sparkly dress and teased hair. It took his breath away, seeing you. Said you were the spitting image of his own mother."

Keep him talking. Keep him talking. Maybe she could forge a connection and get through to him. "Tell me."

He scooped up more dirt but held it in his hand. "You walked around that stage, ankles all wobbly in those heels. Pitiful sight. I sniggered and Harvey jabbed me hard in the ribs."

That day remained a blur. She'd been unhappy about being in the pageant, and she didn't notice much. "My mother wasn't happy with me."

"She was real happy when you tossed that flaming baton in the air. She stood up and clapped."

Jo struggled to make some kind of connection

with Tim so that he saw her as human and not an object. "I was the worst beauty pageant contestant, and she wanted me to be the best."

"Harvey was pleased you didn't perform well. He said you were suited for an intellectual life like his."

"I don't remember seeing you two there."

"We had to be careful. Harvey didn't want trouble. He saw your mother and called her his failed apprentice." He shook his head. "Something made her turn around as we were leaving. She saw Harvey, and I thought she'd faint. We left right away."

His opening to talk gave her hope of a connection.

"I didn't realize my mother knew Harvey until recently. Did he ever talk about her?"

Tim trickled bits of dirt on her belly. Her muscles flinched, which coaxed a smile from him. "Not much. He kept pictures of her, and sometimes he looked at them. I looked at them when he wasn't home. After that day at the pageant he kept pictures of you, too."

She twisted her hands against her bindings, managing only to dig the rope deeper into her wrists and arms. "How did you meet Harvey?"

Tim's body had relaxed and he welcomed talk. "Harvey came into my mother's life when she was in her late twenties. She sold herself to him many times. And then he killed her."

"How old were you?"

"Twelve." Tim raised his gaze toward the moon. "The day she died was the best day of my life. He saved me from a wretched life. I doubt I'd be alive today if it weren't for Harvey."

"He became your father."

"More than a father. My guide. My maker." Dirt trickled out of his fisted hand beside her grave. "He took me out of foster care. He knew I needed a real, permanent parent."

There was a soft side to Harvey Smith. Evil had the capacity for kindness when it suited. "Did he adopt you?"

"No. Nothing formal. But he couldn't have been a better parent." His gaze grew wistful as he scooped up another handful of dirt. "He often said he wanted a son in his own image."

"I can tell you're educated. You're smart."

"Harvey homeschooled me. He didn't like schools. He thought they were prisons. But my education was a better education than anyone in a school could have received. He was patient."

"Many of the schools where he subbed gave him high marks."

"He was a gifted teacher."

"When I spoke to him, he called you Robbie."

Tim's eyes brightened. "I haven't heard that name in a long time. It's good to hear again."

Where she'd been twisting her hands, blood bloomed from the worn flesh.

"He dreamed of us meeting." He frowned. "That's why he pulled you into this case. He knew we'd have to finally meet."

"He didn't know that you'd already made contact with me—that you'd coaxed me into the *Find Christa!* search."

"There's a lot he didn't know. He didn't know I sold you your house. That I kept a key. You know I was in your house when Dayton poked around outside. He couldn't see me. I remembered you'd mentioned someone was bothering you. But I took care of him."

When she stared at him, unable to speak, he added, "I killed him. Nothing fancy. Didn't have time for that. Three bullets to the chest."

She struggled to hold on to her shredding composure. "Harvey would have liked that you looked after me."

"I know. He'd have hated it if that Dayton man had gotten hold of you."

"When did Harvey find out you were back?"

"When he saw the ad in the paper. I knew he'd seen the ad when he sent you and the cops to find Christa. I knew he understood that I'd finally stepped up."

"Stepped up?"

"Killed. Become a man. Ten years ago he gave me that chance, and I couldn't do it."

Killing women was a rite of passage for them. She swallowed anger and fear. "Christa was your first?"

450

"Yes. It's why I couldn't kill her right away. It took time to build up my nerve after I took her."

"Why organize the search?"

A smile tweaked the edges of his lips. "What better way to hide in plain sight? To hear what the cops knew or didn't know. And Scott. Well, the more I got to know him the more I knew he'd be of use."

"What do you mean?"

Terror rose up from the cold earth and saturated her bones. Brody and the others must know she was missing by now. But they were chasing the wrong man. "Where is Scott?"

"Dead in a motel in Austin."

"I don't understand."

"I told him a prostitute had information on Christa's killer. I told him to pick her up and meet me. Once they arrived, it was *pop pop* and problem solved." He shook his head. "The cops will be searching for him for days."

Jo swallowed her panic. "You set him up."

"It really was too easy."

Keep him talking. Build a bond. Find a way out of this mess. "When Harvey spoke about you I heard pride in his voice," she lied. "He said there was no smarter man than his Robbie."

"Really?" For a moment he paused, tears glistening in his eyes. "It's good that in the end there was at least that." He raised his gaze to her and the look of pain reminded her so much of the patients she'd counseled. "You know, we were together for eleven years. I thought he'd love me no matter what. But I failed him that one time, and he tossed me away like I was nothing."

As much as she wanted to scream and rail, she kept her voice level. "You must have been upset."

"I was heartbroken."

"What did you do?"

"I adapted, as he taught me. I reinvented myself. I wanted to kill to prove to him I could do it, but I couldn't. And he was arrested. I came to Austin after he was convicted. I prayed for the courage to kill but I couldn't. It wasn't until I heard he was sick that I knew I had to act. I was running out of time."

Fear tightened her throat. "And Hanna?"

"Poor little Hanna. Confused to the end.

"Do you know I was able to convince Scott that she had information on Christa? He picked her up in my car. Right in front of surveillance cameras. Took her to a motel room but found out she didn't know much. I sent him to see Dusty, Hanna's friend. Those two were always tight when I picked up Hanna. Made sense to clean up two loose ends at once."

She swallowed unshed tears. "Have there been others?"

"I don't think anyone has missed poor Sadie yet."

Her throat tightened. "I know a girl named Sadie."

"I know you do. Fitting that I hunt in your backyard. Makes this more of a family enterprise."

"You killed the girls in my group?"

"You didn't know Christa but I thought it was fitting that you join the search for her." He leaned forward. "Want to know where Sadie is?"

Tears welled in Jo's eyes. She did not want to know. But needed to ask for Sadie's sake.

He grinned. "Is that a yes or a no?"

"Yes," she whispered.

Tim rose and moved several feet to her right. He scraped away the dirt until pale skin caught the light of the moon. Soon he'd unearthed Sadie's face.

Jo shook her head, tears running down her cheeks. "She was only seventeen."

Tim scrambled back toward her. "She was a hard one to coax. Want to know how I got her in my car?" When she didn't answer he smiled. "I told her you sent me to her. I told her you said she could help me find my missing sister."

Misery raked across her heart. As much as she wanted to let the sadness wash over and take her, she didn't. "Tim, you don't have to do this. You don't. Harvey stayed away from me all those years for a reason. He doesn't want me to join him."

"You're wrong, Jo. So wrong."

An odd contentment burned in his gaze as he

stared at her. He rose, reached for the shovel and scooped up a mound of dirt. He dumped it on her legs.

She flinched. "Tim . . . Robbie, don't do this! Talk to me."

"I'm glad we had this time to talk, Jo. I really am. But the time for words is over."

He dumped more dirt on her chest. This time her composure shattered and she screamed.

"Scream all you want, Jo. No one is gonna hear you. Except Sadie, and . . . well, she's not gonna do much about it."

Brody and Santos arrived at the trailer at the end of the country road. The structure was set back off a dirt road a good mile from Rural Route 12. It was lit up as he and the other officers parked, drew guns and converged on the house. Brody motioned for DPS officers to flank the house's left and right sides while he and Santos banged on the front door.

Brody hadn't expected an answer. He tried the doorknob, and when he discovered it was locked he rammed the door with his shoulder. Pain shot through him as the wood splintered. He hit the door again and this time it banged open.

A search of the house turned up empty. No Tim. No Jo. Out back they found the red pickup truck along with two other well-maintained older cars.

"No GPS in the cars," Santos said.

"No." Brody scanned the land around the house. "He buries his victims like Harvey."

"The other victims were off property, away from his house."

Fear scraped at Brody. "I'm betting he's here. He wants to keep Jo close forever."

They moved through the house and out the back door. The other officers had circled around the house and had converged.

On the darkened landscape Brody spotted the distant glow of headlights. "He's out there. About a half mile from here."

Brody considered driving the distance but worried an approach via vehicle would alert Tim and give him time to kill Jo. He glanced at Santos, and the two took off running, the path illuminated by the light of the full moon.

As they hustled down the narrowing path, brush tore at Brody's pants and arms. Once he tripped but righted himself as he focused on the headlights ahead. When they pushed through the brush they found Tim standing, moving a mound of dirt. Shit.

Brody aimed his gun. "Get away from her."

Tim studied Brody and then raised his shovel as if to crush it on her head.

The mound of dirt shifted.

Brody fired, his bullet hitting Tim under his right arm. The impact knocked him sideways and he staggered but he didn't let loose of the shovel. He righted himself and lurched forward as if to make one last attempt to kill Jo. Brody fired once, twice more. Each bullet hit Tim in the chest and dropped him cold.

"Cover me!" Brody shouted to Santos as he holstered his gun, ran to the dirt mound and dropped to his knees. He scraped at the dirt around her face, digging furiously.

"Jo! Jo!" He cleared the dirt from her nose and mouth so she could breathe. "Don't open your eyes. There's too much dirt. Just breathe."

She sucked in a breath and screamed.

It took him several minutes to excavate the earth and when he pulled her out of the ground, she clung to him.

"I know, baby. I know." He pulled a handkerchief from his pocket and wiped the dirt from her eyes. "You're safe now."

Seconds passed and finally Jo opened her eyes. She cupped his face with a muddy hand and kissed him.

He banded his arm around her waist and pulled her to him. "It's okay, baby. It's okay."

Epilogue

Five months later

"God, I am so hungry," Pepper said.

Jo glanced up from the kindling that had smoked briefly and gone out. She'd been striking the flints, hoping to catch a spark and for a brief moment had thought she'd won. Then the fire had gone out.

How the devil had she ended up in the woods with a bunch of cranky, hungry girls trying to start a fire? Because she'd lost what she'd thought had been a sure bet.

The wager had been simple. If the girls in the group all made B's or better she'd take them camping. In all honesty she thought she was safe. But they'd all made B's. Some just barely, but they'd all made the grade.

And so here she was in the middle of nowhere trying to nurse a campfire so they could cook the hot dogs she'd packed.

"The fire will catch, and we will eat soon."

Pepper shook her head. "If that Ranger was here, we'd have a fire."

"He's working." Truth was Jo had not had the heart to ask him to come along. Camping with a half-dozen, streetwise girls was a challenge for her, and she didn't have the heart to ask him to give up one of his rare weekends off. Toss in the fact that the Cowboys were playing the Steelers. Nope, that was asking too much.

"Too bad," Pepper said. "I bet he could have gotten the fire going."

Amber nodded. "I am kinda starving, Jo." She surveyed the open horizon. "Camping looks a lot more fun on television when you're sitting on the couch eating chips."

Jo's stomach grumbled. "Hey, I will get this fire burning, and we will eat. Soon."

"Like *when* soon?" Pepper said.

"Like any minute."

Amber and the other girls grumbled and rifled through a bag of groceries Jo had packed. Despite their grousing now, they'd all had a great day. The hikes through the hill country had been stunning. They'd seen wildlife. Several girls had picked flowers. They'd enjoyed the day and done something rare and precious: acted like kids.

All the girls from the spring class had delivered their babies. A couple had opted to keep their babies whereas Amber and Pepper had chosen to make an adoption plan for their children. Both paths had been riddled with tough emotional decisions, something that came up often in their group meetings. But all were making it. Moving forward. And that, in Jo's book, was a win.

The crunch of gravel had Pepper straightening. "I hear something in the woods."

Amber straightened. "Do you think it's a bear?"

Jo struck the flints together one last time and rose, frustrated. She'd been told this area was a safe place to bring the girls, but *safe* was a term she never took for granted anymore. She reached in her back pocket for her cell. She'd call the cops in a heartbeat if trouble showed up.

The sound of footsteps on the path grew louder and louder. The girls huddled around her, and she clung to her phone.

"Who's out there?" Jo called.

"Jo, where the hell are you?" Brody's voice was clear, deep and full of relief. He emerged at the mouth of the woods. He surveyed Jo and her girls, taking in the unlit fire and raw food. "You girls aren't so easy to find."

She released the breath she was holding and moved from the girls to him. She kissed him on the lips, not caring that the girls giggled and cooed. "What are you doing here?"

"House was too damn quiet. Thought I'd come looking for you."

"You didn't need to come. We got this under control."

He kissed her a second time and looked at the girls. "I bet she's having trouble getting that fire started."

The girls laughed. Amber folded her arms over her chest. "Save us, Ranger. She is starving us to death."

He squeezed Jo's shoulder and moved past her to the unlit fire. Kneeling, he pulled matches from his pocket and lit the fire.

"That's cheating," Jo said.

"I go for what gets the job done, ma'am." The flames quickly danced and licked over the wood Jo had carefully stacked into a tripod. "Though I got to say you stacked yourself a pretty pile of wood."

As the fire grew, the girls gathered around, and Brody showed them how to find the right stick and thread their hot dogs on it. Soon the girls were gathered around the fire, cooking.

Jo folded her arms over her chest, recognizing that this was one of those rare moments in life when all the stars lined up and life felt perfect. She was here. Alive. With Brody. And the world was missing two vicious monsters now that Harvey and Robbie were dead.

Once Brody had freed her from the grave, the cops had secured the entire area. They'd removed Sadie's body from the ground and taken it away. Sadie's father had claimed the body and ordered it cremated. Later, Brody found surveillance images of Sadie getting into Tim's car. Over the next three days they searched the area for bodies, using ground-penetrating radar. They'd found none.

However, the medical examiner, based on Candace Granger's testimony, had gotten DNA from Delores Jones's sister. Mitochondrial DNA had confirmed that the unidentified victim found by the barn had indeed been Delores, the girl Candace had seen bound over thirty years ago. Police believed after Candace fled, Smith had moved the girl to the alternate location where he'd buried her alive before fleeing the area.

Jo had hired a good lawyer for her mother, ready to defend her, but her mother had refused to take a plea agreement. She was actually relieved to have her dark secret revealed. She'd pled guilty to criminal homicide.

Because Candace had been seventeen at the time of the crime, the judge had considered her a juvenile. He'd given her five years probation.

Physically, Candace had pulled herself together. She was back at the shop, working her long, crazy hours as she'd done all Jo's life. However, what Jo now saw was not a woman driven to succeed, but a woman trying to outrun a haunting past.

As much as Jo said to herself the past was the past, it had been impossible to let go. Being out here in the open land conjured memories of the night she'd lain in the earth, dirt weighing on her face, filling her nose and mouth and cutting off her breath.

Brody laid his hand on her shoulder, snapping her from her trance. "So where were you?"

She smiled, shaking off the darker thoughts. "Just watching you with the girls."

He shook his head. "You slipped away from us

minutes ago." He pulled her into his embrace and she let him mold her body to his. He smelled of earth and sky. "He's gone, Jo. He can never hurt you again."

Brody's strength shielded her from the ghosts. "I know."

He squeezed her tighter. "I mean it, Jo. Nothing bad will happen to you on my watch."

She pulled back, smiled and kissed him on the lips. "I know. I know."

He smoothed her stray hair from her eyes. "Marry me."

For a moment she simply stared. "What?"

"Marry me. Again. Let's do it right this time. Church. Family." He looked at the gaggle of girls now staring at them with wide grins. "Friends."

She shook her head. She'd sworn she'd never mention marriage. She enjoyed him in her life and had not wanted to put a cage around him. "It's pretty good the way it is, Brody."

"And it will be better. We aren't kids."

"You're sure?"

"Damn sure."

Tears welled in her eyes before she kissed him. "Yes."

He laughed and hugged her to him. As the girls squealed and circled around them, Brody pulled a ring from his pocket and slid it on Jo's finger. "We'll get it right this time."

Center Point Large Print
600 Brooks Road / PO Box 1
Thorndike ME 04986-0001 USA

(207) 568-3717

US & Canada:
1 800 929-9108
www.centerpointlargeprint.com